Praise for

Out of Nowhere and #1 *New York Times* Bestselling Author Sandra Brown

"I've lost count of Sandra Brown's amazing string of best-sellers, and she just keeps getting better. With *Out of Nowhere*, Brown has swung for the fences and hit a grand slam with this blistering and bracing tale. This is psychological thriller writing of the highest order." —*BookTrib*

"Sandra Brown excels at keeping the tension high and the emotions strong." —Bookreporter

"*Overkill* is storytelling par excellence, weaving complex societal issues into the fabric of a thriller to create a terrific tapestry of emotionally wrought tension. The best book of the summer." —*Providence Journal*

"Brown [turns] up the heat and the suspense [in *Overkill*] in what may be one of her most compelling novels yet. The chemistry between Kate and Zach is off the charts.... [Brown] remains a formidable force." —*The Big Thrill*

"Sandra Brown proves herself top-notch." —Associated Press

"[Brown] is a masterful storyteller, carefully crafting tales that keep readers on the edge of their seats."

—*USA Today*

"Set in 1920, this superior thriller from bestseller Brown firmly anchors all the action in the plot....Laurel and Thatcher are strong and inventive characters, and their surprising decisions and evolving relationship will keep readers engaged. Brown shows why she remains in the top rank of her field [in *Blind Tiger*]."

—*Publishers Weekly*, starred review

"Brown doesn't often delve into historical fiction territory, but she does here with gusto, and readers will practically taste the dusty streets of Foley and feel every rickety bump of the moonshiners' trucks. There are shoot-outs and reformed prostitutes and a no-good hillbilly family, but none of it feels like an empty stereotype—it's just all a lot of fun. Combined with Brown's knack for romantic tension and page-turning suspense, [*Blind Tiger*] is a winner."

—*Booklist*, starred review

"*Blind Tiger* is a winner."　　　　　　　　—AARP

"Suspense that has teeth."　　　　　　—Stephen King

"Brown deserves her own genre."　　—*Dallas Morning News*

"Bold and bracing hard-boiled crime thriller *Thick as Thieves* [is] perhaps [Sandra Brown's] most ambitious and best-realized effort ever....A tale steeped in noir and nuance that's utterly riveting from the first page to the last."

—*Providence Journal*

"A novelist who can't write them fast enough."

—*San Antonio Express-News*

"Brown's storytelling gift is surprisingly rare."

—*Toronto Sun*

"*Outfox* is packed with suspense and love. It is an extraordinarily satisfying and entertaining novel."

—*Washington Book Review*

"Sandra Brown is a publishing icon."

—*New York Journal of Books*

"Sandra Brown just might have penned her best and most ambitious book ever, a tale that evokes the work of the likes of Don DeLillo, Greg Iles and Robert Stone....*Seeing Red* is an exceptional thriller in every sense of the word, a classic treatment of the costs of heroism and the nature of truth itself. Not to be missed."

—*Providence Journal*

"Brown's novels define the term 'page-turner.'"

—*Booklist*

"Sandra Brown is a master at weaving a story of suspense into a tight web that catches and holds the reader from the first page to the last."

—*Library Journal*

OUT OF NOWHERE

OUT OF NOWHERE

SANDRA BROWN

GRAND
CENTRAL

NEW YORK   BOSTON

Grand Central Publishing
Hachette Book Group
1290 Avenue of the Americas, New York, NY 10104
grandcentralpublishing.com
@grandcentralpub

Originally published in hardcover and ebook by Grand Central Publishing in August 2023
First trade paperback edition: March 2024

Grand Central Publishing is a division of Hachette Book Group, Inc. The Grand Central Publishing name and logo is a trademark of Hachette Book Group, Inc.

The publisher is not responsible for websites (or their content) that are not owned by the publisher.

The Hachette Speakers Bureau provides a wide range of authors for speaking events. To find out more, go to hachettespeakersbureau.com or email HachetteSpeakers@hbgusa.com.

Grand Central Publishing books may be purchased in bulk for business, educational, or promotional use. For information, please contact your local bookseller or the Hachette Book Group Special Markets Department at special.markets@hbgusa.com.

Library of Congress Cataloging-in-Publication Data has been applied for.

ISBNs: 9781538742969 (trade paperback), 9781538742976 (ebook)

Printed in the United States of America

LSC-C

Printing 1, 2023

Author's Note

Out of Nowhere isn't a story about death. It's a story about survival.

The destinies of two strangers collide in an instant of unthinkable tragedy. If not for that unpredictable, inexplicable occurrence, it's unlikely that Elle and Calder ever would have met. But because of a caprice of physics, their fates became intertwined.

I didn't particularly want to write a story that begins with a mass shooting. In fact, it's a subject I would ordinarily avoid. I react, as I'm sure you do—as we *all* do—to hearing of another shooting with dismay, repugnance, and abject sadness. Caught in a situation of such incomprehensible ruthlessness, I can't even imagine the terror one experiences.

But, as storytellers are wont to do, I did. Imagined, that is.

I tried to imagine how one copes after surviving such a horrifying, traumatic event. How does one pick up where one's life left off and attempt to rebuild it, reshape it into some form of normalcy when pieces of it are now fractured or missing?

I confess that even as I was writing this story, I knew my words were inadequate to describe the rending of heart and spirit that Elle and Calder were suffering.

To anyone reading it who has come even close to an experience such as that of my characters, I apologize for presuming that I know what it's like. I don't. But I did my best, with as much authenticity and empathy as I could, to portray the struggle of staying afloat in the wake of a catastrophe.

In news reports, "another mass shooting" has become such a familiar refrain that it's far too easy to tune it out, to forget the name of that school, that town, that place of worship, that shopping mall or entertainment venue or office building where lives were lost and others shattered. We as a society, as individual human beings, must never become inured.

So, back to what motivated me to write this story? I suppose it was to honor the casualties. I rank the survivors among them.

Sandra Brown

OUT OF
NOWHERE

Prologue

For the record...

In the unlikely event they catch me, it will be assumed that I am mad.

That will be correct, but only if people are using the word *mad* as a synonym for angry.

To do such a thing as what I'm planning, one doesn't have to be mentally unstable. I'm quite sane. I'm rational. I don't appear or act like a crazed individual, because I'm not.

Irate is what I am.

Fury roils inside me. It has for a while now. Others with a purpose similar to mine make the stupidest blunder possible by announcing to the world what they intend to do before they do it. They air their grievances on social media. They entrust so-called friends with their most morbid thoughts. They commit their maniacal fantasies to paper, drawing ghastly depictions of death and destruction. They fill notebooks with pages of scribbled nonsense that, afterward, psychiatrists and FBI profilers try to decipher in order to pinpoint a motive for their deed, which is usually described as "senseless."

But what's senseless is the analyzing. It's a waste of time and tax revenue. The individual who committed the act wasn't necessarily insane, or afflicted with a personality-altering brain tumor, or suffering a rare chemical imbalance, or cursed from conception with a domineering id.

No. Chances are he was simply pissed off.

That's me. I'm pissed off but good. And I'm going to vent my anger in a way that will be remembered and lamented. But I'm not going to make the mistake of advertising it first. Those other morons who don't exercise patience get captured, or annihilated by SWAT team bullets, or take their own lives.

I have no intention of any of that happening to me. I'm confident that I'll get away with it.

I'll use this gun. It's untraceable. I made sure of that. It's never been used in the commission of a crime. It's portable and easily concealed but no less deadly than an AR-15 rifle.

See? I've thought this through.

There's only one catch, a single, slightly worrisome hitch: I don't know when or where my plan will be implemented. Out of necessity, I'll have to go with the situation, whatever it is, when it presents itself.

But I'm no fool. If the setting doesn't feel right, or there's a large police presence, or any other unfavorable factor, I'll know to scrub the assault and save it for another day.

I've been disappointed by several postponements. The circumstances would seem at first to be ideal, and I would think, *This is it!* Then something would happen that would prevent me from acting. Once it was a thunderstorm. Another time, where otherwise the conditions were ideal, an old man suffered a stroke. Wouldn't you know it? Security guards and EMTs swarmed. I would have been a fool to proceed.

These delays are frustrating and infuriating and leave a bitter taste in my mouth.

But while being unable to choose my time and place is a drawback, immediacy could work to my advantage. I won't give myself away by a slip of the tongue, no accidental tip-off that would alert someone to my intentions or arouse curiosity.

Another benefit to acting in the moment is that when the opportunity does present itself and I realize that all systems are go, I won't have time to get nervous and overthink it. I'll have to act purposefully and without hesitation.

Which is why I stay constantly prepared. I'm vigilant. At the drop of a hat, I'll be ready. When the time is right, I'll know it. And I'll do it.

And the best part? No one will suspect me.

Chapter 1

Y ou claimed to be the best, and, by damn, you are."
Beaming a smile, the CEO of John Zimmerman Industries
handed over a bank receipt. "As of an hour ago, your fee
plus the bonuses you chalked up were deposited into your
account."

"Thank you." Calder Hudson checked the receipt for
accuracy. The account number was correct, and the amount
in front of the decimal point was on the rosy side of six
figures.

"Everything seems to be in order." Calder folded the
receipt and slid it into the breast pocket of his bespoke suit
coat, smiling at the group of upper-management personnel
clustered around him. "It's been my pleasure, ladies and
gentlemen. May I use JZI as a reference?"

The CEO replied on behalf of those assembled. "Of
course, of course. We'll provide a glowing review."

Calder raised an eyebrow. "With an emphasis on discretion."

There was a ripple of chuckles.

"Goes without saying," said the CEO.

Calder nodded with satisfaction, thanked them as a group, then, with the bearing of a cleric doling out blessings, went around the circle shaking hands with each. He wished them a good evening, picked up his briefcase, and left the conference room.

As he made his way to the elevator, he kept his stride and carriage deceptively casual, but inside his head, it was *Mardi Gras, baby!* and he was grand marshal of the parade.

It was a long ride down from the top floor of the steel and glass Dallas skyscraper to the subterranean parking garage, but Calder's blood was still fizzing with self-congratulations as he stepped off the elevator and gave himself a fist pump. His whoop echoed through the near-empty concrete cavern.

As prearranged, his Jaguar had been left in a first-row, VIP parking slot. For three months and change, he'd been tooling around in a rental car and was ever so glad to have his sleek sports model back.

He kissed his fingertips, then tapped them against the roof of the car. "Hello, sweetheart. Miss me?" He shrugged out of his coat and set it and his briefcase in the passenger seat, then started the motor, thrilling to the aggressive growl he'd sorely missed.

He backed out, and, as he took the sharp curves on his climb up the parking levels to the exit, his tires screeched menacingly. "Badass at the wheel," he whispered through a smug grin as he shot out of the garage and onto the city street.

It was after business hours; rush-hour traffic had abated. But no other motorist would have dared to get in his way. Not today. He blew through yellow lights at several downtown intersections before taking a ramp onto the freeway.

He slid on his sunglasses against the blood orange–red streaks painted across the sky by the setting sun, then accessed his phone from the steering wheel.

Shauna answered on the second ring and said, "Helloooo there, handsome."

"Helloooo, beautiful."

"How'd it go?"

"Well, can't say the same for some, but *I* had a great day."

"I can hear it in your voice. It's oozing conceit."

"I'm trying my best to suppress it, but, you know..."

"Yes, I do know. I've heard it before, and it's insufferable."

He grinned. "You suffer it, though, don't you?"

"Don't be smug. Where are you?"

"Headed home. What about you?"

"Home? You're supposed to be on your way here."

Calder's elation dimmed several watts as he now remembered that Shauna had to work this evening. Damned if he could remember what she had scheduled. "You're still at the studio?"

"No, on location at the fair. I'm killing time in the van while the crew sets up for the interview." She huffed with exasperation. "You forgot, didn't you? Honestly, Calder. You said you'd come."

A fair. Right. "I said I would think about it." He hadn't had to think about it. He'd known when he'd told her he would that he wouldn't. He wasn't going to any county fair. "How long will you be?"

"I'm doing the interview an hour before the concert starts. I want to capture some of his backstage energy before his performance. I don't have to stay for the entire thing, but I'll be here for a while yet."

None of what she'd said sat well with him. "I just completed my biggest contract. I'm over a hundred grand richer, and the bigwigs were practically kissing me over the privilege of paying me. I'm ready to get the party started."

"We'll party. It'll just start a few hours later."

A few *hours*?

She was saying, "...because at the last minute, the producer squeezed the interview into tonight's ten o'clock newscast."

"Who's that important? Is the president in town?"

"Better. Bryce Conrad."

"Who's that?"

"Only the brightest rising star in country music," she said, not even trying to conceal her excitement.

"Never heard of him."

"You have so! I told you that he's generally camera shy but that he'd granted *me* an interview. You and I talked about it for ten minutes." A pause, then, "But I knew you weren't paying attention."

"Give me a break, okay? I've been focused on work. This was a high-stakes week for me."

"For me, too, Calder," she snapped. "If you'd been listening, you'd know that my getting a one-on-one with Bryce Conrad was a coup. A big one. *Entertainment Tonight* called this afternoon. They're doing a feature on him over the weekend and may add some sound bites from my interview to it. So, you're not the only one who had a great day, okay? By the way, thank you for asking."

If they continued in this vein, the high he was on would crash and burn. He really didn't want to lose the good buzz he had going to a quarrel over some Johnny-come-lately country singer.

He'd play nice. "Look, I'm sorry. I should have paid closer attention. That's great about *ET*."

Mollified, she said, "Even if they don't air any of this interview, I'm at least on their radar."

"All the more reason for us to celebrate tonight. What's your ETA at home? I'll have the champagne chilled."

"Won't you please come here as planned?"

"To that fair?" He snorted. "Shauna, get serious."

"It's a bit of a drive, but—"

"It's practically in freakin' Oklahoma."

"It's forty-five minutes if you use the express lanes. Please. It'll be fun."

"Compared to what? A colonoscopy? Besides, you'll be working, which will leave me a hanger-on, standing around and playing pocket pool."

"By the time you get here, I'll probably be finished with the interview. Come on. It's a beautiful evening."

"Shauna—"

"I'll leave a pass for you at the north gate. There's reserved parking there, too. Text when you get here, and I'll tell you where to find me. We'll stay through a few songs and then leave. I promise."

"I can't think of anything I feel less like doing tonight than going to a county fair. Good luck with the interview. I'll see you at home. Bye."

Calder clicked off. Anger and resentment had deflated his buoyant mood. He punched up the volume of his car radio, then, irritated by the song selection, switched it off altogether.

Having felt flush with success, he'd anticipated Shauna's hot body and cold champagne to be waiting for him between silk sheets when he got home. A crowded, gritty fairground was as far removed from that fantasy as you could get. He had every right to be pissed.

But after covering a mile or two on the freeway, he eased off the accelerator and grudgingly acknowledged that it was his fault he'd forgotten her commitment tonight. Obviously getting this interview was important to the furtherance of her career, and she was all about that escalation.

When she did get home, she would be sulky if not silent. He'd get the deep-freeze treatment. Forget about sex. Out of the question.

On the other hand, what if he showed up at the fairground unexpectedly and surprised her? He would say, *I acted like an ass. I'm sorry.* Which he wouldn't mean in the depths of his soul, but the apology would, in all probability, create a thaw sufficient to get him laid tonight, which was a priority.

All things considered...

He whipped in front of an eighteen-wheeler, whose driver blasted him with his horn. Calder gave him the finger, gunned the Jag, and aimed it toward the exit.

"Charlie, Charlie, look here. Look at Mommy."

Using her cell phone camera, Elle managed to capture a slobbery, toothy grin as her son glided past her on the mini carousel. On the next revolution, she got several seconds of video of him waving to her, coached to do so by her friend Glenda, who had graciously offered to take a turn on the ride since this was Charlie's fifth time.

When the carousel slowed to a stop, Glenda managed to dismount while maintaining her hold on the squirming two-year-old, who was intent on remaining astride the painted pony. She carried him over to Elle, who relieved her of him.

"Thanks for doing that," Elle said. "If I'd gone one more round, I think I would have barfed."

Glenda laughed. "Over the spinning or the music?"

"Right. Days from now, I'll still have an earworm of calliope jingles."

"Me too, but I wouldn't have missed going for a ride with my favorite cowboy." Glenda patted Charlie on the cheek. It was sticky with cotton candy residue, but she laughed off Elle's apology. "No matter, but I do need to take off. One of the gals texted. They're here, waiting for me in the beer garden with a pitcher of frozen margaritas that they swear is calling my name."

"Go," Elle said as she wrestled Charlie into his stroller. He'd bowed his back and wasn't cooperating. "I didn't count on staying this long, but I think I'm on borrowed time. I feel an exhausted-child meltdown coming on."

She fished Bun, Charlie's flop-eared rabbit, from the compartment on the back of the stroller and passed it down to him. He tucked the stuffed animal under his arm, momentarily pacified.

Frowning, Glenda said, "I wish you could join us girls and stay for the concert."

"Ah, well, me too. But this was a spontaneous excursion. Babysitters are hard to come by on short notice."

That morning, after catching up on laundry and light housekeeping, she'd settled into her home office to work while simultaneously keeping Charlie occupied with toys, books, and his library of *Paw Patrol* videos.

But as the afternoon wore on, he'd turned whiny, demanding her attention, which he'd deserved for being cooped up all day. So, although she'd been on a creative roll, she'd shut down her computer, lifted her son into her lap, and between pecking kisses onto his face asked if he would like to call Glenda. "This is the last day of the fair. Let's see if she wants to go."

Even though he'd only understood "Glenda" and "go," Elle hadn't had to ask twice.

Glenda had welcomed the chance to leave her real estate agency early. "This works out great. A group of friends from my Pilates class is having a girls' night out. We're going to the concert this evening. I'll join you and Charlie, then hook up with them later."

They'd set a time and place to meet just inside the north gate. Glenda, president and CEO of Foster Real Estate, had arrived looking like a model for an upscale western clothing store, wearing a long denim skirt, cowboy boots studded with silver, a fringed leather jacket, and ropes of turquoise beads.

"You make me feel underdressed," Elle had remarked with a self-deprecating smile. "And very mom-ish."

Glenda had eyed her up and down. "If you'd wear one size jeans smaller, your ass would be smokin'."

"Hardly."

"I would trade my butt for yours any day of the week. And don't get me started on your hair. It's just not fair. However, the T-shirt needs an upgrade, and you could use some spangle."

Elle laughed. "Spangle so suits my lifestyle."

For the next two hours, the friends had taken turns maneuvering Charlie's stroller through the crowd. They'd visited the petting zoo, the Christmas market, and various exhibits, leaving the midway for last just as the sun went down and the sky turned a deep violet.

Flashing colored lights on the rides had begun to come on, dazzling Charlie. He and Elle had ridden several rides in the kiddie area while Glenda took snapshots on her phone to text to Elle later. Hands down, the carousel had been his favorite ride. It was a good note to end on.

Now, as Elle hugged her friend goodbye, Glenda said, "I've spotted lots of cute guys around. Put yourself out there, Elle."

"I already have a cute guy," she said as she bent down and ruffled Charlie's dark curls.

"There's no disputing that," Glenda said. "He is a darlin'. Be careful going home. Love you."

"Call me tomorrow and tell me about the concert."

"Will do." Glenda blew them a kiss as she began weaving through the crowd in the general direction of the beer garden.

Elle experienced a twinge of jealousy over her friend's independence and having a Friday night out. But three years ago she'd made a choice, and she hadn't had a moment's regret over it.

When she looked down at Charlie, who was yawning hugely, her heart swelled with pure joy. She bent down and nuzzled his neck. "Mommy loves you bunches and bunches. Ready to go home?"

He kicked against the footrest of his stroller. "Go."

"I'm afraid it'll be slow going." She turned the stroller around as deftly as she could without bumping into anyone.

The crowd grew thicker as they neared the north gate through which they'd entered. Though there were separate turnstiles for entering and exiting, where those who were coming in and those leaving converged, they formed two throngs moving in opposition. Elle and Charlie were swimming upstream of those entering, and eventually their progress was limited to gaining only inches at a time.

"Looks like they're gonna have a good crowd tonight."

The speaker was a gentleman who was shuffling along beside her. He had a round and ruddy face. A horseshoe of gray hair delineated his wide, shiny bald spot. Bridging his nose was a pair of wire-rimmed eyeglasses, the lenses of which reflected the spinning Ferris wheel. At a time when he could have been cranky and complaining, he'd spoken with good humor.

Elle smiled at him. "Bryce Conrad is a big draw."

"Yeah." He winked at her. "I think we're escaping just in time."

She returned his mischievous smile, but her attention was returned to Charlie, who was trying to climb out of his stroller.

"No, Charlie. No, you can't get out."

He resisted her attempts to push him back down into the seat and was having no part of her explanation as to why he had to remain confined. Eventually, she won the battle and straightened up, looking with hope toward the exit and gauging how much longer she could hold out before Charlie had a full-blown tantrum.

"Excuse me."

The irritated mumble came from Elle's other side as someone going in the opposite direction bumped into her. She turned to respond, but he had already moved past. He stood out from everyone else because he was dressed in slacks and a dress shirt. An executive sort, she thought.

That was Elle's last thought before the bang.

It was abrupt and loud.

At first, she thought it was a sound effect coming from one of the thrill rides. When it was repeated, she thought perhaps it was fireworks going off. But they weren't scheduled to start until after the concert.

Confused, she turned to the older man with whom she'd been talking. His hand was at his throat. Blood was spouting from between his fingers. A geyser of it splashed onto Elle.

He staggered, falling hard against her and causing her to reel backward. She caught the push bar of the stroller with her left hand and put out her right to try to break her fall. But on impact with the blacktop, her elbow gave way. Her landing was so jarring, she bit her tongue and tasted blood. She lost her left-handed grip on the stroller.

The older man's momentum caused him to fall against the stroller and propel it forward. It began to roll, knocking into people who were now madly scattering.

Someone shouted, "Shooter, shooter."

It took only a split second for Elle to register that the unthinkable was actually happening. *"Charlie!"*

She lunged forward, reaching out in a frantic effort to get a handhold on any part of the stroller, but it was already beyond her reach and rolling farther away from her. Between her and it was the older man, who had fallen face-down and was now still, a pool of blood spreading beneath him.

In a remote area of her mind that was still functioning, Elle realized that he was dead. But without thinking, without an instant of hesitancy, she crawled over his prone form, her hands and sneakers slipping on his blood. She couldn't gain purchase. Something was wrong with her right arm.

The stroller was being buffeted by the stampede of terrified people. The distance between it and Elle was widening, and she couldn't get to it, to Charlie, to her baby.

Directly in front of her, a man fell, his leg shot out from under him. He bellowed in pain as he went down. Her screams couldn't be differentiated from those of others who were equally panicked and mortally afraid. But she could distinguish those of her child. He was wailing.

"Charlie, I'm coming! Mommy's coming! *Char-lie!"*

A fleeing man wearing a ball cap ran into the stroller, striking the side of it with his knees.

Elle watched in helpless terror as the stroller tipped onto two wheels.

The executive type who'd bumped into her lurched into Elle's peripheral vision, reached out for the stroller, and managed to get a grasp on the bar.

But inertia sent the carriage onto its side and took the man down with it.

He fell atop it.

Elle screamed hysterically.

She heard the raw, primal screams of others. The ground vibrated with the tramping of hundreds of feet.

For Elle Portman, pandemonium turned into a horror movie played out in slow motion.

Which was why she was cursed afterward with remembering everything with such stark and brutal clarity.

Chapter 2

Mr. Hudson?"

Calder wished that whoever the hell was talking to him would shut up and leave him alone. He had a mother of a headache.

He was surrounded by noises and activities he couldn't identify, nor did he want to. People were talking loudly. Impossibly bright light seeped through his eyelids even though he kept them tightly closed. All these hyperactive stimuli were as intrusive as a tornado. His heart's desire was silence, stillness, darkness, oblivion.

"Mr. Hudson? Can you hear me? You can wake up now. Your operation is over."

He sensed motion as the persistent creature—the voice was female—came nearer, bumping into whatever surface he was on, rocking it, and causing the pain level inside his skull to spike off the charts. His right arm was lifted, pressure was applied, and when it was released, the individual said, "My name is Cindy. I'll be taking care of you for the next few hours. The doctor will be in to see you soon. Would you like some ice chips?"

He didn't care what her name was. Who was she, and what was she talking about?

"I'm going to elevate your head a little. Let me know if you feel nauseous."

She didn't elevate his head "a little." She catapulted it from supine to straight fucking up. A stick of dynamite exploded inside his cranium. His stomach heaved. He gagged.

"Here's a bag."

Something cold and foreign was crammed against his mouth. He retched violently. Again and again his guts were wrung out, but nothing came up except sour fluid, which he spat out, uncertain and uncaring if he hit the receptacle or not.

When the spasms finally subsided, she said, "Better now? If you need it again, let me know."

He attempted to raise his arm and bat at Cindy the Witch, who'd pulled him out of a sublime state of nothingness into pure hell, but he seemed to have lost control of his limbs.

Stunned and frightened by that realization, he pried open his eyes and blinked against the blinding overhead light. A figure loomed and receded, loomed and receded, making him seasick until he was able to focus and secure his torturer into place.

A young woman with dozens of long braids was adjusting an IV bag beside what was obviously a hospital bed.

His eyes tracked the IV tubing to the back of his right

hand, where strips of tape secured a shunt. A device with a red light was clipped to the end of his index finger. He supposed it was monitoring something. He became aware that he was breathing through a cannula.

The young woman glanced over her shoulder and smiled at him. "Good. You're with us. Has the nausea passed?"

He tried to speak but only made a croaking sound. His mouth was as dry as dust, and his throat stung from the vile stuff he'd thrown up. He tried again and this time was able to whisper, "Am I in the hospital?"

"Surgery recovery."

"Surgery?"

"You're going to be all right." Cindy patted his right shoulder, then went over to a portable stand with a laptop on it and began tapping on the keyboard.

What surgery? Why did he feel like complete and total shit? What had happened to him, for chrissake?

His memory was sluggish, but things began to come back to him in scraps of recollection that he wasn't sure were chronological. He struggled to piece them together in their proper order until he'd reconstructed the time frame between leaving the office building in downtown Dallas and arriving at the fairground in one of the outlying communities in a neighboring county.

He'd gone there to surprise Shauna. As expected, it had been a mob scene. He had...

Suddenly he heard again the gunfire and was assailed by remembered sights and sounds that seemed surreal. Panicked people screaming, running, dropping, bleeding.

He remembered being struck. "Was I shot?" He was

seized by a horrifying thought that would explain why his limbs were heavy and motionless. "Am I paralyzed?"

The nurse stopped typing and returned to the side of his bed. "You're not paralyzed, Mr. Hudson. You were wounded in the arm. You're getting pain meds in the IV. You can move; you just don't feel like making the effort."

Only then did he become aware of the confining bandage around his left arm and shoulder. He looked back at the nurse, and she must've seen the wild anxiety in his eyes. She patted him again and said, "You're going to be okay."

"Will I lose the use of my arm?"

"You're going to be fine, Mr. Hudson."

He wanted to yell at her to stop saying that. Did he look fine? He put as much oomph as he could muster behind his feeble voice. "I want to talk to the doctor. The one who operated on me."

"He'll be in soon."

He shook his head, detonating land mines of pain inside it. "I want to see him *now*."

"He's still in the OR, working on other casualties of the shooting."

Calder opened his mouth to speak but closed it quickly. A second wave of nausea came on strong. He gulped down the bitter fluid that filled his mouth. "How many were there?"

"I don't have that information."

She was lying, but he lacked the strength to accuse her. "Did some die?"

"I'll bring you a ginger ale. If that doesn't help with the nausea, we can give you something for it."

Her avoidance was answer enough. People had died.

She left by flipping back a flimsy curtain that ineffectually separated his bed from those of other patients. It was a busy place. Staff were going about their duties, carrying this, pushing that. One was wheeling around a mop bucket like a dance partner. Another went past with a rattling cart on squeaky wheels. A young woman in scrubs jogged past, her expression intense. A desk phone rang incessantly, but no one answered it. Outside his range of vision, someone of indeterminate age and gender cried out in either anguish or pain.

He must be having a nightmare. The scenario was too bizarre to be real. People like Calder Hudson didn't get *gunshot* at a *county fair*. People like him didn't even go to county fairs.

But as he settled his head onto the pillow and closed his eyes against the brutal overhead light, he acknowledged that it was all too real.

Other than the headache, he wasn't in actual pain, although he knew he would be when the anesthesia wore off and they reduced the dosage of pain medication.

For now his left arm and hand were blessedly numb and too heavy to move, and, in any case, he was disinclined, and slightly fearful, even to try. Cindy had assured him that he wasn't paralyzed, that he was going to be all right, but could he trust that? Maybe she just hadn't wanted to panic him.

But he was alive.

He could so easily be dead.

He could have died. Today.

Pressure began mounting deep inside his chest and continued to intensify until he feared his sternum would crack open from the strain. His throat grew tight and achy. Random but graphic recollections flashed across his mind's eye.

He made a fist of his right hand to keep it from trembling. Tears leaked from the corners of his closed eyes and rolled down his temples. Against his most stubborn will to withhold it, a sob erupted from between his lips.

——◆——

"Mr. Hudson?"

Calder hadn't realized that he'd fallen asleep, so waking came as a mild surprise. He hadn't intended to sleep. *Must be the medications,* he thought.

Or maybe his brain had simply done him a favor by shutting down so he wouldn't have to dwell on the mass shooting, which somehow, by a trick of fate, he had survived when others hadn't.

He didn't want to contemplate the miracle of why he had beaten the odds. That question was too intricate and complicated for him to deal with right now. If ever.

"Mr. Hudson?"

Unable to put it off any longer, he blinked open his eyes.

The man gazing down at him said, "I'm Dr. Montgomery, chief of the trauma unit here. I treated you in the ER, but I doubt you remember that. Later, I oversaw the surgery on your arm, although others on the team did most of the work. How are you doing?"

The scrubs he was wearing were fresh, so he hadn't come directly from an operating room, but he appeared to have spent long, hard hours in one. He looked very tired. His thinning hair had threads of gray in it, and Calder took comfort in learning that the doctor who'd been in charge of his care wasn't a newbie.

"Dumb question, huh?" Montgomery smiled wryly. "*Under the circumstances,* how are you doing?"

Calder cleared his throat. "What about my arm?"

"The bullet entered here." He indicated a point an inch or so above the crook of Calder's elbow. "It dinged your humerus and exited out the back just beneath your shoulder. It missed the joint, for which you can be grateful.

"All the bone splinters were tweezed out. A vascular surgeon repaired one major blood vessel and restored the blood supply to your lower arm and hand. As gunshot wounds go, you got off lucky. What worried us most was your head injury."

"Head injury?"

"Apparently your head struck the ground. Hard. When they brought you in, you were responsive but remained unconscious. We did a brain scan to look for bleeds, a fracture, or a depression. Didn't find any. You have a bad concussion, and there is some brain swelling, but it's not severe. We can control it with meds and supplemental oxygen." He indicated the cannula.

"I have a bitch of a headache."

The doctor nodded. "That's to be expected. It will dissipate. The neurologist assigned to you will come in later and test your cognition, but you don't appear to be confused. Speech isn't slurred. Is your vision blurry?"

"Not since I first woke up. Takes me a few seconds to focus, though."

"That's normal, too." The surgeon lifted Calder's left hand off the bed. "Can you wiggle your fingers? Like you were playing a piano."

Calder did so against the doctor's hand and had a sudden recollection of impatiently tapping his fingers against his outer thigh as he waited his turn to go through the turnstile that had admitted him into the fair.

If he hadn't been delayed, would he have missed the shooting? If he'd been delayed even a moment longer, would he have been killed? What vagaries of fortune had caused him to be struck by a bullet? What had prevented that bullet from going into his heart instead of his upper arm?

Dr. Montgomery seemed pleased by his ability to move his fingers as instructed and returned his hand to the bed. "Neither I nor the neurosurgeon detected any nerve damage, but alert us to any numbness or tingling anywhere along your arm.

"As insurance, we'll do another brain scan tomorrow. We'll monitor you closely for the next few days and keep you on IV antibiotics to avoid infection, then send you home to take it easy and let your arm heal. In a few weeks, if there are no complications, the orthopedist will prescribe several weeks of PT to rebuild muscle strength and flexibility. You're thirty-seven?"

"Thirty-eight next month."

"Well, you've got general good health on your side. Your vitals are good. Blood work was perfect. You'll have scars where the bullet entered and exited, but the important thing is that you'll heal. In a few months your arm should be as good as new."

"I'm relieved to hear that. Thanks."

The doctor paused, then said, "A psychologist will be in to talk to you about the experience."

"No need for that."

"It's hospital protocol for patients who've survived a traumatic event."

"Well, it's not my protocol. I don't want to talk about the experience. I just want to forget it."

The doctor looked him in the eye long enough for it to become uncomfortable, then quietly said, "In a day or so, the swelling in your brain will subside. But what it recorded today will be there every day for the rest of your life. You acted with courage during the crisis, Mr. Hudson. Don't turn cowardly now. Talk to the psychologist."

Calder lost all sense of time. Staff cycled in and out of his room like circus clowns in a mini car. His temperature was taken. His blood was drawn. Once an hour, he was forced to sit up and huff into a spirometer.

After he puked up the first soft drink, he was offered something to alleviate the nausea. When a nurse arrived with a suppository, he told her to forget it. He'd rather vomit up his toenails.

A nurse who appeared to be about twelve years old came in to check his catheter and measure the amount of urine in the attached bag. It was mortifying.

In between the incessant interruptions, he tried to sleep; he longed for a return to unconsciousness, but his injured arm had begun to throb like an independent life form with a heartbeat of its own. His headache was compounded by all the activity going on around him.

He was told that his girlfriend had been refused admittance because he hadn't yet been interviewed by the police. He felt sorry for the person who'd had to turn Shauna away. She would have gone into orbit. Shauna Calloway of the award-winning channel seven news team wasn't accustomed to being told no.

But he was secretly relieved she'd been denied access. Beyond the humiliation of her seeing him in such a pathetic state, she would be sorrowful, grateful, sympathetic, and solicitous. She had a flair for drama. He didn't have the fortitude to cope with that spillover of emotionality right now.

She would also be curious. She would probe him for information, pester him to give her details, and ask in-depth questions that he wasn't prepared to answer.

Which was why when two strangers entered his room and identified themselves as detectives for the county sheriff's office CID, dread settled over him like a blanket of chain mail.

Chapter 3

The masculine half of the pair appeared to be in his fifties. He was of average height, average weight, average everything except for the traits one would attribute to a detective.

Although his expression tended toward dour, there was no edginess or toughness to him, nothing hard-boiled. He could have been the man who prepared Calder's tax returns. His last name was Perkins. Calder didn't catch his first.

By contrast, there was nothing average about his female partner. She had oversize hair, oversize teeth, and oversize breasts that strained the buttons on the light blue shirt she wore beneath her navy blazer. Her name was Olivia Compton. She wasn't as old as Perkins, but her demeanor was more assertive. Despite the maternal bosom, her aspect was all business.

She asked, "How are you feeling, Mr. Hudson?"

"Like dog shit. How are you?"

A penciled eyebrow arched. She glanced at Perkins, who didn't react at all. When she came back to Calder, she said, "I don't think that response needs elaboration."

"What's CID?"

"Criminal Investigations Division."

"You're here to ask me about the shooting?"

"A necessary evil. Perkins and I understand how difficult this is."

"So why put me through it now?"

"This is only a preliminary interview. We'll keep it brief."

Calder gave a terse nod. He wanted them gone, but he'd been haunted by a question he had to ask. "How many casualties were there?"

"Counting you, twelve wounded, three of those are in critical condition. Five fatalities including the suspect. He died at the scene. Self-inflicted gunshot wound."

Good, Calder thought but didn't say it out loud. "Who was he? What was his beef?"

"We haven't yet released his name, because he was a minor."

"A minor?"

"Sixteen."

"Shit."

"But he'd been booked twice for breaking and entering, once for petty theft, once for selling pot to his friends in middle school. He served two stints in juvie and officially dropped out of high school last year. The day before yesterday, he was hired by the fair to work one of the games on the midway."

Speaking for the first time, Perkins added a footnote. "As to what his beef was, we're trying to determine that."

"Maybe he didn't need a beef," Calder said with scorn. The guy sounded like a loser wanting to generate some respect and recognition for himself, so he went on a shooting spree, killing four people and counting. Calder wished he could peel the skin off the son of a bitch inch by inch. "Was he whacked out on drugs?"

"The autopsy will tell," Compton said. "But he had to pass a drug test before he was hired."

"Those can be rigged."

The agents nodded in grim agreement. Compton said, "We're trying to ascertain what his motivation was, so we need to talk to anybody who might have seen or heard something that would give us a hint. Like if you saw him beforehand in an altercation with someone."

"I didn't make it as far as the midway, and I didn't see an altercation of any kind."

"I was just using that as an example," she said. "Talk us through your experience."

"Now?"

"We'll keep it brief."

So she'd said, but already this preliminary interview had lasted too long. His head was killing him, so was his arm, and his stomach was still queasy. Maybe he should have submitted to the suppository.

He despised being utterly helpless. The detectives had the leverage, the authority, and their facial expressions were as implacable as those on Mount Rushmore, so he had just as well recount what he remembered and get it over with.

"I got to the fairground about—"

Perkins cut him off. "We'd like some background on you first."

"Like what?"

"What we couldn't get off your driver's license. Is the home address on it current?"

"Yes."

"Are you married?"

"No, but I live with my girlfriend."

"What's her name?"

"Shauna Calloway."

The two stopped scribbling on their small spiral note-pads, looked at him, looked at each other, then back at him. "The Shauna Calloway on channel five?" Compton asked.

"Channel seven, but yes."

"Huh. Are you aware that she was doing an interview—"

"Yes. I was going to meet up with her and stay for the concert."

"It was canceled," Perkins offered.

"Have you spoken with Ms. Calloway since the shooting?" Compton asked. "Is she aware that you were wounded?"

"I haven't spoken to her, but somehow she learned that I was shot. One of the nurses told me that she came here to the hospital, but they wouldn't let her in to see me because I hadn't talked to you yet."

Compton said, "Since she and her video crew were on the premises, they were the first to break the story. Within minutes of the shooting, they were reporting live from the fairground."

Shauna would have eaten that up, Calder thought.

He should be happy for her for getting that opportunity. Instead, he felt an inexplicable resentment.

"Who do you work for, Mr. Hudson?" Perkins asked.

"I'm self-employed."

"What do you do?"

He gave them his pat answer. "Consulting."

"Who do you consult?"

"Corporate clients."

His pat answers weren't washing with Compton. "What kind of consulting, Mr. Hudson?"

"It varies from company to company." He rubbed his temples with the fingers of his right hand. "Look, my head is about to explode. Can't this wait?"

"Just a few more questions," she said. "The shooting took place just inside the north gate."

"Yeah, I'd come through maybe a minute earlier."

"You came alone?"

"Alone except for the mob of people also trying to get in. Shauna had offered to leave a pass for me, but I hadn't confirmed that I was coming, so I had to wait in line to buy a ticket. Once through the turnstile, I merged with people trying to exit. It was a madhouse."

"We've seen security camera video," Perkins said.

"The shooter couldn't have picked a better spot to open fire," Calder said. "The crowd was so tightly packed he couldn't have missed hitting a lot of people in a fraction of time. Although when it was happening, it seemed to go on forever."

"Here's the suspect's last mug shot. Do you remember seeing him?" From the pocket of her blazer, Compton produced the picture and held it out to him.

The guy was about what Calder had expected: half-mast eyelids, long, unwashed hair, and a "fuck you" expression. In a few minutes' time, he'd graduated from punk to mass murderer. *Congratulations, asshole.*

With disgust, Calder handed the picture back to Compton. "I don't remember seeing him, but I could have. It was an awful crush."

"What were you doing when you heard the first shot?"

"Working my way through the crowd. Shauna had mentioned that she would be backstage. I was trying to figure out the easiest way to get there."

"When you first heard the shots, what did you think?"

"I thought, some crazy motherfucker is shooting at us."

Again the detectives exchanged a look before coming back to him. Compton said, "We're checking into the suspect's background to see if he had a history of mental illness."

"If he didn't before, he has a history of it now."

Compton didn't respond to that. "You knew right away you'd heard a gunshot?"

"Yeah. My dad is a gun enthusiast. He has semiautomatic weapons that he uses for sport. Less now than he used to, but, growing up, I often went to the range with him. We always wore headsets, but I know what they sound like when fired. What did this guy use?"

"Glock 34."

Calder knew it to be a semiautomatic nine-millimeter, a favorite of law enforcement officers.

"It came with an eighteen-round magazine," the agent said. "It was empty."

So he'd fired his last bullet into his own head, Calder thought.

"Do you own a gun, Mr. Hudson?" Compton asked.

"Only a deer rifle, but I rarely go hunting. The last time was a couple of years ago. The rifle hasn't been fired since."

Perkins said, "You were seen on security cameras hunkering down and grabbing the sleeve of the man nearest you and pulling him to the ground."

"I did? I don't remember."

"He does," Compton said, her eyebrow arching again.

"Is he okay?"

"Thanks to you."

Calder rubbed his hand over his face. "I can't take credit. I acted on impulse."

"You're shown shouting and motioning for people to get down."

"I really don't remember."

"Did you have military training?"

"No. I never served." He tried to situate himself more comfortably on the bed, but with all the tubes attached to him, he was as good as strapped down. "I'm hurting, and I'm tired. I don't remember much. I reacted. That's it, okay?"

"Do you remember going after a baby stroller?"

He closed his eyes. His head hurt more when he tried to think. "Not until just now. Not until you said it."

"Did you know the child?"

"No."

"The parents?"

"No. I'd passed the stroller..."

Thinking back now, he remembered the cumbersome

thing, how annoyed he'd been that it was blocking his path and asking himself why anyone in their right mind would subject their kid to this germy mob scene and try to push a behemoth like that stroller through such a dense crowd.

"Mr. Hudson?" Compton said. "What were you about to say?"

"I, uh..." What had he been about to say? "Uh, moments before the first shot was fired, I'd had to go around it. The stroller." In the process, he'd nudged aside a woman, who he supposed was the kid's mother.

The two detectives were looking at him with the expectation of more to come. "When, uh, when I dropped to the ground, I turned and looked back toward the exit. I think I must've been judging the distance to it. Figuring how exposed I'd be if I made a run for it. Like that. But I don't remember actually *thinking* all that, just...you know. We're talking split seconds.

"Anyhow, I saw this dude barrel into the stroller. I'd thought those things were built not to turn over, but this guy hit it with such force, it tipped over onto two wheels. It was rolling crazily, bumping into people, causing them to stumble." He divided a look between the two. "Again, I guess I acted on instinct and lunged for it."

"You were trying to stop the stroller and it was dragging you over with it when the bullet struck you. Your grimace of pain is clearly visible on the security camera video."

Calder met Compton's incisive gaze, trying to process that information. "I remember an *impact* but nothing after that."

"In spite of your attempt to stop it, the stroller toppled

over onto its side just as you were hit. You fell over it and banged your head on the pavement."

"That explains the concussion."

Compton looked over at her partner. Perkins gazed back at her impassively, but apparently they communicated something, because she drew herself up to her full height and pocketed her notebook.

She said, "They gave us only five minutes. We'll go now, but we'll probably stop by again tomorrow. More often than not, a blow to the head like you sustained affects recall, causes temporary amnesia. Something may occur to you that you haven't remembered yet. You didn't remember the stroller until I mentioned it. If you think of something, please call us immediately."

She laid a business card on the bedside table. "We need information so we can isolate the shooter's motive."

"Does it matter?"

Compton replied, "It does if he was in cahoots with someone else who's still out there." She let that settle, then said, "Get some rest, Mr. Hudson."

As the pair turned away from him, Calder mumbled a goodbye, then said, "What about the kid in the stroller?"

The two detectives came back around. Compton said, "Two-year-old boy. Charlie Portman."

"Was he hurt when that thing went over? Is he all right?"

For the first time since entering the room, she dropped the authoritative persona and looked at him like a regular person. "No. He was struck."

Calder's heart clenched. He looked at the detective with abject appeal, but she added, "He died at the scene."

Chapter 4

Glenda. I won't survive this." Elle bent at the waist, buried her face in the stuffed bunny she'd been holding in her lap, and sobbed into the nubby fabric that smelled of Charlie.

Glenda laid her hand on Elle's back and rubbed consoling circles. "I know you don't *think* you will, but you will. One baby step at a time."

Elle continued to cry and wasn't even aware that her friend had turned off the car and come around and opened the passenger door until Glenda reached in and guided her out.

She stood beside the car and looked at her front door, dreading the moment she would enter the house, knowing that when she did, the reality of what had happened since she'd left it the previous afternoon would slam into her. It might be more than she could withstand.

"Baby steps," Glenda whispered. "Come on."

She never could have made that walk without Glenda's

support, but together they reached the porch. Glenda magically produced her door key, although Elle didn't remember giving it to her. She unlocked the door and gently ushered Elle inside.

There sat Charlie's fire truck on the entry table where she'd placed it as they were leaving for the fair, having convinced him that it was too bulky to fit in the bag they were taking along and assuring him that he wasn't leaving the treasured toy forever, which in his two-year-old mind he was. She'd promised him that it would be there when he returned.

As promised, it was. But Charlie wasn't returning.

She sobbed. Her knees went weak. Glenda took her arm and led her into the living room and over to a wide, upholstered chair. She collapsed into it like a rag doll.

From the perspective of that chair, she spied one of Charlie's sneakers underneath the sofa across the room. The sneaker had gone missing several days ago. She had looked for it everywhere except, apparently, under the sofa.

She must remember to get it later, but for now, all she had the wherewithal to do was sit and look at the small, empty shoe through eyes that filled with fresh tears.

Glenda knelt in front of her. "Do you want something?"

"Yes. I want to wake up and discover that this has been an ungodly dream."

"What can I do for you, Elle?"

"Turn back time?"

"I wish with all my heart that I could. But I can't."

"Then there's nothing. Besides, you've done enough already. You must be exhausted. Go home."

"Not a chance."

"You don't have to stay."

"I'm herc, and I'm staying."

She stood and went over to the sofa, where she sat down and tugged off her cowboy boots. Her fringed jacket came off next; then she began unwinding the ropes of beads from around her neck.

Glenda was wearing the same clothes she'd had on when she'd arrived at the fair. At some point in the past twelve hours—Elle couldn't remember precisely when—someone, whom she didn't recall, either, had provided her with a set of scrubs and a pair of rubber flip-flops to exchange for her clothes and shoes, which were stained with blood. That of the older man she'd chatted with, and Charlie's.

Her healthy son had had a sturdy little body. She'd often teased him about it as she playfully poked him in the belly. But he had felt very small, defenseless, and fragile when she'd clutched him to her, screaming prayers that he would take a breath, make a sound, that she would feel a heart-beat. His sweet body, the one that had chugged around so energetically and industriously, had remained unmoving and limp. Lifeless.

She gave another harsh sob.

Glenda dumped the strands of beads on the coffee table and went back to Elle's chair. "You're taking a shower while I scramble some eggs. After you're fed, I'm giving you one of the sedatives you refused to take earlier and putting you to bed."

Glenda hauled her up out of the chair. When Glenda was in managerial mode, it was easier to go along than to balk, so Elle didn't argue or put up any resistance as she was pro-pelled out of the living room and down the hall.

"Do you need help with that?" Glenda pointed to the cold pack on Elle's right elbow.

"It's just Velcro. I'll manage."

"Okay. Undress. I'll get the water going."

Glenda left her standing in the center of her bedroom, where everything was so familiar, but nothing would ever be the same. She removed the cold pack and laid it on the end of the bed, then mechanically began to take off the scrubs.

When Glenda returned from the bathroom, Elle was down to her panties. Her bra had been too bloodstained to salvage. "It's ready for you," her friend said. "Take as long as you like. I'll be in the kitchen." She pulled the door closed behind her when she went out.

Although Elle longed for the restoration a hot shower could provide, she was reluctant to wash off the last physical vestiges of her son. His scent, the sticky imprint of his hand on her cheek, the smear of drool that had dried on her neck.

Knowing it had to be done, she stepped into the shower stall and stood directly beneath the spray, head bowed. She let it beat down on her for a full minute before opening her eyes. The water swirling around her feet toward the drain was tinged pink with her child's blood.

Not until the water ran clear did she reach for the soap and begin to wash.

Glenda forced her to eat some of the breakfast she'd cooked, then gave her a pill, strapped a fresh cold pack to her arm, and tucked her in. The sedative was effective. She went almost instantly to sleep. When she woke up, she enjoyed a few precious seconds of forgetfulness before memory blasted in.

Gauging by the slant of the sun coming through her bedroom window, it was late afternoon. Still a bit fuzzy from the medication, she dressed and left her bedroom.

In the living room, Glenda had her large leather-bound day planner lying open on her lap. She was talking on her cell phone, confirming a two o'clock appointment for the following day.

"Thank you. We'll be there." She clicked off and set her phone and calendar aside. "I took the liberty of scheduling you an appointment with the funeral director."

"I appreciate that, but I don't know when they'll release his... his body. I was told it could be several days."

"When they do, you'll have the preparations already behind you."

Elle sat down, leaned back in her chair, and gazed up at the ceiling, thinking of all the arrangements she needed to attend to, how exhausting those chores would be, and how unmotivated she was to do a damn thing.

After a lengthy pause, Glenda tentatively resumed. "Your parents are due in at eight-thirty this evening. I scheduled a car to pick them up at the airport, bring them here, and then wait until they're ready to go to the hotel, where I've reserved them a room."

At Elle's request, Glenda had called them from the morgue to deliver the news. It was an impersonal and insensitive way to inform them of their only grandchild's death, but, at the time, Charlie had looked so cold and pale that to leave him alone would have felt like abandonment.

Glenda had reported that her parents, who lived in Michigan, had heard of the mass shooting on CNN, but, of course, they never would have dreamed that Charlie and she were victims.

It had been the middle of the night when Glenda had called them, but they'd told her they would book themselves on the next available flight and would text her their itinerary.

Glenda said now, "Of course you have the option of having them stay here with you."

"I suppose I should extend the offer."

"Do you want them here?"

She gave a feeble smile. "Not really."

"Then don't offer, Elle." Glenda leaned forward and said with earnestness, "Get this straight. You don't have to cater to anyone except yourself. You don't have to be stoic or an example of how to grieve elegantly. You don't have to do or be anything you don't want to."

"Except to go on living."

"You don't mean that," Glenda said softly. "I know you don't. Think of the awful legacy that would lay on your precious Charlie."

When Elle didn't respond, Glenda took a deep breath and continued with the practical matters. "I also notified Laura."

Laura Musgrave was Elle's literary agent.

"At first, she was in shock; then she became distraught. She wanted to speak to you immediately. I told her you were sleeping but that I was certain you would contact her soon. She plans to fly down for the funeral. We're to send her the details when we have them."

"I'll call her in a while. There are so many people I need to notify."

"Taken care of," Glenda said. "I got into the contacts on your phone and made a list of first-tier friends and acquaintances, people I thought you would want notified sooner rather than later. I sent all the info to my staff. They're making those calls on your behalf."

"What about Jeff?" Elle asked.

"I didn't know how you'd feel about that, so I left him out."

"He's my ex-husband. Word will get around to him."

"Which, to my mind, relieves you of an awkward conversation."

Elle extended her hand in a gesture of gratitude. "You've been busy while I was knocked out. Did you get any rest?"

"I took a nap."

"Thank you for handling things."

"Don't thank me yet."

Elle withered. "What?"

"Since the fairground isn't within a city limit, the investigation falls to the county sheriff's office. Detectives want to talk to you, but they're extending you the courtesy of coming here rather than having you go to them. If you hadn't woken up when you did, I would have had to wake you. They're due here soon."

"The culprit killed himself," Elle said. "What is there to investigate?"

"I guess you'll find out."

Just then a phone rang, and Glenda said, "That's yours. Want me to get it?"

"Please."

She answered Elle's cell phone, which was sitting beside hers on the coffee table. After identifying herself, she listened, then said, "She's unavailable, especially to the media, and how did you get her number, anyway?"

More listening, then she covered the mouthpiece. "Shauna Calloway. Channel seven. She said to tell you that she's a close personal friend of Calder Hudson."

"Who's that?"

"The name doesn't mean anything to you?"

Elle shook her head.

"Me, either." Glenda went back to the phone, through which Elle could hear a woman still talking in clipped, imperative tones. "I don't care who you're friends with. Ms. Portman is unavailable for comment. Don't call again." Glenda clicked off and huffed, "Honestly. Pushy bitch."

"It will be all over the news, won't it?"

"It already is, Elle." She motioned toward the television. "Do you want to—"

"No."

"I didn't think so, which is why I haven't watched, either."

The doorbell rang. Swearing under her breath, Glenda said, "It's Grand Damn Central Station in here." She went to the front window and peered out.

"A man and a woman who I would bet are the expected detectives. They're right on time." She turned back to Elle. "Are you up to this? Say the word and I'll barricade the door."

"It won't be any easier later."

"Talking to cops is never easy. I have a lot of high-profile celebrity clients, remember. Occasionally one gets into a scrape. Police provide a much-needed public service, but keep in mind that they have their own agenda."

Elle looked down at her ragged jeans and one of her T-shirts that needed an upgrade. "Am I at least presentable?"

"Who gives a shit?"

Elle blurted a humorless laugh. "Let them in."

Glenda left her, went into the foyer, and answered the door. Introductions were murmured. Glenda said, "I'm Elle's friend Glenda Foster. Is this absolutely necessary right now?"

More murmuring, then the shuffle of feet as the two detectives came inside. They preceded Glenda into the living room. She introduced them as Detectives Perkins and Compton. "This is Elle Portman." She motioned them into a pair of armchairs.

Compton dragged hers several inches closer to the easy chair in which Elle sat. She tipped her head toward the compression sleeve on Elle's arm. "How is it?"

"Nothing bad. I landed hard on my elbow and caused temporary numbness. Like when you hit your funny bone, except about a hundred times worse. It'll be all right."

She'd been told all that by the intern in the ER after her arm was x-rayed. Her elbow hadn't been dislocated. No bones were broken. Her arm had been wrapped in the cold pack and put in a sling. She'd been given prescription-strength ibuprofen to take for inflammation and then released...to reunite with Charlie in the morgue.

Her attention was brought back to Compton, who was speaking softly. "On behalf of everyone in the sheriff's department, I want to extend our deepest sympathy, Ms. Portman."

"Thank you."

"Detective Perkins and I realize what an intrusion our visit is and apologize for the necessity of it."

"Why is it a necessity? Word filtered down while I was still in the emergency room that the shooter had taken his own life at the scene."

"We're trying to establish his motive."

"Then I'll help you any way I can," Elle stated. "Because I want to know why. *Why* did my son die that way? *Why*?" Her voice cracked. She covered her face with her hands and began to cry into them.

In an instant Glenda was beside her with a box of tissues. "Do you want some water? Anything?"

Elle pulled a tissue from the box and blotted her eyes. "Nothing, thanks."

"I'm sorry, Ms. Portman. You've suffered a terrible loss. Words are inadequate."

She met Compton's gaze and nodded a thank-you. "You are exactly right. Words are inadequate, so don't waste them. What I want, need—*demand*—is an explanation beyond the banal. Since you're investigating, I charge you with finding out why he did it."

Chapter 5

Compton remained calm, no doubt having heard similar mandates from victims of violent crime. "We have personnel working day and night, in conjunction with state authorities, to provide you with answers as to why this individual did what he did. We can't bring your son back, but, I assure you, Ms. Portman, that we wish to give you whatever closure we're able."

She reached into the pocket of her blazer. "The suspect." She passed Elle a photograph.

It was a mug shot. The young man staring back at her embodied hostility and insolence. He was smirking with contempt. "His name?"

"It's being withheld because he was only sixteen, and we've yet to locate a parent or guardian. He'd been in trouble since puberty and had a police record." She gave Elle a rundown of the teen's criminal history.

Glenda muttered a profanity under her breath and said, "And this miscreant was walking among us?"

"He didn't have any outstanding warrants," Perkins said. "His fingerprints were linked only to his previous arrests."

"That's a huge comfort," Glenda said, glaring at him. "I feel much better now."

The detective remained unmoved by her sarcasm.

Compton continued. "He skipped out on his probation officer in Houston over a year ago and definitely worked the system."

"Dysfunctional system," Glenda said.

"He was crafty enough to get himself employed at the fairground. But they didn't check the information on his application form very well, if at all. His name was authentic, but the New Mexico driver's license he used for his ID was fake. He filled in a Dallas zip code, but the street address doesn't exist, which makes it extremely difficult to track his recent actions, including those of yesterday afternoon.

"We're trying to learn where he went and who he saw prior to the shooting. Had he posted rants or grievances on social media? He didn't have activity like that on his phone, but it could have been a burner that he used only to make calls. He could have had a computer tucked away somewhere. We're investigating all that because there may be others involved that we don't know about."

"You mean accomplices?" Elle asked.

"Well, in this situation, that's a broad term. The suspect might have been commissioned, dared, or threatened by a radical group with an agenda. Under duress, he martyred himself. Or he acted entirely alone, a victim himself of ridicule, shaming, romantic rejection—"

"Sociopathy."

Compton, who'd apparently had it with Glenda's editorial comments, shot her a dirty look before coming back to Elle. "Or he could have been mentally ill to one degree or another. We won't know his circumstances until we locate his next of kin or acquaintances."

"Where are you with that?" Elle asked.

"Not far, I'm afraid. There were only a handful of contacts in his phone, and those we've spoken with claimed not to have seen or heard from him in months."

"And you're taking their word for that?"

Compton shot Glenda another dirty look. "Of course not. We're following up, but it's taking time, because these few individuals are scattered over several states, leading us to believe that the suspect was a transient." She hesitated, then with reluctance said, "There's something else that's working against us."

"I can hardly wait," Glenda muttered.

"I told you he was cagey. He must have known where the fairground security cameras were located, and he avoided them, except for those near the game booth where he was working.

"Between customers, he's seen going in and out of the tent there, probably to smoke marijuana. It was found on him. Three minutes before the first shot was fired, he's seen looking around furtively, then slipping into the tent where his body was found. But we haven't yet detected him in the crowd firing the weapon."

Hearing all this incensed Elle. "In which case, you have nothing, absolutely nothing to go on."

Compton said, "Determining a motive may not be timely or easy, but we won't give up, Ms. Portman. The first thing we must determine is if he was a disillusioned loner or a disciple willing to die for a cause. Did he have partners who helped camouflage him in that crowd? That would be particularly worrisome because we have no idea who they might be.

"We also need to determine if he fired randomly, not caring who he hit. Or did he/they have a specific target, and the other victims, like your son, were collateral damage? That's why it's necessary for us to interview anyone who might recently have had even a passing connection to him."

"I don't recognize him at all," Elle said as she took one last look at the face of her son's murderer before returning the picture to the agent.

Compton replaced the photo in her blazer pocket, then asked Elle if she would relate what she recalled of the minutes leading up to when the first shot was fired. "The more details you can remember, the better. Let us decide whether or not they're significant."

"Well, I said goodbye to Glenda at the kiddie carousel and started—"

"Excuse me." Compton turned to Glenda. "You were also there?"

Glenda explained their arrangement to meet and her plans for the remainder of the evening. "I peeled off and headed for the beer garden."

"Did you hear the shots?"

"No. But soon after I'd joined my group, people began coming into the pavilion and shouting about a shooting. Then police officers swarmed in and contained everyone. For *hours*. We were given very little information."

"The officers wouldn't have had much information at that point."

"I guess," Glenda said in response to Perkins's remark. "But the news reports certainly weren't censored. All of us were watching on our phones, and the visuals being broadcast actually made everyone even more anxious. Families had split up, just as Elle and I had. Not to know if a loved one was a casualty... Well, you can imagine the anxiety.

"Worse for me, Elle wasn't answering her phone, and I knew she would have if she could. My best hope was that she and Charlie were being contained in an area like I was and that perhaps she didn't have possession of her phone. But when I finally did hear from her, she was calling from the emergency room."

During the telling, her voice had turned rough with emotion. "She was hysterical. No one was with her. As soon as everyone in the beer garden was cleared to go, I raced to the hospital. After she was released, we went to the morgue. We were told they don't usually let loved ones in to see the body, but under the circumstances..." She paused and looked miserably at Elle.

She said, "They uncovered his face for me."

"She couldn't be with him, but she didn't want to leave him there alone. We stayed. I drove her home early this morning."

A pall settled over the four of them. Perkins coughed

behind his fist. Compton scribbled something on her spiral notepad, then asked Elle to describe her actions from the time she and Glenda had separated.

"Charlie was becoming cranky. I was eager to get him home, but we were stalled because of the bottleneck at the gate. There was a man standing next to us. He and I'd had a brief exchange. When I heard the shot, I turned to him." She raised her hand to her throat. "He...uh..."

"He was slain by the first shot fired," Compton said.

Having the gentleman's death confirmed sent a spike of pain through Elle's chest. "What was his name?"

"Howard Rollins. You didn't know each other?"

"No. But he was friendly and seemed good-natured." Sadly, she added, "I thought he would make a good character."

The agents looked at each other in puzzlement. "A good character?" Perkins asked.

"Elle writes and illustrates children's books," Glenda said.

Quick to clarify, Elle said, "So far only one has been published. I'm working on the second. I liked this man's..." She made a circular motion over her face. "He had a kindly face. Like a Santa Claus without the beard." She bowed her head and said huskily, "I saw him die."

When she didn't immediately continue, Compton asked if she needed to take a moment.

"No." She raised her head, then tilted it back and sniffed. "Let's just please...Can we...finish soon? How much more do you need to know?"

Compton's prompting was gentle, but, nonetheless, she

gave Elle prompts that forced her to verbalize memories she would rather wish away.

"I could hear Charlie crying, but I couldn't get to him. Then his stroller was tipped over by a man who barreled past it. He didn't stop. He ran on.

"Then a man dressed in business clothes lunged from behind me and tried to catch the stroller from teetering, but it had too much momentum. He went down with it. At that point, I didn't know that he'd been shot." She rubbed her temple. "My right arm had lost all feeling. It was useless, but somehow, I managed to crawl over to the stroller."

"Had the shooting stopped?" Perkins asked.

"No, but it seemed to be coming from farther away. Although, in truth, I wasn't even thinking about that at the time. Only about getting to my child. The man who'd fallen over the stroller was large, tall. I couldn't see Charlie at all. I was screaming his name and trying frantically to reach him. He... he was no longer crying."

After a lengthy silence that was fraught with emotions forcibly contained, she resumed in a low monotone. "Suddenly I was surrounded by people who had rushed to my aid. The gunfire had stopped. Several men lifted the man off the stroller and laid him on the ground." Abruptly she stopped and asked Compton, "Was he dead?"

"No. He survived."

"That's good." Elle meant it sincerely, but her voice was faint because her mind had already returned to the most horrific moments of her life. "A man with elaborate tattoos on his arms helped me pull Charlie out of the stroller. The paramedics—a young man and young woman—appeared. It seemed they were there very quickly, but I could be wrong. Time seemed either to be suspended or racing like fast-forward.

"They worked on him. They worked on him even while in the ambulance on the way to the hospital. Even when they knew there was no hope, they kept working on him. I could tell they were distressed because they couldn't bring him back."

She lost control then and began to sob, taking heaving breaths that racked her entire body.

She was aware of Glenda going into overdrive and ordering the detectives to leave. Even they deferred to Glenda. They stood.

"I'm sorry, I'm sorry," Elle gasped, looking at them in turn. "I know it's your duty. I want you to do your duty. I want to know why he did it. How *could* he? I'll help you. I will. But I can't talk about it anymore right now."

"We understand," Compton said. "We'll be in touch, but for now we have what we need. Your account corroborated Mr. Hudson's."

Elle darted a glance toward Glenda and saw that she too was surprised to hear that name repeated within half an hour of hearing it for the first time from Shauna Calloway.

"Mr. *Hudson*?" Elle said to Compton.

"Calder Hudson, the man who was shot while trying to stop your son's stroller."

On a short exhalation, Elle said, "Oh. How awful of me.

I hadn't even thought to ask his name. You said he survived, but what's his condition? Is he going to be all right?"

"He's going to be fine. He was shot in his left arm. The bullet passed through." Compton looked over at her partner. Perkins gave her a subtle nod. Then Compton came back to Elle and looked at her with empathy. "It was the bullet that killed Charlie."

Chapter 6

Calder, before you have a knee-jerk reaction, hear me out, okay?" Shauna spoke quietly, but she was fairly shivering with pent-up energy, like a puppy who'd been ordered to stay.

She'd arrived ten minutes earlier. For eight of them, she'd hovered and fussed over him. Fluffing his pillow, offering him the lidded cup with the bent straw from which he had obligingly taken a sip of ice water, asking if his arm was miserable, if his headache was any better, if his vision was completely back to normal.

Over the past two days, she'd come to visit him three times, and he'd grown increasingly unhappy to see her. She brought too much *flutter* with her.

Television viewers who hadn't known her before the fairground shooting had come to know her since. Her touted live coverage at the scene, practically as the tragic event was unfolding, had considerably increased her visibility on the local channel and had achieved network exposure as well.

She signed autographs for starstruck nurses and orderlies. She granted them selfies taken with her, usually offering before they even asked. Her Instagram and Twitter accounts must be melting from overuse.

He didn't begrudge her this major feather in her cap. She'd earned it. He just wished she would bask in the glow of her new celebrity status somewhere other than his hospital room. At least during this visit, she'd kept the door closed and hadn't invited into his room anyone seeking to take a picture of her and him together. Hell would be frozen over for millennia before that happened.

When he'd finally convinced her that he was as comfortable as he could possibly be under the circumstances, she'd dragged the room's one chair closer to his bed, perched on the edge of the seat, and finally got down to what he suspected was the reason for the nervous intensity he'd sensed the instant she'd entered the room.

He turned his head on the pillow and looked at her. "What?"

Her chest expanded with a deep breath. "I brought a production crew here with me. They're waiting downstairs for my signal. I have the hospital's permission. Now that Detective Compton has your official statement, she gave me the green light." She clasped her hands beneath her chin and gave him a pretty-please smile. "Let me interview you."

While seconds ticked past, he merely looked at her, then said, "On camera? For TV?"

"Well, yes and yes."

"Well, fuck and no."

"You agreed to hear me out."

"No, I didn't. And this isn't a knee-jerk reaction. If I pondered it from now till Doomsday, I'd still say no."

"Calder, your name comes up in every news story about the shooting. People attribute their survival to you. You're big news, and I'm a news reporter who also happens to be your girlfriend." She spread her arms wide. "I couldn't dream of a better scenario."

He thought he might need Cindy to bring him the upchuck bag again. "Signal your crew."

"Really?"

"Really. Tell them they can pack up their gear and get the hell lost. I'm not doing it."

"Calder—"

"People *died*, Shauna! Christ!" He pinched the bridge of his nose and squeezed his eyes shut. He was hoping that she would leave, but when he lowered his hand, she was as she had been, except more subdued... by possibly one degree.

"I'm aware of that," she said softly. "Right now they're only names. Grim statistics. I want to present the stories behind the names. Let people know who they were in life. I want to make them real."

"Trust me. They were real. They bled."

"See? That's jarring in its honesty. That's what you should tell the audience."

He chuffed, disbelieving that she still didn't get it. "I'm not saying a fucking thing into a microphone for any fucking camera. Now, can we drop it, please?"

She rested her back against the chair, saying nothing

while she fiddled with the gold chain dangling from her neck. Then, quietly, she spoke. "The ME released the little boy's body. His funeral is the day after tomorrow."

Calder looked aside.

"It's tragic."

"Yeah."

"You did everything you could to try to save him, and the effort almost got you killed."

"Yeah."

"It was fate, Calder. It was his time." She said it in a way that implored him to accept it. "It was…"

"I know what you're trying to say. I've said it to myself a thousand times. But…" He clenched his teeth, took a breath. "I don't want to talk about it, okay?"

"You're depressed. The psychologist told me to expect that."

He turned back to her. "What psychologist?"

"The one here at the hospital."

"You talked to Dr. Sinclair without—"

"At her invitation," she said, cutting him off. "She invited survivors' family members, and, in our case, the 'significant other,' to attend a meeting. Naturally, she didn't go into the specifics about her sessions with each of you. She spoke in generalizations about the stages survivors of a traumatic event go through and what we as loved ones can expect. Depression. Nightmares. Mood swings. That kind of thing."

"Textbook stuff."

"Exactly. Psych one oh one. Certainly nothing for you to get upset over. You've had two sessions with her. What was your impression?"

That she could see straight through my bullshit.

Buying time away from that unsettling thought, he reached for the unwanted cup of water and sipped. To fill the silence, he shook the ice, took another drink, and replaced the cup on the tray bridging his bed.

When he ran out of delaying tactics, he said, "Both times, she did most of the talking. Wanted to know about me. You know, family background, my interests, education, religious affiliation if any."

He shrugged with feigned indifference. "Then she said basically what she told you in that meeting. You can expect this, don't beat yourself up over that, cut yourself some slack, give yourself time. I'm paraphrasing, but that was the gist."

Shauna sat up straighter, appearing relieved. She even gave a light laugh. "I came away from the meeting thinking, 'She doesn't know the Calder Hudson I know.' You'll rebound in no time."

She smiled sweetly as she reached for his hand and squeezed it. "I have my moments, too. Sometimes I'm overtaken by what could have been, and I get weepy. I shudder when I think of how close I came to losing you."

"So do I." He squeezed her hand in return, then released it. "I know you're disappointed, but I'm not going to apologize for turning down the interview. It just wouldn't feel right. Maybe one of the other survivors would be comfortable doing it. I'm not."

"I've already recorded one with a young woman who was at the fair with her mom. After the first shots, they got separated in the stampede. The mom got out okay. The police think the daughter was the last one who caught fire before the gunman killed himself. She was in the vicinity of the tent and got shot in the calf. Rotten luck for her."

"Rotten? She's lucky to be alive."

"Of course," she said with a trace of exasperation. "I only meant— Never mind. The interview with her will be on the six o'clock news tonight if you want to watch it." She motioned toward the television mounted on the wall just under the ceiling. "Have you even turned the TV on since you got moved into this room?"

"I haven't felt like watching."

"Even my reports?"

"I saw it as it happened, Shauna. I don't need to see snippets of it on TV. The images remain very clear inside my head." He didn't want to argue with her about it, so he followed up with a question. "What are they saying about him? The shooter."

"Very little. We're getting the basic runaround. 'It's an ongoing investigation. No comment.' I have sources in every branch of law enforcement. They've all gone mute. They won't even release his name until they locate and notify his next of kin."

Since that was the line he'd gotten from Perkins and Compton during his meeting with them, he didn't pursue it.

Shauna gazed around the room as though looking for something else to talk about. "Who sent the flowers?"

It was a lavish bouquet. At his request, an orderly had removed the most fragrant blossoms, which were intensifying his headache and making him queasy.

"JZI. The CEO has left two voice mails, expressing shock

and concern for what happened to me less than an hour after I left their offices."

"Have you called him back?"

"I texted a thank-you for the flowers."

"Have you talked to anyone, Calder? What about your folks?"

"We've talked twice, and we text throughout the day. Dad feels guilty. As if his cancer treatments aren't a good enough reason not to come. Mom's a basket case. She's stretched so thin that I'm as worried about her as I am about him. I emphasized that she's where she needs to be and that I'm fine."

His parents lived in La Jolla, California, where his dad's ideal and well-earned retirement had been cruelly inter-rupted by a diagnosis of leukemia. It was a curable type but required daily infusions for several months. Calder didn't expect or want them to travel halfway across the country to sit by his bedside. It would be a grueling trip for them, and when they got here, what could they do except fret? They could do that in California.

"Would you like for me to call them?" Shauna offered. "Reassure them that you're all right?"

"No. Mom would just suspect that you're hiding a terrible truth about my condition."

"You're probably right," Shauna said, giving him a wan smile. "Your voice mail must be at capacity. Do you want me to return some of the calls for you?"

"No thanks. I'll get to them."

She looked doubtful of that. Rightfully so. He didn't intend to return calls any time soon. Even the best of friends would press him to give them a down-and-dirty account of the shooting, and he wasn't ready for that.

Shauna said, "Maybe talking to some of your baseball teammates would cheer you up."

They were a group of successful professionals who played in a ragtag league that was more about talking trash and drinking beer than batting and catching. "They're a rowdy pack," he said. "I'll get with them when I feel better and regain some strength."

She looked disappointed in his lack of enthusiasm but didn't comment on it. "Has anyone told you when you'll be released?"

"Tomorrow, possibly. If not, then the day after."

"Be sure to give me plenty of notice. I'll be here to drive you home. Your precious Jag is already safe in the garage. I handled that for you."

He hadn't even thought about the retrieval of his car from the dusty fairground parking lot.

Shauna was telling him that their housekeeper had stocked the kitchen with his favorite foods. Shauna had canceled his upcoming dental cleaning and an appointment with his tailor. When she wound down, he said, "Thanks for seeing to all that."

"You don't have to thank me." She ran her fingers through his hair. "I want you back home. I want you well soon."

"Me too."

She leaned down and brushed a dry kiss on his lips, then checked her watch. "I need to get a move on. I've booked an interview with the minister who's going to officiate that funeral. God help him. Literally. I mean, what do you say?"

Having only half listened to everything else she'd been rattling off, upon hearing that, he was instantly alert. "The little boy's funeral?"

Shauna picked up her oversize bag and carried it across the room to the counter where the sink was. "They've already announced that it'll be a private service. Media will be kept a block away from the church. Of all the stories, his is the most poignant because of his age." She moved aside the garish bouquet to better access the mirror above the sink and began to tweak her hair.

Calder cleared his throat. "Do you know if they have other children?"

"There is no 'they.' The mother is a single parent, and whoever the father was"—she spread on lip gloss—"is no longer in the picture. Charlie—not short for Charles, just Charlie—was her only child."

She capped the lip gloss and zipped the tube into a cloth pouch, which she dropped into her bag, then slid the wide strap onto her shoulder. Turning back to him, she said, "I've tried twice to speak with the mother—"

"What's her name?"

"Portman. Elle Portman." Her glossy lips twisted into a frown. "She's got this harpy taking her calls. So far I've gotten nowhere with her. Not even when I invoked your name."

He almost came up out of the bed. "Invoked *my* name?"

"I thought if she knew of our connection—"

"Don't do that again."

She opened her mouth as though to come back with a retort to his brusque order but must have thought better of it. She waited several beats, then said in a calm and level voice, "I didn't think you would object."

"But you didn't ask, did you? And I object a hell of a lot."

"I told the woman on the phone that I was a close personal friend of yours. That's all. If it makes you feel any better, your name didn't make a dent. She hung up on me."

"Can you blame her?"

Again she seemed to be on the verge of saying something else, when instead she looked at her watch again. "I've stayed too long. You look tired. I'll check in on you later. Get some rest."

Then she was gone, eagerly on her way to prepare for her coverage for a curious public of the private funeral of the two-year-old that he couldn't save.

Chapter 7

——◆——

Elle pulled into a metered parking slot in front of the precinct office of the sheriff's department. She'd been asked to appear there at three o'clock. The flags out front were flying at half-staff in honor of the casualties of the Fairground shooting.

It had occurred a week ago today. Over the course of those seven days, it had achieved capitalization status in print and had been designated with a hashtag on social media. News networks were still doing follow-up stories.

But for those not directly involved, it was a notch in history. Millions of people had resumed their everyday lives as though in Elle Portman's universe there hadn't been a catastrophic event on the scale of the sun burning out.

She'd arrived ahead of the assigned time, so she let her car idle while she gave herself a few minutes to reflect on the past week.

Glenda had returned to work this morning, but only after Elle had insisted. When pressed, Glenda had admitted that time-sensitive matters were demanding her attention at Foster Real Estate.

"But I hate for you to go to that meeting alone. What do you think it's about? Did Compton give you a hint?"

"No. When she called this morning, she began by apologizing for imposing on me during this 'difficult time' but asked if I could meet with her and Perkins again this afternoon."

"Asked. But was it optional?"

"I don't think so."

"Maybe you should take a lawyer with you, Elle. I could make some calls."

"No, no. It's nothing like that."

Still looking dubious, Glenda had said, "If you change your mind, I only need a moment's notice. Otherwise, I'll see you back at the house, say sixish? I'm sick of all those casseroles people have brought, so I'll pick up something for our dinner. What would rev up your appetite?"

Elle had been waiting for an opening like that. She'd placed her hand on her friend's arm. "Thank you, but I don't need you to stay over again tonight."

Glenda had squinted one eye and appraised Elle with the shrewdness of a diamond merchant. "Don't need me to or don't want me to?"

"Please understand. Since the shooting, I've been surrounded by people. Well-meaning, caring, compassionate people, and I'm so grateful for their many kindnesses. But I haven't had any time alone."

"You mean time alone with Charlie," Glenda had said softly. "I get it." She placed her hand on top of Elle's where it rested on her arm. "Say the word. You know I'll come running."

Her friend had been indispensable, but Elle was desperate to be by herself in her house among Charlie's things, surrounded by his spirit. She wanted and needed to reminisce in solitude, to sob without courteous restraint, to grieve in private.

Sandwiched between her parents and Glenda in the front pew of the chapel, she had endured her son's funeral with fragile dignity. It had been a beautiful service.

But the loveliness of the music, the minister's message of hope, and the plethora of flowers banking the small casket didn't buffer the fact that her baby was sealed inside it, that she would never again experience his smiles and tears, his scent, the sound of his unintelligible chatter, the bubbling joy of his laughter, the weight and warmth of his body against hers.

Glenda had made all the arrangements for the catered reception following the interment. Elle's house had been abounding in sympathy, almost to a level that had made her claustrophobic. She'd gotten through it.

She'd even withstood the stilted conversation with her ex, Jeff, and his new wife, Lesley, whose short, tight black dress wrapped her distended abdomen like a bandage, making it all the more prominent.

Elle hadn't wanted to invite them to the funeral, but when Glenda had told her that Jeff had called to ask if they would be welcome, Elle had said, "Of course." She didn't care enough about his marriage and pending fatherhood to have made an issue over their attendance. If she had, she'd have looked peevish.

He'd seemed ill at ease when he and Lesley had made their way over to her and extended condolences. He'd sipped nervously at a glass of scotch as Lesley had looked at Elle with soulful eyes and said, "The heartbreak you must be suffering." As she ran a caressing hand over her pregnant belly, she'd made a *tsk*ing sound. "I just can't imagine losing this little one."

Before Elle could respond, Jeff had offered to bring her a glass of wine, and when she'd declined, he'd given her an awkward hug. She'd thanked them for coming. As Lesley teetered away on her stilettos, clinging possessively to Jeff's arm, Glenda had rolled her eyes at Elle and poked her finger down her throat.

As people had begun to leave, she'd left Glenda to see them off while she withdrew to bid goodbye to her agent, Laura, who'd said, "Be kind to yourself. Don't rush the grieving process. Don't worry about the book."

"I confess that it's been the last thing on my mind."

"The publishing house understands and supports you one hundred percent. I'll be calling frequently to check on you."

Her parents had left the next morning. Despite their offer to remain for a few more days, she'd urged them to get back to their two cats, whom they'd left alone. She'd been secretly relieved to wave them off. They weren't intentionally demanding, but keeping them content had required energy she didn't have.

Also, deep down, she knew they had never fully endorsed her decision to have Charlie.

When she'd told them of her intentions, her mother had furrowed her brow. "Are you sure you want to do this, Elle? Under the circumstances?"

The question had been posed in an undertone, as though the circumstances were so unsavory she didn't dare speak of them out loud for fear of their being overheard.

Now she said aloud, "I wouldn't have missed him for the world, Mother." With the same amount of emphasis, she switched off her car and slammed the door shut after she got out.

Inside the precinct, she went through security screening. Compton had told her that she and Detective Perkins could be found on the third floor. The elevator emptied her into a serviceable but unattractive lobby, where a female deputy was seated at a desk.

"Can I help you?"

"I'm Elle Portman, here to see Detectives Compton and Perkins."

"They're with someone else right now, but I'll let them know you're here. Go down this hall," she said, pointing. "At the dead end, take a right. They're in room three-oh-six. Have a seat in the hall, and they'll be with you shortly."

"Thank you."

As Elle turned away, the woman said, "I'm very sorry for your loss, Ms. Portman."

Elle gave her a weak smile of thanks and started down the long hallway. At the dead end, she turned right and then came to a halt so abruptly she could have walked into an invisible wall.

She recognized him instantly. He was seated in a chair

about midway down the hallway. His knees and feet were widespread, his head bent low. He was staring at the floor.

His right hand was cupped around his left elbow, lending support to the bulky sling in which his arm was cradled. He was wearing a dark, herringbone-patterned blazer over a white shirt and black jeans. The empty left sleeve of his blazer hung off his shoulder.

Elle's heart began to beat erratically, her palms turned damp, noisy buzzing filled her ears. She couldn't account for these absurd physical reactions to seeing him, except that it was so unexpected.

The intersection of their destinies had been random and fleeting, and she hadn't anticipated it ever happening again. At least not before she'd had an opportunity to consider and rehearse what she would say to him should the occasion ever arise.

He hadn't noticed her. She thought about retreating to prepare a brief speech, but she didn't want to be late for the appointment. She also didn't think that any amount of preparation would make this easier. Taking a deep breath, she forced herself to continue down the hall.

As she neared him, he glanced up and acknowledged her presence with a curt hitch of his chin, then directed his gaze back to the floor space between his shoes. Boots, actually. Black ostrich cowboy boots.

Being as unobtrusive as possible, she sat down in one of the chairs along the opposite wall, facing him. She couldn't help but wonder about the nature of the thoughts that had him so absorbed.

She had a direct view of the crown of his head. At its

center was a whorl like the eye of a hurricane from which his wheat-colored hair fanned out. He had thick eyelashes and well-shaped brows that were drawn steeply together to form a vertical dent above his nose. His jawline was firm and well defined. It contracted and released as though he was grinding his teeth.

He must have sensed her scrutiny. Nothing in his position changed except for his head, which he raised suddenly, looking directly at her.

Caught staring, she had to say something, and it came out gruffly. "Mr. Hudson?"

Chapter 8

When he'd heard someone approaching him, he'd reacted with a glance. His brain had registered only that the individual was female; then he'd dived back into that bottomless, lightless pool of rumination in which he'd been submerged for a week.

He hadn't become fully aware that she'd sat down across from him until he'd felt the intensity of her stare, weightless but palpable, like a breath against his face.

He'd raised his head, and their gazes had collided, and immediately he'd been arrested by the unusual color of her eyes.

Then she'd said his name.

And with the precision of a lightning bolt that had nearly knocked him off his chair, he'd been struck with the realization of who she must be. Jesus. When he'd gotten up this morning, he sure as hell hadn't expected this. He wasn't ready for this! But it was happening, and there was no getting out of it.

As resigned as a man facing a firing squad, he drew himself up straight. "Calder Hudson."

"Elle Portman."

"I assumed."

She was observing him with such rapt curiosity, he flicked his gaze away. He looked down the long hallway in one direction, then in the other. No rescue in sight.

When he came back to her, he hesitated, then said, "That wasn't quite the truth. What I just said. I didn't assume who you were. I *knew*. Something…" He exhaled a gust of breath, made a dismissive motion with his hand, then plowed his fingers through his hair. "I don't know how I knew. I just did."

She shifted in her seat and looked toward the door of room 306 as though willing the detectives to materialize. And where the hell were they, anyway? He'd dreaded having another meeting with them, but this was worse. This was sheer torture. She was looking at him again.

"You didn't know me by sight," she said. "Because you didn't really see me." Apparently she realized his confusion because she added, "You didn't recognize me from the fair."

"Oh. No, not from the fair. I remember bumping into you, but, no, I didn't really see you."

He felt like a shit for having to admit it, but he realized that he couldn't lie to her while looking her in the eye, although, before seven days ago, lying artfully had been the ability he'd been proudest of.

"No reason you should have noticed us, of course," she said. "If it hadn't been for the stroller, you wouldn't have."

There was nothing to say to that. It was another statement of fact that put him in a bad light.

"It was blocking your path, and you were already
irritated."

"Was I that obvious?"

Her lips formed a hint of a smile. "You were to me. I
noticed you because you weren't dressed for the fair. I sensed
that you were annoyed and not at all happy to be in that
crowd."

"You're right, but how did you get all that in only a couple
of seconds?"

"I'm observant and have excellent recall."

"Enviable traits."

"Or a double curse."

He didn't touch that. One misstep here could take him
down a rabbit hole, so he didn't ask why she considered
those traits to be curses, because he could guess the reason,
and, thank God, she didn't elaborate. He didn't think he
could sit through an elaboration.

They lapsed into a strained silence, strangers with an ele-
phant the size of Everest between them. Also connecting
them.

Making even brief eye contact had become uncomfortable. He hunched over again and resumed his examination
of the terrazzo floor. Beads of sweat slalomed down his ribs.
His skin felt stretched too tight, and it itched from the inside.

In his peripheral vision, he noticed her casting another
anxious glance toward the office door, which remained
firmly shut. She looked at her wristwatch and murmured,
"They said three o'clock."

"Compton and Perkins?" When she nodded, he said, "They told me to be here at two forty-five."

"It's ten after three. You haven't seen them yet?"

He shook his head.

"Do you know why they asked to see us?"

"No. You?"

"No." She looked down into her lap. She pulled her lower lip through her teeth a few times, then, raising her head suddenly, said, "I thought you were dead."

Always one with a glib comeback, he blanked. He couldn't think of a thing to say.

"There were people who were suddenly there. Helping. When . . . when they lifted you off the stroller, they stretched you out on the ground."

"I don't remember any of that."

"You were very still."

"When I fell, I was knocked unconscious."

"There was a lot of blood on you."

"A blood vessel in my arm got clipped. They repaired it in surgery."

"I see." Her throat was pale and slender. It worked with the effort to swallow. "I couldn't tell if it was your blood or Charlie's."

He needed to get the fuck out of here. He *really* needed to get the fuck out of here. Before the sweat he was leaking from every pore began to soak through his clothes. Before he ran completely out of oxygen. Before his eyes produced tears.

Again, he swiveled his head, looking for an exit sign.

"How long were you in the hospital?"

He turned his attention back to her. "Five days."

"How is your arm now?"

He looked down at it as though needing to consult it before replying. "It'll be okay. In time. After some PT."

"No residual damage?"

He shook his head and croaked out, "No. They don't think so." *Unlike you.*

He looked into her dewy eyes and held them momentarily, then looked down at his right hand as he restlessly rubbed it up and down his thigh. "I'll be honest with you, Ms. Portman. I'm at a complete loss here. I don't know what to say to you. It'll either sound insensitive, or insincere, or like the babble of a complete ass who doesn't have a clue as to what you're going through. Anything I said would just be *wrong.*"

"You don't have to say anything. It's I who—"

"Yes, I do. I do. I have to tell you how goddamn sorry I am about your little boy. I wish like hell…I wish…" He gave a shake of his head, which he hoped would convey the helplessness he felt.

She said, "You wish that Charlie had survived, and thrived, and gone on to live a long and wonderful life. You wish you could roll back the clock and decide not to go to the fair that evening. You wish you'd been stopped at a railroad crossing, which would have delayed your arrival. You wish that the young man who shot at us had never been born."

Calder drew in an unsteady breath. "You expressed it well. Perfectly, in fact. But wishing it away doesn't work, does it?"

No.

Her lips formed the word, but it was inaudible because she'd lowered her head to blot her eyes and nose with a tissue she'd taken from the handbag in her lap. He had an impulse to reach across and touch her hand, to express the sorrow and regret that had been gnawing at his guts like a rat ever since he'd been told that the child had died.

But any such gesture would be inappropriate. And, even if it was the height of etiquette, he doubted she would welcome it. So he stayed as he was while she composed herself.

With a final sniff, she brought her head up. "What compelled you to jump up and go after the stroller?"

He rolled his shoulders before remembering that reflexive movements like that made his arm hurt like a son of a bitch. She must've noticed his grimace because she quickly asked if he was in pain.

"Not all the time."

"Aren't you on pain medication?"

"I take it before I go to sleep. Before I *try* to go to sleep."

She gave him an understanding smile and a nod. "You were about to say?"

"Why did I go after the stroller? Honestly, I don't know. I've been asked a dozen times by the doctors, the nurses, the shrink, my—"

"Alison Sinclair?"

"You've met Dr. Sinclair?"

"She came to the morgue that night and sat with me for a while. She called again the next day, but I wasn't up to talking to her then. She was kind enough to come to my house after Charlie's funeral. We had a few minutes together. She told me about the group therapy sessions she's scheduled."

"Yeah."

"I missed the first one because of Charlie's funeral. How was it?"

"I didn't go. That kind of thing isn't for me."

"No? What did Dr. Sinclair say about that?"

Again, he shrugged without thinking, and again it hurt like hell. "She's a therapist. Naturally, she encourages it."

"I got the impression that attendance is mandatory."

"No."

"She couldn't talk you into joining?"

"No."

"Hmm."

The dialogue ended on that soft *hmm*, but the silence that followed had the texture of steel wool.

With hesitance, she said, "I interrupted what you were saying."

"About what?"

"Everyone has asked why you went after the stroller. The doctors and nurses, et cetera."

"Oh. Yeah. My parents asked me about it. They commended me, but, you know, they're my folks. They turned right around and said I shouldn't have taken the risk. My girlfriend thinks that, too."

"Shauna Calloway."

He reacted with a start. "How did you know that?"

"She's asked to interview me. I've declined. She's dropped your name each time she's called."

"*Each* time? How many?"

"Four times, I think."

He was outraged, especially on behalf of Elle Portman. "I

had nothing to do with her calling you. Nothing. In fact..."
He stopped there, unwilling to talk about Shauna with her,
although he had plenty to say on the subject. "I'm sorry you
were made to deal with that on top of everything else."

"Actually, a friend was fielding my calls. She refused on
my behalf."

He was glad that this friend, referred to by Shauna as a
harpy, was running interference with the media.

As for Elle Portman herself, she didn't come across as a
harpy, but not as a shrinking violet, either. When she'd said
she wished the boy who'd shot at them had never been born,
she'd left no doubt that she meant it.

She wasn't a militant type, though. More like the student
council president, who every guy in school wanted to bone
but who was too wholesome to corrupt. Or to even try to
corrupt. It would be like drinking communion wine in order
to get wasted.

For one with such fair skin, her hair was a dark contrast.
It was pulled back, so it wasn't until she'd turned her head
away that he'd seen the long ponytail, almost as thick as his
wrist, rippling down her spine.

Shorter strands, just as wavy, framed her face, adding to
its overall delicacy. Her wide-set eyes weren't as clear as they
might have been had she not been crying a lot recently, but
they were the color of—

"What did you tell them when they asked why you lunged
for the stroller?"

He drew his mind away from trying to choose the elu-
sive descriptive word for her eye color and focused on the

question she'd asked. "I told them I didn't make a conscious decision. I didn't think about the risks or anything else. I reacted, that's all."

"You tried to save my child, Mr. Hudson," she said softly. "I wouldn't dismiss that brave effort as 'that's all.'"

Chapter 9

The door to room 306 suddenly opened, and Perkins stepped out. He greeted them with a half-assed *hi*, then reached back to hold the door open for a woman who emerged on crutches. As she entered the hallway, she nodded self-consciously at the two of them.

Compton followed her out. Seeing them, the detective said, "Thank you for waiting. I trust you two have introduced yourselves. Elle Portman, Calder Hudson, this is Dawn Whitley."

Calder, recognizing her, came to his feet. "I saw your interview."

Feeling guilty for having turned down Shauna to go on camera himself, he'd watched the interview the night it had aired. Of course that was before he knew that she had continued to pester Elle Portman and had brought up his name *each time.*

The Whitley woman's control of the crutches looked precarious, but she came toward him, smiling timidly. "I'd never been on TV before. I was so nervous. But Miss Calloway put me right at ease. She was very sweet and considerate. She told me that you two lived together but weren't married yet."

It made him mad as hell that Shauna had exploited their personal life for her benefit, but that wasn't this lady's fault. He smiled at her. "No one would have guessed you were nervous. You handled yourself well."

"I cried a lot."

"That didn't detract from what you were saying."

Elle Portman stepped forward. "I'm afraid I didn't see your interview."

"That's okay."

"I heard that it was compelling. How is your leg?"

"I haven't quite gotten the hang of walking on crutches, but I'm not complaining." Her expression was almost contrite, and Calder could identify with the survivor's guilt she felt when in Elle Portman's presence. "I'm as sorry as I can be about your son."

"Thank you."

"I'll probably see you at one of the group sessions." She formed it as a question.

Elle responded with a yes.

The woman looked expectantly at Calder. He gave her a noncommittal nonsmile but said nothing.

"Well, my husband and mom are waiting for me downstairs. It took both of them to get me in the car."

Compton said, "Thank you for coming in, Mrs. Whitley. I know it was an inconvenience. We'll be in touch."

"I'll see her out and come right back," Perkins said. He trailed the injured woman's ungainly progress down the hallway.

Compton turned to Calder and Elle. "I had these appointments scheduled fifteen minutes apart, but she arrived late. I'm sorry you were kept waiting so long. Can I get you anything to drink? Coffee? Water?"

Both declined. Calder said, "Why are we here?"

"I'd like to know that, too," Elle said.

"I scheduled an appointment for each of you survivors, and for at least one family member of those who were killed. Detective Perkins and I wanted to speak with each of you individually, but you're the last two, so, in the interest of time, I'll tell you together if that's all right."

"Fine by me," Calder said and looked at Elle, who gave a nod of agreement.

"Then please have a seat." Compton motioned them back into their chairs. She sat down in one of the extras.

When they were settled, she said, "There's been a development in the investigation, and I wanted you to be made aware of it before it goes public during a live press conference, which will begin in..." She consulted her wristwatch. "Forty minutes." Looking at Calder, she added, "No doubt Ms. Calloway will be covering it."

Calder had no doubt she would be, too, but he didn't remark on it.

He asked, "What's the development? Have you located the suspect's next of kin?"

"No. But the purpose of this press conference is to go public with his identity and picture, hoping that someone who knows him will come forward." She looked at them in turn, then said, "But he'll be cited as another casualty, not as the shooter."

"What?" Elle gasped. "He committed suicide."

Compton shook her head.

"It took you a week to check for gunpowder residue?" Elle said.

"That only happens on TV shows, Ms. Portman," Compton said with a half smile. "Powder residue is helpful but not conclusive. A gun is fired, the powder can go anywhere, get on anything or anyone." Looking at Calder, she said, "If you and your dad spent time at a shooting range, you should know that."

"I did. When you told me in the hospital that it was a suicide, I took your word for it."

"How did you make such a mistake?" Elle asked.

Compton said, "Well, for a mass shooter, that's almost become the standard escape route. Secondly, the wound to his head. At first sight, it was consistent with that of a suicide. But we now believe that his murderer walked up and put the muzzle to his temple."

"But that's another assumption," Elle said. "How do you know you're right?"

"Another indicator of suicide, in most instances, certainly something we always look for, is what's called a cadaveric spasm."

"What's that?" Calder asked.

She crooked her index finger. "The last signal the brain receives is that of pulling the trigger. Death is instantaneous. The index finger remains seized up. His wasn't, not on either hand."

Calder looked over at Elle, who looked back at him. He went back to Compton. "That's it?"

"No. This is what took so long. The ME's determining factor was the physics. The suspect's arrest records described him as being left-handed. The trajectory of the bullet indicates that it couldn't have been fired by a lefty. The ME consulted respected colleagues and ballistics experts, whose opinions were unanimous. The suicide was staged. It was rapidly done, obviously. But done well enough to fool first responders and give the culprit time to get away during the mayhem that followed."

"If it wasn't him, then who was it?" Elle demanded, her voice cracking. "Who murdered my son?"

Compton looked aggrieved. "I regret to tell you that the suspect remains at large and is presently unknown."

———

The detective's statement left Elle speechless. She looked over at Calder Hudson, who appeared to be as dumbfounded as she.

Compton broke the taut silence by suggesting that they leave the building before the press conference got under way. "Unless you want to be hounded by reporters, which I don't suppose you do."

Perkins came toward them from the end of the hallway and overheard her as he reached them. "They're already arriving and claiming spots. I'll escort you out the back way."

"I would appreciate that," Elle said.

Calder gave a brusque nod. He appeared to be enraged and barely able to keep his anger in check.

Elle shook hands with Compton and thanked her for the update. "It wasn't what I wanted to hear."

"It wasn't the news I wanted to break to you, either."

"What are you going to do besides change the young man's status from shooter to victim?" Elle asked. "By the way, what was his name?"

"Levi Jenkins. As for what we're going to do in regards to the investigation, we'll review every video from every security camera yet again. We'll go over statements we obtained from eyewitnesses like yourselves, and appeal to the public to—"

"Enough bullshit," Calder said. "You'll be starting from scratch. That's essentially it, right?"

He had said precisely what Elle was thinking except in a tone much harsher than she would have used.

To Compton's credit, she responded candidly. "Yes. We're no happier about it than you are, Mr. Hudson."

Acting as a diffuser, Perkins said to Compton, "I'll escort them out and meet you down there."

Compton nodded. To Calder and Elle, she said, "I'll keep you apprised of developments." With no more than that, she retreated into the office and closed the door.

Perkins wordlessly indicated that Elle and Calder follow him. They fell into step behind him as he threaded his way through the third floor's maze of hallways to an elevator at the back of the building, designated as being for sheriff's personnel's use only. He punched a code into a keypad to bring it up.

They rode down to the ground floor in silence, although Elle could feel anger emanating from Calder like heat waves. She reasoned that he was struggling to contain a variety of simmering emotions: Frustration. Impatience. Despair. Rage.

She was experiencing all those, plus some. Indefinitely, if not forever, they'd been cheated of getting closure. It was a devastating blow.

As they got out of the elevator, Perkins motioned them toward an exit. Adjacent to it were restrooms. "If you'll excuse me," Elle said and gestured toward the women's room. "I'll see my way out from here."

She exchanged a look with Calder, but he didn't say anything so neither did she. She turned away and went into the restroom, locked herself in a stall, and had a meltdown.

It wasn't nuclear, as others during the past week had been. But it was violent enough to make her torso ache as she sobbed out her grief and outrage.

But mindful that her car was parked in front of the building and that her time to escape ahead of the press conference was dwindling, she forcibly brought herself under control.

At the sink, she made a cold compress out of paper towels and used it to dab at her flushed face, then held it against her stinging eyes. It did no actual good in terms of making her look better, but it was soothing.

She left the restroom and exited through a door that was so heavy she had to put her shoulder to it. It opened onto a sidewalk that divided a parking lot on the left from a grassy lawn on the right.

The sidewalk ended at the street, where Calder Hudson was looking down at his phone and pacing along the curb, his empty left sleeve swinging at his side.

Perkins was nowhere in sight.

She headed for the parking lot. Cutting across it would put her in front of the building near the row of meters where she'd left her car. But after taking no more than a few steps, she acted on impulse and changed course.

When Calder noticed her coming toward him, he put away his phone and took off his sunglasses. Right away, he noticed that she'd been crying. Concern deepened the dent between his eyebrows. "Are you all right?"

"Are you?"

"No. I'm furious."

"I had a crying jag in the ladies' room. It helped. Not much, but some."

He was tapping his sunglasses against his thigh in agitation. "I'm mad as hell. I'm just not sure who I'm mad at."

"That's the way I feel. I'm seething, but I don't know what to do with it." She made a helpless gesture. "We wait it out, I guess."

"I guess. Although waiting something out isn't my forte."

The autumn sunlight highlighted features that the fluorescent overheads inside the building hadn't. It picked out the lighter strands of his hair. His eyes were hazel, though more green than brown. There was a sprinkling of pale freckles across his cheekbones. They were an interestingly pastoral feature on an otherwise uptown face.

But she shouldn't be noticing any of this. She quickly

looked over her shoulder. "My car is parked in front. Where's yours?"

He indicated the sling. "I can't drive until the doctor signs off. I came by Uber. I just called for another. He's on his way."

"Do you live far?"

"On the fringes of downtown. In a high-rise. You?"

"Fort Worth."

"Fort Worth?"

She gave a light laugh. "You say it like it's the frontier."

He grinned. "Isn't it?"

"To someone who lives in a high-rise near downtown Dallas, I guess it seems that way."

"I didn't mean it offensively."

"No offense taken. I love where I live. It's the perfect home for—"

She broke off before speaking Charlie's name. Calder seemed to realize why she'd stopped. He didn't prompt her to continue. She crossed her arms over her middle and directed her words to the section of concrete between her bargain-brand flats and his ultra-expensive boots. "I feel so bad for thinking and saying the things I did about Levi Jenkins."

"Yeah, me too. When I was told that the shooter had killed himself at the scene, I was in surgery recovery, miserable. I remember being glad that he'd spared society the trouble."

She raised her gaze back to his. "It doesn't sound as though he was a solid citizen, but his is another unanswered-for death."

"That eats at me." Still holding on to his sunglasses, he pressed the thumb and index finger of his right hand into his eye sockets. When he lowered his hand, he said, "I can't stomach the possibility that the shooter might get away with it."

"I want retribution for Charlie."

"You should have it. You deserve it." He said it without any qualification, his features unyielding with resolve.

Distracted by motion beyond him, she said, "Is that your Uber?"

He glanced behind him at the approaching car. "Yeah." Coming back around, he said, "Are you going to be all right?"

"My car's not far. I still have time to make a clean getaway."

"No, I mean..." He compressed his lips, tapped his thigh with the glasses, searched her eyes. "I mean overall. Are you going to be all right?"

She blinked, her eyes lowering fractionally away from his. When she met his gaze again, she said, "Eventually."

She gave him a rueful smile, but he didn't smile back. For what seemed like a long time, they just stood there looking at each other, at this juncture not knowing what more there was to be said.

The Uber driver lowered his car window. "Hudson?"

"Me," he said, but without taking his eyes off her. He lowered his voice so only she could hear him. "That list of wishes we talked about earlier? Add to mine that I wish my arm had stopped that bullet."

Her throat constricted, and she feared she might begin

crying again. "If I don't see you again, I want you to know that I'll always be grateful to you for trying."

She extended her hand. He looked down at it, then back into her face, then back at her hand as his closed around it. They shook. She kept it brief, then withdrew her hand. "Goodbye, Mr. Hudson."

I take a bow because…

"We're uncertain at this time if the unknown suspect was acquainted with Levi Jenkins, or in league with him, or if Jenkins served as a scapegoat to throw first responders off track while the individual who committed this heinous crime made good his escape."

So says the austere head of the Sheriff's Office CID department.

This is the third time I've watched a replay of this afternoon's press conference. It's the best sitcom I've seen in ages. The egg on this guy's face is priceless.

"Hey, genius, it was what you in law enforcement call a crime of opportunity."

One presented itself, and I seized it. That's not to say that I hadn't been patiently watching and waiting for it. It was worth the wait. It was perfect. Wrong place, wrong time for some, including Levi what's-his-name. But if I'd handpicked a suitable scapegoat, I couldn't have done better.

The department head goes on. "We're continuing to try to locate next of kin or someone acquainted with Levi Jenkins. If anyone seeing this photo recognizes him, please notify the authorities."

Cue the mug shot of Levi, an unwashed, worthless pothead if I've ever seen one.

"The shooter acted quickly but effectively to stage the suicide, making Levi Jenkins the last victim."

"You say that with such undeserved reverence. You just showed us his mug shot. He was a drain on society. Now he's a saint? Please. No one will miss him. No one *has* missed him."

Becoming bored, I fast-forward through the section where the guy takes questions. Nothing of substance came from any of his answers. Even the rank and file of grim-faced law enforcement officials standing behind the podium looked pained by some of his blatant sidestepping.

"You've got nothing on me, do you? You're afraid that your viewing audience, of which I'm an avid member, knows it."

I hit Play when the recording gets to Shauna Calloway. I was a fan of hers even before her coverage of the shooting. She asked about the firearm found in Jenkins's hand.

"Has it been confirmed that this was the weapon used in the shooting?"

"Yes. All the bullets fired came from this weapon. It's a semiautomatic pistol. Thirty-eight caliber."

"Has its ownership been traced?"

"Shame on you, Shauna. That's such a dumb question."

He replies, "No. And we haven't connected it to any other crime. But we're turning over every stone, following every lead."

"Exactly what leads are you referring to? You don't have any. Not one. You should shut up before you embarrass yourself further."

"Even trace evidence can provide us with a valuable clue," he says.

"Trace evidence? Knock yourselves out. Waste taxpayers' money."

"However, our most reliable asset will be a witness." Steely eyed, he scans his listeners as though looking for a witness among them. "Someone who saw something that they probably don't even realize is a clue into the identity of the suspect. There's a number appearing on your screen. Please call it if you have any information, no matter how insignificant it may seem. Each call will be taken seriously. Your identity will be kept confidential."

Annnnd here comes the big finish. An impersonation of J. Edgar Hoover.

"We'll find the individual who committed this unspeakable crime—"

"Good luck with that, J. Edgar."

"—and see to it that justice is served for the victims and their families."

I hit Stop, Rewind, Replay. It's worth sitting through the whole farce to hear that last line. It's the epitome of irony.

Chapter 10

Calder let himself into his thirty-second-floor condo and headed straight for the built-in bar. The surface of the countertop, like every surface in the place, was as sleek as a mirror and cool to the touch. The glass shelves above it were invisibly lined with strips of LED lighting, preset to provide a soft glow. Everything was top of the line.

That included the bourbon that he splashed into a crystal glass. He shot it, then poured another. "Sue me," he said, raising the refill to the pharmacist who had cautioned him against combining his pain medication with alcohol.

Not that the prescription pills did a damn bit of good without liquid reinforcement.

He carried his drink into the living area, slumped down onto the sofa, and picked up the TV remote. It was always set on a sports channel unless Shauna had come along behind him and changed it.

Sure enough, an MLB game was on. Third inning, no score.

It was top of the ninth and Calder was on his fourth undiluted whiskey when the door lock clicked and Shauna came in. Automatically, she tapped a wall switch that turned on all the lamps. The lighting was subtle. Nevertheless, Calder scowled against it.

Spotting him, she said, "Why are you sitting in the dark?"

"I didn't realize I was."

He hadn't noticed that the sun had gone down even though two walls of the spacious living area were composed of floor-to-ceiling windows that overlooked the Dallas skyline, now alight against a late-evening sky.

She set her large bag on the console table and stepped out of her heels. "I was getting worried. I called to check on you several times."

"I turned off my phone."

"Were you sleeping?"

"No."

"Have you eaten anything today?"

"No."

"Calder—"

"I'm not hungry."

She came over and sat on the opposite end of the sofa from where he was slouched. She noticed his booted feet propped on the acrylic coffee table. That was against house rules, but he couldn't get his boots off one-handedly, and he hadn't wanted to bother going into his bedroom to use his boot jack. Shauna was wise enough not to remark on the transgression.

Instead, she glanced at the TV and asked, "Close score?"

"I really haven't been paying attention."

"Did you watch the press conference?"

"No."

"I left you a voice mail about it. You should have watched it. The big announcement was that—"

"I know what the announcement was. Compton and Perkins scooped you. I heard the news straight from them."

"They came here?"

"I went to them."

"When?"

"This afternoon. At two-forty-five to be exact. But it took longer than fifteen minutes."

By now she'd noticed more than that his feet were on the coffee table. At some point, he had wrestled himself out of his blazer and had slung it inside out over the back of a chair. He'd also untucked his shirttail and undone several buttons.

After taking in the uncustomary messiness, she said, "How did you dress yourself without help? Was Stella here?" she asked, referring to their part-time housekeeper.

"No. I managed."

"Please tell me that you didn't drive yourself."

"I took Uber. Both ways. Okay?"

"Where did they meet with you?"

"Same precinct where the press conference was held."

Her eyes rounded. "You were there at two-forty-five and knew about the press conference? Why didn't you let me know you were there? You could have stuck around and—"

"And given you another opportunity to nag me about going on TV? No thanks."

Her reserve snapped. "What's the matter with you? Why are you being so hateful?" She leaned forward and sniffed. "Are you drunk?"

"I'm trying my best." He reached down and picked up the highball glass, which had been out of her line of sight. He'd set it on the floor within easy reach of his right hand.

"Honestly, Calder." She exhaled a gust of annoyance, left the sofa, and stalked over to the bar. With a lot of clatter, she took a bottle of vodka and ice cubes from the appliances under the counter and poured a drink. She added a wedge of lime and took a hefty swallow before returning to the sofa. She didn't sit. She stood over him. "You're not even supposed to be drinking."

"I wasn't supposed to be at that goddamn county fair, either."

She fell back a step and gave a bitter laugh. "Oh, I've been waiting for that. I insisted that you come, so it's my fault that you got shot."

He set his glass on his stomach, holding it with his right hand. "No," he said softly and with remorse. "It wasn't your fault. The asshole who did it is to blame. Now I don't have the satisfaction of knowing that he's dead, or even who he is."

She sat down close to him and placed her hand on his thigh. "The announcement stunned everyone at the press conference. I can only imagine how upsetting this news must have been for you, for all of you who were directly affected."

"That's why the detectives called us in individually. I guess they were worried about how some would react when told."

"How did you react?"

"I wanted to hit somebody, but I didn't know who. Probably a good thing. I can't afford another injured arm."

"I'll drink to that." She clinked her glass against his, but he didn't pick up on her attempted levity.

He said, "The woman you interviewed was there."

"Dawn Whitley?"

"We met in the hallway."

"How was she?"

"Chatty."

"What did she say?"

"That you and I are living together but aren't married yet."

"Well? Aren't we?"

"Why was that important for her to know? What did that have to do with the subject of the interview?" He gave her a baleful look. "I specifically asked you to keep me and our relationship out of it."

She removed her hand from his thigh and raised her chin defensively. "The interview with her had already been recorded when you laid down that law."

He wanted to back her into a corner and tell her that he knew about her subterfuge, about all the times she'd approached Elle Portman, but he didn't want to bring Elle into their argument. "Don't do it again."

"You've made your point."

"I thought I had the first time."

Shauna left that alone and changed the subject. "Did you talk to the people in Seattle?"

"Not yet. I'll call them tomorrow."

"They'll be shocked when you tell them what's happened to you, why you won't be there as scheduled."

"I'm sure."

"Will they let you postpone until after you've finished rehab?"

"Probably. If they don't, fuck 'em. I don't need the job."

She thunked her glass onto the coffee table and stood up. "I think you do. I think you need to resume everything that was an aspect of your former life. But first off, you need to sober up."

"I'm not through drinking yet."

"You're plastered. I'm going to fix you something to eat, and you're going to eat it if I have to force-feed you."

"I told you, I'm not hungry," he said, raising his voice.

"Well, I'm starving," she said, raising hers louder.

"Be my guest." He gestured toward the kitchen.

"Fine. Sit here and wallow in whatever it is you're wallowing in." She retrieved her shoulder bag and shoes, then stomped from the room.

Calder was unmoved by their argument and uninterested in making peace. So what if he was being a shit? She had gone against his express wishes about using his name as leverage to get interviews. The Whitley woman seemed to have been okay with talking on camera, but he was certain that others shared his and Elle Portman's reluctance to make their personal suffering available for public viewing.

Shauna would never understand because she hadn't experienced the upending calamity they had. Resume every aspect of his former life? *That may take more than a measly seven days, Shauna.*

He should shout that at her. Or maybe confide it to her earnestly and humbly, beseeching her to understand. But he didn't have the urge to do either. He feared that no matter what he said, she would never get it.

A strikeout ended the ball game. He fumbled around to find the remote and switched off the TV, then rested his head against the firm back of the sofa and closed his eyes.

He must be drunker than he'd thought, because he started thinking about rainbows, about the blurred line on the color spectrum where green merged with blue after blue had borrowed a pale shade of violet from its other neighboring stripe.

He thought about how one hue faded into the other in an ever-changing melding. Which of those colors dominated at any given moment was dependent on the light.

The light and the angle of her head. And the sheen of tears that had always seemed to be on the brink of spilling over the black, black lashes of her lower eyelids.

The description of her eyes that had eluded him earlier came to him now, and he whispered, "Like opals."

Chapter 11

Two months later...

Does anyone want to lead us off today?" Dr. Alison Sinclair looked around the circle of twenty or so people in attendance.

The group therapy sessions were conducted in a basement room of the medical building where she shared a practice with four other psychologists. All were well qualified, but, in Elle's opinion, Dr. Sinclair's calm disposition was perfectly suited to guiding this group.

They met once weekly. During the meetings, she had gently urged each of them to talk through their impressions of that fateful day, as well as to share how they were coping—or not—with its aftereffects.

No one responded immediately to her invitation to launch today's discussion. There was a nervous shifting of feet, the squeak of metal as someone squirmed in his chair, a couple of dry coughs.

Then, after a full minute had passed, someone blurted, "I'm mad as hell."

Elle knew from the previous meetings she had attended that the middle-aged man had survived the shooting without a scratch, but his wife had been critically injured and was still hospitalized because of recurring infections and other complications.

Having gained everyone's attention with his outburst, he said, "What the hell are the police doing? It's been two months. Sixty days, for crying out loud. And they haven't even identified the suspect."

There were murmurs from others who were likewise disgruntled. One even ventured that Levi Jenkins had been the culprit after all, inciting others to chime in and express their frustration and anger over the seeming ineptitude of those investigating the shooting.

The first man said, "My wife isn't out of the woods." He was a big, burly man, who used a beefy fist to wipe away the tears streaming down his ruddy cheeks. "I could still lose her, and, so far, the person responsible for her misery is as free as a bird."

The young woman sitting next to him put her arm across his shoulders, squeezing them and whispering, "Dad," as she passed him a box of tissues.

Dr. Sinclair waited a moment, then said, "Several of you here today lost a loved one. How do you feel about the suspect still being unidentified, much less apprehended?"

Everyone looked toward a grieving couple, who now leaned into each other. The woman began to cry against her husband's chest. Their daughter, a freshman in college, had been killed.

A young man whose wife of only three months had fallen beside him didn't move or make a sound and kept his head down.

Although Elle had attended the meetings on a regular basis, she had yet to contribute anything, because she feared that she couldn't get through her account without falling to pieces.

"Elle?" Dr. Sinclair said. "Anything to say?"

Glenda had urged her not to hold back. "What's the point of going to the sessions if you don't let it out? You have a heartrending story to tell. Tell it. Not only because it'll be cathartic to you. It also might help someone else there. That's what these sessions are about, right? Sharing and supporting?"

With her friend's words echoing inside her head, she began in a wavering voice. "I lost my son. His name was Charlie. He was only two years old. He was the love of my life."

Once she started speaking, the words poured out of her. She told about how they'd come to be at the fair, about parting from Glenda and then getting caught in the crush at the gate.

Her eyes remained dry until she told them about Howard Rollins. Elle had since learned that he'd been a widower, but she had met his two daughters at the last session. They were here again today and began weeping softly as Elle described his kindliness and joviality.

She skipped the details of how he'd died and went on to describe the sequence of events, much as she had several times to Compton and Perkins. Throughout, she remained as factual and unemotional as possible.

"Charlie had become cantankerous and was trying to

climb out of his stroller. I reached down and pressed his shoulder, pushing him back into the seat." She paused momentarily. "I told him he couldn't get out, that there were too many people. If he got out, he could get lost."

She looked around the circle in an appeal for them to understand. "See, this stroller is bulky. I couldn't carry Charlie and push it through that crowd at the same time." She put her hand to her mouth. "If only I'd lifted him out..." She couldn't go on until she'd swallowed hard and taken a deep breath. "But I didn't. Instead, I buckled him in."

When she stopped there, you could have heard a pin drop. It seemed that no one in the room was even breathing, except for her. Her breaths were coming in gasps that sounded noisy in the silence.

"Then the first shot rang out."

She told them about the instant she realized what was happening, of falling to the ground as Howard Rollins collapsed against her, of watching helplessly as Charlie's stroller got farther and farther out of her reach.

"A man who was fleeing ran into it, colliding hard enough to tip it onto two wheels. Another man—his name is Calder Hudson—came from behind me and tried to catch it. That's when he was shot." She paused to take a Kleenex from her pocket and used it to blot her eyes.

"He fell on top of the stroller, and it went all the way over. Charlie was inside it, but the bullet penetrated and hit him. I want to believe that he died instantly."

Following another weighty silence, Dr. Sinclair said, "Everyone here can appreciate how difficult relating this is for you, Elle."

She nodded.

"Do you have anything to add, Mr. Hudson?"

Elle's head snapped up. She looked at Dr. Sinclair, then swiveled around. He was standing just inside the door, in shadow beneath a soffit, looking self-consciously aware that every eye in the room was now trained on him.

His eyes connected with Elle's. As though speaking only to her, he said, "I didn't want to interrupt."

"I'm glad you've joined us." Dr. Sinclair indicated an empty chair between two that were occupied.

With apparent reluctance, he walked around the circle toward the appointed seat and sat down, nodding to the person on either side of him, one being the burly, outspoken man. He shook Calder's hand.

"Do you have anything to contribute to Ms. Portman's account?" Dr. Sinclair asked.

Calder gave a curt shake of his head.

The therapist looked at Elle. "Please continue."

Whereas before, when the words had seemed to form themselves, her thoughts were now too scattered to think. "That's all today."

"Very well." Dr. Sinclair moved on to someone else. A few others spoke, including Dawn Whitley. She shared that her husband expected her to "resume relations" now that she was no longer on crutches. "I'm just not ready for that yet." She asked if anyone else was having that particular problem, but if anyone else was, they didn't speak up. Dr. Sinclair eased them on to another topic.

Elle listened attentively to everyone who spoke, but she was acutely aware of Calder sitting across the circle from her. Wearing a black leather jacket over a black T-shirt—the classy kind that had to be dry-cleaned—he was better dressed than anyone else there. If for no other reason, that made him conspicuous, and he seemed keenly aware of that. Dr. Sinclair must have sensed his discomfort. As soon as she adjourned the meeting, she approached him and drew him off to the side of the room for a private chat.

As people began to drift out, a good number of them stopped to speak to Elle. She was given hugs, condolences, and encouraging words that sounded like platitudes but which she knew by now were sincere.

Then Elle found herself alone. Others were mingling. Dr. Sinclair was now speaking privately with the couple who'd lost their daughter. Calder was at the snack table, filling a Styrofoam cup with coffee from a thermal dispenser.

Elle walked over. "Hi."

He turned to face her. "Hi."

"You changed your mind."

"Last-minute decision. That's why I was late."

"Honestly, I didn't think you would ever come."

"Honestly, I didn't think I would, either."

"Well, welcome."

"Thanks." He raised his cup in a mock toast, then took a sip. "Have you been coming regularly?"

"Yes, once I thought I could endure it. But this is the first time I've spoken. On my first visit, I dashed out as soon as it was over."

He gave a wry grin. "I would have if Dr. Sinclair hadn't waylaid me."

"I believe she was genuinely pleased to have you."

"She said she was." He took another sip of coffee and glanced down at the table. "Would you like a cookie?"

She glanced at the platter of dried-out chocolate chip cookies. "They don't look very tempting. How's the coffee?"

He grimaced. "I'd pitch it, but I don't want to be ungracious." He did, however, set the cup down on the table and slide his hands into the rear pockets of his jeans.

"Oh," she said. "I just realized. Your sling is gone."

"For a couple of weeks now. I was glad to be shed of it."

"Your arm is healing okay?"

"Not fast enough to suit me, but the doctors say it's right on target." The instant the words left his mouth, he hissed, "Oh, shit," and ran his hand over his mouth and chin.

"No matter," she said and instinctively reached out to touch his arm in an *It's okay* gesture. But she pulled her hand back before making contact. "It happens to me, too."

"Really?"

"Um-huh. I catch myself making a gun-related analogy all the time."

"I'm glad I'm not the only one." He looked down at the table again, then glanced over his shoulder toward the exit.

She figured that he was eager to leave. "Well, it was—"

"I could—"

They started at the same time, stopped at the same time, then he motioned for her to go ahead. "I was just going to say that it was good to see you. Here, I mean. Without the sling and all."

"What about you?" he asked. "How have you been?"

"All right. Considering."

"Yeah. Considering. That's a big word these days."

She tilted her head and took in the strain on his face. In a softer voice, she asked, "How have *you* been?"

"Drunk."

"Oh."

"But only on bad days."

"On good days how are you?"

He met her gaze straight on and said with a self-deprecating snuffle, "Drunk*er*."

"I'm sorry, Calder." And now she was embarrassed and wanted to say *shit*, because she'd used his name when before she'd only ever called him Mr. Hudson, and she could tell that he'd noticed the slip.

However, he didn't acknowledge it. "So, what I'd been about to say was that I could use a cup of coffee." He looked down at the abandoned cup. "Real coffee. You want to...?" He didn't finish but raised his shoulder and a corresponding eyebrow.

Elle looked out across the room. Dr. Sinclair had left, leaving only a trio who had formed a prayer circle. They were sitting together holding hands with their heads bowed.

"Don't feel obligated," he said.

"No, no, coffee sounds good."

"Great. After you." As he motioned toward the door, he smiled.

It was her first glimpse of the suave charm he must have exuded. Before.

Well, now this...

During an interview with Dr. Alison Sinclair about post-traumatic stress, Shauna Calloway had weaseled out of the therapist that she's conducting group sessions for the Fairground shooting victims.

Like that was a bombshell. Isn't that a step in the playbook?

It's become a hobby of mine to observe the attendees as they arrive and leave the meetings. Some go in looking dejected and disconsolate, and fifty minutes later emerge looking restored.

Others enter looking hopeful and come out looking like they've been beaten with a chain.

This ebb and flow of emotions fascinates me. I can't help but wonder what triggers their misery one day and a renewal of spirit the next. Perhaps something like a birthday or anniversary that reminds them of who or what they've lost. Or possibly a call from a friend asking how they're doing. I'll bet that 99 percent of the time they say, "I'm fine."

But they don't mean it. It's a fat lie. How could they possibly be fine? I wreaked havoc on them. I rained hell down on all of them. Life as they knew it will never be the same.

I don't feel bad about that at all.

Because no one takes into account my suffering, my hardship, the hell I was put through that drove me to do what I did. If people were aware of my circumstances, they might not be so quick to judge.

But, as expected, I'm being analyzed by people who don't know me and never will. I'm referred to as "criminal." "Evil." "Mentally ill." I had braced myself for that, remember?

Some would regard this current spying on my victims as perverse, as a sick thrill. They'd say I'm victimizing these people all over again. But I can't seem to help myself. It's titillating.

Especially today.

I was surprised to see them walking out of the building together. Then she pulled her car behind his as they drove out of the parking lot. That raised my eyebrows. Wouldn't it have raised yours? I mean, the scenario is captivating. One bullet. His arm. Her kid. Talk about titillating!

And, in light of his relationship with the TV reporter, which she made certain everyone knew of, doesn't this Hudson-Portman pairing feel a bit clandestine? It does to me. I'm intrigued. So I'm going to follow them and see where this leads.

Chapter 12

As they left the office building, Elle said she would follow him in her own car. Calder didn't contest that plan, although he kept one eye on the rearview mirror, fearing she might change her mind and veer off.

He didn't want to go to a well-lit, highly trafficked place.

Instead, he drove to a bar near the Southern Methodist University campus that was on a side street off the beaten path. It was a neighborhood hangout, as old as time, not chic or trendy.

But what really recommended it was that he'd never brought Shauna here.

It was a stone structure with ivy-covered walls and mullioned glass windows. It could have been mistaken for the home of a tenured professor. Only a small neon sign above the arched doorway designated it as a tavern.

As Elle alighted from her car, he noticed her wariness. He said, "Yes, they make a mean old-fashioned. But also, superior coffee."

The interior was pleasantly dim, redolent with the yeasty aroma of beer. He ushered her to a corner booth, then went over to the bar and ordered two coffees.

As he slid in across from her, she said, "Cozy spot."

"I used to come here when I was at SMU, ostensibly to study."

"And instead?"

"Drank beer and chatted up coeds."

"What was your major?"

"Drinking beer and—"

"Chatting up coeds."

They laughed; then he asked her where she'd gone to university. "Michigan, but I came to Dallas as soon as I graduated, encouraged by my friend Glenda, whose father owned a residential real estate company here. You probably know it. Foster Real Estate."

"Of course."

"Glenda and I got our licenses. I never had much heart for it, but Glenda excelled and took over the agency when her father retired. She's very successful. Glamorous. She's married and divorced two of the wealthy men she's sold houses to."

"Presently looking for number three?"

"Always."

"Are you still in real estate?"

"No. I happily got out of it when I moved to Fort Worth and had Charlie."

"What do you do now?"

"I write children's books."

He hadn't expected that. Nothing even remotely like that. His amazement must have shown, because she laughed. "What?"

"I've never met a writer before. No, I take that back. I met a sportswriter who was hanging out in the nineteenth hole during a golf tourney. He smoked cigars and drank a lot and looked nothing like you."

"I don't have the luxury of hanging out in the nineteenth hole. I toil at a computer and a drawing board."

"Making up stories?"

"And then illustrating them."

"For storybooks. Like picture books."

"Yes. Just like that."

He was intrigued. "How does that work, exactly?"

"Well, I stare into space and daydream a lot. When something good —what I think *could* be good—comes to mind, I write it down. The next day when I reread it, I either keep it, edit it, or toss it and try again."

"What are your stories about?"

"I'm working on the second book of what I hope will become a series. It's about a community of clouds."

"Clouds."

She nodded. "They live in a wide area of the sky. Conflicts arise when they become separated, either by a natural happenstance like a storm or by a trouble-making cloud. They must create ways to reconnect and stick together for everyone's betterment."

"Ah. There's a subtext."

She smiled, looking pleased that he'd derived that. "There is, but the stories are written to engage and entertain young children—preschool, basically—who have notoriously short attention spans. The moral of the story is subtly woven into the antics of the clouds."

"I'm impressed. That's very creative."

"Thank you." Her soft smile became wistful. "Although I haven't been creative lately. Even after two months, I can't seem to pick back up, get into any kind of rhythm."

"I know that feeling too well."

The bartender brought over steaming mugs of freshly brewed coffee. "Smells delicious," Elle said. Then, as she stirred milk into hers, she asked, "What do you do?"

"My job? Consulting." She gave him the expected expectant look and he said, "It's boring. Nothing nearly as interesting as writing kids' books."

She must've caught the hint that his occupation wasn't something he wanted to talk about, because she didn't pursue it. She lifted the mug of coffee to her mouth and blew into it.

He was certain she hadn't intended for it to be provocative, but his belly quickened, and he was so distracted by what her lips were doing, he drank from his mug without blowing on it first and scalded his tongue.

After taking a more careful sip, he asked her if she'd heard from Compton or Perkins.

"Not a word."

"Me either," he said. "I've called, but they're always unavailable and haven't called me back. I take that to mean that the investigation has stalled, big-time."

"Had you come into the meeting yet when the group talked about that?"

"No. What was said?"

She gave him a brief recap. "The man seated next to you was the first to speak out, but I believe he expressed what most everyone was thinking."

"What were you thinking?"

She wrapped both hands around her coffee mug and stared into it thoughtfully. "I'm desperate for my child's murderer to be caught and punished. But a part of me just wants it all to go away, to be over and done with." Back at him, she said, "Does that sound crazy?"

"Not to me. I understand the contradiction. I'd like to see the bastard drawn and quartered. But going through a trial, and everything that it would entail—motions, rulings, postponements, appeals. It could drag out for years, and we— anyone who was involved—will be dragged along with it."

"It's a dismal thought, isn't it?"

"Yes, but not as dismal as the thought of him getting away with it." He propped his forearms on the edge of the table and leaned toward her. "I have dreams about it."

Her nod encouraged him to continue.

"They're not about the shooting specifically, but there's something I can't finish, somewhere I can't get to, and time is running out. Like that."

"Failure dreams. They're common."

"Sure. My most frequent one is that I'm searching for my baseball glove. The umpire has already cried, 'Play ball,' everyone is waiting for me to take the field, and I can't find my glove.

"But these recent dreams are different. They make me wonder if my retelling about the shooting has made it familiar by repetition. Am I recounting it by rote and overlooking a minor detail that could be huge, that could be the one thing that nails the shooter?"

"Like what?"

He gave her a grim smile. "I don't know. That's just it. I've always been a problem solver, able to work out a knot. I can't work this one out, and it's frustrating as hell because I want the son of a bitch to be punished to the fullest extent of the law. I want to punish him myself. *Wrathfully.* I think about it all the time."

She looked at him with compassionate sadness. "Even if he is found and punished to the fullest extent, I'm afraid that day will always be a preoccupation for those of us who survived it. Like a brand, it'll be there for the rest of our lives."

"When I was still in recovery, the trauma surgeon came to check on me. He told me the same thing, in virtually those same words. It'll always be with me." He fiddled with the paper napkin beneath his mug. "I don't know if I could do what you did."

"What did I do?"

Now that he was getting to the heart of the matter, he wanted to make sure they wouldn't be overheard. He looked around the bar. There was only a smattering of customers, but just then a pair of older men came in, laughing together. The bartender greeted them by name and began drawing two mugs of draft beer even before they were settled on their bar stools.

Calder took in the obvious friendship between the two

men, their ease with each other, the bartender's familiarity with his regulars. In that moment, Calder envied them. He'd almost forgotten what it felt like not to be wallowing—Shauna's angry but accurate word—in the suffocating aftermath of the shooting. Like quicksand, there was no escaping it, and the harder he fought it, the deeper he sank.

Elle was leaning toward him in anticipation of what he'd been about to say. She was focused directly on him as though completely unaware of their surroundings, as though he were the only person in the world.

But he didn't want to be the only person in the world. He wanted her to be there with him.

Unsettled by a sudden but undeniable yearning, he angled back slightly and cleared his throat. "What did you do?" he said, repeating her question. "You opened up to the group in a way that I never could."

"At what point did you come in?"

"You were saying that Charlie was the love of your life."

"True. I went to a lot of trouble to get him."

Calder was unsure how he should respond, or if he should at all. But he wanted to know. "Shauna covered Charlie's funeral for channel seven. In passing, she mentioned to me that you're single."

"Divorced."

Shauna had also told him that the boy's father wasn't in the picture. "Has your ex been around to help you through this? As Charlie's dad, you'd think—"

"Charlie wasn't his."

"Oh. Sorry. I see."

"No, I don't think you do." He sensed that her smile

was at his expense. "I was a couple of years past thirty. I wanted a baby. Jeff, my ex, wanted to wait, wanted to get better established in his job first, wanted to be able to buy a larger house, a bigger car." She took a breath. "But what he wanted most was a much younger personal trainer at his fitness club."

He opened his mouth. She held out her hand. "No, don't say anything. It's too cliché. He got the girl, I got an express-lane divorce, then immediately began taking the steps necessary to conceive Charlie."

He was curious, but it would be rude to ask, so he arched an eyebrow.

She laughed at the implied question. "I went through dozens of men. Hundreds maybe. Night after night...I snuggled up with a catalog of sperm donors."

"Oh," he said with chagrin.

"See? I knew it wasn't what you were thinking. Charlie's conception was purely clinical."

"Damn. We were just getting to the good part."

She smiled and he smiled back; then she looked pensively down into her coffee again. "Once I knew I was pregnant, I never gave the donor another thought. He was a nameless number with all the desired traits, interests, and physical characteristics, but I didn't think of him as a *person*.

"Since the shooting, he's come to mind frequently. Somewhere there's a man who'll never even know that Charlie was conceived, that he was beautiful and sweet and clever. And then he was killed in the Fairground shooting." After a pause, she said, "Actually, I think the donor would rather not know that."

Calder agreed but didn't say so. "Did your ex marry the girl?"

"He brought her to the funeral. The irony? She's out-to-here pregnant." She formed a circle with her arms above the tabletop.

"I hate that cocksucker."

She laughed. "You sound like Glenda."

"She's your best friend?"

"The best of besties. That night, she came to the hospital as soon as she could. If not for her, I don't think I would have gotten through it."

"In the group session, you stopped before you got to that part. What happened at the hospital? If you feel like talking about it."

"It's okay."

Calder wouldn't have encouraged her to proceed and was somewhat surprised when she turned reflective and began to speak. He was even more surprised by how badly he wanted to hear the rest of her story.

"I had a minor injury that was dealt with in the ER." She told him the extent of that and then related what had happened when she and her friend got down to the morgue. "Even when they told me I needed to go, I couldn't leave. There was a ferocious thunderstorm. I used it as an excuse to stay longer. Glenda and I sat in a cold corridor until after daybreak.

"Eventually, inevitably, I had to surrender him. The attendant was considerate, even apologetic. She told me that I would be notified when Charlie was transported to the funeral home. Transported," she said with distaste. "Like he was cargo, not my little boy."

She propped her elbows on the table and placed her fingertips at her temples. "But the worst of it, the very worst, was when the stroller got away from me, and I could hear him screaming but couldn't get to him. I dwell on that more than I do on the moment I had to accept that he was gone.

"He had to have wondered where I was, why wasn't I there, why—"

"Shh, shh, shh." Calder reached across the table and took one of her hands, pressing it between his. "Elle?" She raised her head and looked at him. "Don't blame yourself for not taking him out of the stroller. Given the situation, it was the right decision. You know that."

"I don't blame myself, exactly. But I do have to live with it." She gulped, swallowing with effort, and eventually brought herself under control. "I'm sorry. So sorry. What a spectacle. Is anybody looking?"

"I don't know. I don't give a shit."

She released a spontaneous breath that was almost a laugh and blotted her wet cheeks with the back of her free hand. He was still holding her other between his.

She sniffed and smoothed back loose strands of hair. "Lord! How many buckets can one person cry?"

"No one is counting."

She gave him a look of gratitude and continued to gaze into his eyes. Which is how he knew the instant she realized that he was rubbing his fingers across the back of her hand, because her breath caught, and she looked down at their hands and slowly pulled hers away.

She straightened her shoulders and looked at her watch,

motions that signified a withdrawal beyond the reclaiming of her hand. "I should be going."

"Will you do me a favor first?"

"If I can."

"Will you show me a picture of Charlie?" When she failed to respond, he feared he'd made a terrible blunder. "Look, sorry, I shouldn't've—"

"No, no it's fine. Of course. I just…" Flustered, she took her cell phone from an outside pocket of her purse, accessed her photos, and began to scroll through. "I've only got about ten thousand, but this is one of my favorites. It was taken on his second birthday."

She held the phone out to him, and he took it. Upon seeing the child's face, Calder had anticipated choking up, but the smile Charlie had flashed at the camera was infectious, and he couldn't help himself from smiling back. "Was he always this happy?"

She laughed. "No. Trust me, he had his moments."

Calder pointed at a lumpy thing clutched beneath the boy's arm.

"What's that?"

"That's Bun. Short for Bunny. Selfishly, I wanted to keep him, but Charlie was never without him, so, at the last minute, I put him in the casket."

They shared a look, then Calder returned to the picture. "He got your hair."

"Yes. But his eyes were like melted dark chocolate. Nothing like mine."

Hers had been tear-washed and were reflecting the wavering light from the candle on the table. "Yours would be hard to replicate." They held him spellbound for a moment, then he passed the phone back to her. "Thank you for showing me."

"When you asked, I was taken aback. Most people are so uncomfortable talking to me about him, they're hesitant even to say his name. No one has asked to see his picture. So thank *you*."

She replaced her phone in her purse. Calder asked if she wanted a refill of coffee, but to his disappointment, she declined. He said, "In hindsight, maybe we should have ordered the old-fashioneds and just gotten skunked."

She laughed as she scooted out of the booth. He left a twenty on the table and waved a thanks to the bartender as they walked toward the door. The two buddies turned on their stools and wished them a good evening. They probably assumed they were a couple.

As they walked to their cars, Calder kept his hand hovering above the small of her back. He told himself it was a precaution in case she lost her footing where the sidewalk was buckled by tree roots.

But who the hell was he kidding?

When they reached their cars, which were parked side by side, she nodded toward his Jag and said, "Snazzy."

"Snazzy? You need to put that word in one of your stories."

"I'll keep it in mind," she said, smiling up at him.

He stepped around her and opened the driver's door of her compact SUV. He noticed the child seat was still belted into the back seat. Attached to it was a toy steering wheel.

She didn't get in immediately but stood facing him in

the wedge of the open door. "Will you be at the next group session?"

He winced. "I don't think so. I felt conspicuous."

"You were a bit."

"I shouldn't have come in late."

"It wasn't that. People are in awe of you."

"In awe?"

"You're attributed with saving lives."

"They're giving me a lot more credit than I deserve. In any case, I'll never talk about it publicly. I appreciate what some people get out of those meetings, but I just can't see myself—"

"You don't have to explain. No judgment."

"Thanks."

She nodded, then said, "Well..." She looked beyond him, toward the building, before coming back to him. "I liked the place. Thank you for the coffee."

"You're welcome."

"I hope I didn't embarrass you with all the tears."

"You didn't."

She gave him a faint smile. "Take care of yourself."

"You too. Be careful driving home."

"I will. Goodbye." She turned to get into the car.

"Elle?"

She came back around.

There was no valid reason for him to detain her further except that he didn't want to say goodbye. He didn't want to see her drifting away from him like one of her storybook clouds.

She stood very still, her expression inquisitive. And here he was, known for his elocution, unable to vocalize anything.

Words would have sounded hollow, anyway. So he did what felt right. He pulled her into an embrace.

There was a split second of surprise and resistance on her part; then she seemed to wilt into compliance. He drew her closer, so close that in order for them to retain their balance, they had to shuffle their feet forward until his were separated only wide enough to bracket hers between them.

Their bodies aligned. Contours shifted to fit into shallow depressions. Then they settled.

Her arms curved under his to encircle his waist. His hands moved in tandem up and down her back; then one slid under her ponytail and molded itself around her nape, while the other stayed in the dip above her hips. And stayed longer. And pressed, securing her front against his where it counted. And from that meeting place, a fever spread.

He lowered his head and placed his lips against the pulse that beat in her temple. He whispered gruffly, "What I have to live with, Elle, is that the bullet I survived killed the love of your life."

Chapter 13

No sooner had the front door swung shut behind Calder than Shauna appeared, coming from the direction of the bedrooms. "There you are. I was beginning to think you'd lost your way."

She was wearing a slinky lounging outfit. It was in the style of a track suit, except that it was made of silk and clung so well that it was evident she was wearing nothing underneath.

She linked her arms around his neck and kissed him. He returned the kiss but kept it short and didn't go back for seconds. He released her and shrugged off his jacket. "Something smells good."

"It could be me." She struck a pin-up girl pose. "Is it an exotic floral scent?"

"More like an Italian kitchen."

"Oh, then it's Stella's lasagna. It's in the warming drawer.

But if this new fragrance I'm wearing doesn't enchant you, as it's guaranteed to do, I'll demand a four-hundred-and-fifty-dollar refund from Neiman's."

"Don't get a refund. It's nice."

"Thank you. But this proves the adage about the way to a man's heart. Would you like a drink before dinner? I can pour you a bourbon, or if you'd rather go straight to the Brunello, it's already decanted."

"Let me think about it. I'm going to wash up." He hooked his jacket on his index finger, slung it over his shoulder, and headed across the living area.

"Calder, what the *hell?*"

He stopped and turned around. It was clear from her tone and stern expression that she was good and pissed because he hadn't responded to the seduction scene she'd staged: the do-me-now outfit, candles scattered throughout the room, romantic music emanating from concealed speakers.

He said, "I see you've gone to a lot of trouble. I appreciate the effort. I do. But I'm just—"

"Just what? As you know, I detest lasagna. It's fattening peasant food. But I asked Stella to make it because it's one of your favorites."

She pinched up the flimsy fabric of her top, then let it go with a snap. "I don't much care for this outfit, either, but you gave it to me for Christmas because you said you got a boner just thinking about getting me out of it. I dabbed my erogenous zones with that frigging expensive perfume. All this in the hope of sparking some response from you. And you turn your back and walk away. For the love of God, Calder! What is wrong with you?"

He huffed a bitter sound and lowered his head, shaking it. "You mean besides cheating death?"

She threw her head back and looked up at the ceiling. "I know, I know. You got shot. I didn't. Because it didn't happen to me, I can't empathize with what you're going through, mentally and emotionally."

Even though her words dripped sarcasm, he said, "Thank you," then turned and resumed his original course.

But she didn't give up that easily. She strode over, hooked her hand in his right elbow, and yanked him around. "It's been two months. How long before you're normal again?"

"Is there a countdown?"

"Let me rephrase. Are you *ever* going to be normal again?"

He heaved a sigh. "I'm tired, Shauna. Can we talk about it tomorrow?"

"You're always tired."

"I've been recovering from a gunshot."

"And I've been patient. I've held my tongue. But this conversation is long overdue."

His temper flared. He tossed his jacket onto the nearest chair and placed his hands on his hips. "*This* conversation? It's that specific? What exactly is *this* conversation?"

"The one about your inability to get over this. Which I think is actually an *unwillingness* to get over it. You sit for hours and stare at the TV without the audio. Your friends have reached out, but you've put them off until they've given up on you. When was the last time you and I went out? I can't even remember.

"You drink way too much, eat way too little. I don't know

how well you sleep, or if you do at all, because we haven't shared a bed since the night before the shooting."

"My arm—"

"Your arm, your arm. I've heard at least a dozen times that your arm needs time to heal, it's awkward to sleep with, it aches during the night, and you'd keep me awake trying to find a comfortable position." She snorted. "You never showed any concern for the comfort level of our positions before."

"Ha ha. Good one."

"Your aching arm was a valid excuse for a while, but…" She backed down, took a breath, and asked in a quieter voice, "Are we ever going to have sex again?"

"I finish PT next week."

"That's not what I asked you, but as long as you brought it up, do you plan to continue abstention even after PT?"

"I'm not planning anything. I'm taking it one day at a time."

"Well, this is a day. Today is a day," she said, making downward stabs with her index finger. Then, once again, she reined in her anger and placed her hand on his shoulder.

"I miss you, Calder. I miss your droll humor, the high you're on when you come in from a hard workout, your vitality. I miss sex with you." With uncustomary shyness, she said softly, "It doesn't have to be a marathon. It doesn't have to be vigorous. We'll be careful. And once we're into it, I'll do my best to make you forget about your arm, forget about everything. It'll do you good. Leave it to me." Smiling suggestively, she reached for his crotch.

He caught her by the wrist. "I can't get my dick straight until I get my head straight."

"You can't get an erection?"

"It's not physical. I can get it up. I just—"

She jerked her hand out of his grasp. "You just don't want to."

He breathed in deeply, exhaled slowly. "What I don't want to do is pretend to you that everything is back to normal and that I'm all right, when I'm not. I can't..." He looked around at the atmospheric setting she'd created and spread his arms wide. "This is great, but I can't enjoy it. I can't enjoy anything right now."

"You could if you would allow yourself to. God forbid that you resume your life, our life. And heaven help you if you actually enjoyed it. If you did, think of all the guilt you'd have to bear."

"Yes. I would. You're finally getting it."

She deflated, folded her arms across her middle, and looked down at the floor. "I appreciate your honesty at least. Survivor's guilt *is* a thing. It was the topic of one of my post-shooting reports. I interviewed that psychologist at the hospital. You should talk to someone about how to get over it."

"I did."

She raised her head and looked at him with surprise.

"I went to Dr. Sinclair's group therapy session today. I didn't talk. I listened. Believe me, you and I aren't the only ones grappling with all this. Everyone there is finding it hard to get back on track."

"Maybe I should go with you to one of the sessions."

She'd offered with sincerity, but he almost laughed out loud. He couldn't envision her in the midst of that bereaved group. Besides, he wouldn't trust her not to be calculating which of them would make the best human-interest story. As someone was pouring their heart out, she would be thinking Emmy.

He said, "Thanks for the offer, but I'm not going back."

"Truthfully, I don't think you belong there, either. You're nothing like the rest of those people."

"Right. I felt conspicuous." That was a straight answer. Almost everything else he'd said since coming through the front door had been an equivocation. Feeling guilty over that, he reached for her hand. "You do look great tonight. I still think that outfit is hot, even if you don't like it."

"What about the perfume?"

"Tough one. It's a toss-up between it and the lasagna."

Encouraged, she smiled. "Why don't you relax and have a glass of that wonderful wine while I fix our dinner plates?"

It was an olive branch that he didn't have the heart to reject. "Deal."

While they ate, she talked about a plum investigative report she'd been assigned, then went on to describe a trip to Italy she wanted the two of them to take.

"I've been reading about this fabulous place, an ancient monastery or winery or something. Anyway, a nobleman from somewhere, who has tons of money, bought it and has converted it into a boutique hotel. I was thinking we could go after you wrap up the job in Seattle. How long do you think that will take?"

"I canceled it."

She had passed on the lasagna and was eating only salad. With that unexpected announcement, she set her fork on her plate and looked at him with bewilderment. "When?"

"A couple of weeks ago."

"Why?"

"The management was getting antsy for me to start. I couldn't go to Seattle until I finished PT. I did what I felt was the honorable thing and gave them an easy out by advising they get someone else. I even recommended a few candidates."

"Calder—"

Before she could say more, his cell phone rang. Seeing the name in the LED, he answered immediately. "Detective Compton?"

"Is this a good time?"

"Hold on. I'll be right with you." He pushed back his chair and stood. "Leave the dishes. I'll clean up after I take this."

Her expression hard-set, she reached for her glass of wine. "Don't worry about it."

Since his release from the hospital, he'd been camped in the guest bedroom. He went in and closed the door, sat down on the end of the bed, and put the phone to his ear. "I'm here. Do you have news?"

"I wish I could tell you that we have our suspect in custody, but unfortunately that's not the case. Perkins and I would like to talk to you tomorrow."

"About what?"

"I'd rather not go into it over the phone. Would four o'clock be a convenient time?"

"Same place as before?"

"Yes."

"I'll be there."

He was about to disconnect when she asked, "How are you getting along, Mr. Hudson?"

"I'm doing okay."

She hesitated, as though knowing he was lying and was about to address that. Instead, she ended with a terse "See you tomorrow."

The shower in the guest bath didn't have all the directional showerheads and gewgaws as the one in the master, but he stayed in it for a long time.

From the shower, he went straight to bed and turned out the light. When Shauna tapped on the door and spoke his name, he didn't answer, pretending to already be asleep.

He heard the master bedroom door close and knew that she would soon be propped up in bed with her phone and laptop, avidly scanning every venue of social media, on the lookout for a breaking story.

Her nonstop drive had been one of the qualities that first attracted him to her. Second only to her tousled-blonde-knockout looks, of course. They had met at an engagement party for mutual acquaintances. Their chemistry had been immediate and fiery. They'd dated for six months before deciding to take the next step and move in together.

He'd known exactly what he was signing on for. Shauna was ambitious, vain, and self-centered. But he was like that, too, if not more so. That was why the relationship had worked so well. In any given situation, be it sex or choosing a sandwich condiment, each had known what to expect from the other. What he was now feeling—or not feeling—wasn't her fault. She hadn't changed   he had. He didn't blame her. He wasn't angry with her.

He was indifferent.

Which was worse. What she was sensing from him was apathy.

There was a basis for every slight she'd accused him of tonight. Most of the excuses that he'd offered up had been not only weak but flat-out lies.

When he'd come in tonight, he hadn't been tired. He'd been despondent because he'd had to say goodbye to Elle.

He'd told Shauna he couldn't enjoy anything, but he'd enjoyed that hour spent with Elle. Most of the subjects they'd talked about had been somber, soul-searing, heart-wrenching, but in her company he'd felt a peacefulness that he hadn't experienced since the shooting.

No, even before the shooting, neither he nor his life could be described as peaceful. Had he ever felt content? Rarely, if ever. He'd always been in a rush to get somewhere, to start this or finish that. He'd been the go-to man, the problem solver, the whiz kid with all the answers, on call and in charge.

The shooter hadn't cut down that Calder Hudson, but the experience had. It had humbled him. Shauna couldn't accept that. She certainly wouldn't want to hear that he didn't want to return to being that guy.

He thought Elle would understand. She wouldn't badger him to return to normal. She wouldn't try to accelerate his recovery. She would be empathetic.

Or, that was, she would have been before tonight. Now, though, he wasn't sure what she thought of him.

Because when he'd released her from his embrace, she'd looked stunned, a little apprehensive, a lot confused. Without a word, she'd climbed quickly into her car, pulled the door shut, and had driven away as though the devil were chasing her.

He'd had no business kissing her. Not that it had been a real kiss. After whispering against her hairline, he'd kept his lips there, that's all. Only to demonstrate his earnestness. They may have been parted a little, but a guy had to breathe, and he'd kept them in place and unmoving. Not for very long, either. Just perhaps long enough for it to have felt like a kiss. Long enough for him to want nothing more than to relocate his lips to hers, which he'd been obsessing over since she'd taken her first sip of coffee. He was almost certain that they were as soft as they were pink and full and that when they separated invitingly, his tongue would discover that her mouth was luscious.

"Jesus." He reached behind his head and drew his pillow over his face to stifle a groan.

He'd told Shauna the truth about one thing: He could still get it up.

Chapter 14

Shauna was in her cubicle in the warren of the newsroom, doing research on the current affairs story she'd been given to investigate. It was about how scamming the elderly had become epidemic.

She'd been flattered to have it assigned to her. The story could be told in a way that oozed pathos, which was always good for ratings. Everybody had a grandma with dementia.

But now that she was into it, she was looking for a hook or angle that hadn't been used by ten thousand other reporters also seeking to engage and enrage their viewing audiences.

She was reading a newspaper story about a couple who'd transferred all the funds from their bank account into another on the promise that their life savings would be tripled in a matter of days.

Shauna felt more scorn than pity for the victims. "How

dumb do you have to be?" she mouthed, just as her cell phone rang. "Hello?"

"You didn't hear this from me."

She recognized the nasal drawl of one of her secret sources within the sheriff's department in the county where the Fairground shooting had occurred.

Billy Green's face was pitted with acne scars, and he had chronic bad breath, but he was enough of a weasel for his information to be reliable, and he was in lust with her, which never hurt.

"Who is this?" she said, which of course made him cackle. "Whatcha got for me?"

"The woman whose kid died in the Fairground shooting? The baby in the stroller that got shot when your boyfriend—"

"Elle Portman. What about her?"

"I don't know, but something."

It irked her that the best story about the shooting had yet to be told. A child's involvement heightened the drama of any story. This one also had a cosmic/karma/fate/divine intervention overtone that she could milk for all it was worth.

Damn the Portman woman for not thawing on giving her an interview. And damn Calder in general. Double damn Calder.

She was still furious over last night's rejection and wanted to scream when she thought of all the trouble she'd gone to and then had gotten nothing in return.

Calder hadn't even become angry enough to make a good fight out of it. And she knew he hadn't been asleep when she'd knocked on the guest bedroom door. She'd heard him tossing and turning all night.

But never one to let her personal life get in the way of her work, she grabbed a tablet and pen and began jotting down the nitty-gritty of what her snitch was telling her.

"They're behind a closed door as we speak," Green said.

"Elle Portman and who else?"

"The homicide detectives, Compton and Perkins."

"Fabulous," Shauna grumbled. Throughout the investigation, that pair had been excessively tight-lipped.

"They're there at your precinct?"

"Yeah, that's how I know." He took a breath, then whined, "Why don't you break up with that rich asshole? What's he got that I don't?"

"A full head of hair."

"Hey, that hurt."

"What time did she get there?"

"The Portman woman? Five minutes ago."

"Thanks for calling me so soon. It's a good tip. Call me back if you learn more."

"Natch."

"And I'm the only one you're giving this to, right?"

"I wouldn't cheat on you, sweetheart."

"Thanks, Billy. I owe you a beer."

"You always say that, but you never come through."

"If I get Elle Portman to grant me an interview, I'll buy you two beers."

"Someplace dark and private. Wear a skirt."

"Goodbye."

She clicked off and looked thoughtfully at the sketchy

notes she'd taken on the scam story. The news director had promised her a week's worth of promotion and a prime-time broadcast slot.

But old people getting screwed out of their pensions because of their own stupidity didn't excite her.

She pushed back her chair and reached for her shoulder bag.

"I don't understand." Elle looked at Compton and Perkins in turn. "I'm happy to cooperate. I want to. But I've told you everything I remember. You have it all recorded. Why did you ask me to come back and go over it again?"

Compton had called her last night, asking if she would return today for yet another interview. She hadn't specified the reason for it except to say that it was "important." As before, Elle hadn't felt that it was optional.

Compton said, "First off, thank you for coming. We realize that it interrupts your workday. It's also an emotional drain each time you're asked to recount that day."

Actually, her workday suffered more from writer's block than this interruption.

But recounting the incident was more than an "emotional drain." It was like scraping the scab off a wound with coarse sandpaper. While it had been cathartic to relate her experience at the group therapy session yesterday, the retelling had also awakened a thousand horrible reminders of it. Then later with Calder—

Calder.

She'd been so shaken by those last few minutes with him that she didn't even remember her long drive home to Fort Worth. His abject despair, which had been evident in what he'd whispered to her, had left her feeling sorrowful for him.

The other matter, the embrace, had left her dazed.

Since Charlie's death, she had been hugged more times than she had been in her entire lifetime up to that point. But no other hug had felt like that. None had come close to what it had been like to be held against him, tightly and needfully and with want.

If it had been nothing more than a warm hug of condolence, she wouldn't have run from it. Instead, she'd fled, not from him but from what he'd made her feel.

Just thinking back on it now made her restive.

But she didn't want the detectives to think she was nervous because of them. Refocusing, she said, "Anything I tell you now will be what you've already heard in our previous conversations."

Compton said, "You've been exceptionally thorough and accurate, Elle."

Always before, she'd been Ms. Portman. The familiarity was like a caution light. They wanted something from her. She couldn't imagine what.

Compton was saying, "The information you've provided coincides with the security camera videos, which our analysts have broken down into fractions of fractions of seconds. It's because your recall is so precise that we wanted to talk to you again."

Lucky me. "All right. But I'm still in the dark as to why."

"It was actually Perkins who picked up on something." Compton motioned toward the dour man, who, after a cursory greeting, hadn't said another word. "I'll let him explain."

He didn't become animated, but he did amble around the corner of the desk and prop himself against it to be nearer her. "You mentioned that we had recorded your statement. We recorded everyone's. Compton and I have watched and listened to those interviews over and over again. On about the tenth pass, I noticed that a few of you mentioned something that others hadn't."

"I'm sorry. A few of who?"

"A few of you survivors."

"I see. What did we mention?"

"The man who ran into the stroller and nearly knocked it over."

Elle said, "There were so many people around the stroller, I'm sure that most of those you interviewed told you about him."

"Uh-huh. Many did."

"Then what makes my mention of him noteworthy?"

"Take a look." Compton turned the open laptop on the desk toward Elle. "It's jerky. Scoot a little closer so you can see better."

Elle did as asked. Compton hit a few keystrokes, and a video began to play in extreme slow motion. Compton said, "At this point, the shooter had fired four shots. The first killed Mr. Rollins. The next three came in rapid succession. Two were misses, partially because of Mr. Hudson's yanking those around him to the ground. The fourth shot caught a man in the thigh."

"Yes. I remember seeing him fall."

"This video picks up seconds after that."

The images were of people scrambling in terror. They were difficult for Elle to watch, although she'd seen them through her mind's eye a thousand times.

As she'd told Calder, those were the worst moments of the entire experience, to watch in helplessness and horror as her child became unreachable. At least the video played silently. She didn't have to listen to Charlie's screams as she did in her nightmares.

The individual in question came into the frame. "That's him." He was seen barreling into the stroller, but even as it began to topple, he kept going. He didn't slow down. He didn't look back. "He might have caught it, I think," she said absently. "Of course, he was panicked, literally running for his life."

"Seconds after he ran past, Mr. Hudson enters the frame and grabs the push bar of the stroller. Simultaneously, he's struck. Both he and the stroller go down, him landing on top of it."

Elle flinched.

Compton stopped the video, turned the laptop back around, and folded her arms over her expansive bosom. "Describe the man who banged into the stroller."

Confused, Elle looked at the two of them. "You just saw him."

"Yes, but I want you to tell me again what *you* saw. What was he wearing?"

"Khaki pants, a navy-blue windbreaker, a faded red baseball cap."

"What kind of shoes?"

"I only saw him from the knees up."

"Did you get a good look at his face?"

"No. Only in profile."

"Facial hair?"

"I don't think so. Nothing like a full beard."

"Ethnicity?"

"White."

"Height?"

"A little above average, but that's only a guess."

Perkins said, "He's caught in one freeze frame with Calder Hudson. Hudson's six feet three inches. Gauging by that, we put this fellow at around five ten."

"I would say that's in the ballpark," Elle said, "but I couldn't swear to it. He didn't strike me as either distinctively tall or short."

"Thin or heavy?"

"Again, not remarkably one or the other." She held up both hands, palms out. "I'm being of no help to you. Can you give me a hint of what you're looking for?"

"Let's keep going," Compton said.

"He really was only a blur," Elle insisted. "I was focused more on the stroller and the likelihood of it tipping over."

Compton ignored that and said, "How old would you guess he was?"

"Judging by his agility alone, I would say late twenties, early thirties. But he must have been older."

"What makes you think so?"

"His ponytail was gray." She knew immediately that she'd hit bingo, because the detectives exchanged a telling look. "Is that significant?"

"Out of all the eyewitnesses we interviewed, you're one of

only five who mentioned this guy's ponytail," Perkins said. "And in every instance, it was off-handedly referred to and at a different point of their narrative. That's why it took us so long to pick up on it."

"You're absolutely certain that he had a ponytail?" Compton asked.

"Absolutely certain."

"You saw in the video that he was wearing a baseball cap."

"His collar was flipped up, but I could see that his ponytail was coming out through the opening in the back of his cap."

Compton turned the laptop back around toward Elle. "Like this?"

She tapped a couple of keys. A photograph appeared on the screen. It was of a faded red baseball cap with a gray ponytail trailing from the opening. "Exactly like that," Elle said. "The ponytail is fake?"

"One of those novelty caps like you buy at a truck stop, usually with a ribald slogan," Perkins said. "Easily obtainable."

"Yes, I've seen them," Elle said, "and they rarely fool me. But he was running so fast. And with everything else going on, it never occurred to me that it was fake hair. Where was it found?"

Compton took a deep breath. "This crime scene presented numerous challenges. Thousands of people attended the fair that day. Anything, the smallest item, was potential evidence. Crime scene units from all over the area were assembled and organized, then were assigned sections of the fairground, which, when you include the parking lots, encompasses nearly thirty acres.

"The officers first had to photograph their section, and then begin the painstaking process of collecting evidence. It had been a beautiful day, but there was a storm that night with rain and high wind, elements which further compromised the scene and hampered progress.

"I'm telling you all this to excuse how the cap was initially dismissed. Upon inspection of it, a strand of human hair was found inside it. It didn't belong to the ponytail, which is synthetic. The DNA of that hair didn't match Levi Jenkins's. Nor was it flagged by any criminal database. Consequently, the cap was catalogued but passed off as debris left by someone fleeing."

Elle said, "Or it could have been dropped days before the shooting and nobody had bothered to pick it up."

"That could very possibly be the case," Compton admitted. "But when Perkins realized that five of you had mentioned a man wearing a cap matching this one, we went back to the crime scene photos taken that night within hours of the shooting. We put them under a microscope and spotted this cap in one of those photos. It was on the ground very near the tent where Jenkins was found.

"But that wasn't where it was collected by crime scene techs two days later. It was in a different location some distance away from where it had been photographed."

"It had been moved?" Elle asked.

"We blame the strong wind for that," Perkins said. "Although, with a crime scene that large and that many people on site, anything can happen to a valuable piece of evidence." He added glumly, "And too often does."

Elle divided a look between them. "All right. I'm following you so far, but what does it boil down to?"

Compton said, "Let's say the culprit came across Jenkins, who was stoned, who didn't even realize what was happening, and certainly didn't resist when the pistol was placed against his head. This individual hastily made it look like a suicide, ran from the tent, and merged with the frenzied, stampeding crowd, losing the cap in the process, maybe deliberately dropping it to be trampled."

"We don't have any idea who this individual is," Elle said.

"No, but when we do isolate a suspect, this cap and the human hair found in it could prove to be incriminating evidence, especially if you five can testify that he's the man you saw in the vicinity of where Howard Rollins and your son were fatally shot. It could lead to a conviction. Our ultimate goal."

Elle wet her lips. "So then, this is a breakthrough?"

"A sliver of daylight, but it's a starting place. We have personnel trying to track down the origin of the cap and trace it to the owner. But think of it as hunting a unicorn. It's grunt work, and slow going, and we're doing it as covertly as possible."

"Why?"

Again the detectives looked at each other. Perkins gave Compton a subtle nod. She came back to Elle. "Even though we're getting hammered by the media for not catching the guy yet, we're not going to announce that we have this lead. But these things have a way of getting out no matter how hard we try to keep a tight lid.

"If it is leaked that there's been a development, we're going to downplay the significance of it. We're not going to reveal what it is, and we're definitely not going to name the witnesses who put us on to it."

"Thank you for that consideration," Elle said. "I'd rather be kept anonymous. I've turned down every request for an interview."

"Elle," Compton said, leaning in closer to her. "Keeping you anonymous isn't only a courtesy to protect your privacy. Whoever this whack job is, he's still unidentified and at large."

Suddenly Elle intuited what this signified, and it caused her heart rate to jump.

Compton said, "You provided the clue that could nail him. If you remembered that detail about him, what else might you remember that would lead to his capture? We're keeping your identity under wraps for your safety."

Chapter 15

Calder was within a few yards of the precinct entrance when Elle came out.

Upon seeing each other, they halted simultaneously. Neither moved for several seconds; then Calder tipped his head toward an out-of-the-way spot at the side of the main doors.

Her hesitation was obvious, and he knew it must be because of their parting at the bar last night. But then she walked toward him, fell into step, stopped when he did, and faced him when he turned to her.

"Hi," he said.

"Hi."

"Thanks for coming over. I thought you might avoid me."

"Why would I do that?"

"Now that you didn't, it doesn't matter."

After that, they stood and stared at each other without saying anything. A whisper of wind caught at a loose strand of her hair and brushed it against her lips, fantasies about which had kept him awake most of the night. In an unconscious gesture, she pushed the wayward tendril back onto her cheek.

He flicked his gaze away from her mouth. "Are you here at Compton's request?"

"She called me last night."

"Me too. You've met with her already?"

"Her and Perkins. We just finished."

"What's it about?"

"I'm not supposed to talk about it with anyone. But since they asked you to come in also, I assume it relates to the same subject."

"Why the two of us?"

She gave a faint smile. "That's what I'm not supposed to say."

"Is it something bad?"

"It's, uh—"

"Sorry. Scratch that." He shoved his hands into the pockets of his leather jacket. "I shouldn't be pressuring you for information if they asked you not to talk about it. I guess I'll learn what it's about soon enough."

She nodded and glanced toward the entrance. "I shouldn't keep you."

"You're not. I'm a few minutes early." Quickly, he added, "Am I keeping you from something?"

"No, I'm not on a deadline."

"What about your book?"

"Well, there is that."

Their chuckles were followed by another lull, during

which he debated with himself. Before he could change his mind, he said, "Actually, Elle, it does matter."

"What?"

"The reason I thought you might avoid me. It had to do with what I told you last night just before we left each other."

"Oh." Her eyes turned soft. "The bullet you couldn't stop. The burden of guilt you live with."

"It's a heavy one."

"Calder." She placed her hand on his sleeve. "Who knows why things happened the way they did. They just did. Please don't blame yourself for not dying."

"I'm trying to come to terms with it, you know? But it's tough."

"I don't blame you. If I don't, can't you forgive yourself?"

"I promise to work on it."

She smiled and gave his arm a little squeeze before letting go. "You shouldn't be late for your meeting. Take care."

"You too."

He was in discussion with Compton and Perkins for half an hour. As he exited the building, he couldn't suppress an effervescent hope that Elle was still there.

She wasn't.

Shauna was.

Fuck!

She was sitting on a concrete bench, her ever-present shoulder bag at her side. She sat with her legs crossed, the top one swinging like a lazy pendulum. For once, she wasn't busily navigating her phone. Her gaze had been fixed on the door through which he'd just come, keying to him that her being here wasn't happenstance. It was an ambush.

"Hello," she said.

"Hey."

She nodded down toward the bench. "Have a seat."

He scanned their surroundings to see how many people were around to witness what he anticipated would be an ugly scene. He spotted no more than a handful of people, and all were out of earshot and going about their business.

He sat down. "What brings you here?"

"The same as you, I would imagine."

"What do you imagine?"

"That there's been a breakthrough in the investigation of the shooting."

"You have a source in this precinct," he said, and not in question form.

"I believe I knew that there'd been a development even before you did."

"It was easy enough for you to deduce, Shauna. You were sitting three feet from me last night when Detective Compton called."

"Did she tell you then what was up?"

"No."

"She wanted to inform you in person?"

He spread his hands as though to say *I'm here.*

"After talking to her last night, why did you hide out in the guest room? Why not tell me that you had been summoned to meet with her and Perkins?"

"Because I didn't want to get the third degree like I'm

getting now. And before you try to drub out of me why they wanted to see me, understand right now that I can't talk about it."

"Can't or won't?"

"Both."

"But you talked to Elle Portman about it."

For the first time since joining her on the bench, he turned his head and looked straight at her.

"At least I assume that's what you were talking about in your little two-person huddle. Of course, you could have been talking about something else entirely."

She pointed across the street. "I was parked right over there, so I couldn't miss your arrival. I wasn't all that surprised to see you because it explained Compton's call. I was about to get out of my car and hail you, when Elle Portman came through the exit and the two of you had that... *moment*."

She paused, lowered her chin, raised her eyebrows. "Care to comment?" When he said nothing, she continued. "I'm sure you know the moment I mean. The one when you both stopped dead in your tracks, deer-in-the-headlights fashion, and then sort of gravitated toward each other as though drawn by an irresistible compulsion to be closer." Again, she paused. "Still nothing to say?"

"We saw each other yesterday at the group therapy session. Since it was my first time, she came over to me. We chatted. So, naturally when we saw each other today—"

"I'm not blind or stupid, Calder. I know what I saw, so don't waste your bullshit on me."

"You don't have a monopoly on bullshit, Shauna. You think I don't know that all those trips you took to Austin—"

"I told you why I had to go back and forth. I was covering the abortion bill debate."

"And fucking your cameraman. Your married-with-children cameraman." He chuffed. "You called or texted me several times a day. Since you rarely do that while working, it was easy enough to figure out the reason for this sudden outpouring of affection. I could smell the bullshit through the phone."

"You're guessing."

"No. I'm not." He gave her a look that dared her to try to lie to him.

She held on to her indignation, but when she saw that he wasn't going to yield, she said, "That was months ago. Why didn't you accuse me then?"

"Because I didn't care."

She swelled up like a puff adder. "So why bring it up now? To salve your guilty conscience?" She made a scornful sound. "You should have seen the way you watched her as she walked away. As though *pining*. Is she the reason we haven't had sex in two months?"

"No."

"Or why you while away hours each day in front of a silent TV? Or why you canceled a six-figure contract, why you do nothing constructive with your time, but only drag around and mope?"

"I did something constructive this morning."

"Oh, really? What?"

He stood up. "I moved out."

"I'm sorry, Laura. I know it's not the status report you wanted to hear."

After returning home from the meeting at the precinct, Elle had sat down at her computer, determined to produce something. Even if what she wrote was terrible, she needed the confidence booster of writing *something*. She set herself a minimum goal of composing at least two lines of dialogue.

But after several hours of staring into space, dwelling not on her storyline but on her two meetings at the precinct, the one that had taken place inside and the one with Calder outside, she had gathered her courage and called her literary agent. Better that she preemptively notify Laura of her lack of progress than wait in dread for Laura to inquire.

Laura was understanding. "Elle, your work ethic surpasses that of any other writer this agency represents. And because you thrive on the storytelling itself, I know that you're more frustrated by this dry spell than anyone. You lost a child. No one expects you to jump right back in."

When her pregnancy was confirmed, Elle had acknowledged to herself that selling real estate wouldn't be compatible with having an infant. Glenda had tried to persuade her to take a leave of absence, to give herself several months to think it over before taking such a giant leap that included a new career path in addition to motherhood and relocation.

But Elle's mind had been made up. Unbeknownst to Glenda, she'd been ready to make a change even before Charlie was conceived.

While pregnant, she'd undertaken the nesting process. During the day, she'd worked on the house. Her evenings were spent making notes for her first book.

She had submitted an outline to Laura's agency the day before going into labor. Charlie was four months old before she heard back. The voice mail message, left two days earlier, had been straightforward. "My name is Laura Musgrave. Your story concept is charming. Let's talk." Elle had called her immediately.

Now, in reply to Laura's attempted soothing, she said, "It is very frustrating. I need to lose myself in something. I thought that resuming work on the book would be grounding, that it would give me something else to focus on and help keep the grief at bay." She placed her head in her hands and massaged her temples. "What does the publisher say about the delay?"

"They're not worried."

"Laura. I'm a grown-up. Give it to me straight."

"All right. I did get a call from your editor yesterday. It was a gentle probe, but a probe nonetheless."

"Will they ask for their advance back?"

"No. Lord, no. We're nowhere near that point. He asked about your progress only for the purpose of scheduling the publication. Art, marketing, sales, every department wants to know when they can expect this second book. Which should be very good news to you. They're eager to get it out there in the marketplace, which is hot for Betsy books."

"What is he thinking in terms of a pub date?"

"Fall of next year. Edging toward the holidays would be ideal."

"Coveted timing for a release."

"Exactly," Laura said. "He's going to hold open several slots and will choose one when you deliver."

"Fantastic. No pressure."

In her *Stay calm* voice, Laura said, "We didn't etch a date in stone. There's some flexibility, and you've got plenty of time to complete the book."

"Ordinarily, yes. But not at the rate I'm going."

"If you try to force it, you'll just get stuck worse."

"That's a discouraging prospect."

"Are you sleeping enough?"

She confessed to waking up several times a night, listening for Charlie, thinking she'd heard him.

"Are you eating enough?"

"Enough to get by."

"Drinking enough?"

"I hydrate."

"I meant liquor."

"I don't think booze is the solution to my problem."

"All the greats were drunks," Laura stated, and when Elle laughed, she added, "I'm serious. It's an irrefutable fact. Name a classic, any classic. The author—"

"Wasn't writing about precocious clouds."

"No, but his or her head was always in one."

Elle's doorbell rang. "This conversation has deteriorated, and the UPS man is at my door."

"Is he cute?"

"I'll call you in a couple of days."

"Have some faith in yourself, Elle. I do, and so does the publisher."

She disconnected. The banter had done her good. She was still smiling as she made her way to the front door and pulled it open.

He wasn't what she would call *cute*.

Chapter 16

Calder Hudson wasn't cute. He wouldn't walk into a room and put people at ease by cracking jokes and glad-handing. He would walk into a room and make everyone wish they had the self-possession he did. He made it appear so effortless, it was intimidating.

Elle wasn't intimidated by him, but, upon finding him on her porch, there was no denying the balloon-bounce of sensation in her midsection. "I thought you were the UPS man."

He nodded and said deadpan, "I get that a lot."

Spontaneously, she laughed. Maybe he could crack a joke. "My neighbor went out of town and asked me to watch for a delivery, so..." Running short of breath, she let a shrug suffice.

"Am I intruding?"

"No. I was just wrapping up a business call with my agent."

"How'd it go?"

"That depends on your outlook. Glass half full or half empty."

"Try me."

"The publisher wants the second book sooner rather than later, but mainly because the first is selling well."

"Definitely half full, and I'm partially to thank." He held up a brightly colored tote bag bearing the logo of a local bookstore. "Will you sign my book?"

She was astonished. "You bought my book?"

"Two copies."

"For who? I mean for whom?" A niece or nephew? A son or daughter she didn't know he had?

"One is for me," he said. "The bookstore discounts the cover price if you donate a second copy to their children's reading program."

"On behalf of the reading program and myself, thank you for your generosity."

"You're welcome." He paused. "Does it entitle me to come inside while you're signing my copy?"

She was both happy and flustered over his unexpected appearance coming so soon after their chance encounter at the precinct. But it had been presumptuous of him to just show up. "You should have called first."

"I was afraid you'd say no."

That was said without a grin or joking lilt. He no longer looked quite so self-possessed and intimidating, and, in spite of her common sense, she was flattered that he'd sought her out.

She stood aside. "The living room is on your left."

He stepped into the entry and squeezed past her, walked down the short hall, and turned into the living room. She followed and stood beside him, viewing the room as a stranger might—as a cosmopolitan stranger like him might—and wondered what he thought of it.

He surveyed it leisurely and seemed to take special notice of the overstocked bookshelves, framed photos of her and Charlie, the potted plant that had outgrown its corner adjacent to the window, the chenille throw she'd left bundled up in her chair.

She raised her arms to her sides to encompass the room. "It's homey."

He smiled. "It looks like you."

"God help it," she said with a self-deprecating laugh. "I wasn't expecting company. I'm in my work clothes."

After returning home from the precinct, she'd changed clothes, intending to spend the remainder of the afternoon and evening at her desk. Her work uniform consisted of stretchy, comfortable leggings and a loose-fitting top.

"You look great."

She was about to protest the unwarranted compliment, when she decided not to make a big deal of her casual appearance. After all, he'd come unannounced. Nor did she want him to think that she was fishing for compliments.

"First time I've seen you without your hair pulled back," he said.

"I was getting a headache, so I shook out the ponytail."

Made self-conscious now, she gathered her hair at her nape and pulled it over her shoulder, knowing that it would still look like an unruly mess.

She wished she had on lipstick. She wished her sneakers were new chic ones instead of old standbys. She wished her sweatshirt had the spangle that Glenda had recommended. She wished she looked more sophisticated and less domesticated.

She wished he looked less mouthwatering.

"Please," she said, motioning him toward the sofa.

Calder had begun to think she would never ask. "Thanks." He set the book bag on the coffee table and sat down in the center of the sofa.

"Something to drink?" she asked.

"I'm okay, thanks."

She moved to an upholstered chair, which he determined was her favorite spot. Beside the chair was a small table. On it were a paperback book and a mug with a tea bag string dangling from it. Before sitting down, she picked up a throw from the seat and draped it over the back cushion.

The room was cozy with *stuff*. He realized that the condominium he'd moved from this morning hadn't had any stuff in it. Top-of-the-line furnishings and objets d'art that a decorator had placed just so, but not everyday things you'd pick up and handle without worrying about leaving fingerprints. His would be on the TV remote. The whiskey decanter. Not much else.

It had taken him less than two hours to pack his personal possessions. Clothing and shoes had taken a majority of that time. He'd cleared out everything else with very little effort because he hadn't had much to clear out.

Except for the items he could pack into two suitcases that would fit in the trunk of his car, he'd boxed up everything and left it all in the storage unit in the building's parking garage, along with his two bicycles, snow skis, skateboard, baseball gear, and other toys. He'd told the building superintendent that when he had a new address, he would send a mover for it all.

The super had eyed him speculatively. "So this is a permanent move?"

"Yes."

"What about Ms. Calloway?"

"Not my business. You'll have to ask her."

He gave the guy a two-hundred-dollar tip and drove away feeling like he'd gotten a reprieve from a life sentence.

"You had your meeting with Compton and Perkins?"

Elle's question pulled him back into her livable living room. "Yeah."

"And?"

"It was hard to take it all in. You know how Perkins gets wound up and goes on and on."

She looked at him with surprise, and then they both laughed. It imbued him with a sense of satisfaction that he'd made her laugh twice since his arrival. Given her youthful and unseasoned appearance, one would expect her laugh to sound like jingle bells. Instead, it was as throaty as a cello and sexy as hell.

He'd often wondered what her hair would look like when

it wasn't bound. Now that it was rippling over her shoulder in loose waves, he wanted to sink his fingers into it and—

"You know what I think?"

Caught thinking with his libido, he said huskily, "About what?"

"The Compton/Perkins team."

"What do you think?"

"Perkins deliberately doesn't say much in order to make you forget he's there. He's the more cerebral and analytical."

"While Compton is talking, he's observing."

"Uh-huh. Closely watching for reactions, listening for giveaway inflections. Compton is as sharp as a tack, too, but I think he's her senior. She defers to him before revealing anything of consequence."

Calder thought back on the occasions that he'd been with the two. In particular, he remembered when he was in the hospital, and Compton had looked toward her partner as though asking his permission to share that Charlie Portman hadn't survived. His gaze flicked to a framed baby picture of Charlie on the end table.

"I think you're right," he said in response to her observation. "They instructed me not to discuss this new lead, the same as they did you. But will you report me if I cheat?"

She shook her head and motioned for him to proceed.

"What do you make of it? Did that guy stand out to you?"

"Only because he nearly knocked over the stroller."

"I don't even remember mentioning the ponytail, but they played back that part of my recorded statement. I'd said, 'A guy in a ball cap with a fake ponytail.'"

"You recognized it as a fake?"

"Not consciously, but I guess it registered as such because that's what I told them."

"Do you know who the other three key witnesses are?"

"No. You?"

"No. I wouldn't have known that you were one of the five if we hadn't run into each other outside. I don't think they would like that we're talking about it. They wouldn't want us comparing notes or influencing each other's memory."

"Probably not," he said. "But what harm can come of it? Something you say might spark something in my memory, and vice versa."

"So coming here to get your book signed was only a ploy. You really wanted to get my take on the investigation."

"Hell no. My priority was to get your autograph."

"How did you know where to find me?"

The blunt question took him off guard. Out of habit, his initial reaction was to evade it with a double-talk answer. But he decided to tell her straight.

"Shauna told me that she'd asked you several times for an interview, so I was certain she had your contact info stored in her phone. I don't have access to that, but when I got out of the hospital, I snooped around her workspace at home. I found your name, address, and phone number scribbled on a notepad."

"Why didn't you just ask her for it?"

"Because I had insisted that she leave you alone. After our rather heated discussion about that, if I had turned around and asked how I could contact you, she would have wanted to know why."

Speaking low, she said, "*I* would have wanted to know why."

He averted his gaze to the tag on the tea bag string. "While I was still in the hospital, I thought about writing you a note or something. You know, let some time pass first, a week or two, then reach out to tell you how sorry I was about your son."

He let that settle, then looked at her directly again. "That was before we came face-to-face there in the hallway at the precinct. I came away that day thinking that I'd botched it for sure, but that I'd said everything I had to say, everything I knew to say, so I never followed up on writing you the note.

"But after what we learned today, I was glad I'd held on to your address. I could come here and talk to you privately about the hush-hush lead and ask what you thought about it."

"Why didn't you just call to ask?"

"I could have, but I wanted to...uh...talk about it face-to-face." *My face to your face.*

"Oh."

"You know, because it's such a tricky subject. We're not even supposed to be talking about it."

"Right." She dampened her lips. "And it's harder to catch nuances over the phone."

"That was my thinking. You miss expressions and inflections." He waited a tick, then said, "Like last night."

Her chest visibly hitched. "What about last night?"

"Well, I don't think the conversation we had in the bar would have been as meaningful, at least not to me, if it had been over the telephone. I took away much more from it by being there. With you."

Their gazes held for a ten count, then her eyelids lowered,

shutting off direct contact. The atmosphere had become so thick, he either had to breathe deeply or pant. Instead, he gave a dry laugh. "And if I had called, I wouldn't have gotten my book signed."

He leaned forward and took the copy of *Heavens to Betsy* from the bag. "I assume Betsy is the main character."

Looking relieved of tension, she smiled. "Yes. She's the cloud with life lessons to learn."

"How old is she?"

"Six. And a half, as she makes sure you know. Generally, she's well-behaved and obedient, but occasionally she makes bad choices that result in consequences which affect not only her but also her family and friends."

"By the end of the story, she acknowledges her blunders and makes amends."

She narrowed her eyes. "Did you read the last page first?"

He laughed. "No. I swear. Lucky guess."

"Spot on, though. Maybe you should be writing the books. Want to swap jobs?"

He maintained his smile, but her question cut him to the quick. "I'd have no idea how to write a story, especially one for kids. And you wouldn't be any good at my job." Realizing how offensive that sounded, he added, "Believe me, Elle, that was a compliment, not a put-down."

The seriousness of his tone dispelled the humor. Solemnly, she said, "All right."

She didn't demand an explanation. She'd simply accepted the truth of his words. He wanted to tell her how much he appreciated that but didn't want to linger on the topic of his work. He didn't want to talk about it with her, because

he was having a hard enough time conducting internal dia-
logues about it with himself. Since the shooting, his thoughts
about returning to work had been conflicting.

To change the subject, he said, "You also do all the art-
work in the books. That's amazing."

"My publisher urged me to get an illustrator, but I held
firm. I know what each character looks like. They live in
here."

In order to tap her temple, she moved aside the mass of
hair, then let it fall back into place over her left breast, the
fullness of which was barely discernible underneath the
baggy sweatshirt. The concealment was maddening. For a
moment he was sidetracked by an arousing fantasy of doing
away with it.

She was saying, "If I handed my characters over to
another artist, they would become his or her interpretation.
I could never settle for that."

"What's the title of the next book?"

"It will be volume two of the *Heavens to Betsy* series, but
I don't have a title yet because I don't have a story." She
assumed a sad, defeated aspect and stared down into her lap.

"Every now and then, I'll feel a tingle of inspiration, but
the minute I try to convert the random thought into words,
I get distracted by a memory of Charlie, which will lead to
another, and by the time I force myself to concentrate, the
idea has evaporated."

"You'll get there."

Her head came up, and she gave him a wan smile. "I had
better. In the meantime, thank you for this purchase." She
reached across for his book. "Do you have a pen?"

He checked the inside pocket of his jacket. "No, sorry."

"A writer should never be without a pen. There's a drawerful in my office. I'll be right back." She stood and headed out of the room.

He came to his feet. "Okay if I tag along?"

Chapter 17

———◦◉◦———

She looked hesitant.

He said, "I'd like to see where you get creative."

"I'd like to see that myself."

He took the dry remark as license to follow her from the living area into a hallway. They passed a room with an open door. Although no lights were on, he saw that it was furnished with a crib and matching chest of drawers, a rocking chair, bins of toys. *CHARLIE* was spelled out in block letters attached to the wall above the crib. Since she didn't point out the room to him, he went past it without commenting.

Nor did he say anything about the bedroom on the other side of the hall. It too was unlighted, but it had to be hers. He caught a whiff of vanilla and thought it must be from a scented candle. Or maybe her body lotion.

The bed was made. He imagined it unmade, with her and rumpled sheets. His reaction was instantaneous and imperative, an onslaught of mistimed lust. He couldn't or wouldn't act on it, but it was damned hard to put in reverse.

At the end of the hall, she entered the only room in which lights were on. It had a desk with a computer setup and a drafting table littered with drawings in various stages of completion. Others had been tacked to a wall covered entirely with cork.

She took the Betsy book over to the desk and located a pen. "Do you want only my signature, or do you want it personalized?"

"Personalized, please. Mind if I take a look?" He gestured down at the drawings scattered across the drafting table.

"Help yourself. They're only sketches." She opened the book to the title page and bent over the desk to sign it.

Dear God.

He quickly turned away from that tempting sight and began shuffling through the drawings of her characters. They were clever. The clouds had expressive faces, their personalities depicted by features such as a beauty mark and long eyelashes for the diva, a beetled brow for the thunder-cloud, apple cheeks and a missing front tooth for Betsy. All were instantly engaging.

Then he came to a drawing that caused his stomach to drop.

"Here you go." Elle had finished signing the book and had extended it to him, but when she saw what he held, she set the book back on the desk, walked over, and stood beside him.

Together they looked down at a sketch she'd drawn of Charlie. With strokes of pencil lead and artful shading, she had captured his happy countenance, tousled curls, bright eyes.

Quietly, she said, "I tried to explain my predicament to my agent."

"What predicament, specifically?"

"It's difficult for me to write about an animated sun, a benevolent moon, and clouds, and stars who live in a pastel universe where problems are easily resolved and everything always turns out happily, when, in the real world where we live, there's so much darkness, and ugliness, and violence, and sudden, needless deaths that you aren't braced for. The make-believe I write is so far removed from reality I feel like I'm selling a lie to children."

He slid his hands into the pockets of his jacket, mostly to keep himself from touching her. "Kids need the make-believe, don't they? To balance all the bad shit they're exposed to? I think so. Your stories will leave people feeling hopeful and upbeat. Positive. That's something to take pride in, Elle."

"I used to, but the endeavor seems trivial now. To a laughable degree."

"I assure you, it's not. If you leave people feeling good, that's huge."

She looked at him as though she sensed that he had much more to say on the matter. But when he didn't continue, she drew a deep breath and exhaled it slowly.

"The trauma has left all of us more introspective, hasn't it?" she said. "It's understandable that we're viewing things differently. Remember, one of the group members talked about the shifts in his perspectives on everything, every aspect of his life. I knew exactly what he meant. I dwell on concepts, abstracts, more than I did before."

"Such as?"

"The weighty ones. Love, tolerance, forgiveness, gratitude, compassion. They've taken on greater significance."

"Whew, that's deep."

She laughed lightly. "Smaller things have also taken on greater significance."

"Name one."

"Well, let's see." She tapped the side of her chin. "A good cabernet? I bought one that the man in the wine shop told me is to die for. Want to give it a taste test?"

"Another time." He came nearer and cupped her face between his hands. "This is what I've been dying to taste test."

He lowered his head and settled his lips on hers, then rubbed them apart. Her tongue tantalized his by playing shy. He lifted away only far enough to look into her eyes. "Elle?"

"I'm sorry. I haven't—"

"What?"

"Been alone with a man. Not in a long time."

"You were alone with me last night."

"Not quite alone. And not like this."

"No, not like this. But close to this. And this is all I've thought about since. Let me taste, Elle. Please."

He eased his mouth down to hers, giving her time to protest, praying she wouldn't. He tried a different slant, and this time her lips were more pliant. Their tongues touched. When his slid into her mouth, she gave a purr of permission.

He lowered his hands from her face to her waist, drawing her against him as he had when he'd embraced her the night before. This time, however, as though her form had been sculptured onto him, adjustments were unnecessary. On contact, they fit together so familiarly and perfectly, they breathed sighs into each other's mouths.

He deepened the kiss, slipped one hand under the roomy sweatshirt, and splayed it over her bottom, lifting her against him until he filled the notch of her thighs. Filled it well.

She gasped and angled her head back, breaking the kiss. He ducked his head in an attempt to recapture her mouth, but she placed her hands on his chest and pushed against him.

"Elle," he groaned. "What?"

"I won't cheat with you. I've had it done to me. I refuse to participate."

"Shauna? She isn't a factor. She and I are over. I moved out."

She swallowed and panted softly, "Really? You did?"

"Yes."

"When?"

"Recently." Then he cursed under his breath and admitted wryly, "This morning."

"*This* this morning?"

"Early. After last night, after you and I—"

"Does she even know yet?"

"Yes."

"Was she upset?"

"Livid. But only because I denied her the satisfaction of kicking me out. Since the shooting, we've unraveled. She was impatient with my inability to snap out of it. I was resentful of her impatience. She doesn't understand what I'm going through. Not at all."

Elle eased out of his arms and backed away. "But *I* do."

He didn't immediately catch her implication, but when he did, he was swift to dispel it. "No. *No.* I didn't come to your door tonight with a hard-on for *understanding.*"

"I think that's exactly what you did. If it's consolation— a consolation prize—you're after, go find another warm body."

In a flash, she left the room. He charged after her.

———

"I came here because I think about you constantly."

She gave a bitter laugh. "Since yesterday?"

"Since the first time I saw you."

Elle stopped short and turned around. He'd been so close on her heels, she nearly bumped into him. Still skeptical, she held his gaze as she backed into the living room and took up a position in front of the dormant fireplace.

He came farther into the room but wisely kept his distance. "That day at the precinct, when I took my first good look at you, I thought, 'Damn,' as in 'Damn. Those eyes. Those lips.'

"But in the next heartbeat, less than a heartbeat, it slammed into me who you must be. The little boy's mother. What a shitty twist of fate that was, because I knew you wouldn't want anything to do with me."

"I didn't feel that way. I never felt that way."

"I did." He placed his hands on his hips and hung his head, looking down at the floor. "See, I have this issue with failure."

"I find that hard to believe. What have you ever failed at?"

He raised his head and, in a barely audible and rueful voice, said, "Nothing. That's the issue. In third grade, I set a goal to sell the most fund-raising candy bars, and I did. In high school I made the varsity baseball team as a freshman. I became an Eagle Scout.

"Despite the beer drinking and girl watching, I graduated SMU summa cum laude. I set up my consulting service, and it took off. I've never failed to achieve anything I've attempted." He took a stuttering breath. "Except for the one time when it was a matter of life and death. I failed to stop that goddamn bullet."

She whispered, "I've asked you not to do that to yourself. It wasn't your fault."

"No?"

"You were trying to save him."

"Yeah, and that might have been what got him killed. I keep thinking that maybe, subconsciously, I wanted to be a hero. You know? My natural inclination has always been to take charge, get her done, make it happen, whatever *it* was. After the first gunshot, that instinct took over.

"Maybe, if I'd dropped like I was yelling for everyone else to do, if only I'd stayed put..." He looked at her helplessly. "Instead, I lunged up and chased after Charlie's stroller. That action might have been what drew fire toward us."

Elle covered her face with her hands. She felt remorse for the guilt he carried, but more than a few times she also had called into question his spontaneous action and the ramifications of it.

She didn't blame him for his valor, but the "what-ifs" were innumerable and insurmountable. Each was an obstacle between them. She feared they always would be.

Lowering her hands, she met his tormented eyes. "Because of the fateful circumstances of Charlie's death, I think you genuinely feel an emotional connection to me. But you're mistaking the nature of it, Calder. You're mistaking it for being—"

"Sexual."

"Yes."

"No. There's no mistaking this." He flicked his hand toward his pelvis. "I feel an emotional connection to everybody who was affected by that shooting, but I don't think about them around the clock, and thoughts of them don't keep my right hand busy at night."

She rolled her lips inward, then tried again. "Your relationship with Shauna has suffered—"

"Died."

"This development in the investigation has further embroiled us. It's another shackle that's keeping us from moving on. I resent it. I know you must, too. You're dealing with a lot of—"

"Shit."

"Yes! That's my point. It's only natural that you would turn to someone who relates to how it feels when your world, the life you knew and gloried in, disintegrates within seconds."

He waited, seeming to consider all that, then said, "Valid

points, Elle. Seen from your perspective, I get where you're coming from. But the *only* reason I went to that group therapy meeting yesterday was in the hope that you'd be there. I couldn't think of another way to see you that wouldn't look contrived.

"After the time we spent together last night, I had to see you again, and *not* because I wanted understanding. I didn't want to wait for the next group session, but I needed another plausible excuse for tracking you down. That's when I thought of your book. Perfect. I went to the bookstore between moving out of my condo this morning and going to the precinct this afternoon."

"You'd already bought the book when we saw each other there? Why didn't you tell me? I could have signed it then."

"That's why I didn't tell you. I was holding it as my ticket to seeing you again." He raked his fingers through his hair. "I grant you that it is bad, bad, bad timing. The complexity of the situation, how freaking bizarre it is, doesn't escape me. I can see how you might think that I'm confusing emotions. I swear I'm not.

"For two months, sixty-something days and nights, I've thought of you. I've fantasized about a hundred things we could do together, and I believe the attraction is mutual." Lowering his voice, he added, "When we held each other last night, we generated heat."

She gave a small but noncommittal nod.

He tilted his head toward the hallway behind him. "And you did—briefly—kiss me back."

With a slight motion of her shoulders, she conceded that also.

"Right. In my sex fantasies, you are into it as much as I am. In my daydreams, you don't let the complicating tie that binds us keep us from tearing our clothes off." He must've read the shock in her expression, because he added, "Oh yeah. I've imagined us like that. A lot. As recently as when I looked into your bedroom and saw your bed."

He paused, shifted his stance, changed his tone of voice. "But if for one second you doubt my reason for wanting you that way, then it's not happening, Elle. I don't do one-sided sex, and I sure as hell don't want you doing me a favor out of compassion."

His monologue had made her feverish. The wanting he professed wasn't at all one-sided. She longed to walk over to him and resume the kiss that she had halted. She wanted to take it further. Take it to her bed.

She had to force herself to say what she felt she must. "As things are, while we're having to deal with so much right now, I think it would be a mistake to add...that."

He looked at her for a long moment, then nodded. "Take care of yourself." With no more than that, he walked out.

She followed him through the entry to the front door, which he opened himself. He didn't look back as he started down the walk toward his car parked at the curb.

She closed the door and pressed her forehead against the wood, taking in gulps of air in an effort not to weep. She'd made the correct decision, but God, it hurt.

She trusted in Calder's integrity. She didn't believe that he would purposely leave her with another serrated wound to her heart. What she mistrusted was the male mind-set that sex was a cure-all. She feared that, to him, it would represent the last link in their connection, that he would regard it as a reckoning with her and closure with Charlie's death.

Once she slept with him and he'd gotten her out of his system, then what? She wouldn't deceive herself into thinking, hoping, that there was a future for them. How could there be?

She was worlds apart from what he was accustomed to. She wasn't a Shauna Calloway type. What did he really see in Elle Portman except that she was the mother of the child for whose death he felt responsible?

As she stood there anguishing, the doorknob she'd been clutching turned in her hand.

She flinched, let go of it, and backed away. The door was pushed open, and Calder stepped inside.

He didn't say anything. He only looked at her, knowingly and hungrily, as he slowly pushed the door shut. They remained in that tableau, their breathing accelerating, then simultaneously surged toward each other.

Growling her name, he fisted a handful of her hair and used it to tilt her head back for his kiss.

Chapter 18

There's mortification, and then there's mortification.

The former would apply to an everyday-variety embarrassment.

The latter to having heedless, reckless, hottest-ever sex with a man who then fled with the speed of light. A slam-bam without even a thank you, ma'am.

Forehead resting on the heel of her hand, Elle groaned.

"Knock knock?"

The sudden voice was loud and unexpected, causing Elle to jump and almost topple off her drawing table stool. Hot coffee sloshed from her cup onto the leg of her pajamas. She recognized Glenda's voice.

Glenda is here? Now? Elle barely contained the burble of hysteria that threatened.

"Elle? Okay to come in?"

No, not okay. She positively, absolutely could not see

anyone right now. Certainly not her perceptive best friend. Should she tell her she had a stomach virus, Covid, Ebola? But then Glenda would want to nurse her, hover, coddle, insist that she see a doctor. Make matters worse.

All this went through Elle's sluggish mind with relative speed, and she concluded that she would just have to brazen it out. "I'm in the office. Come on back."

Hastily, she took inventory of herself and realized what a shambles she must look. Calder couldn't keep his hands out of her hair and had left it a tangled mess. Clumsily, she gathered it at her nape and twisted it into an unsecured knot.

She ran her hand over her chest as though to ensure that her T-shirt was still there and would conceal the whisker burns on her breasts. Memories of Calder's fervent mouth washed over and through her and she whispered, "Oh God, oh God."

She dabbed at her lips. They still felt swollen. Did she have a mark on her neck? How mortifying would that be? She hadn't noticed one when she'd taken a guilty glimpse of herself in the bathroom mirror, but she might have missed it.

Her eyes were red from crying, but if Glenda commented on that, she was ready with a valid excuse.

"Good morning, you."

Putting on a brave face, Elle swiveled her stool around and faced her friend with feigned gladness. "Good morning. You're out early."

Glenda tilted her head quizzically. "It's after ten."

"No. Really?" Elle gestured toward her drawing board. "I was working on some sketches. Lost track, I guess."

Glenda looked her over. Naturally, she homed in on the coffee spill.

Elle forced a dry laugh. "You startled me with your knock knock."

"I'm sorry. Did you burn yourself?"

"No, I'm fine."

"I would have rung the bell, but I noticed that your front door was ajar."

He'd left the door ajar? But then, that wasn't so surprising.

"It was?" she asked, playing innocent. "Huh. I stepped outside earlier to check for a package my neighbor was expecting yesterday. But it wasn't delivered. I'd promised to keep an eye out for it. I guess the door didn't shut behind me. It's been doing that lately. Sticking without closing all the way. You have to push it."

Stop talking! Liars got caught by overexplaining. Glenda had the cunning of a fox and the nose of a bloodhound. If she continued to blather like this, she would give herself away. "Whatcha got?" she asked, motioning toward the small white sack Glenda had brought with her.

"Have you been crying?"

"A little." *No, not a little. A lot. Hours of horribly ugly boo-hooing.*

"What set you off?"

Elle picked up the sketch of Charlie that she and Calder had looked at together and showed it to Glenda, who placed her hand over her heart.

"Oh, how sweet. I haven't seen that one."

"I drew it just a few days ago. This morning, when I looked at it, it brought on a few tears."

"I can see why. It's so him."

Elle nodded as she returned the sketch to the table and asked again about the sack.

"Half a dozen chocolate-covered doughnuts, fresh from the bakery. I brought them in the hope that you'll indulge in a calorie or two. You need to put some weight back on. You're still scrawny."

Calder hadn't seemed to think so. Scrawny hadn't been included in the sexy litany he'd groaned as he'd penetrated her.

"Elle?" Glenda nudged her arm. "Here." She passed her a wrapped doughnut, then handed over the sack.

"Aren't you having one?"

"I don't need the carbs. And, anyway, consider them an apology for interrupting while you're working. I'm glad to see that you're sketching again."

"Baby steps, remember?"

"Baby steps. But you reported for work this morning without even taking the time to dress. I consider that a healthy sign and a good start. Maybe a sketch or two will get the creative juices flowing."

"Let's hope. I got a pep talk from Laura yesterday."

"She's much more worried about your well-being than she is about the book."

Elle stopped licking the chocolate icing from her fingers and set the doughnut down. "How do you know what my agent is worried about?"

"Busted," Glenda mumbled. "Dammit." She sat down in Elle's desk chair and turned to face her. "Laura and I compared notes."

"About me?"

"Don't get mad. She called me, and it was a well-intentioned conversation on both our parts. We're worried about you."

"Why? This is what grief looks like, Glenda," she said, pointing to her face. "I can't just spring back like the two of you obviously expect me to."

"No one expects—"

"I'm going to need a minute, all right?" Elle was stung by the thought of the two women in whom she most often confided discussing her grieving process. "I resent your talking behind my back."

"We weren't gossiping, Elle. We expressed to each other our concern for you. That's all."

"Well, when one of you has a child, and he gets shot and dies, come back and tell me how easy it was to get over." The instant the words left her mouth, she wished desperately to recall them. She lowered her head and took several deep breaths. "That was a wretched thing to say. Forgive me, Glenda."

"You're forgiven. The minute I came in, I saw that you were upset and distracted."

Glenda didn't know the half of it.

After a lengthy silence, Glenda asked how the group therapy was going. "Are you deriving any benefit from it?"

"I suppose I am, because I keep going back."

"Maybe you should see someone independently."

"I've had a couple of private sessions with Dr. Sinclair."

"And?"

"They're private."

Glenda thumped her forehead. "Right. I shouldn't have

asked. In fact," she said as she stood up, "I should be going and let you get back to work. Eat the doughnuts. All of them. Gorge. Sugar binge."

"Glenda." As her friend walked past on her way out, Elle reached for her hand. "Wait. Don't go. I apologize. My distraction has nothing to do with you. Something happened yesterday that left me rattled."

"What was it?"

"A meeting with the detectives."

"About what?"

"I'm not at liberty to talk about it, which is the main reason it rattled me."

"Something to do with the investigation?"

"Yes, but please don't ask me about it, because I can't tell you. All I'll say is that my conversation with them brought on the hurt all over again. That's why I'm not myself this morning."

"You're entitled to an off day. To a thousand off days. It didn't help that on this one I barged in on you."

"That doesn't excuse my rudeness. I know that you and Laura aren't gossiping and that your concern comes from the heart. I haven't even thanked you for the doughnuts. Stay and have one with me. I'll brew a fresh pot of coffee."

"Thank you, but I can't. I have an appointment in half an hour. But in exchange for the doughnuts, I will take a book."

"A book?"

"The daughter of one of my sales agents is turning four years old today. For her birthday, I promised her a signed copy of *Heavens to Betsy*."

Elle watched helplessly as Glenda went back to the desk

and picked up the copy left there last night by Calder. She hopped off her stool and rushed over to the desk. "That one's been flipped through several times. I'll get you a new one."

"It'll be fine." Glenda turned to the title page and was about to pass the book to Elle, when she noticed that it had already been signed. She lifted the book closer to her face, stared at the inscription for what seemed an ice age, then looked at Elle and searched her eyes as she asked quietly, "How many Calders do you know?"

Busted herself, Elle replied huskily, "Just the one."

"Hmm. And how well do you know him?" When Elle remained guiltily silent, Glenda closed the cover, replaced the book on the desk, and turned back to Elle with an obvious but unposed question.

Elle reminded herself to brazen this out. "The day before yesterday, he came to the group therapy session. It was his first time there. We chatted at the refreshment table. He asked if I would sign—"

Glenda held up her hand. "Lying would be pointless, Elle. First of all, you're a pathetic liar. Secondly, your dishabille makes sense now. I recognize a rough 'morning after' because God knows I've had many. So, I'm in no position to judge."

"Why do I feel like there's a 'however' coming?"

"Look, I'm thrilled that you got laid. But *him*? Are the two of you a good idea?"

Elle went back to her stool at the drawing table and sagged down onto it. "No."

"The circumstances are—"

"Unorthodox."

"To say the least. They make it kind of…I don't know… murky?"

"Very." Then, in her defense, Elle added, "It's not like we planned it. It just sort of…happened."

"Oh, dear. Spontaneity." Glenda sighed as she sat down on the desk chair again. "It must have been bloody good." Elle looked over at her, and Glenda smiled wryly. "If it had been god-awful, you would have said so by now. You would look relieved. Like, curiosity slaked, but never, ever again. You wouldn't look as miserable as you obviously are."

Elle could think of nothing to say to all that except to elaborate on just how bloody good it had been, which she wasn't about to do.

Glenda's brow was furrowed. "Beyond what relates to the shooting, what else do you know about this guy?"

"Very little. He's intelligent, mannerly, well spoken. He dresses tastefully and expensively, lives in a high-rise, and drives a Jaguar."

"That describes my gynecologist. What does Calder Hudson do?"

"Consulting of some sort, but he doesn't talk about his work."

"I wonder why. He's obviously successful, but when I goo-gled him, nothing much came up. Nothing recent except mention of him in coverage of the shooting."

Elle looked at her with dismay. "You googled him?"

"Early on. When he was being hailed a hero. Just like you, he ducked the press. No picture, not even a quote. He's a ghost on social. Unless he's a double agent for the CIA, I find that odd, especially considering who he lives with. Speaking of, what about *her*?"

"I asked."

"Before or after the spontaneity?"

"Sort of in the middle."

"Hmm. And?"

"He told me they had split."

Unable to bear Glenda's worldly-wise and pitying look, Elle lowered her head and pressed her fingers against her forehead. "I know, I know. Stupid me. But he was…" She took a shaky breath. "He brought his book here to be signed. We talked. We'd said our goodbyes. He was leaving. In fact, he was already out the door, and then he came back, and we just…"

She stopped there. If she couldn't explain the immediate combustion to herself, how could she possibly explain it to anyone else, even her best friend?

She certainly didn't want to describe Calder's departure, which he'd taken with supersonic speed. While she was still tingling all over and trying to catch her breath, he'd left the bed as if the bedspread had caught fire—the bedspread on which they'd been in sexual congress only moments before. They hadn't taken the time to turn back the covers.

Humiliated nearly to the point of choking, she said, "I don't want to talk about it anymore except to say that it won't be happening again."

"Are you sure?"

"Absolutely sure."

"And you're okay with that?" Glenda was looking at her like she already knew the answer.

Elle's cell phone rang, sparing her from having to reply.

"You're in no condition to talk to anyone," Glenda said. "Let it go."

Elle glanced at the readout. "I can't. It's Detective Compton."

"Crap. Then I'll leave you to it, but I'll check back later. Bye." Glenda blew her a kiss and left the room.

Elle answered her phone.

Without preamble, Compton said, "Elle, listen carefully. You need to pack a bag and—"

"Pack a bag?"

"Essentials only. Enough for a few days."

"Where am I going? What's happened?"

"Remember meeting Dawn Whitley? The woman on crutches."

"Of course. She's in the therapy group."

"She received a death threat this morning."

"*What?!*"

"She's one of you who saw the ball cap guy, and all five of you have been identified."

"You said our names wouldn't be disclosed."

"That was the plan, but—"

"Elle!" Glenda rushed back into the room, looking out of breath. "What the hell is going on? There are two sheriff's deputies at your front door. They said they're here to escort you."

Chapter 19

Calder hadn't slept at all. But as he shifted his position in the unfamiliar bed, he glanced at the clock on the nightstand and, seeing the hour, determined that he had delayed facing the day long enough. Facing himself.

Kicking off the covers, he got up, used the bathroom and pulled on a pair of boxers, grabbed his phone, then went in search of caffeine.

The apartment complex was ranked the most exclusive temporary housing to be had in the metroplex. Yesterday, he'd leased the only unit available and had paid for one month in advance.

As advertised, it was outfitted with all the bells and whistles. He was indifferent to most of the amenities, but in the compact galley kitchen, he discovered a coffee maker and—God bless the previous occupant—several pods of dark roast.

He brewed a cup and carried it into the living area, stepping around his suitcases, which he hadn't yet unpacked. His laptop had been charging overnight on the dining table. He checked the inbox of his emails but didn't see anything that demanded an immediate response.

His new residence had a sleek gym on the second floor and a heated pool on the rooftop. He should avail himself of one of them and get in a workout. But he couldn't generate any enthusiasm for the idea and used his left arm as an excuse not to overexert.

Although he'd had no problem using it to support himself above Elle as she'd arched up—

Shit!

He carried his coffee over to the broad window. It overlooked a congested freeway, not the man-made lake featured in the online ad for the complex. Standing there watching vehicles battling for yardage around road construction, he muttered, "Hero, my ass."

What must Elle be thinking of him this morning? No doubt she was calling him every name in the book. She had reason to.

He'd run.

He cursed himself lavishly and obscenely as a damn coward. Then, having exhausted his repertoire of vulgarities, to no effect, he set his coffee cup on an end table, backed up to an ottoman and sat, placed his elbows on his knees, plowed all ten fingers up through his hair, and held his head between his hands.

It would be a mistake, she'd said.

Fine, he'd thought.

He wasn't a beggar, sure as hell not where women were concerned. Besides, he'd just gotten rid of one pain-in-the-ass female. Why would he seek another relationship that was already ten times more complicated? He wouldn't. No thanks.

But he'd gotten only halfway to his car before he'd stopped.

Did he really want to leave it like this? Two months ago, no question. Two months ago, he would have been halfway home by now.

If he went back—just sayin'—he risked making a colossal fool of himself. *So just leave, you dumb shit.*

On the other hand, she'd said it would be a mistake. She hadn't said she didn't want to. Hadn't said, *No way in hell; get serious.*

With that in mind, he'd turned around, having no idea whether she'd even let him back inside, or what he would say to her if she did.

But the door had been unlocked, and when he'd stepped into her small entry, all he'd had to do was look into her eyes and recognize a desire that matched his own. The instant they'd touched, yearning had given way to urgency.

Her mouth: hot, delicious, receptive, even greedy. Her hands: bold, searching, all over him.

Under her baggy sweatshirt was skin like warm satin. A scanty, lacy, see-through bra. The stuff of wet dreams, but bothersome as hell when trying to get his mouth around her nipple, already raised.

He would have been fine with the couch, the wall, the floor, but, still glued together, they'd somehow stumbled their way into her bedroom.

Clothing had been an aggravation, but she did manage to wiggle out of her leggings and underwear. He'd unbuttoned his shirt but didn't waste precious time taking it off. Within a second of levering himself above her, he'd gotten his belt unbuckled, his zipper down, his slacks shoved past his hips.

She'd been wet, but tight, and had felt so good when he'd pushed into her that he'd shuddered and said...something. Hadn't he? Maybe.

He'd pressed into her until he couldn't press any farther, then began thrusting. He'd braced himself on his hands, arms straight, back arched. Her hands clutching his ass insistently. It had been hard and fast and vigorous, breath-stealing and heart-pounding, and then they came.

Jesus, it had been amazing.

Only when his arms had folded beneath him, and he'd settled on top of her, and had buried his face in her fragrant neck, had nipped her soft skin with his teeth, had heard her sigh his name as she whisked her lips across his cheekbone, had felt her sweet body go languid beneath his weight had he realized that this hadn't been the strategized, customized, guidebook-step-by-step-until-climax fucking he was accustomed to.

No, he'd been seized by a primal streak of possessiveness and had lost himself to it. His need to claim her, have her, become one with her had been primordial. He had mated.

The Calder Hudson of old had cast off things he no longer liked or had use for. Shoes, neckties, tennis rackets, cars, women. Once they were out of his life, he never thought of them again.

There, feeling Elle's heartbeat against his, he realized that he'd found something he wanted to keep, something that, on an elemental level, belonged to him and that he couldn't do without.

And that scared the shit out of him.

In order to prove himself wrong, he—bloody fucking coward that he was—had abandoned her body, her bed, and her house without even a goodbye.

He was jerked back into the present by the ringing of his cell phone. It was almost a welcome reprieve from his self-castigation. But then he looked at the ID. Compton. "Screw that." Whatever she was calling about, he wasn't in the mood. Eventually the phone fell silent.

His coffee had turned cold, so he headed toward the kitchen to make another cup. Midway there, his phone began ringing again. "Goddamn it." He went back for it, snatched it up, and barked an ungracious hello.

"Mr. Hudson, do you recall our conversation of yesterday afternoon?"

No good morning. No nothing. Compton sounded as ill-tempered as he was. "Of course."

"Do you remember our *directive* that you not to speak to anyone about it?"

"Of course."

"When we said *anyone*, we meant it. We did not exclude Shauna Calloway."

"Neither did I."

She gave a harrumph of doubt that seemed to come from deep within her heavy bosom. "Pack an overnight bag. A pair of deputies will be waiting outside your building to pick you up in fifteen minutes. Max."

"Wait a minute, wait a minute. What's going on?"

"Like you don't know."

"I don't know."

She huffed and puffed, then said, "The five eyewitnesses whose names we wanted to keep tightly under wraps?"

"Yes?"

"Your girlfriend broadcast them. Thanks to her, one has already received a death threat."

Conniption fits are being had all over...

This morning, Shauna Calloway became the town crier.

Via local and national news programs, millions of people learned from her that there had been a breakthrough in the Fairground shooting investigation.

She didn't specify what that breakthrough was, which means she doesn't know. If she did, she would have reported it. However, even without that crucial detail, she was so hyper, she'd barely taken a breath. Basically, she conveyed that this was a Big Deal.

To everyone else, maybe. But this development doesn't worry me in the slightest. If it was that substantial a breakthrough, I would be in manacles and wearing orange right now.

The upshot of Calloway's story was that "five key witnesses" had met separately with investigators yesterday. It was sheer speculation on her part, although she made it sound like fact (you know how they do) that these witnesses, either singly or collectively, had provided a clue that had "injected energy into what had become a lethargic investigation."

What shocked me was that she actually named names! She identified those five key witnesses. That can't have gone over well with the sheriff's department and state agencies who're desperate to capture me. As if that weren't already a daunting commission—doomed to fail—now they have key witnesses to protect.

It tickles me that Calder Hudson is one of them, when Shauna

Calloway has made the public well aware of her "close personal relationship" with the hero of the shooting. What is he thinking about the story she broke this morning? She made him a target for dangerous and deranged me.

I wonder… Did she blow the whistle on him and Elle Portman because she found out that they've been sneaking around together?

Maybe I'm reading too much into what I saw. Maybe all they discussed inside that quaint tavern was what they'd experienced since that day at the fairground. Did he lend a sympathetic ear as she reminisced about her little boy? Maybe he begged her forgiveness for being unable to save him. Does she fault him for not dying in place of her child?

A thought-provoking question, isn't it?

She has actually endeared herself to the public by shirking the spotlight. It's become common knowledge that she's the author of a popular children's book. Shauna Calloway showed a copy of it in her report this morning. Ms. Portman could be capitalizing on that exposure. She isn't, which I believe is part of her allure. She's avoided public exposure and, by doing so, has become everyone's tragic sweetheart of the Fairground shooting.

What I wonder is: Has she become Calder Hudson's sweetheart?

I suppose stranger things have happened.

But nothing stranger springs to mind right offhand.

It does concern me a bit that they had their heads together two days ago. Then the very next day, yesterday, each spoke privately with the lead detectives. Now, suddenly, after two months of nothing, there's a breakthrough.

Of course, one incident may have nothing to do with the other. Still, it's worth a worry. I haven't reached this point by being careless. Knowledge is power, and knowing what's up with them could be useful to me.

What I do know, because I saw it with my own two eyes, is that the goodbye hug they gave each other outside that bar didn't look strictly platonic.

So, to be on the safe side, whether or not their secret partnership is romantic in nature, I probably should interrupt it. Permanently.

Now that Shauna Calloway has blabbed their names, the sheriff's office will no doubt circle the wagons and make my interference more of a challenge than it would be otherwise.

Unfortunately for them, I love a challenge.

Chapter 20

The upstairs room of the house to which Calder had been transported by the taciturn deputies was butt ugly and overheated.

He'd spent the past five minutes in it with Compton and Perkins, explaining to them why he was no longer at the address to which they'd been about to send those deputies to collect him. They had been diverted to his temporary living quarters and had arrived within the specified fifteen minutes. Max.

He'd been ready. He'd showered and dressed quickly, then had had to sort through the contents of his suitcases and pack what he thought he might need into the smaller of the two.

The deputies had asked that he turn over his cell phone and laptop to them. "Why?"

"Protocol."

They went a few rounds like that. All his arguments against "protocol" fell on deaf ears. His request to follow his escorts in his own car had been denied, as had his request to know their destination.

It turned out to be an old, large two-story house situated in the center of a heavily wooded and isolated property about ninety miles east of Dallas and two counties over from their department's jurisdiction. Which they also refused to explain.

During the drive there, he'd pretended to doze in the back seat of the unmarked sedan and didn't waste his breath asking more questions of or arguing with the laconic pair.

He had saved his protests for Compton and Perkins. Summing up his explanation for his recent change of address, he said, "Now you know. I broke up with Shauna and moved out of the condo we shared. I didn't have the TV on this morning, so I didn't know anything about her broadcast until you called and told me."

As ever, Perkins's reaction was that of a drowsy cat. He blinked once, slowly.

Compton was glaring at Calder as she repeatedly turned a pencil end over end on the dented metal desk that separated them. Click went the sharpened tip; thump went the eraser.

"Why didn't you tell us about your breakup and relocation when we saw you yesterday?"

"Because my personal life isn't any of your business."

"The devil it isn't," she said. "It's definitely our business to know if you spoke to Ms. Calloway following our meeting yesterday."

"In fact, I did. She was waiting for me outside the precinct as I left."

"So she knew you were there."

He explained that Shauna had seen him when he'd arrived and had waited until he came out.

"What was she doing there?"

"She'd learned about the breakthrough, although she didn't know what it entailed. At least she claimed not to."

"How did she hear about this development?"

"She admitted to having a source inside the precinct."

Even Perkins reacted with a start. Compton said, "Which department?"

"I don't know."

"Did she tell you who this individual—"

"No. And before she'd tell you, you'd have to cut out her tongue."

Perkins surprised Calder by mumbling, "That could be arranged."

Compton dropped the pencil she'd been toying with and linked her hands on the desktop. "Mr. Hudson, did you tell Ms. Calloway, or give her any hint, about what we discussed?"

"No."

"Nothing?"

"Nothing."

Compton again looked at Perkins, but Perkins was staring at Calder in that impassive way of his, which was beginning to grate. "I didn't tell her a fucking thing," he said with succinct emphasis.

"I wouldn't have even if she had prodded me, but she didn't, because I told her straight off that I couldn't talk about what was said in that meeting. I don't know where she got her information, but it wasn't from me. Now, that's the last declaration of innocence you're going to get from me. If you want to grill me on this further, I'm calling my lawyer." He leaned back in his chair and crossed his arms over his chest.

Perkins was the next to speak. "Who broke up with whom?"

"It was my doing."

"How did she take it? Was your parting amicable?"

"We didn't shake hands and wish each other well, no."

"Hostile, then."

"You could say. Her parting words were 'go fuck yourself.'"

After another taut silence, Compton said, "Calder, is it possible that she leaked this story in retribution for your breakup?"

Maybe Compton only wanted to defuse his anger, but he was surprised that she had addressed him by his first name, and in such a soft and confidential tone.

Her question, however, came as no surprise at all. It had occurred to him that Shauna had pulled this stunt in retaliation for his attraction to Elle. But he hadn't wanted to acknowledge, even to himself, that she would do something so vindictive and harmful, and not only to him. She'd put the lives of people who weren't even involved into jeopardy.

It was a disturbing thought, but he kept it to himself and avoided giving the detectives a direct answer to the question. "I can't comment on Shauna's story because I haven't even seen it. What exactly did she report?"

"That we'd conducted closed-door meetings with five witnesses to the shooting. That's it in a nutshell. But she editorialized, saying that you five were obviously key to the investigation and that you had been recalled by us for a specific reason. She also identified each of you by name."

He dragged his hand over his face. "And one of us has already received a death threat?"

"Dawn Whitley. You met her outside our office at the precinct."

"The lady who'd given Shauna an interview and was so enamored of her."

"The irony of that hasn't escaped us."

"Will there be blowback on Shauna?"

Compton gave a bitter laugh. "If we issue any kind of official reprimand or bring her in for questioning, she'll raise a hue and cry about First Amendment rights. Her colleagues will be envious of her for getting the story, but they'll also rally in her defense. Meanwhile, the culprit is laughing up his sleeve, and we're left with five lives to safeguard."

Calder looked down at his suitcase standing beside his chair. "Safeguard for how long?"

Before Compton could respond, the telephone on the desk rang. Perkins punched a blinking button, and a male voice came through the speaker. "The other two are here."

Perkins thanked the voice, clicked off, and moved toward the door. He said to Compton, "Give me five minutes; then we'll explain it to them as a group. You may want to use this time to…" He hitched his chin toward Calder.

"Yes, I will."

Perkins went out and closed the door behind himself.

"What was that about?" Calder asked. "Use this time to what?"

"To speak to you alone."

"About what?"

Shauna might have ratted out Elle and him, although he didn't see how anything personal between them would affect the investigation. And would Shauna own up to losing her man to another woman? Unlikely.

Whatever this was about, Compton was in dread of it. She left her chair and walked over to an antique water cooler. "Want some?"

"No thanks."

She filled a plastic cup from the belching machine and brought it back to the desk. After she had sat down and taken a drink, she asked, "Have you returned to work yet?"

He forced himself to hold her incisive gaze. "Not yet. When I finish PT."

"Hmm. Your last client was a company called JZI for short, wasn't it?"

He waited a beat and then gave a dry huff. "You're not really asking for verification, are you?"

"No." She settled more heavily into her seat. "You should've told us in the beginning what you do. Your vagueness only made us more curious about the nature of your corporate consulting. Digging into your career history turned out to be quite an adventure. We ran into roadblock after roadblock. Why? Because your clients are bound by a nondisclosure clause."

"For reasons I'm sure you understand."

"Yes, I do. The specialized consulting you do could generate hard feelings, deep-seated resentment, and, if someone took it to the limit, reprisal."

Made uneasy by that observation, Calder said, "What are you getting at?"

"Do you have any enemies?"

"Not that I'm aware of."

"Modesty doesn't suit you. Mr. Hudson. Considering your success, isn't it more probable that the number of people holding grudges against you is in the hundreds? Perkins and I think so. Consequently, we believe your business records of the last few years warrant a thorough review."

He opened his mouth, but she cut him off. "We anticipated your reluctance to share, Mr. Hudson, so..." She took an official-looking document from her briefcase and held it up. "We got a court order that allows us to review the files on your laptop."

It wasn't lost on him that he was back to being Mr. Hudson.

Chapter 21

S ince this morning's broadcast, Shauna had been fielding calls one right after the other. Therefore, she didn't first check the ID before answering the incoming call by pressing the button on her steering wheel.

"Shauna Calloway."

"You threw me under the bus."

It was her sleazy source, Billy Green. "I did no such thing, and I won't."

"No, but you've created a shit show in this precinct, in the whole damn department. If anybody finds out that I'm the one who fed you that information—"

"They won't find out unless you panic, behave like a moron, and give yourself away."

"Yesterday, there was a handful of personnel from other agencies working with Compton and Perkins," he said rapidly and furtively. "All part of the task force investigating the shooting along with our CID. Now the place is crawling—crawling, I'm telling you—with DPS troopers, Texas Rangers, you name it. The attorney general's office was on the phone with the sheriff, who's gone apeshit, on the verge of a stroke, someone said, and—"

"Calm. Down." She could imagine him sputtering, spraying spit, wiping the greasy sweat off his high forehead.

"Calm down, she says." Lowering his voice to a creaky whisper, he said, "The whole goddamn department is on edge. Everybody's suspecting everybody. All because of you."

"No, all because of you wanting to get up my skirt. Right? There wouldn't have been a story causing the havoc you describe if you hadn't given me those names yesterday."

He admitted no complicity. "You did yourself no favors, you know."

"I bagged the big story. That's my job."

"Yeah, but now your Mr. Jaguar with the full head of hair has a bull's-eye between his broad shoulders. Did you think of that?"

"He'll be protected. All of them will be."

"Says you."

"What do you say?" She laid the trap subtly, betting that he would step into it, and he did.

"They were rounded up. Lickety-split."

She deliberately downplayed that. "Naturally they would be. That's hardly a headliner." She waited, listening to him breathe while he weighed his options and considered whether impressing her was worth taking another risk.

Finally, he said, "They've moved them somewhere.

Your dickhead boyfriend, the lady whose kid died, and the woman you interviewed in the hospital."

"What about the other two?"

"I don't know."

"Come on."

"Swear. All I've heard is that those three have been relocated to a safe house."

"Where?"

"I don't know. Swear to God."

"I don't believe in God," she said, "and I seriously doubt that you do."

"Someplace out of the county. That's all I know, and that's the truth."

"Can you find out where?"

"Haven't you been listening? I would bet my left nut that there are appointed spies in this building trying to sniff out the snitch."

"You're being paranoid, Billy."

"Uh-huh. This is different. This isn't like the time you asked me to get the exact amount of money a CEO took from the corporate kitty to pay his call girls for blow jobs.

"This shooting investigation wasn't going gangbusters anyway, but you really fucked it up. Somebody hung a channel seven poster in the lobby and put a dart through the picture of you, right between your eyes. Everybody who works for this department would like to strangle you."

"Not everybody." She inserted a strategic pause, then said, "Look, if you're this scared of being found out, let's shut down. I'll find a replacement. There are plenty who've vied for the opportunity."

"Who?"

"You know I can't say. I never reveal a source. Which I've proven to you today. Correct me if I'm wrong." Another well-placed pause. "See? I could have turned on you to prevent darts being thrown at my picture, but I didn't. Now hang up and act normally, and you'll remain anonymous."

"I stay your guy, right?"

"You stay my guy. You get a gold star if you find out the location of that safe house."

"I can't, Shauna. Not today. Jesus. I'd be cutting my own throat to even try."

She didn't say anything.

After a time, he said, "It won't be easy, but I'll try."

"Which is why you're my guy."

"No promises. I'll try. But if I come through, two beers, a skirt, no panties."

She hung up on him. He was disgusting, and the fool probably would give himself away.

No great loss. Telling him that he could be replaced hadn't been a bluff. There were plenty of starstruck cops longing to get up her skirt.

Elle was a little carsick from having ridden in the back seat, and her head was reeling from all that had happened in such a brief period of time, beginning with Glenda's ill-timed visit, then Compton's stunning call, culminating in leaving her home, towing a roll-aboard that Glenda had packed for her while she'd showered and dressed.

In looks and passivity, the two deputies serving as her escorts were interchangeable. They'd given her their names and showed her their badges, but she'd been so shaken by the turn of events, she hadn't distinguished one from the other.

When they confiscated her cell phone, they'd been subjected to Glenda's diatribe about their fascist tactics. "How are we supposed to communicate?" she'd demanded.

One of them had said, "You're not."

From her house in Fort Worth, it had been almost a two-hour drive to the rambling structure they were now approaching on a bumpy gravel road that cut through dense woods. Beyond asking if the car temperature was comfortable for her and telling her to let them know if she needed a restroom stop, the two in the front seats had said little during the entire trip.

Now, as the serviceable sedan rolled to a stop, the deputy on the passenger side said, "Here we are," and alighted to open the back seat door for her. He carried her roll-aboard up the front steps of the house.

The door was opened by a burly man who introduced himself as Deputy Weeks and his older, more weathered partner as Deputy Sims. They wore uniforms and badges that designated them as deputies of the sheriff's office in a county east of Dallas.

The one who'd delivered her wished her good luck and returned to the car. He and his partner drove away.

Sims asked if she needed anything.

"Water, please."

He ambled off to get it for her. Weeks said, "They're not

quite ready for you. You can wait in here. Detective Compton said to remind you not to talk to each other about the case."

The room into which he led her was a spacious living room, furnished with what appeared to be pieces picked at random from thrift stores. No regard had been given to aesthetics.

The only person in the room was Dawn Whitley, who was sitting on a chintz sofa, nervously rocking back and forth against the back cushions, her eyes skittish. When Elle walked in, the other woman looked at her as though she represented rescue.

"Ms. Portman," she cried out softly.

She was a regular at the group therapy sessions. Everyone had applauded when she arrived without her crutches for the first time. Now, as she left the couch, Elle noticed that she still walked with a slight limp.

She clasped Elle's hand, squeezing between their palms a tissue she had twisted into a damp wad. "I'm glad to see somebody I recognize. I'm so scared."

Elle gently turned her toward the couch and walked her back to it. They sat down side by side. "Are you all right?"

The other woman shook her head. "I can't stop shaking." She held out her hand to show Elle the tremor.

Elle was curious to know what form the death threat she'd received had taken, but, before she could ask, Sims returned with her requested water. He scooted aside a stack of outdated magazines on the end table near Elle and set the bottle down. She thanked him. He said, "You bet," and left the room.

Deputy Weeks positioned a straight chair beneath the

wide arched opening separating the room from the central hallway and sat down. He took out his phone and began idly scrolling through it, but Elle got the impression that he'd been posted to watch them and make certain they heeded the order not to talk to each other.

Elle took a moment to get her bearings. The room had a high ceiling made of stamped tin. Thick drapes had been tightly drawn over all the windows. Four mismatched chairs surrounded a game table. On it were a checkerboard, a Monopoly game, a box of dominoes, and several decks of cards. In one corner was a television, which had a large screen but looked generations old. The bookcase was stuffed with paperbacks, their pages yellowed, their covers curled at the corners.

People had been made to pass idle time here.

Dawn leaned sideways toward her. Speaking in an undertone out of the side of her mouth, she said, "Did you meet with the detectives yesterday?"

Elle responded with a slight nod.

"I'm sure they cautioned you, the same as they did me, about the danger we're in. Can you believe Shauna Calloway announced our names?"

Actually, Elle could, but she didn't say so.

"She must be really two-faced. She'd been so nice to me. And why would she put her own boyfriend's life in danger?"

Elle made a motion with her shoulder that could have been interpreted any number of ways. To avoid further mention of Calder, she whispered, "We shouldn't be talking, remember."

"I know, I know, but aren't you afraid?"

Deputy Weeks, who'd been staring into his phone, raised his head and looked over at them, Dawn's frantic whispers having come to his attention. Elle looked guilty by association. "Ladies," he said.

"I was just asking Ms. Portman if she knew where the restroom is," Dawn said.

"Down the hall and on the right. Do you need it?"

"Not right now. I just wanted to know where it is when I do. Sometimes my leg slows me down."

"Let me know," he said, and went back to his phone.

After that, Dawn fell silent but continued to twist the tissue. She flinched at every sound. The death threat must have been credible for her to be this frightened and for Compton and Perkins to have been so swift to respond.

Without any warning of his approach, Perkins appeared in the archway. "You made it here okay?"

The two of them nodded.

"Where are the others?" Dawn asked. "Has something happened to them?" Her lower lip trembled.

"They're all safe," he said. "After our meeting with Mr. Cooper yesterday, his family thought it best to make a preemptive move. They took him out of state last night. His folks have been notified of Shauna Calloway's broadcast this morning. So have the local authorities there. They'll be keeping a close watch on him."

"He's in our therapy group, Ms. Portman," Dawn said. "You know, the young man who lost his wife of only a few months?"

Elle nodded, although she hadn't known his name till now. He'd never spoken and had sat through each session in a near catatonic state. She was glad to learn that he was out of the fray.

"Have either of you met Molly Martin?" Perkins asked.

Dawn shook her head. Elle said, "I didn't meet her, but she sent me a sympathy card, which was awfully kind of her."

"She's a senior lady," Perkins said. "She became very upset yesterday by what we had to tell her. Last night at home, she suffered a cardiac episode and was taken to an area hospital."

"Is she going to be all right?" Elle asked.

"She's stable. She'll be placed under guard. Calder Hudson, whom you've both met, is with Detective Compton upstairs. We'll be down shortly." He left with no more fanfare than he had appeared with.

Dawn nudged Elle's arm and whispered, "I'll bet Mr. Hudson is chewing nails over this, don't you?"

"I...I wouldn't know."

"How long—"

"Dawn, please. I don't know any more than you do."

Actually, she did. She knew that Calder had a birthmark on his right shoulder. She'd kissed it while he was still full and heavy inside her, while his breath was humid and hot against her skin, while—

Hearing the approach of a heavy tread on the hardwood floor, she looked toward the archway. Calder strode into the room, sighted her immediately, and practically nailed her to the couch with his gaze.

Chapter 22

Her heart skipped as she thought back on the feel of his breath and lips and hands and inert weight anchoring her to the bed before his abrupt desertion. But she kept her expression implacable and regarded him with cool indifference before turning her head away in dismissal.

He walked past the deputy without even acknowledging him, although Weeks had stood up and moved his chair out of his path. Compton and Perkins followed him in.

"Have a seat, Mr. Hudson."

Out of the corner of her eye, Elle saw him walk over to the chair Compton had indicated and practically throw himself into it.

"I told you," Dawn whispered. "You can tell he's mad."

Deputy Weeks dragged forward two of the game table chairs for Compton and Perkins, then propped himself against the wall just inside the arch. Sims was lurking in the hallway.

Compton began. "We know you're all disoriented, afraid on some level, and probably a little put out with us for taking you away from your homes so abruptly. But after it was revealed this morning that you are key witnesses—"

"By his girlfriend," Dawn Whitley said, shooting a look toward Calder.

Compton said, "Mr. Hudson has assured us that he did not share any information with Ms. Calloway."

He seemed unmoved by both Dawn's remark and Compton's defense of him. He sat with his arms folded over his midriff, his legs outstretched and crossed at the ankles, his attention focused on the upturned toe of his ostrich boot.

Compton continued. "Ms. Calloway has a source inside the precinct. An internal investigation is under way to smoke him or her out. It's hoped that the individual will be identified soon and dealt with accordingly."

She paused before going on. "Our first objective will be to learn if additional information was leaked to Ms. Calloway or to anyone else. In the meantime, we're in damage control mode. You've been brought to this safe house for your protection. We're hopeful your stay here will be short-term."

"Define short-term." The words rumbled from Calder's chest. "'Hopeful' doesn't inspire my confidence. Are you actually saying that this arrangement is indefinite? Because that's not going to work for me.

"When we were upstairs, you told me that two witnesses are being guarded in controlled environments. Why can't we three have a guard outside our residences or something like that? It would suck, but it would be better than being shut away out here."

"Because safeguarding you three is more critical."

"Why's that? What makes us special?"

"You three pose the greatest threat to the shooter. You because of your personal relationship with Shauna Calloway."

"*Which is over*," he said tightly. "I thought I'd explained that."

"You did. But the unsub doesn't know that you've ended it."

Dawn sucked in a quick breath.

Weeks raised his eyebrows.

Calder seethed but didn't offer a comeback.

Elle tried to imitate Perkins and remain sphinxlike, which was difficult because Compton turned her attention away from Calder and onto her. "Since it's been publicized that you authored the Betsy book, you've gained a high public profile."

"Which I've never sought. I want the book to be popular, not me."

"Your self-effacement is admirable, Elle. But, like it or not, your recent notoriety would appeal to an unbalanced individual wanting to make a statement."

Perkins chose then to speak. "You'd be a trophy."

"You're single and live alone," Compton added. "We can't chance his getting to you."

Then she focused on Dawn. "During your television interview with Ms. Calloway, it was obvious that the two of you had established a rapport."

In a thin voice, Dawn said, "Well, she was just so nice."

"I'm sure she was. You served her purpose very well. Your

descriptions were detailed; you held little back. Now she's exposed you as a key witness." Compton shifted in her seat and leaned forward toward Dawn.

"If I were our unsub, I'd be worried about what else you remember from that day, a fact or two that could be ferreted out of you. Perkins and I believe that's why it was you who received the death threat."

Dawn clamped the soggy tissue against her mouth and whimpered, then began to cry in earnest.

Elle said, "What form did this death threat take?"

She had addressed the question to Compton, but Dawn blurted, "A voice mail."

Looking at Elle and Calder in turn, Compton explained. "He called her cell phone. She had the presence of mind to notify us immediately."

"How did he get my number?" Dawn asked.

"If he's smart enough to pull off what he did at the fairground, he's smart enough to get a telephone number," Compton said.

"It was awful," Dawn blubbered. "He said—"

"Let's let them hear it for themselves," Compton said. "We had to take Mrs. Whitley's phone as evidence, but I recorded the voice mail." She accessed her cell phone and put it on speaker. The nasal voice said, "You got off light the first time, lady. Keep your mouth shut, or you'll get it in the head just like that tattooed dude in the tent."

Compton clicked off. "We tracked the phone's location. It was found in a culvert. Obviously tossed there after having served its purpose."

Calder said, "How do you know that wasn't a crank call?"

"'Tattooed dude,'" Compton said. "In our descriptions of Levi Jenkins, we deliberately omitted his tattoo for just this reason. To weed out the cranks. It was here," she said, pointing to the side of her neck. "It wasn't there in his mug shot, so he must've gotten it since that arrest. Our shooter saw it when he killed him." She slid her phone back into her pocket.

"My apology," Calder said.

"It was a reasonable question. It's also reasonable that you asked about the length of your stay. As to that, the task force is busy trying to find each of you a private accommodation, which we couldn't manage to do immediately. We hope to place each of you where you can have some normalcy."

"What's the timetable on that?" Calder asked.

"Possibly as early as tomorrow."

He opened his mouth to speak, seemed to think better of it, and resumed the broody contemplation of his boot… when he wasn't casting broody looks at Elle.

Dawn, who was still weepy, timidly raised her hand, and Compton called on her. "Can I let my husband know that I'm okay? The deputies who came to the house wouldn't tell us anything, not even where they were taking me. Frank was fit to be tied."

"We brought a new prepaid phone to replace yours. Once it's charged and usable, you can call Mr. Whitley."

"And my mom?"

"Ask your husband to notify her. All of you will be allowed to call a family member or friend who'll naturally be worried about you. But please, for everyone's safety, keep the call brief and, most importantly, don't tell anyone where you are."

"How could I tell when I don't even know?" Dawn said.

A phone chirped. It turned out to be Perkins's. He glanced down at the readout, then left his chair and walked out into the hallway.

Compton watched him leave, then turned back to them. "You'll be assigned bedrooms for tonight. There are two up, only one down, so you'll be put in that one, Mr. Hudson. It has a private bath. Ladies, you'll share a bathroom, but I'm sure you can work that out.

"You're free to use this room, but if you want to go outside for some fresh air, ask one of the deputies to accompany you. The kitchen has already been stocked with snacks. Dinner will be brought in. You can eat together, but, at any time, please don't discuss any aspect of the case or what you saw or heard that day at the fairground.

"Through no fault or action of your own, you've become very important to this suspect's capture and identification. At trial, your testimonies could help win a conviction, but a strong defense attorney will attempt to make the jury doubt the accuracy of your memory. It needs to be clear and consistent with your initial statements to us. Don't let it be clouded or influenced by something someone else says. Does everyone understand that?"

They nodded in unison.

"Good."

Just then Perkins reappeared and said, "Calloway's source is blown."

He didn't name him but described him as a civilian

employee, not a deputy, a "glorified gofer." His duties gave him access to every office in the building, making it easy for him to glean information from what he saw and overheard.

Calder said, "Shauna wouldn't have given him over. How'd they find him out?"

"He turned himself in. Said she'd reneged on their deal."

The two detectives left for the drive back to Dallas to question the man themselves.

The batteries in their phones had been removed while in the custody of the deputies. Elle and Calder had theirs returned with the batteries temporarily replaced, and Dawn was given her replacement phone. Again they were admonished to call only one person close to them who would want reassurance that they were all right. Weeks told them to keep it short.

Elle called Glenda. "I can't tell you anything except that I'm fine."

"Where'd they take you?"

"I can't tell you, Glenda, and, honestly, I don't know exactly. They may move us again tomorrow."

"Us? *He's* there?"

Against her will, Elle glanced across the living room toward Calder, who wasn't using his phone. He was zeroed in on her.

"Elle?"

"Yes, he's here, but we haven't spoken."

"What does he think of his girlfriend's dirty trick?"

"We haven't spoken," she repeated. Then, "Glenda, the deputies guarding us are signaling me to wind up."

"Wait, Elle. I have something to tell you before you hear it from someone else." She took a breath. "Jeff's fitness queen had their baby last night."

A question formed on Elle's lips, but she couldn't bring herself to ask it.

Glenda said softly, "It's a boy."

It felt as though an arrow had pierced her heart. How could God be this cruel?

"Elle?" Glenda said. "Sweetie? I hated like hell to tell you, but I—"

"No, it's fine. But I have to go. I'll call you back when I can. Love you."

She hung up before Glenda could say more and dazedly passed her phone to Weeks when he approached her and extended his hand for it.

Soon after that, she and Dawn were shown to their bedrooms upstairs and instructed to settle in.

Elle's room overlooked the front of the house and the narrow road that connected it to the two-lane state highway by which they'd arrived. Beyond the clearing in which the house was situated, there was nothing to see except for piney woods.

With nothing else to do, she stretched out on the bed, stared at the ceiling, and surrendered herself to a tide of sorrow.

Reasonably she knew that the birth of Jeff's child had no relevance to Charlie's death. But somehow this new life made Charlie seem more dead. The pain of it was so bitter, she couldn't even cry over it. Her eyes burned, but they remained dry. She couldn't produce one tear to mitigate her anguish.

Of course, she'd used up a lot of tears last night after Calder's flight.

"Damn you," she whispered. He'd robbed her of dignity; now he was robbing her of the luxury of weeping. Add that to the growing list of reasons to despise him.

And the staring. Every time she'd looked in his general direction, he'd been homed in on her, and, even when she wasn't looking his way, she could feel his watchful stare.

After he couldn't wait to leave her last night, what was the close scrutiny about? Guilt, perhaps? Did he feel remorse over his lusty seduction followed by his breakneck getaway?

She shouldn't care at all about what the heartless, selfish bastard was thinking or feeling. She was belittling herself by giving him any consideration at all.

Nevertheless, as she drifted off to sleep, she was thinking about him, about his face above hers, flushed and taut, eyes hot, breath hectic, when the introductory contractions of her orgasm pulsed around him.

Chapter 23

Elle was roused by a knock on her bedroom door. Groggily, she got up and opened it to find Weeks. "I came to take your dinner order."

"What are my choices?"

"Whatever extras you want on your burger."

Forty-five minutes later, the carry-out was delivered by a third deputy, who was startlingly young. A bit bug-eyed, he gaped at Dawn, Calder, and her; then Weeks sent him on his way.

They gathered around the dining table in the kitchen where the deputies drew Calder into a conversation about the national baseball playoffs and each team's chances of winning the pennant.

During a lull, Calder idly dunked a french fry into a puddle of ketchup in his burger basket. "How many of you are there?"

Weeks stopped chewing, swallowed. "How many of what?"

"Men," Calder said. "Eyes and ears. Guns. Besides that kid who brought the food, how many of you are protecting us?"

"The kid's just an errand boy. He's deputized, but, you know, his uncle's a city councilman. It's just Sims and me on duty. We drew the short straws." He guffawed. "No offense."

"None taken."

Calder smiled, but Elle thought of a wolf who'd spotted an unwary rabbit. He said, "I imagined tough guys in SWAT gear, crawling around out there in the woods, watching the house through night vision binoculars." He stretched back in his chair and chuckled. "I guess I've seen too many movies about covert operations."

The two deputies laughed with him. Weeks said, "Naw, just us."

"But officers back at your office are monitoring the security cameras, right?"

"You noticed 'em, huh?" Weeks said, seemingly amused.

"In the treetops on either side of the turnoff."

Weeks winked at Sims and said to Calder, "We made 'em obvious so they'd serve the same purpose."

"As what?"

"As real cameras," Sims said. "They're dummies."

"Huh." Calder looked over at Elle, who silently communicated that she shared his apprehension.

Sensing it, Weeks said, "Hey, not to worry. Y'all are safe. Nobody comes out here."

"Why not?" Calder asked. "Are the dummy security cameras that much of a deterrent?"

"First off, the house is hard to find."

Calder nodded. "It must be at least a mile back to the state highway."

"Less than a half," Sims said, reaching into his shirt pocket for a toothpick.

"Really?" Calder said. "When we drove it this morning, it seemed farther."

"Because there's no landmark to gauge the distance by," Weeks said. "All pine trees look alike. Unless you're a park ranger or something."

"Is that road the only access to the house?"

"The only direct access. But it's not like people are beating the door down to get into this place."

"How'd the sheriff's office come to own it?"

"A few years back, several regional agencies chipped in to buy it to use as a safe house for valuable witnesses like y'all, or women who escaped their abusers. You know, like that."

"Well, it's certainly ideal for hiding people, sitting out here all by itself," Calder said. "No neighbors for miles."

"Nearest is the Millers' ranch. That's at least five miles," Sims said around the toothpick.

"Besides its being remote," Weeks said, "the place has a dark history." He bobbed his eyebrows.

Calder laughed. "Don't tell me. It was a brothel."

"No."

"Speakeasy and gambling hall?"

"Wrong again."

"It has a ghost?"

Dawn looked at Weeks with wide, frightened eyes.

Weeks grinned. "It's not haunted, Mrs. Whitley. Not that I know of. But back in the nineties—"

"It was the eighties," Sims said.

Weeks looked at the older deputy and cocked his head to one side. "You sure about that?"

"Positive. My daddy was a deputy then. He was in on the cleanup." He removed the toothpick from the corner of his mouth and pointed it for emphasis. "It was the eighties."

"Cleanup of what?" Calder asked.

"Family feud," Weeks said. "One branch of a white-trash clan got crosswise with another branch."

"Over the property?"

Weeks shook his head. "A litter of bird dogs. That's what started it, anyway. It escalated from there. Resulted in a shootout at an abandoned filling station."

"Where's that?" Calder asked.

"As the crow flies, about a mile and a half from here. That way." He hitched a thumb over his shoulder. "It was the O.K. Corral all over again. When the smoke cleared, eight were dead. Those that survived died in prison."

"My daddy discovered the bodies of two women here in the house," Sims boasted. "They'd killed each other. With the *same pistol.*"

Calder said, "Wow. That is a dark history."

"After that, nobody wanted anything to do with this place," Weeks said. "Bad mojo. Scares people off, you know?" He looked across at Elle and motioned toward her burger basket. "Are you gonna eat the rest of your fries?"

They all helped to clear the table; then Weeks offered them the use of their phones again. "Keep it to three minutes. Just a good night."

Dawn happily drew aside to call her husband.

Calder said, "I'm good," and asked if he could make a pot of coffee.

Elle also declined to use her phone. She considered calling her parents but decided against it. Three minutes wasn't enough time to explain her current situation adequately. A hurried summary would leave them distressed, not reassured.

Nor did she want to call Glenda again and be interrogated about Calder or provided with unwanted details about Jeff's newborn son.

After Dawn surrendered her phone again, they all went into the living room, where Weeks tuned the TV to one of the playoff games they'd discussed over dinner.

Dawn discovered an abandoned book of crossword puzzles and applied herself to filling in the ones left unfinished. Elle chose a mystery novel from the bookcase.

After spending the earlier part of the day staring at her with the single-mindedness of an eagle, Calder seemed indifferent to her presence, except for when he'd looked at her to get her take on the dummy cameras.

He'd removed his familiar leather jacket and was wearing a plain white shirt, the tail untucked, the cuffs rolled back. He'd grown just enough scruff to make him look rough-and-tumbly delectable. She hated him for it.

No longer broody and temperamental, he seemed relaxed. He'd gotten increasingly chummier with the deputies and even anted up a five-dollar bill when Weeks suggested a friendly wager on the outcome of the game.

Elle observed the founding of this comradery with a skeptical eye. It was out of keeping with how artfully he had played the deputies at the dinner table. Neither of them seemed to have realized that it wasn't the house's history that he was interested in. He'd let them think they were impressing him with their knowledge, when actually he'd been mining information from them.

When he wanted something, Calder Hudson could be charmingly disingenuous. She should know.

When the trio of men boisterously objected to one of the umpire's calls, she'd had enough. She replaced the novel in the bookcase. "I'm turning in."

"Me too," Dawn said. "These puzzles are too hard."

Both Calder and Weeks said good night, but neither took their eyes off the television. Sims reluctantly left the party to escort Dawn and Elle up the enclosed staircase. After giving each of their bedrooms a cursory check, he wished them a good night and went back down.

Elle let Dawn have the bathroom first. When she came out, she paused in the open doorway of Elle's room. "I'm glad you're here, Elle. I mean, I'm not *glad* about any of it, but this would be really awkward with all the—" She motioned down the staircase.

"Testosterone."

The young woman smiled. "Frank's got a jealous streak. He told me that Mom wasn't crazy about me going off to parts unknown with two strange men, either. Both like knowing there's another lady here."

"I'm glad there's another lady here, too," Elle said. "Good night."

"See you in the morning."

To Elle's relief, Dawn went into her room and closed the door. She'd feared that Dawn would want to treat tonight like a sleepover.

She took her turn in the bathroom. When she came out, she noticed that all the lights were still on downstairs. Even after she'd turned out the lights in the bedroom and had gotten into bed, she could hear the TV and the muffled voices of the men coming up through the floorboards. The game must have gone into extra innings. It seemed never-ending.

Eventually, blessedly, the television was silenced. Conversation dwindled, then died. Although all became quiet, she had trouble falling asleep. She was still awake, lying on her side facing the windows, when she smelled leather, like Calder's jacket. She sensed a shift in the air.

She rolled onto her back just as he planted his knee beside her hip on the mattress, leaned over her, and cupped his hand over her mouth. "Don't say anything, just listen."

She swatted his hand away. "Like hell I will. Leave this room *now*, or I'll shout this place down."

"Elle. Shh. Please." He clasped her head between his hands and lowered his face close to hers. "After last night, I can't even imagine what you must think of me."

"I promise that whatever you can imagine, it's worse." She began pushing against him, trying to unbalance him, dislodge his knee from against her hip, break his hold on her. "Let go of me and get out of here."

"Goddammit, that's exactly what I'm going to do. This

is a disaster—another disaster—waiting to happen. I'm getting out of here, and you're coming with me."

"Not if my life depended on it."

"It *does*. Those men downstairs might be good-hearted good ol' boys, but you heard them. They're here because they drew the short straws. They're ill-equipped. They're lax. Protect us? Forget it."

"Over the burger baskets, you were pumping them for information, weren't you?"

"You saw through that?"

"Clearly. But you beguiled them."

"I'm very good at it."

"I know that too well."

"Elle, last night—"

"Don't."

"Fine. We don't have time to argue now anyway. Come on, get up, we're leaving."

"I wouldn't go anywhere with you."

She placed her hands on the undersides of his arms and pushed up, dislodging his hands from her head. He hissed, and she knew the move must have hurt his injured arm, but she used that moment of distraction to scramble off the other side of the bed. She rounded the end of it and rushed toward the door.

He caught up to her before she could open it and sandwiched her between it and him. He crowded in behind her, placing his hands firmly on her waist to hold her in place. His lips against her ear, speaking to her in a rushed, harsh whisper, he said, "Do you want that asshole to get the best of you?"

The shooter. That's who he was talking about. "He already got the best of me. Charlie."

"He may not see it that way, Elle. He may want you, too. Just like Perkins said, you'd be a trophy. Think of the fame he would achieve. First the boy, then the mother. Even if he's caught, he'll have gotten the last laugh."

He took her by the shoulders and turned her around, lowering his face to within an inch of hers. "We're sitting ducks here. You've got to trust me on this."

"I don't trust you to do anything but manipulate people."

"I've already admitted that I have that talent. I'm a shit. And you don't know the half of it. Last night, I walked out on you after some rocket-launch sex. Revile me for that. Boil me in oil. I deserve it. But first I'm getting you out of here if I have to drag you. Now, are you going to make this hard or easy?"

She hated giving in to him, but in spite of herself, she was swayed by his arguments. "Damn you."

"Easy, then," he said, relaxing a bit. "Good."

"When should I be ready?"

"We're going now."

"*Now?* It's the middle of the night."

"No better time. Hurry. Get dressed."

"I won't leave Dawn."

"I heard her coming downstairs but didn't let her see me because she would start talking, asking questions. We'll grab her on our way out. Let's go."

She stepped around him, reached for the pair of slacks she'd been wearing all day, and pulled them on over her boxer pajama bottoms. She tugged on a sweater over her tank top.

Calder had felt around in the dark on the floor beside the bed and found her discarded sneakers. He passed them to her. As she worked her feet into them, she asked, "Where are the deputies? They'll try to stop us."

"If we're quiet, we'll be out before they realize it. Sims is sitting in the hallway, asleep in his chair. Last I saw Weeks, he was in the living room, feet up, on his phone, probably—"

He was interrupted by an eruption of gunfire and a blood-curdling scream.

———

For an instant, they froze. Then, "*Shit!*" Calder propelled Elle toward the closet, opened the door and pushed her inside.

She lunged out. "Dawn."

He pushed her back into the closet. "Do not come out, and I fucking mean it." He slammed the door shut.

"Calder!"

He had to ignore her, because all the while, the *pop, pop, pop* of gunfire and shattering glass was unrelenting, and so were Dawn's screams.

He flung open the door to Elle's room and ran along the dark hallway, barely catching himself from tumbling down when he reached the top of the staircase. He teetered there, fighting his instinct to plunge headlong into the fight as he had at the fairground.

But the action might draw more fire, put them all in greater danger. If he was dropped by a bullet, he'd be of no help to anyone, just like he'd been of no help to Charlie.

But, fuck it all, he couldn't do nothing.

He descended the stairs with caution. He called out to Weeks, to Sims, to Dawn. No response, except for Dawn, whose screams could be heard above the deafening barrage of bullets and hailstorm of shattered glass. He figured the shooter must be firing through the row of three windows behind the kitchen table.

All the lights in the kitchen had been shot out, but there was a blue-white glow. The refrigerator light. Dawn had left the door of it open. She must be pinned down, in mortal danger. It would even the playing field if the shooter didn't have that light.

He shouted, "Dawn, if you can, shut the fridge door!"

But the light stayed on. If he showed himself in the kitchen he'd immediately be fired on. Where the fuck were Weeks and Sims? What could he do without a weapon, without—

Dawn's screams abruptly stopped. As though a switch had been flipped.

After another rapid series of shots were fired, the gunfire also ceased. The abrupt silence was almost as eerie as the explosive racket. Calder envisioned the shooter reloading in anticipation of another opportunity to kill.

Hearing the creak of old wood behind him, Calder spun around. Elle had made it halfway down the stairs. Furious, he made an emphatic motion with his hand for her to go back up. She mouthed Dawn's name. He raised his shoulders, then repeated the gesture for her to return upstairs.

She looked mutinous, but she began backing up the stairs. He waited until the darkness at the top of the staircase obscured her; then he bent at the waist and crept toward the kitchen.

But even before he reached the doorway, he saw Sims's body sprawled on the floor, his torso blown to bits.

Calder didn't think twice. He took the unfired six-shooter from the dead man's hand and, with a bloodlust that shocked even him, emptied the cylinder into the darkness beyond the broken windows.

Chapter 24

Compton watched Perkins dip his hand into a bag of potato chips and crunch a mouthful. "How come you can go through bag after bag of those and not get fat?" she groused.

"Life's unfair."

"You're telling me."

After returning from the safe house, they'd grilled the weasel Billy Green. He'd admitted that he'd passed along nickel-and-dime information to Shauna Calloway in the past and swore that the names of the material witnesses were the biggest bonanza he'd ever given her.

Their greatest fear was that he'd heard about the baseball cap or had learned the location of the safe house and had shared one or both of those pieces of information also. But after spending an hour coming down hard on him, their gut feeling was that disclosing the names of their witnesses had been his swan song.

He was fired and got a Do Not Pass Go escort out of the building. He was lucky not to have been tarred and feathered. Everyone who worked in any capacity for the sheriff's department, in any of the precincts, had been outraged over the embarrassment his betrayal had caused.

"I mean, it's not as if the whole goddamn world isn't already crucifying us," the sheriff had been quoted as saying. It was a justified boom of fury, because, nationwide, it was open season on his entire operation.

Heretofore it had been a role model for other law enforcement agencies of comparable jurisdiction. But because the Fairground shooter was still at large, the sheriff's office was now being harshly criticized.

None were more aware of the microscope they were under than Compton and Perkins, the department's senior homicide detectives. The CID, and in particular the two of them, were taking a beating.

They desperately needed a break. Even a person of interest would be a boon, a development they would gladly share with the media themselves. The provenance of the ball cap was still being tracked, but doggedness took time, and time consumption was increasing the pressure applied to them.

One crack, though slim, was the nature of Calder Hudson's "consulting" work and the implications it might have. When they learned what his job entailed and how successful he was at it, Perkins had ventured, "The shooting began in the area where he was. Could he have been the target that day and all the others collateral?"

Compton had been dubious and had said so. "If somebody

was that pissed off at him, why not just murder him in his house or as he crossed the street?"

Perkins hadn't relented. "Still worth following up."

Having no other lead to follow, they went about obtaining Calder Hudson's files.

When Compton had informed him of their intention to review them, he had staunchly disclaimed the notion that an individual in his records bore him such a bloodthirsty grudge.

"Besides, remember the nondisclosure clause? There are hundreds of names in those files, and half don't even know who I am."

Considering the volume of material—Hudson had had clients in two dozen states and three countries in Europe—it did seem to be a long shot, especially since they really didn't know what they were looking for.

A handful of part-time deputies had been recruited to pitch in, but after they knocked off for the day, she and Perkins had felt obligated to put in some overtime themselves, even though their day had included the round trip to the safe house and the wringing out of Billy Green. They were tired, grungy, grouchy, and sleep deprived.

As Perkins ran his finger down one list of names, he asked, "How's your husband?"

"I don't remember."

He chuffed his version of a laugh.

"I called him twice today," she said around a yawn. "The dog's sick. He had to take her to the vet. He's more worried about her than he is about me."

"Go on home," he said. "I'll stay awhile." A confirmed bachelor, he had no one waiting on him.

"Another thirty minutes," she said.

He pushed the bag of potato chips to within her reach. She didn't thank him but began absently eating them as she continued perusing her own list. For several minutes they shared a companionable silence, then Perkins said, "Draper."

Compton raised her head. "Hmm?"

"Draper, Arnold M."

"What about him?"

"I'm thinking." He rocked back in his swivel chair and tapped his folded hands against his chin.

Compton's cell phone rang. "Hold the thought." She licked salt off her fingers and reached for her phone. She saw the readout, checked the time, and frowned as she clicked on. "Weeks?"

"His phone, but Weeks is dead."

"Calder?" Compton whipped her head around and looked at Perkins, even as she switched over to speaker. "Say again?"

"Weeks is dead. So is Sims. Dawn Whitley, I don't know. She's unaccounted for."

Having heard all that, Perkins grabbed the receiver on the desk phone and began punching in numbers.

Compton asked Calder if he'd called 911.

"Just before I called you."

"Are you all right? What about Elle?"

"Neither of us was hurt."

"What in God's name happened?"

"You'll need a good crime scene unit to figure it all out. But the gunfire came from outside through the kitchen windows. I'd just seen Dawn in there, so I figure the shooter was aiming for her.

"Sims had posted himself in the central hallway. When the shooting started, he must've run toward the kitchen but only made it as far as the door. Multiple wounds but hard to tell how many. His torso is mush.

"Weeks was next, I guess. Last I saw him alive, he was in the living room. Now he's lying dead in the hallway. He was hit in the throat. Lots of blood. Since he didn't make it into the kitchen before he was shot, I'm guessing it was a rifle. Based on the rapid fire, it was the kind that means business."

Perkins had been following the conversation while maintaining contact with the other sheriff's office to whom Calder's 911 call had been directed.

Perkins covered the mouthpiece of the desk phone. "Tell him they're about ten minutes out. Not to touch anything. Keep his head down, and make certain he identifies himself when they arrive. They'll be gunning for the individual who put two of their men down."

"Did you hear all that?" Compton asked.

"Yeah," Calder replied. "But I've already touched the bodies to check for pulses. I may have stepped in some blood and tracked it. I took Weeks's phone and Sims's pistol."

Compton pressed her hand to her forehead. "Had it been fired?"

"Not when I took it. It has been now."

"You returned fire?"

"Six shots."

"Did you hit him?"

"I don't know."

"Let's back up. What about Mrs. Whitley? You say you and she were in the kitchen when it started?"

"She was. I was upstairs."

"And Elle?"

"Upstairs."

Compton looked over at Perkins to see if he'd caught that. His raised eyebrows indicated that he had.

Calder was saying, "First blast of gunfire, Dawn started screaming."

"Was she hit?"

"I don't know. More shooting. Lots of shooting. Windows exploding. It lasted, I don't know, two minutes maybe. I'd stowed Elle in a bedroom closet and gone downstairs. The only light was coming from the open fridge. I found Sims, then Weeks. No sign of—"

"Are you certain they're dead?"

"They're *dead*. No sign of Dawn, but she didn't respond when I told her from the stairwell to shut the fridge door to kill the light. She was screaming like a banshee. And then she stopped. Chopped off. Like he'd gotten her with a clean shot once she went out the back door."

"The back door?"

"I got to the kitchen and shut the fridge, but not before I saw that the back door was standing open with a trail of blood leading out. There was broken glass all over the floor, all over everything. She could've been bleeding from cuts or bullet wounds. No way of knowing. I couldn't see but a few feet beyond the door out into the yard, and I didn't want to risk turning the light back on."

"He was still out there?"

"In order to find out, I'd have been shot."

"You didn't see him?"

"No."

"But you returned fire."

"In anger. I wasn't really aiming at anything. I couldn't see anything. I just wanted the motherfucker to know that he's on borrowed time."

Compton rubbed her forehead again. "Any vehicle?"

"I'll get to that. But at the time, I got a sense that he was still there, waiting for the rest of us to show ourselves. In addition to our guards, he would have been expecting five of us, right?"

"I assume."

"I stayed where I was and listened but didn't hear a thing, nothing to indicate that Dawn was alive, nothing that would give away his position if he was still there. Not knowing if he was or not, or what kind of firepower he had left, I went back upstairs."

"Elle was unharmed?"

"If you consider her second shooting in sixty days not to be harmful." He waited a beat before adding, "We managed to escape."

"How?"

"That small room where you and Perkins interrogated me before everyone else arrived? Remember there's a door that opens onto an exterior staircase? We went out that way."

"I didn't notice a door or a staircase."

"Well, I did. Want to know why? Because I was already looking for an escape hatch. This setup was a fucking joke. Why didn't you have badasses protecting us? Like the marshal's service?"

"They're federal."

"They're federal," he muttered. "Between those deputies, they had two six-shot revolvers and a rifle, and it was propped against the front doorjamb. The security cameras out there are for show."

"You have every right to be angry and upset."

"You're fucking right I do," he shouted.

"Vent later, Calder. I'll listen. But right now I need you to stay steady. Are you and Elle away from the house?"

"Yeah, we made it across the clearing and into the woods. I called 911, and then you."

"Do you feel safe there?"

"Partially. The vehicle? I can't describe it, but as we were running across the clearing, it was speeding down the road that leads to the highway. All I saw were taillights, but I think he's gone."

"How'd the car get there without somebody hearing it coming?"

"Sims was asleep. Weeks was diddling with his phone. He's still got his ear pods in. And I was . . . upstairs."

Compton took a breath. "Okay." She looked over at Perkins, and he held up his hand, fingers spread. "They're five minutes out," she said to Calder. "We'll tell them to look for you in the woods. Which direction from the house?"

"The side with the exterior staircase. Whichever that is."

"Stay hunkered down till first responders get there, but

when they do, if you're ordered to come out with your hands up, do it. Surrender that pistol you took off Sims. Turn yourselves over to the highest-ranking officer. He or she will see to it that you're protected."

"You mean like they've protected us so far?"

"Until Perkins and I can get there."

"You and Perkins, who didn't realize you had a jabberwocky in Shauna's pocket? He was right under your noses."

"All right, point taken. We messed up. We underestimated. But you and Elle are material witnesses to two crimes now. Two very bloody crimes. You're valuable. We'll protect you." When he didn't come back with a rebuttal, she said, "Calder, are you listening?"

"Yeah."

"Are you going to heed what I say?" Again, an answer wasn't forthcoming.

Perkins nudged her arm and slid a sheet of paper in front of her. On it, next to a circled name, he'd written: *Ask him.*

She said, "Calder, who's Arnold Draper?"

Chapter 25

Calder immediately disconnected. *Arnold Draper.* He repeated the name several times inside his head, but it rang no bell.

He didn't know what was up with that, but sorting it out would take contemplation he didn't have time for. He had to get Elle and himself as far away from here as possible before the cavalry arrived and they were placed under "protection" again.

While he'd been talking to Compton, Elle had been huddled against him, shivering from the chill as well as from the most recent trauma she'd experienced. Her teeth were chattering, but she hadn't spoken a word.

However, when he hauled back his right arm and threw Weeks's phone as far as he could into the woods, she came to life. "Why'd you do that? We'll need that phone."

"I have ours."

"You do?"

"I'll explain later."

He took their phones out of the side pocket of his jacket, shook off the broken glass that each had been covered in when he'd retrieved them, suspended the reception of cellular data and powered down each, then replaced them in his pocket.

"Here. Take this." When he tried to pass her the large revolver he'd taken off Sims, she recoiled. "Come on, Elle. Take it and keep it handy."

"Why? You told Compton the shooter was gone."

"I could be wrong. It's loaded. Safety's set. If you have to fire it, don't forget to unlock the safety. See?" He demonstrated and tried again to hand it over.

She shook her head. "You keep it."

"I have Weeks's."

"You didn't tell Compton that."

"No. I didn't tell her I took bullets from his gun belt, either." He'd already reloaded the pistol he'd fired. "Take the damn gun."

When she didn't, he cursed and crammed it into the side pocket of her jacket.

The argument had cost a valuable minute. All the while he'd been listening for sirens announcing the arrival of first responders to his 911 call. "Okay, let's go."

"Go? You agreed to stay here."

"No, I didn't. We're hooking it, just like we were about to do when the shooting started."

"But that was before this was a crime scene. Leaving the scene of a crime is a crime."

"What's a crime is promising key witnesses protection and then falling way short." In the distance, he heard the wail of sirens. "We gotta go." He grabbed her hand, but still she resisted. He swore again. "Elle, I'm getting you away from here."

"I didn't ask you to."

"I'm not giving you an option. You're mad at me. More than mad. But you're coming with me. Now. Got that?"

After devoting a few precious seconds to thinking it over, she let herself be pulled along behind him as he set out at a jog, running in a northerly direction, the opposite of where he'd told Compton they were.

"Why not take the deputies' car?" she asked.

"I didn't have time to search for the key. Besides, how far do you think we'd get in that? We'd probably meet first responders on the road to the highway. Or the shooter, expecting that's what we'd do. Either way, we're better off in the woods on foot."

He realized that was easy for him to say. Elle's stride, being much shorter than his, required her to take more steps, but she kept pace. Barely. Because they were weaving their way through the pine forest, where the trees grew straight and so close together their trunks resembled a stockade. The forest floor was inherently hazardous because of undergrowth, woodsy debris, and uneven terrain.

It would have been rough going in broad daylight. But it was dark. And, as if the gods weren't heckling them already, it had begun to drizzle.

Elle had become short of breath, but she said, "I feel like

we're deserting Dawn. What do you think happened to her?"

"I don't know."

"You think she's dead, don't you?"

"Maybe she ran like we did, got across the clearing, and into the woods to hide. Maybe she was wounded and unconscious. Or maybe she was unable to answer when I called to her because she knew if she did, she'd be giving away her position to the shooter. There is an endless number of possibilities."

Behind him Elle stopped so suddenly he lost his grip on her hand. He turned quickly. She was standing upright. Rigid, actually, her hands balled into fists at her sides. "Dawn is dead, isn't she? That's what you really think."

He placed his hands on her shoulders and squeezed them firmly. "Yes. I think the odds are good." He dipped his knees to bring himself eye level with her. "I don't want the same to happen to you, to us. Which is why we had to leave and why we have to keep going."

"Oh, I'll keep going. I swore to myself, to Charlie, that I would do everything within my power to get justice for him, even if I die in the process." She raised her fists and beat them against Calder's chest. "*Why can't they catch him?*"

He hoped no one was on their trail because her shout, bouncing off every solid tree trunk, would have echoed its way back to the house. Not that he blamed her for her rage.

"He'll be caught, but I don't want you to die in the process." He pulled her to him and hugged her tightly but released her immediately and reached for her hand again. "We've got to keep moving."

He'd hated leaving without knowing Dawn Whitley's fate just as badly as Elle did, but he had no guarantee that the gunman had fled. He might only have been trying to make it look like he had in order to draw them out.

But whether he was behind them or not, Calder knew for certain that lawmen were, those who'd promised them sanctuary, failed to provide it, and yet pledged it again. Screw that.

As earnest as the efforts of Compton and Perkins, Weeks and Sims, and the behind-the-scenes personnel had been, they'd been outclassed, outsmarted, and outgunned by the Fairground shooter.

Shauna's report had been as tempting as Eve's apple. He'd gone for it, swiftly and with a vengeance. The boldness of the attack on the safe house was an indication of his resolve. Calder was as resolved—damn the consequences—that he and Elle get away and regroup someplace safe. Or at least safer.

But first he had to get them out of this freaking forest. He wasn't even certain they were still going in the right direction, and he didn't want to risk turning on his phone to check. He didn't share that worry with Elle, though. Her breathing had become increasingly labored.

He wasn't overexerted yet, but with every step, he repeated the name that Compton had tossed out to him. Apparently she thought it would mean something to him, but it didn't. In his mind, it was like a roulette ball that spun and bounced around the wheel but never found a pocket in which to land.

He had a disturbing intuition that he was running from that, too.

The cool front that had ushered in the precipitation had also caused the temperature to drop. The drizzle had become a steady rain, which made their footing riskier and obstacles in their path more difficult to see and avoid.

One of those obstacles caused Elle to stumble. She caught herself before she fell, but when he stopped and turned to check on her, she panted, "How much farther?"

"Not much. We only had a mile and a half to cover. You good?"

With determination, she nodded and fell into step behind him again. "Do we have a destination?"

"The abandoned filling station Weeks mentioned."

"It's probably not even there anymore."

"The station doesn't have to be there. Only the road it was on. If we can find the road, do you think your friend would come pick us up?"

"Glenda? Yes."

"Would you trust her not to tell anybody?"

"She would never."

"You're certain?"

"Positive."

"Okay, we'll call her."

"How did you get our phones back?"

"When I went into the kitchen, before I doused the fridge light, I noticed them on the kitchen counter where the deputies had left them. I snatched them before coming back upstairs."

"Nothing escapes you, does it? The security cameras in the treetops, the door to the outside stairs, our cell phones. You take notice of everything."

"I noticed your navel piercing."

He wasn't sure Elle heard that. In any case, she didn't respond.

Not long after that, they came out of the woods and crossed a narrow ditch onto the road that Calder had anticipated would be there. He allowed himself only time enough to regain his breath, then took his phone from his jacket pocket. As he was rebooting it, Elle asked why he'd used Weeks's phone to call Compton.

"So she wouldn't know right away that I had mine."

When his phone was ready for use, he said a prayer for good cell service. Three bars. He accessed a GPS app that showed their location. He took a screen shot, then handed his phone to Elle.

"This is a county road, and, according to the map, there's a consolidated school not far from where we are. We'll shelter there. Text that screen shot to Glenda, then call her. Tell her that after this call, I'm turning the phone off again. If we have to move, we'll call or text her. Do you think Compton might contact her, looking for you?"

"It's likely. She's met Glenda and knows she and I are closer than family."

"Okay, tell Glenda to watch for a tail. Tell her to hurry but not to risk getting stopped for speeding. I know it's a lot to get across, but make it short, Elle." As an afterthought, he said, "Put her on speaker."

Elle might have all the trust in the world in this friend who was closer than family, but it wasn't his family, and he wanted to judge her integrity for himself.

It took five rings for her to answer, her voice muffled as though buried in a pillow. But when she heard Elle's voice, she was instantly awake and began sputtering questions.

Elle promised to give her the whole story later but urged her to stop talking and listen, which she did. Elle finished by telling her to check her text messages for directions to their location. "Did you get all that?"

"Yes, but, Elle, are you going to get into trouble for running away?"

"We were in life-threatening trouble where we were."

"Good point. What about *him*? Are you two—"

"We're fine," she said quickly, her gaze swinging up to Calder's. "Grateful to be alive."

"He's listening, right?"

"Can you please bring me a jacket or coat? I grabbed mine at the last minute, but it's soaked through. It, my wallet, and phone are all I have with me."

"Of course. Anything else?"

"Whiskey," Calder said.

He took his phone back and disconnected but didn't turn it off immediately. As they walked along the shoulder in the direction of the school, he accessed his contacts. No one named Draper was among them.

As he slid his phone back into his pocket, he told Elle, "If I use my VPN, they can't track it. At least I don't think so. They can get our cell records, but I think it requires a warrant, and that'll take a while. In the meantime, the less we use them, the better."

They found the K-through-twelve campus, but it sat atop an incline that was too far off the road to suit Calder. "Let's stay here." He led Elle into the school bus stop.

The shelter was open on all sides except for the back, which had a plexiglass shield. It and the metal roof kept the rain off. They collapsed onto the bench.

"What happens if a car comes along?" Elle asked.

"It's so quiet out here, it'll announce itself before it gets here. We'll hightail it into that grove."

The silence was broken only by the patter of rain on the roof and their individual shifts on the hard bench seeking a more comfortable position. Calder's leather jacket squeaked as he went to take it off. "Here, Elle, put this on."

Looking straight ahead rather than at him, she said, "The lining will get wet. I'm fine."

She looked cold and bedraggled, but he didn't press it. After a time, he said, "Earlier, when Weeks let us use our phones, you made a call. Who to? Your parents?" She didn't answer. "It's none of my business, of course."

She exhaled with annoyance. "I called Glenda."

"Hmm. Is that when you told her about last night, and us? Or am I wrong in assuming that I'm the *him* she scornfully referred to?" She turned her head, her lips parted and ready to speak, but he stopped her. "Don't try denying it. I was observing you, Elle."

"You were rudely staring a hole through me."

"Which is how I know you got upset by something she said to you. I was closely watching your face."

"Why?"

"Primarily because I like looking at it."

She rolled her eyes.

"And secondly, I was gauging your expression, because the last time I was looking into your face and gauging your expression, you were in the throes of a long and clenching orgasm."

She glared daggers at him. "That must've made you feel proud."

"It made me feel like the king of the fucking jungle." She didn't roll her eyes at that, maybe because of the dead seriousness of the declaration. He let it hover, then said, "When I came, I thought my heart was going to burst."

She ducked her head, but he placed his finger beneath her chin and tilted it up, forcing her to look squarely at him. "And it still wasn't enough."

Without expression, she held his gaze for a moment, then lifted her chin off his finger. "That must be why you stuck around for so long afterward, why I couldn't get rid of you and practically had to kick you out the door. Oh, no, wait. You left in such a hurry, you didn't even pull the door all the way shut."

This time, she stopped him from speaking by holding up her hand, palm out, directly in front of his face. "I know. You're a shit. Boil you in oil. Which, granted, isn't a bad idea. But there's no need to belabor the point. I told you it would be a mistake, but we did it, and biologically it was—"

"A seismic shift."

"Momentarily pacifying. It's done. History. We don't have to talk about it anymore."

"The hell we don't."

"I don't. Not now or later or ever."

He'd learned from experience that dealing with someone who was this angry was pointless. They tended to take a stance and only dig in deeper. It was better to back off and wait for another opening.

Of course, Elle wasn't just "someone," but their current circumstances weren't conducive to having a heart-to-heart like they needed to have.

He wasn't going to surrender on one point, though. "During that phone call, what did Glenda say that upset you?"

"Don't flatter yourself into thinking it was about you."

"Then what was it?"

She looked aside, and he thought she would refuse to share. But then she turned back to him. "Jeff and his wife had their baby. A boy."

He flopped back against the plexiglass, making it wobble as, softly but emphatically, profanities poured out of him.

When they stopped, Elle said, "It doesn't matter."

"It does matter. It matters a whole hell of a lot. Come here." He put his foot on the bench and raised his knee, opening his lap. He held the sides of his jacket apart.

She shook her head. "No thank you."

"Come on, Elle. You have every reason to detest me, but it'll take Glenda a while to get here, and you're shivering."

She wrestled with indecision, then inched closer along the

bench. He drew her against him and wrapped her inside his jacket. "Lay your head down."

"My hair is soaked. I'll get your shirt wet."

He cupped her head and pressed it down. Eventually she folded her legs up on the bench, rested her cheek against his chest, and relaxed against him. Given her frame of mind, he didn't hold her as snugly as he wanted to, but as tightly as he dared.

But still, it felt good. Her elbow was wedged in his crotch and her breasts—braless—were soft against his ribs, except for her nipples, which weren't soft. At all.

He was probably going to hell for thinking along erotic lines. But he could very well have died tonight, and he was probably going to hell anyway, so why not think dirty?

After a time, she said quietly, "She surprised me with doughnuts."

"Hmm?"

"Glenda. This morning she dropped by unannounced. I didn't tell her about last night. She figured it out when she discovered the signed copy of *Heavens to Betsy* you left behind."

He hugged her a little closer, tipped his head down, and whispered against the crown of her head, "Remind me to get that from you."

Chapter 26

They were there for almost two hours before Glenda arrived.

Twice they'd left the bus stop to conceal themselves in the nearest copse of evergreens. Once, a mean-looking state trooper's SUV had whizzed past. Its flashing emergency lights had signaled its approach, giving them time to slip into the darkness of the dense grove.

The other time, they'd heard a helicopter. From their cover, they saw its searchlight skimming over the treetops, but it never got near enough to pose a real threat to them. Neither wanted to venture whether it was searching for the shooter who'd killed two lawmen, or for them. Calder supposed both.

They were anxious, exhausted, stiff with cold, wet, as miserable as two people could be when Glenda's luxury SUV began slowing down as it approached the school campus. Calder stepped out from the bus stop and flagged her down.

As Elle hastily made the introductions, Glenda helped her into a quilted jacket. She then looked Calder up and down, said, "Pleased to meet you," and handed him a bottle of Jack Daniel's. "Anybody will drink that," she added, her tone insinuating anybody who was lowbrow enough.

With attitude, he cracked the seal and took an indecorous swig, then climbed into the back seat. Elle got in up front on the passenger side and moved the seat forward to give him more leg room. Once they were headed back toward Dallas, Glenda began demanding details.

After listening to their harrowing tale, she shook her head. "Unbelievable. What now? What are you going to do? What can I do? Should I call Daddy? He could provide private security for you. Tough guys *nobody* would mess with. He could jet you off to someplace tropical and safe. He could also send a battalion of lawyers and have them sue the asses off everyone responsible for this fuckup."

"Hold off on all that for now," Elle said wearily but with humor. "I'm less interested in punishing them than I am in bringing my son's murderer to justice."

"Well, of course."

"I just don't know how to go about it."

Glenda caught Calder's eye in the rearview mirror. "What about you, Mr. Hudson? What do you think you should do?"

"I think you should call me Calder. I think Elle and I need time to wrap our minds around what happened at that safe house. We've been running on adrenaline. I haven't given it much thought except to escape it. But now...how in the hell did the shooter learn where we were?"

"It had to be from someone within one of the two sheriff's departments," Elle said. "Shauna's source?"

Calder was skeptical. "It's quite a stretch between leaking info to Shauna and being in cahoots with the shooter. Someone referred to as a 'glorified gofer' doesn't feel like a fit."

"Then back to the original question," Elle said. "Who gave us away? How did he find us?"

"By some means yet unknown," Calder said thoughtfully. "A means no one has considered."

"That's an even more frightening prospect," Elle said.

"Exactly what I was thinking." Calder dug his thumb and index finger into his eye sockets. "But I'm really too tired to think straight. The first order of business should be some sleep."

Elle turned around to look at him. "They'll be watching our houses. Yours, too, Glenda."

"I thought of that," Glenda said, reaching across the console to pat Elle's knee. "I took the liberty of making a plan for you. I brought the keys to a house we keep guest-ready for out-of-town clients who come to shop properties in the area. Celebrities, sports stars, and such, who want to stay under the radar and not check into a hotel. It's got every amenity imaginable and is more hush-hush than that so-called safe house they put you in."

She paused. "If you're worried about the sleeping arrangements, it's got two master suites in opposite wings of the house. Besides, you're grown-ups who've already done it."

Upon reaching Dallas, she drove them to an imposing house on an expansive lot in an imposing neighborhood where every lot was expansive. She used a remote to open the garage, then led them in through a multipurpose utility room and beyond it into a chef's fantasy kitchen.

"I brought food from my pantry and fridge. Basics, mind you. I'll put everything away while you're cleaning up. You'll find the bathrooms are well stocked with toiletries."

She'd carried in a duffel bag and now handed it to Elle. "There are several changes of clothes in there. I also brought a hairbrush, lip gloss, blush, and mascara. Which is all she needs, right?" she said, addressing the question to Calder. "It's demoralizing."

Continuing with him, she said, "No clothes for you, I'm afraid, but you can use the laundry to wash and dry yours, and there are spa robes in the guest room closets, so you'll be decent while you wait." She pointed him down a hallway. "Why don't you take the suite on this side? I'll get Elle settled into the other."

Calder went to his assigned suite. As described, the house did have every amenity imaginable. He found the spa robe and took it with him into the utility room, where he shucked his clothes, put them in the washer, and set it on a short cycle. He hung up his jacket and hoped that by morning it and his boots would be dry.

By the time he had scrubbed in the luxurious shower, the washing machine was on the spin cycle. He waited until it was finished and transferred his clothes to the dryer.

Then he took the bottle of Jack with him into the kitchen, where Glenda was busily moving about, unloading tote bags of food. She laughed when she saw him in the spa robe with his bare feet and hairy calves.

He said, "I'm lost and need directions to the pedi chairs."

Still laughing, she said, "What you need is a glass." She took one from a cabinet and brought it to him.

"Thanks."

"Ice, water, Coke?"

"After the night we've had, the neater the better." He tipped the bottle toward the glass.

She picked up a glass of white wine she'd been drinking and raised it in a silent toast, then resumed unpacking the foodstuffs. "I hope you like chicken salad. It's my house-keeper's secret recipe," she said as she placed a sealed plastic container in the refrigerator. "She made it fresh yesterday. And..." She pulled out another container. "She also baked a batch of brownies, which are so decadent that I don't typi-cally share them. You should feel privileged."

He leaned back against the counter, crossed his bare ankles, and sipped his whiskey as he watched her.

"I was thinking," she said, as she placed apples and oranges in a wire bowl. "I could send someone out tomor-row to buy clothes for you. Not someone from the agency, because Compton will probably have people watching it. I was thinking of my hairdresser. She owes me a favor."

Over her shoulder, she confided, "I paid the fine for her DUI. Not for her sake, but for that of my hair. What would I have done with my roots while she was in jail? Anyway, write down your sizes." She passed him a pad of Post-its and a pen. "Shirt, pants, undies." She looked down at his feet. "Shoes?"

"Sneakers. My boots might not dry out overnight." He wrote down his sizes, then placed the Post-its on the counter within her reach. "Think you could get us some prepaid phones? A couple of burners would come in handy."

"Great idea! I wouldn't send my hairdresser for those, though. I could use the guy who keeps all the electronics in this house working. He should go to two different stores, so it won't look suspicious. And buy them with cash." She bumped the pantry door shut with her hip.

"Oh! Do you need cash? I forgot that. Neither of you should be using credit cards or ATMs. That's the first thing they'll look for. I'll bring you some legal tender tomorrow."

By then, she'd finished emptying the last tote bag. "There. All done. You've got provisions." She beamed him a smile and picked up her wineglass.

"Glenda, what are you keeping from Elle?"

She nearly choked swallowing the wine. She blinked several times and played dumb. "Pardon?"

He moved nothing except his hand to swirl the whiskey in his glass. "What are you keeping from Elle?"

"What are you talking about?"

Without taking his eyes off her, he shot his drink and set the empty glass on the counter. "You're trying too hard."

"Trying too hard?"

"To be her best friend. Even going so far as to chummy up to me, and I know that's bogus. You're hiding something."

Her eyes narrowed on him as she set down her wineglass and placed her hands on her hips. "Who do you think you are? You don't know me. You barely know Elle. And given the circumstances under which you met her, having sex with her is, frankly, weird. Unless you think your cock is so magical it would make up for the bullet that *you* couldn't stop."

He lowered his chin almost to his chest and mumbled, "Transference of wrongdoing." Classic narcissism. He hadn't come off his relationship with Shauna without taking some knowledge from it. He was immune to the insult as well as to Glenda's haughty and accusatory glare.

Airily she asked, "Excuse me, what did you say?"

"That you remind me of someone."

"Obviously someone you dislike. Who?" Then she lowered her hands from her hips and gave a wave of dismissal. "You know what? Never mind. Why am I even honoring this with further discussion? You don't know what you're talking about, and I certainly don't. Whatever, you're way off base."

With absolute confidence, he said, "No, I'm spot-on."

"You've known me for how long? Yet you have the nerve—"

"Not nerve. Experience."

"At what?"

"At spotting a suck-up." Lowering his voice, he said, "You're trying too hard to convince Elle that you're her bestie. What don't you want her to know, or even suspect?"

She clung to her arrogance for several moments before beginning to lose her grip on it. Sensing that, he zoomed in for the kill. "Maybe her husband wasn't the only one who was unfaithful."

She took a deep breath, looked toward the ceiling, then

back at him. She rolled her lips inward and held them like that, then eventually relented. "Elle left town for a week to visit her parents. I'd just gotten my second divorce. Jeff came over to console me, and..." She gave a small shrug.

Calder had suspected something like that. For Elle's sake, he wanted to slap the shit out of this woman. For Elle's sake, he said, "Don't ever tell her."

From the open doorway, Elle asked, "Tell me what?"

Chapter 27

———⚬———

Elle walked into the kitchen, sensing that the atmosphere between Calder and Glenda was practically crackling. It was a wonder their hair wasn't standing on end.

But Calder smiled and said, "I was begging her not to tell you how scared I was tonight."

"You put up a brave front," Elle said. "You were also a bully."

"I had to get us through those woods."

"A challenge for sure," Glenda said. "And it had to have been exhausting, so I'm going to head out and let you two get some sleep. The car in the garage? Use it."

Calder asked who it belonged to.

"Basically, to Daddy, but it's registered to an LLC, which owns a small percentage of another LLC, on and on through God knows how many layers, so nobody will be looking for it. The key is in it."

Calder said, "There's a laptop in my bedroom, but I need the password."

"This chart covers everything." She opened a kitchen drawer and took out a laminated sheet of paper. "There's one of these in each of your nightstands, too. It's got the security alarm code, passwords to the various computers, smart TVs, Wi-Fi, the whole shebang. The guy I told you about? He's the general overseer of the house. His number is on here if you have a question about something. He's on call 24/7."

"Is he discreet?"

She snuffled. "We've put up the raunchiest of the raunchy in this house. He's a vault. His job depends on it. Anything else?"

Elle said, "I need to call my parents. How safe is the landline?"

"Again, it's in a company name. The only problem you'll have is if your parents mistake it for a spam call and don't answer."

Calder said, "Compton and Perkins will expect Elle to reach out to you in some manner, so there may already be surveillance on your house."

"I prepared for that. This, uh, gentleman I know will swear to anyone asking that I was with him for several hours this evening."

"Looks like you thought of everything. Why am I not surprised?" Elle went over to Glenda and pulled her into a hug. "You came through for me again. Thank you. A thousand times over."

"Same here," Calder said. "Thank you." Calder extended his hand.

As they shook, the two appraised each other. To Elle the handshake looked like the sealing of a tenuous truce.

Glenda turned back to Elle for one final hug. "You know where I am. Call me if you need anything."

Then she was gone, and Elle was left with Calder in an unfamiliar kitchen that suddenly seemed to take on the proportions of a cathedral. She was left with Calder in nothing except a bathrobe.

Pushing aside the forbidden thoughts that surged to mind, she said, "Fetching getup."

He grinned. "You're one to talk." He tilted his head and looked her over. She was wearing a modest pair of flannel pajamas that Glenda had lent her. "Are you in there somewhere?"

"Glenda is more . . . filled out than I am. In a good way."

"That's a matter of opinion."

The implied compliment caused her stomach to do a little somersault. "She does have a way of taking things in hand, doesn't she?"

"She should be marshaling troops."

"All this." She raised her arms at her sides. "When we were running through those woods, I didn't expect for the night to end like this."

"No. It could've been much, much worse. I'm feeling survivor's guilt all over again."

"Me too. After Dawn and I went upstairs, you spent time alone with Weeks and Sims. Did they mention having families?"

"They didn't say. I didn't ask. But I got the feeling they were looking upon that assignment as a boys' night out."

"I hadn't really thought of them until I was in the shower just now. Then the realization hit me. They were killed because of me."

"Not because of you. Of any of us. Blame their superiors. Those two were the wrong men for that job. They weren't qualified or equipped to handle a worst-case scenario. Their higher-ups never should have placed them in that situation. It was a recipe for the disaster that resulted."

She nodded, sighed, then indicated the bottle of whiskey on the counter. "May I have some of that?"

"Sorry. I should have offered." He walked over to a bank of cabinets. Beneath the terry cloth robe, his backside was well defined. Last night, when he was grinding his pelvis against her, she'd kneaded those firm glutes, making them contract even tighter as she'd arched up to take him deeper.

When he turned and walked back toward her with a glass, she kept her line of sight well above the robe's low-slung tie belt. He poured her a whiskey along with a refill for himself. Eyes locked, they clinked glasses, then drank.

Rebelliously, her body made her acutely aware of and responsive to all of Calder's attributes underneath the robe: his skin and form, his scent, the raw masculinity. She'd experienced it but had been denied time to explore and savor.

His rejection had stung, as did the whiskey now. It burned all the way down, but after the past few turbulent hours, she welcomed the sedation she hoped it would provide. She had escaped with her life. The deputies, and likely Dawn, hadn't.

As she tried to speak, she realized her voice had been made husky by the bourbon. Or perhaps emotion. "Calder, thank you."

"You're welcome. But it's not my whiskey."

"No," she said with a soft laugh. "Not for that. For—"

A ding sounded. "The dryer. Hold the thought. I'll be right back. Better attired." He set down his glass and left her.

While he was gone, she took a tour of the kitchen, looking at everything, registering nothing. Just as during the aftermath of the shooting, tonight's happenings seemed surreal. The stuff of outlandish dreams or an episode of someone else's life. Surely not hers. Elle Portman, escaping with her life, but running from the law? Who was that woman?

What had happened to the writer of children's books and the mother of Charlie, where a bad day would amount to an inconvenience, not a catastrophe? Spilled juice, not spilled blood.

Her mind went 'round and 'round like the carousel during Charlie's last ride. Her thoughts were blurred, fleeting, and difficult to catch, just as it had been hard to capture a picture of him on the painted pony as he'd glided past her, moving out of sight and beyond her reach.

Calder returned, dressed in his jeans and white shirt, but barefoot. "My boots are going to take a while."

"Will they be ruined?"

He shrugged. "I have a boot guy that will soften them up." He picked up their whiskeys and passed hers to her. "Drink up." They each took a swallow. He said, "The dryer interrupted what you were about to say."

"Oh, I was trying to thank you, not for the whiskey, but for getting me safely away from that place."

His expression softened. "Elle—"

Before he could continue, she raised a hand to stop him. "What were they talking to you about upstairs?"

"Hmm?"

"At the safe house. Compton and Perkins met with you separately. What was that about?"

His gaze darted away from her before coming back. "Shauna. It took some doing to convince them that my relationship with her was over and done with and that I hadn't been her source for that story."

"I see." Because he couldn't quite meet her gaze, she got the distinct impression that he was holding something back, but she didn't probe. "Before I forget," she said, "that pistol you forced on me is in the nightstand drawer in my bedroom."

"Good. Keep it close."

"Compton and Perkins will demand both of them back."

"Yes. But tomorrow. First, let's get through the night." He looked down at the floor and ran his hand around the back of his neck. "It's crazy. Us talking about pistols that I lifted off two dead men. Never in a million years would I have predicted I'd be doing something like that. Or any of it. All of it. Everything that's happened to me since I went through the turnstile at the fair. I saw none of this coming. And— What?" he said when she began to laugh.

"Just minutes ago, I was thinking along the same lines. Whose life is this that I'm living? Surely not mine."

He smiled wryly. "Beats the hell out of me, too. You think you have a handle on things, on your life, on your future, then…you get zapped with something that an instant before would have been unthinkable."

They reflected for a moment, then she asked what he thought would happen tomorrow.

"Two lawmen were killed in the line of duty," he said. "That will incite an angry reaction from the general public as well as from the law enforcement community. Whoever killed them will be public enemy number one."

"Do you think it was the Fairground shooter?"

"He used a semiautomatic handgun. I'm almost positive those deputies were killed with a semiautomatic rifle. Either the same person is skilled with both, or it was someone else."

"What does your gut tell you?"

"You have to ask? The timing of tonight's attack is the giveaway, I think." Speaking more softly, he added, "I don't think he's going to give up, Elle."

"No. But I'm not giving up, either." She gave him an emphatic look, then took one last drink from her glass before setting it on the counter. "However, I'm exhausted right now, and it's going to be a short night. I'll see you in the morning."

She turned to go, but he hooked his hand around her elbow and drew her close to him. "Sleep with me."

"No, Calder."

"Just sleep."

She gave him an arch look. "I've learned the hard way how effortlessly you maneuver. I'm not as gullible, naive, or malleable as you seem to believe. You see, I knew that Glenda and Jeff had slept together."

He was stunned, and it must have shown, because she smiled. "I knew within an hour of my return from that trip out of town."

"What gave them away?"

"As you said, they were trying too hard to please me. The overcompensation made it glaringly obvious."

"After that betrayal, you're still friends with her?"

"In my heart I knew my marriage was over already. I didn't love Jeff anymore, and I knew he didn't love me. But I knew Glenda did. I know she *does*. It would kill her to know that I know, so please don't ever tell her."

Just when Calder thought he'd seen every facet of Elle Portman, she revealed another as fascinating and intriguing as all the rest. Her youthful appearance and genteel demeanor threw people off. She had more depth and strength of character than anybody he'd ever met.

She also had a steely will, which was particularly vexing tonight.

With regret, he went alone to his master suite. He consulted the chart that provided all the codes and set the security alarm. From the telephone extension in his bedroom, he called his parents, waking them. Because of the hour, they were alarmed. He was quick to tell them that he was safe. After giving them a watered-down account of the day, he still had to talk both of them off the ledge, but eventually they calmed down enough for him to reassure them that he was all right.

"What about the young woman you escaped with?" his mother asked.

He looked toward the doorway of his bedroom, hoping that Elle would appear there. It remained open but empty.

"Like me, she's shaken up, but physically all right. We were both damned lucky to get out of there. Of course, I guess we're considered fugitives. There's that."

He asked about his dad's treatments and was told they were yielding positive results. He desperately wanted to believe that. He promised to keep them updated. "And for godsake, don't believe everything you hear on the news. If it doesn't come directly from me, doubt it."

After saying goodbye, he was tempted to get on the room's laptop and conduct a thorough online search for one Arnold Draper. But if Draper wasn't in his personal contacts, it was doubtful he'd ever had a connection to the man. Anyone even semi-important, such as the maître d' of his favorite restaurant, was always added to his contacts.

Besides, he was exhausted. He got into bed and switched off the bedside lamp. But when he closed his eyes, desire for Elle clawed at him, making him restless and hot. He threw off all the covers except for the sheet, and then he shoved one leg out from beneath it even as his hand slid under it and ventured toward his groin.

That's how Elle found him when she burst into the bedroom. "Calder! Are you awake? Turn on the TV."

Awake? He was hard and throbbing, and every cell in his body had become a blaring trumpet. He was definitely awake and happily processing how well timed her arrival was. But to watch TV?

When he didn't react quickly enough, she rushed over to the nightstand, clicked on the lamp, and picked up the TV remote. "Dawn is alive."

"Thank God. Thank *God.*"

"That's not all." Elle was looking at him in a way that was out of keeping with the news. "Police officers in their community were dispatched to notify her husband of the attack on the safe house. They found him dead."

Chapter 28

———◆———

Calder looked at her blankly. "Dead? What the hell?"

"As you thought, Dawn went out through the back door of the safe house. In her panic, in the dark, she ran into one of the metal poles holding up the clothesline and knocked herself out. That's why her screams ended so abruptly. First responders found her, brought her around. She was dazed and disoriented. They took her to the nearest hospital."

Elle sat down on the edge of the bed and turned on the TV inside a cabinet on the opposite wall. An all-news channel was broadcasting remotely from the safe house as well as from the Whitleys' home in a Dallas suburb. The perimeters of both houses had been cordoned off. Within the crime scene tape, there was much activity.

She said, "I was watching in the other room. This is a replay of what I've already seen." She gave a slight shudder.

"The images are horribly reminiscent of everything that was taking place after the Fairground shooting."

"Don't watch any more. Just fill me in." She relinquished the remote to Calder when he reached for it and turned down the volume. He rubbed her forearm, which had broken out in chill bumps.

"The coroner pronounced Weeks and Sims dead of multiple gunshot wounds. After the discovery of Dawn's husband's body, her mother insisted that she be transported back to Dallas. She was admitted to a hospital here for tests and observation."

"What's her condition? Is she going to be all right?"

"I think so. Physically. But she's suffering the shock of her husband's body being found in their living room."

"How'd he die?"

Elle heaved a breath. "He was shot in the same manner as Levi Jenkins. It had been made to look like a suicide, but the authorities have all but ruled that out and are investigating it as a homicide."

Calder dragged his hand over his scruffy jaw. "Jesus Christ."

"Compton was interviewed at the safe house crime scene. She told the reporter—"

"Not Shauna, I hope."

"No."

"That's a wonder. Go on."

"The reporter kept pressing Compton about us, our whereabouts and welfare. Rather tersely, she got across that she'd spoken to you by phone and that you'd assured her that you and I had escaped unharmed. That's paraphrasing."

"That was it?"

"No. Looking none too pleased, she admitted that our whereabouts were currently unknown and asked that anyone with information please call the sheriff's office immediately. She expressed concern for our safety."

"A little late for that."

"True. I wouldn't want to be in her shoes. Naturally, the reporter asked if investigators were linking the shooting at the safe house and the murder of Frank Whitley to the Fairground shooting. Compton tried to waltz around it but ultimately conjectured that upon learning the names of the five key witnesses, the Fairground shooter sought out Dawn Whitley at her home. Frank Whitley, who knew the location of the safe house, must've given it up under duress. That's how the shooter knew where to find us."

"How did Whitley know our location?" Then he winced. "Dawn told him when she called him."

Elle smiled sadly. "I wouldn't put it past her, Calder. She must've taken mental notes along her way there. She told me her husband was beside himself when she left with the deputies for a secret location. If she did indeed tell him, she'll never forgive herself. She would have done it to reassure him, never expecting that it would get him killed. Weeks and Sims, too."

"It wouldn't have made a difference if her husband knew or not, Elle. If he told or not. The minute the shooter showed up at their house, Whitley was a dead man. The shooter wouldn't have left behind someone who could identify him later."

He glanced at the TV. A uniformed man was now being interviewed. "Who's that guy? What am I missing?"

"A detective for the police department in the municipality where the Whitleys live. They have jurisdiction and will conduct that investigation. But in league with the sheriff's office."

"Maybe that crime scene will produce something useful to Compton and Perkins. The shooter left the weapon like before?"

"The same kind as the one used at the fairground."

"He's a confident son of a bitch," Calder said. "He's got gall, and he's good." His jaw tightened. "But not that good. He'll mess up. He probably already has. Somebody's just got to find that incriminating mistake."

"I'll keep the TV in my room on in case they break with something." She made to get up from the bed, but Calder caught her by the hand.

"You're sleeping here."

"We've been through this." She tried to wrest her hand free, but he held on.

"That was before. This guy is resourceful. Ruthless. Has balls of brass, and he's growing more and more sure of himself. Taking greater risks."

He rolled to his side and made certain the loaded pistol was still on the nightstand where he'd placed it before going to bed. Turning back to Elle, he said, "Hit the lamp. You're sleeping within my reach."

At Elle's insistence, they'd been lying at least two feet apart when they went to sleep. But at some point in the few intervening hours, their legs had become entwined. Her hands were trapped between her chest and his, and her head tucked beneath his chin so closely that she came awake to the warmth of his breath wafting over her face and his fingertips strumming her spine beneath the pajama top on loan from Glenda.

She didn't miss any aspects of her marriage to Jeff, God knew, but she had missed having a masculine presence around. Absent from her life now was that uniquely male essence that contrasted and complemented her femininity. She realized now how much she'd missed the intimacy of sharing a bed with...manliness.

Everything about this sleeping arrangement with Calder felt so good, she was reluctant to disrupt it. In no hurry to disengage, she moved only her head, drawing it from beneath his chin and tilting it back to look up at him. He was awake, watching her.

He stopped the idle caress of her backbone, pulled his hand out from under the pajama top, and laid his index finger vertically against her lips.

Without any preamble, he said, "I didn't run out on you because I didn't like it, Elle. I ran because I liked it too much."

She pushed his finger off her lips. "Is this a prepared 'it's not you, it's me' speech?"

"I prepared a speech, but I doubt it'll come out the way I want it to." He paused, scrubbed his tousled hair with his knuckles. "I can't explain it like a poet would. I don't think in terms of abstracts and concepts. The work I do is about assets and liabilities, nothing quixotic. My brain deals in facts, figures, practicality. So forgive me if I stop trying to make it pretty and speak bluntly, okay?"

"I'd prefer it."

"Good." He hesitated before starting again. "After that warm hug we shared outside the bar, I talked myself into believing that fucking you wouldn't be an experiment, that you weren't just a curiosity, an anti-Shauna, a salve for the aftereffects of the shooting, an itch I had a hankering to scratch. That...that my wanting you went deeper than all that. That's what I told myself."

"That's what you told *me*."

"That's what I told you." He sighed and ruefully shook his head. "But when I was inside you, I realized that all those rationales that I'd so meticulously stacked up were actually self-delusions, denials."

"Of?"

"Of just how meaningful it would be. What happened between us on your bed actually wasn't a test drive. I didn't want to leave, not your body, not your house, not you. And realizing that scared the hell out of me. That's why I left."

"On winged feet."

"Yeah." He picked up a strand of her hair and rubbed it between his fingers. "Tonight, when you were out of the room, Glenda said that my wanting to have sex with you was, under the circumstances, weird. I guess if you apply enough psychology to it, it would seem like that."

"It seems like that to me, Calder."

"I swear to you that if the Fairground shooting had never happened, and if we'd met at some other time and place, nothing weird about it, I would still have been blown away by you. I would have wanted you. You've gotta believe that, Elle."

"I find it hard to believe. You've just admitted that you lied in order to have sex with me."

"Not lied exactly."

"Then what? What would you call it, exactly?"

"Justifications that I made work to my advantage."

"So manipulation."

"Shit. You're not going to let me off this hook, are you?"

"No."

He laid his forearm across his forehead. When he lowered it, he said, "All I can tell you is that last night wasn't a sign-off. It did mean something, a lot of something, and made me want you even more."

"Why, Calder? What can I possibly bring to your table?"

"You. You bring you."

She gave a dry laugh. "Me and my cloud with long eyelashes and an insecure Mr. Sun who lives in fear of becoming a white dwarf? How would that fit in with your facts and figures and practicality?"

He lowered his face closer to hers. "We fit hand in glove, Elle. A very tight glove."

Although his words and tone caused an involuntary flutter low and deep inside, she angled her head back away from his. "That's manipulative."

"Sorry. But it's also true. Deny it, and you'll be the liar."

Frustrated by her own susceptibility to him, she said, "My fantasy fiction aside, I can be practical, too. I don't think you and I, as a couple, are meant to be."

He rested his head against the headboard and thought for a moment. "What if we were?"

"What?"

"What if our being a couple *was* meant to be? What if we had met in another place and time? Zing, bam, sparks fly. We were hot for each other. Couldn't keep our eyes and hands off each other. In addition to the fanfuckingtastic sex, we liked each other as companions. All systems were a go.

"Then out of nowhere tragedy struck. Someone close to one or both of us died, and our life together was turned upside down. Poof. Would you compound that loss by throwing *us* away?"

"Of course not." When she heard her own response, she began to backtrack. "It's not the same."

"It's the same except that we met after the tragedy, not before. That damn bullet is always going to be there, Elle. We can't change that. What we can do is decide the amount of control it has over the rest of our lives. I want you. If last night was any indication, you want me."

He stroked her cheek, low, near the ultra-sensitive corner of her lips. "A tragic circumstance brought us together. Will you let it be the one and only thing that keeps us apart?"

"That sounded prepared."

"It was," he said, smiling with chagrin. "It was going to be my summation. But that's what it boils down to, Elle."

She had to admit that it was a strong argument, but she resented how easily he'd snared her. "I'll have to give it some serious thought."

"That's fair."

"There's a *lot* to think about."

"I realize that. I've thought about it for two months. You've had two days."

"So I'll need time."

"Granted."

"And I won't be rushed."

"No pressure."

"When I compare my lifestyle with yours—"

"We'll create *our* lifestyle."

"I'm afraid."

"Of what?"

"Another irreparable heartbreak."

"I understand why you would be, but you don't have to be."

"The timing of this is the worst possible."

"It is, yes."

"What if—"

"Elle," he interrupted quietly. "A free piece of advice. When the other party is saying yes to everything, stop negotiating." He palmed her jaw and aligned his lips with hers. "Otherwise, the other party might detect a weakening of your position."

Then he was kissing her, his tongue sleek and searching, and she was lost and she knew it. Paradoxically, she reveled in her misguidedness.

One intoxicating kiss evolved into another without any separation of their mouths. With a hand on the small of her back, he pulled her more securely against him and wedged his knee between her thighs. She slid her hand past his rib cage and down the yummy trail.

Then, with a start, she yanked her hand back. "Where's your underwear?"

"On the floor, I think," he mumbled as he sought her mouth again.

"This whole time, you haven't been wearing underwear?"

"It's been pure hell." He reached beneath the covers, found her hand, and molded it around his penis. "Till now."

They stroked together; then he withdrew his hand and gave her free will. When she whispered, "I want to see," he bicycled his legs to push off the covers.

Lord, he was gorgeous. Each muscle was long and toned, skin tightly stretched over his lean frame, a perfect dusting of body hair that changed texture and narrowed into the satiny stripe that bisected his lower torso and pointed toward his sex. Not that it needed anything to call attention to it.

It was hot-blooded and hungry. A bead of semen clung to its straining tip. She swiped it onto the pad of her thumb, lifted it to her mouth, sucked it off.

Calder watched with eyes that grew dark and intense. He growled, "I think you're writing the wrong kind of books."

After she suggestively pulled her thumb from her mouth, he sealed it with another passionate kiss. Then, breathing hard, he said, "I want to see, too," and began unbuttoning the pajama top. It was so large for her, it was easy to shrug off and leave crumpled beneath her.

Eyes fixed on her breasts, he started on the pajama bottoms. The loose elastic band made it easy for him to work them over her hips and down her legs. He whipped them off, and they went sailing.

Then, becoming unrushed, his hand lightly and slowly skimmed her leg up from her knee all the way to the top of her thigh. He rested his warm palm on her mound.

Just that, no more, before continuing the path upward. He drew a lazy circle around her navel with the minuscule hole on the rim of it. His eyes met hers with an unspoken question.

"A girls' weekend trip to New Orleans got a little wild. At the time, it seemed like a good idea."

"It was a good idea," he said, giving her a wicked smile. "It was a fabulous idea. I love the idea. What was it?"

"A diamond stud. Well, zirconium."

"You still have it?"

"I had to take it out when I got pregnant."

"Hmm."

He touched the tiny hole with the tip of his tongue, then continued his exploration. His hand moved up to her breast, which he cupped and lifted as he bent his head and claimed it with his mouth. He drew it in deep and tugged strongly. His tongue was deft against her nipple, by turns flirty and then fervent.

Elle's back arched in an appeal for more. His fingers had readied her other breast, and while applying the same sensual treatment, he slid his hand down the center of her body to the vee of her thighs. Again, he rested his hand there, his palm radiating heat as he lightly ground it against her.

When his fingers tapered to slide into her cleft, she sighed and parted her legs. He lifted his head from her breast and turned to watch as he slipped his fingers into her. He monitored each stroke as though wanting to get it just right and make the most of each caress.

Sometimes his fingertips tarried just at the entrance, moving only slightly, leaving her in breathless anticipation. Sometimes they withdrew completely and waited for an imploring whimper from her before penetrating again.

She became tightly wound by pleasurable sensations and began to rock her hips against the heel of his hand. He brought his gaze back to her face, giving her a lusty look as his fingers continued to caress from the inside while his thumb played over and around the spot that most craved his touch.

"I'm gonna kiss you here," he whispered in a darkly seductive voice. His thumb pressed and spiraled, and her body jerked with the onset of an orgasm that she fought to withhold. "But not until I have a lot of time. Which isn't now."

He pulled his hand away, settled himself between her thighs, and groaned her name as he pushed into her in one purposeful glide. He filled her but continued to lean in until they were completely grafted. She contracted around him, and he hissed.

"Please don't move yet, Elle. If you do, I'll come, and I don't want to come until I've fucked you, and I don't want to fuck you until I've said this."

Forearms supporting him, he held her head between his hands. His breath was hot against her face, his eyes glassy with arousal. She could feel his heartbeat against her breasts as well as deep within her.

"I want you. Don't doubt that. Maybe, in some small part, it does have to do with this." He tipped his head toward the scars on his left arm. "But even if it does, does it matter? It brought us together. From the moment I looked up and saw you, looked into your eyes, I recognized you. Innately. I knew you immediately, knew that I had to be with you. Like this."

To illustrate his point, he flexed his hips. She reacted with a corresponding move. He groaned, "Aw, Jesus. I asked you not to move."

Before it became too late for both of them, he levered himself up and began to thrust.

Chapter 29

Glenda woke up to a ringing sound. She automatically reached for her cell phone before realizing that her doorbell was chiming. She checked the time on her phone. It was a little before six a.m.

Immediately thinking of Elle, she got out of bed and pulled on a robe as she hurriedly went through her house toward the front door. When she reached it, she looked through the panel of glass flanking it.

Looking back at her were Compton and Perkins. Perkins stared, unblinking and expressionless. Compton looked the worse for wear. Her big hair had deflated, and dead leaves were stuck to the mud that caked her sensible shoes.

She said, "Let us in, please, Ms. Foster. We need to talk to you."

"If it has to do with Elle and last night's debacle, I already know. I saw it on the news hours ago. Your incompetence knows no bounds, does it? I can only hope and pray that Elle is safe. If she is, it's no thanks to you and that bunch of East Texas hayseeds you put in charge of guarding her. Although I am deeply sorry that two of them were killed. And that young woman's husband, of course. Do you think the same person is responsible?"

"The investigations are still too fresh to draw conclusions."

Asking for more information would be pointless. Compton deflected, and Perkins was a brick wall. But there was only one explanation for their being on her doorstep.

She gave the knot of her robe's belt an emphatic yank. "If you came here expecting to find Elle, you've wasted a trip."

Perkins finally spoke up. "You were away from your house last night."

She glared at him through the glass panel. "With tragedies unfolding one right after another, you had nothing better to do than put surveillance on my house?"

As unflappable as a statue, he said, "You weren't seen leaving, but you returned at two-thirty-four a.m."

"I'm impressed, Detective. Even I couldn't have told you what time I got home."

"Where were you, Ms. Foster?"

"None of your damn business." Then, thinking about the honey/vinegar adage, she said, "But if you must know, I was out late at a friend's house. Not Elle. Another friend. A male friend." She arched her eyebrow, implying *Get it?*

"I didn't learn about the shit show at that safe house of yours until I got home and turned on the TV. I immediately started calling Elle's phone and continued calling for over an hour. She hasn't picked up or called back, leading me to believe that she doesn't want to be found just yet, and who could blame her?"

The two on her porch remained unmoved. Compton repeated, "Let us in."

"And have you stomping through my house in muddy shoes for nothing? I don't think so. Watch my lips. Elle. Isn't. Here."

"If that's true—"

"It is."

"—then she could be in even greater danger," Compton said. "Is she with Calder Hudson?"

Glenda's breath was momentarily arrested, but she tried not to give that away. "That's what you said in your interview on TV. So you tell me. Is she? Did they escape together, or was that supposition on your part?"

"How much do you know about him, Ms. Foster?"

"I know his girlfriend has a big mouth. If not for Shauna Calloway, Elle wouldn't be in danger of her life."

Compton exchanged a glance with Perkins before coming back to her. "We're as worried about Elle's safety as you are, especially in light of Mr. Whitley's death, which appears to have been a homicide."

Glenda thought that over. "Between him and Elle, the common denominator is the Fairground shooting."

"It hasn't been established yet that these two crimes are related, but even a tangential connection seems likely." She let that sink in, then said, "I ask again, is your friend with Calder Hudson?"

Glenda looked at them in turn. "Is all this about

him?" Neither responded, only maintained their infuriating passivity.

Decision made, Glenda disengaged the alarm, unbolted the door, and opened it. "I'll make coffee."

———◆———

Calder eased himself away from his spooned position with Elle, trying not to wake her. Also trying not to be tempted to wake her. God knew she needed the sleep.

Their trek through the woods had been a mere warm-up for their sexual exertions. In between bouts of ardent coupling, they'd rested while lazily exploring each other. They kissed endlessly.

That cycle of lovemaking had continued until their bodies had demanded a time-out. Heavy eyelids and languid limbs ultimately betrayed them. They'd fallen sleep.

But now, just by watching her in a deep slumber, he became aroused. His body was reawakened to how much pleasure it had derived from hers. What a delightful surprise to discover that her wholesome aspect concealed an incredibly carnal lover.

Every inch of her was sensitive to the touch of his fingertips, lips, tongue. He'd been ravenous. She'd been inviting and generous, responding without inhibition even when, after minutes of nuzzling between her thighs, he'd made good on his promise to kiss her on that most delicate spot when he had the time. He'd taken a lot of time.

Shauna prided herself on being a hot number in the sack.

She didn't come close to Elle's secret smolder. Her full lower lip only got plumper when kissed, sucked, bitten. Her unusually colored eyes became downright sultry during foreplay. He now knew that her laugh didn't only sound sexy. It had a cello-string vibration that he wanted to bottle, so he could apply it, as she had, to his beseeching cock.

With a muffled groan of self-denial, he got up and slipped into the bathroom. Making as little noise as possible, he showered and dressed, then, in stocking feet, left the suite for the kitchen.

The cabinetry included a desk nook furnished with a laptop, which he booted up using the password on Glenda's chart. After making coffee, he sat down at the desk and began his search for Arnold Draper.

Assuming that Compton had unearthed that name from his own work files, he accessed them from the cloud, ran a search, and found Draper, Arnold M. (Milton) in a client's file from four years ago.

Out of hundreds, Calder never would have remembered the name or the man. He never would have met him. He never would have wanted to know him.

But did Arnold Draper know *him*?

What other reason would the detectives have had for flagging Draper out of so many? Or had they picked that name at random to use as a ploy, to give him a vengeful enemy to worry about after he'd defied their authority and left the crime scene at the safe house?

Almost as soon as that possibility crossed his mind, he dismissed it. Playing mind games seemed unprofessional and out of character with the two investigators who were committed to capturing the Fairground shooter, even more so now after last night's deadly occurrences.

It was their sworn duty to capture the guy. Calder's commitment to catching him was more personal but no less unshakable. If Compton and Perkins thought that this Arnold Draper was a lead, then he wanted to follow it himself, if only to disprove their speculation that Draper was someone seeking retaliation against him.

He desperately wanted to prove them wrong. It didn't bear thinking about that the shooting had been an act of retribution against him.

He felt a pang of guilt for not sharing this with Elle. If something enlightening turned up, he would let her know about Draper immediately. But if this exploration led nowhere, why cause her additional worry?

Within the file where he'd found Draper's name, he knew there would be paperwork pertaining to him. In a few keystrokes, he'd accessed the man's profile.

Four years ago, Draper had been living in Des Moines, Iowa. Marital status, married. Religious preference, none. Level of education, two years of community college but no degree. According to his date of birth, he would now be sixty-eight years old.

Sixty-eight? Could an average sixty-eight-year-old who was even moderately fit have been running so full-out that he'd nearly upset Charlie's sizable, bottom-heavy stroller? There were men in that general age group who ran marathons and climbed mountains, but that degree of fitness was atypical.

A gray ponytail would coincide with a man that age,

but the relevant one was fake. The man in the baseball cap could have had red hair, or ebony-black hair, or no hair.

"Dammit." Frustrated, Calder leaned back in his chair and stared into the monitor, thinking.

Something about this Draper had stood out to Compton and Perkins, which had caused them to mention his name, and not in passing, but at the height of a crisis situation. But what was that *something?*

He went through the entire file he had compiled for that particular contract. He studied it page by page, scanning notes he'd made, emails he'd sent and received. He drew no direct connection between him and Draper.

"Maybe Compton and Perkins are blowing smoke," he said under his breath.

He got out of his own files and went to an online person-finder. He narrowed down the various fields by city, state, and age group. No Arnold Milton Draper was presently living in Des Moines. Or in the whole state of Iowa.

There was, however, a link to other states where Draper, at some point in his life, had resided.

Calder's heart picked up speed. *Leave it alone. Leave. It. Alone.*

But of course he didn't. He couldn't. He clicked on the link.

Texas.

Chapter 30

—◦◉◦—

To Calder's supreme frustration, he couldn't go to the next level of information on Draper without having to pay for the service. Cursing, he clicked on the icon for one of the online payment options. When it opened, he typed in his user name and password.

No soap. Since he was using an unrecognized device, he was being sent a temporary security code by text. *Shit!* He would have to turn on his phone. The alternative was to use a credit card, but as Glenda had noted last night, credit card usage would be the first thing Compton and Perkins would look for.

He didn't want the detectives to know that he was running a search for the name they'd dropped. They would interpret that to mean that Arnold Draper was a valid concern.

Although, if he was being honest with himself, he was concerned. He was afraid that Compton and Perkins were already privy to something terrible, that they had uncovered a link between him and the Fairground shooting.

The thought of that made him queasy, but if proof of a connection was going to be sprung on him, he needed to know what he was up against and be somewhat prepared.

He went into the utility room where his jacket was still drying and got his cell phone out of a pocket. Back in the kitchen, he'd almost reached the desk nook when a shrill sound froze him in his tracks.

It was a rude awakening, to say the least.

Elle sat bolt upright. The landline extension on the nightstand had an uncommonly loud and obnoxious ring. She grabbed it before her eardrums burst. "Hello?"

"Thank God it's you who answered," Glenda said. "Are you all right?"

"I'm fine. If I don't sound fine, it's because you woke me up. What's your excuse? You sound out of breath."

"Are you in your bedroom?"

"Uh…"

"Is he with you?"

"He has a name, Glenda. It's Calder." She looked at the empty side of the bed. "And no, he's not with me."

Either she didn't catch Elle's testiness, or she ignored it. "Where is he?"

"I suppose in the kitchen. I smell coffee. What's the matter?"

"There's been a development."

Based on her friend's apparent anxiety, Elle braced herself for bad news. "Have they found out where we are?"

"No. Well, sort of."

"Glenda, *what*? You're scaring me."

"Just sit tight. We'll explain when we get there."

"We?"

"Compton and Perkins."

If she had said Beavis and Butt-Head, Elle couldn't have been more shocked. Or more disconcerted. "Why are you with them? What's happened?"

"We're on our way. ETA ten minutes. In the meantime, play it cool with him, okay?"

"With Calder?"

"Play it cool, *okay*?"

"Okay." The instant Glenda hung up, Elle said, "Not okay."

She threw back the covers and clambered out of bed. She didn't bother to locate the pajamas last seen being flung by Calder over the side of the bed. Instead, she grabbed the spa robe that he'd been wearing and pulled it on as she rushed from the room.

When she entered the kitchen, she noticed two sounds at once: the beep a telephone makes when it's been left off the hook and the revving of a car engine.

After confirming that Calder had left without notice, Elle took a hasty shower and dressed so she would be at least presentable—and not smell of sex—when Glenda and the two detectives arrived.

Now, from where she sat on a bar stool at the kitchen island, she heard the front door being unlocked and footsteps scurrying inside. "In here," she called. The trio hurried into the kitchen and took a look around. Coming up empty, they all focused on Elle.

"He's not here," she said. "He's gone."

Compton muttered a curse word. Perkins, who was perennially expressionless, looked thoroughly irked. Glenda was the first to recover her voice. "*Gone?*"

Their consternation over his disappearance couldn't compare to what Elle was experiencing, which could only be described as shell shock, along with crushing heartache.

She kept her expression and tone of voice as matter-of-fact as possible. "As soon as I hung up from Glenda, I came in here to the kitchen. There was that," she said, indicating the cordless extension lying on the countertop, "and I heard the car starting up in the garage. By the time I reached it, he was gone."

"He stole the car!" Glenda exclaimed.

"Calder wouldn't *steal* the car. He's just using it. Which you invited him to do."

"I didn't invite him to use it to run from the law." With asperity, she asked, "Why are you defending him?"

"Why are you being so quick to judge?"

"For crying out loud. Isn't it obvious that he was listening in on the phone and overheard that we were on our way here? He cleared out. Pure and simple."

"I'm afraid it's neither pure nor simple," Perkins said.

Speaking directly to Elle, he said, "Much more serious than this morning's vanishing act is last night's. After tampering with and lifting evidence, he left the scene of a double homicide, and so did you. The deputies' service revolvers are missing. Did you take them?"

Elle nodded dumbly.

"Where are they?"

"One in each bedroom. Calder insisted I keep one handy."

"Are they loaded?"

Realizing that the gravity of her situation extended beyond Calder's skipping out on her again, Elle gave another nod.

Perkins turned to Glenda. "Do you know the car's make, model, and license number?"

She produced the information sheet from its drawer and handed it over. "Call the guy at the bottom of the page. He'll know all that."

Perkins said to Compton, "I'll put out an APB." He moved to the far side of the room and got on his phone.

Elle felt as if the ground were shifting beneath her and that at any moment she might plunge into a fathomless sinkhole. She asked Compton, "Are you going to arrest me?"

"Are you going to cooperate?"

"If I can."

"Did you see Mr. Hudson this morning?"

She hesitated. They hadn't fallen asleep until dawn, so, technically she had seen him—all of him—this morning, but she shook her head. "Glenda's call woke me up. I guess Calder picked up the kitchen extension at the same time and overheard what she told me. It does appear that he then left in a hurry. He took the laptop."

She indicated the desk nook where a half-full cup of coffee had been abandoned. "Before you got here, I checked the utility room. His jacket is gone, and so are his boots." Her voice went thready on the last few words.

"When did you last see him?" Compton asked.

Again she sidestepped. "After Glenda left us last night—"

"Which I regret. I should have known better. I had a gut feeling all along about—"

Compton held up her hand to shush Glenda. "Go on, Elle."

"We went to our separate rooms. I was keyed up, couldn't sleep. Actually, I was a bit afraid."

"Of Hudson?"

Elle looked at the detective with dismay. "What an unfounded and appalling question. Why would you even ask such a thing? I can't explain Calder's behavior this morning, but last night he risked his own life in order to protect mine and was deeply disturbed because he couldn't protect Dawn.

"I wasn't afraid of him. I was frightened because the suspect you've failed even to identify is still out there," she said, making a broad sweep with her hand, "and is bent on killing us. I was under the same roof with two men who were gunned down. Don't you think my fear was justified, at least a tad?"

Compton looked chagrined but didn't apologize. "Please go on."

Elle had to think back to where she'd left off. "Unable to

sleep, I turned on the television and saw all the news coverage. I went to Calder's room, woke him up, and told him about Mr. Whitley. We were both disbelieving. How is Dawn?"

"Not good. You know she was transported to a hospital here." Elle nodded. "Perkins and I went to see her as soon as we got back to Dallas from the safe house. By that time, a police chaplain had already told her about her husband. She was devastated, barely coherent, but it was crucial that we question her about what went down at the safe house."

"And?"

"She pretty much confirmed what Calder had told me over the phone, although she didn't know that Weeks had been killed. She witnessed Sims being fatally shot. That's when she tried to escape."

"Did she see the shooter, the car, anything?"

"No. It was dark as pitch outside. She was running blind and didn't see the pole. It knocked her senseless. She's got a concussion and cuts on her feet. None that serious."

Elle asked, "Had she told Frank where she was?"

Compton looked rueful. "We didn't even have to ask before she broke down and confessed. She blames herself for the murders."

"If she'd been at home, she would have been killed along with her husband."

"We emphasized that, but..." Compton sighed. "They're keeping her in the hospital for at least another day. Her mother is with her, and we posted a guard outside the door of her room.

"We've also doubled the guards on Mr. Cooper and Mrs. Martin. So far there haven't been any more death threats, unless you or Calder have received one we don't know about."

Elle shook her head, but Compton was searching her eyes for a telltale sign of lying. "We shut our phones down."

"Yes, I realize," the detective said. "Why did Calder take the pistols off the deputies?"

"He saw their bloody bodies. He assumed that Dawn had met the same fate. We didn't know if the shooter had given up on us or if he was right behind us. So take a wild guess as to why Calder took the pistols."

Compton caught her snideness. "You've lost faith in us. I get that. But we're very much aware that all five of you are still vulnerable. Let us do our job, Elle. You came out okay this time, but taking matters into your own hands was foolhardy."

"It didn't seem so at the time."

"Don't do it again."

"I understand."

"Does he?"

She was saved from having to answer as Perkins rejoined them. "APB is in the works. He can't have gone far. His head start was only about ten minutes."

Glenda had been standing by, following the lengthy conversation with obvious impatience. She said now, "When are you going to tell her?"

"Tell me what?" Elle asked.

"Mr. Hudson—"

Glenda cut Compton off. "You can attribute the Fairground shooting to Calder Hudson. Everyone who was killed or injured that day, those deputies last night, the Whitley man, our sweet Charlie..." Her voice cracked. "They're all dead because of him."

Chapter 31

Calder was new to evading capture, but even the most inept fugitive from justice knew that flight was priority number one.

Glenda had told Elle that she and the detectives would be at the house within ten minutes. They would discover him gone, question Elle, and then immediately initiate a broad-stroke search that would have every cop within a fifty-mile radius on the lookout for the SUV he was driving. Its convoluted ownership notwithstanding, it wouldn't take long to locate. By then he needed to be away from it, so every second counted.

Of course, that plan would leave him afoot. Then what? Fuck if he knew. He might have had years of experience maneuvering, as Elle had called his tactic, but he was playing this by ear.

From the freeway, he spied one of those mammoth gas stations that took up a lot of real estate along the access road. In addition to having one hundred fuel pumps, it boasted no-wait restrooms, an acre of shopping opportunities, a liquor store, and numerous eateries. Every variety of car and truck came and went around the clock. With any luck, all that vehicular activity would provide camouflage.

Calder took the exit and navigated the crowded parking lot, yielding to pedestrians and dodging drivers competing for parking spaces. He found a space between a bus-sized RV and a dually pickup. To anyone else, it was undesirable, but it served his purpose of hiding something in plain sight.

Working quickly, he transferred everything from the pockets of his leather jacket into the pockets of his jeans, then folded the jacket and stuffed it beneath the passenger seat. It was pricey. Anyone wearing it would be more easily noticed and remembered than a guy in a wrinkled white shirt. He left the key fob under the floor mat.

With the laptop he'd borrowed from the house tucked under his arm, he walked along the access road to the next nearest commercial complex, which included more modest gas stations, several restaurants, and a chain hotel. He picked the hotel.

When he entered, trying to look like a registered guest with a right to be there, the young woman at the check-in desk didn't even glance up from her computer monitor.

The lobby expanded into a multistory atrium. The bar and café were presently closed. No one was in there except for a custodian pushing an electric buffer across the floor.

Off to one side of the spacious area was a room designed

to serve as a temporary office for guests. He chose the work-space nearest the window, so he'd have a view of the front parking lot.

He turned on his phone and the laptop. While waiting for them to boot up, he took a moment to catch his breath. He'd been in a state of high anxiety ever since the blare of that damn phone in the kitchen had almost given him a heart attack. He'd reached it just as it had stopped ringing, but he'd clicked it on to see if Elle had answered.

When he heard Glenda's breathless, panicked voice, he'd figured she was calling to tell them that their hiding place had been discovered and to get the hell out. In preparation for having to make a quick getaway, he'd rushed toward the bedroom to hustle Elle along.

But then Glenda had asked her if *he* was around. Whatever he'd been about to contribute to the conversation died on his lips. The call pertained to *him*, not impending arrest.

Furiously but silently, he'd listened as Glenda issued Elle what sounded like a warning. She was coming to Elle's rescue, and she was bringing Compton and Perkins with her.

He'd had a split second to make a decision, and it was a dilly.

If he'd stayed, he would have been corralled, which meant he would have been of no use either to Elle or to himself.

But skipping out came with serious consequences. To the detectives it would appear that he was avoiding arrest for leaving the scene of the crime at the safe house. Elle—God, Elle—would think him the lousiest son of a bitch in the world for deserting her again. This after the night, the passion, they'd shared.

But damn it, he'd had to go, and go right then, without taking time to explain. Otherwise, he couldn't have continued his sleuthing into Arnold Draper. He would have been unable to determine what that name had implied to the pair of detectives.

He could only hope that all of them, especially Elle, would understand his purpose for leaving and ultimately forgive him for it.

All that had flashed through his mind as he'd backtracked into the utility room to grab his jacket and boots. Those in hand, he'd returned to the kitchen only long enough to pull on his boots, disconnect the laptop from its power source, and set the phone extension on the counter…but not before hearing Elle's "Okay," when Glenda had admonished her to play it cool with him.

Just like that, based on her unfaithful friend's obscure hint that *he* wasn't to be trusted, Elle had agreed. He hadn't had time to explain. Therefore, to her, it would look like a repeat of what had happened before and that all the reservations over their relationship that she had itemized last night were proving to be warranted.

That disheartening thought was now interrupted when his phone lit up and signaled that he'd received the promised text with a temporary pass code. On the laptop, he reentered the people-finder website and typed in the temporary code, which enabled him to pay the necessary fee to continue.

With a click, another page of information on Arnold Draper opened. No arrests or police record. No DUIs. He'd never declared bankruptcy. He wasn't in hock to anyone. The guy appeared to be your average law-abiding citizen.

There was a list of possible relatives. None of the names on it were familiar to Calder. Draper had lived at two addresses in Dallas. He'd been at the most recent one for the past two years. There was a telephone number, but Calder was hesitant to use his phone unless absolutely necessary. Besides, he wanted to get a feel for Draper before Draper became aware that he was being felt out.

But Calder needed transportation and only hoped that if a manhunt for him was already under way, he was still ahead of it. He had to take the chance of hiring a car.

When he and Shauna had started living together, he'd created a dummy business for the purpose of obtaining a credit card that she didn't know about. He'd rarely used it, but he'd had the foresight to open a separate Uber account with it.

He used it now to summon a car and spent five anxious minutes waiting on it. As soon as he saw the car pulling into the parking lot of the hotel, he strolled through the lobby, past the inattentive young woman at the desk, and out the revolving door.

As he climbed into the back seat of the gray sedan, he and the driver exchanged cursory greetings and verified the destination address. Then they were off.

Fortunately, the driver appeared uninterested in his passenger. They made the twenty-minute trip in silence. But Calder knew he would be remembered later for challenging the driver as he pulled into a semicircular driveway and brought the car to a stop in front of a redbrick building. The architecture was Colonial. White fluted columns flanked a large front door. Above it was a sign with black cursive lettering.

"Excuse me," he said, "are you sure this is right?"

The driver pointed to the GPS screen on his dashboard, nodding vigorously and repeating in heavily accented English, "Yes, yes."

"All right, thanks." Calder got out, not knowing what to think or what to expect. It was with mixed emotions that he started up the shallow set of steps to the entrance.

Elle had been startled speechless by Glenda's implicating declaration about Calder.

Before she had recovered enough voice to ask what she could possibly mean, Compton had given Glenda a stern look and said, "We'll get to that." And had stressed, "In time. Now, where would be a convenient place for us to talk with Elle alone?"

Glenda had led them into a media room from which she'd been promptly ejected.

For the past hour, Compton and Perkins had been putting Elle through the drill that had become all too familiar. They'd pressed her for information on what had happened at the safe house. What had she seen, what had she heard, why had she left the scene when it was obvious that the crisis was over?

"It wasn't at all obvious."

Perkins asked her about the weapons Calder had taken, and she repeated to him what she'd already told Compton.

When she finished, Perkins said, "You believed Calder Hudson better capable of protecting you than we were."

"He was. When Glenda arrived to pick us up, we were cold and rain-soaked but alive."

"Ms. Foster corroborated that," Compton said. "She told us that you looked 'ragged' but were otherwise okay."

"Then explain to me why a shadow of suspicion has been cast over Calder. What basis did Glenda have for blaming the Fairground shooting on him? The suggestion had to have come from you. Which dumbfounds me. It's as preposterous as your asking me earlier if I was afraid of him."

Perkins spoke up, asking quietly, "If it's that preposterous, why isn't he here, Ms. Portman? Why did he leave without a word?"

Elle's throat grew tight. She shot up from her chair. "I need to take a bathroom break. Excuse me." Before they could object, she left the room in a rush, bumping into Glenda as she rounded a corner in the hallway.

"Elle?"

Elle brushed past her without stopping. "I need a few minutes."

She returned to the bedroom, shut the door behind her, and leaned against it. After having held herself together for more than an hour, the emotional logjam in her chest broke apart.

She clamped both hands over her mouth and screamed into them. Despite her determination not to cry over Calder, tears practically spurted from her eyes until they were streaming down both cheeks.

Damn him! *Why?* Why had he done this to her again? After all the tenderness and sweetness and passion they'd shared last night, how could he desert her again?

Elle, a better question would be why you continue to let him.

That question, which she had subconsciously asked herself, drew her up short. Yes, why *was* she? The more she thought about her susceptibility, the angrier she became. Certainly at him, but she was even angrier at herself.

Her gullibility ended now. She should have heeded her initial caution, listened to the voice of reason. She should have listened to Glenda.

Nevertheless, she gave no credence to Calder's having anything to do with the shooting. Something was terribly wrong there. Regardless of how she felt personally, she would do what she could to rectify that misconception.

She went into the bathroom and washed her face with cold water, then walked back through the bedroom, a little better prepared to face the music.

As she approached the bedroom door, there was a soft tap on it. "I'm coming." She opened the door expecting Glenda but finding Compton.

"We retrieved the pistol in the other suite from the nightstand drawer where you'd left it. I came for the other one."

"Oh, it's on the——" She turned to indicate the table at the side of the bed on which Calder had slept. The pistol wasn't there.

When she and Compton returned to the media room, Glenda was setting a bowl of fresh fruit and a plate of brownies on the counter of the wet bar. Perkins was wrapping up a call on his phone. "Okay, thanks." He clicked off. "They found the vehicle."

He told them where. "Key fob was in it, so obviously he had no intention of stealing it," he said, addressing that to Glenda. "A leather jacket with a monogram of his initials on the lining was found under the seat. No sign of him. Did you get the pistol?"

Compton glanced at Elle. "It wasn't where Elle last saw it. We searched the bedroom and bathroom." She shook her head.

Perkins's only reaction was to slide his hands into his pants pockets. "Nothing else to report?" Compton asked.

"They're canvassing, but there could have been a hundred or more folks on and off that parking lot since he was there."

"What about security cameras?"

"They show the vehicle being driven in and him leaving it. Last seen, he was walking north along the access road, but then he disappeared from their scope. They're going to start canvassing other businesses in that direction."

"Or maybe he hitchhiked from there," Glenda said. "Bummed a ride from a long-haul trucker. He could be in Oklahoma by now."

Perkins took Glenda's droll comments seriously. "Could be." Back to Compton, he said, "Guys in the office are checking for credit card use, ATMs. We'll run him down."

"In the meantime, what's he up to?" Glenda asked.

Three inquisitive pairs of eyes focused on Elle, who'd been following the conversation without contributing to it. "I have no idea," she said.

"He didn't say anything to you last night about what he planned to do in light of the safe house incident?" Compton asked.

"No. I asked him what he thought tomorrow—today—would bring. He said there would be fallout over the deputies being killed, but if he had a personal agenda, he didn't share it."

"Am I interrupting?"

The four of them turned toward the doorway. There stood Calder.

Chapter 32

At first they were all too stunned to speak; then everyone began talking at once. Except for Elle. Regardless of what she'd resolved after her crying jag only minutes earlier, at the sight of Calder, her heart swelled with relief, not angst.

His eyes connected with hers and held, while Perkins watched him through calculating eyes, Glenda muttered scornful remarks about car theft, and Compton fired a volley of pertinent questions.

He finally looked away from Elle, disregarded Glenda, and addressed the two detectives. "Arnold Draper isn't your guy."

"How do you know?" Compton asked.

Calder, as though riled by the question, got right in her face. "Why did you drop his name to me last night?"

"You mean as you were fleeing the scene of a double homicide?"

"She dropped his name because I asked her to," Perkins said.

"*Why?*"

"At the time, to bait you, to gauge how you would react."

"I figured that out for myself," Calder sneered. "So all of this was a fucking hoax?"

In a voice loud enough to override the other three, Elle said, "*Who is Arnold Draper?*" With anger and accusation, she gave each of them in turn a hard look, landing on Calder. "Obviously this is important, so why didn't you tell me about it last night?"

"Because I didn't know anything last night."

Going back to the detectives, she said, "If this concerns the murder of my son, I deserve to know what you're talking about. Who is this person Draper?"

"He's a patient in a memory care facility." Calder's calm and unarguable tone stifled the detectives. "I was just there. That man didn't shoot anybody."

"You expect them to take your word for this?" Glenda said. "You're a private eye now?"

Elle whispered, "Glenda, please."

Calder turned to face her. "You don't like me, and that doesn't bother me in the least. I don't care for you, either. But we've got a shitload of stuff to talk about here that concerns Elle, who you do care about. So unless you can contribute something enlightening or useful, please either shut up or go away entirely."

"This is *my* house, remember."

"And I've thanked you repeatedly for the use of it. You went above and beyond for us last night. I don't know what's behind your snarky wisecracks, but they aren't helpful, not to anybody, but especially not to Elle."

Ever the diplomat, Compton said, "We do need to ask your forbearance, Ms. Foster. Thank you for the snacks and for the use of this room."

Glenda saw the detective's intervention as the dismissal it was. She huffed. "Make yourselves at home. Enjoy the brownies."

After she left, Perkins waited a beat, then said, "I need to call off the APB."

Calder said, "Her SUV—"

"It's been found."

"Intact?"

"So I'm told."

"I left a jacket—"

"Officers retrieved it. You'll get it back."

"Thanks."

"Give me the pistol." Perkins extended his hand.

Calder hesitated, then raised his shirttail and pulled the revolver from his waistband at the small of his back. He handed it to Perkins, who said nothing but stepped away to use his phone to call off the search for Calder.

Compton said, "Let's sit."

Elle took a chair. She was glad Calder had returned of his own volition, but she wasn't yet ready to share a sofa, or anything else, with him.

Compton began by asking where he'd gone after parking the SUV.

"I walked to a nearby hotel. I needed time on the computer. By the way, I put the laptop back in its place in the kitchen on my way in. Glenda can't accuse me of stealing it."

Perkins rejoined them, sat down on the arm of the sofa, and said to Calder, "You beat them by four minutes."

"What? Who?"

"The deputies we dispatched to check out Arnold Draper, formerly of Des Moines, now a resident of Dallas."

"We put in time on the computer, too," Compton said to Calder.

"I figured you would," he said. "I wanted to get to Draper before you got to me. That's why I was in such a hurry and left without notice this morning." He gave Elle a meaningful look before going back to Perkins. "Did the deputies you sent see him?"

"No, but they talked to the administrator of the center, asked about Draper's level of cognition, and when told, dismissed him as a suspect. They were also told that, other than his wife, Draper hasn't had a visitor since his admittance two years ago. What a coincidence that the deputies showed up asking about Draper within minutes of his nephew doing the same."

Compton harrumphed. "Nephew?"

Calder said, "I talked my way in. An attendant showed me to the rec room and pointed out Draper to me."

"What did you say to him? How did you introduce yourself?"

"I didn't. He and his wife were sitting together on a couch. She was clipping his fingernails and chatting away, as though he was taking it all in."

He shook his head sadly. "Intruding would have served no purpose, would it? They never knew I was there. Thank God. I called for a car to bring me back here."

Elle said, "I'm still in the dark. Why were all of you interested in this man?"

"As it turns out, they weren't," Calder said. "They picked his name at random to mind-fuck me, and it worked."

"Actually, I didn't pick it at random," Perkins said. "Last night, while Compton and I were going through your files, I—"

"Excuse me," Calder said. "I'm in no position to ask a favor, but before we go any further, could I have a few minutes alone with Elle?"

The request startled her. "Why?"

"Because I would like for you to hear all of this from me."

"All of what?"

He looked at the detectives. "Please?"

Compton shook her head. "Sorry. We've cut you a lot of slack, but we can't allow material witnesses to compare notes during an active investigation."

"Give me a break," Calder said. "You know it's too late for that. Besides, your investigation isn't what I want to talk to Elle about. I promise not to run off."

The two consulted each other with one of their now familiar unspoken exchanges, then both stood. Compton said, "Five minutes."

Calder watched them go, waited for the door to close behind them, then turned to Elle. Before he could say anything, she asked, "Hear all of what from you?"

"Elle, I'm sorry about this morning."

She steeled herself and repeated succinctly, "Hear all of what from you? If it's sweet nothings, I don't want to hear them."

"Elle." Eyes full of regret, he silently appealed to her. When she didn't bend, he sighed. "Understood." He let a few seconds elapse before continuing. "Remember yesterday, that private conversation upstairs with them?" He tilted his head toward the door.

"It wasn't about your breakup with Shauna?"

"It was, but there was also something else."

"Sounds serious."

"I believe you'll think so. Which is why I've avoided talking about it with you."

He got up and, looking down at the floor, paced a circle. He then walked over to the built-in bar where Glenda had left the refreshments. So far they'd gone untouched. Calder picked out an orange from the bowl and bounced it in his palm.

"It's about what I do for a living." He dug his thumbnail into the orange and tore off a chunk of the rind. "I'm a corporate hit man." He pitched the piece of orange skin into the small sink, then looked over at her. "Do you know what that is?"

"I... I'm not sure."

"Well, follow closely." He tore off another piece of the orange peel and also pitched it. "Companies in financial straits hire me to come in and analyze their operation. Time management, productivity, assets and liabilities. The whole shebang. I ingratiate myself with the employees, become one with them so that they'll talk to me candidly about their bosses, coworkers, and the job in general.

"After several months, when I'm satisfied that I've been thorough, that my projections will save the company thousands, often millions, of dollars in salaries alone, I recommend which employees should be let go, because, in my expert opinion, they not only contribute little, but they're a drain on the budget. They're dispensable. Deadwood."

He turned and looked at her directly, as though to ensure that she was comprehending him, then resumed peeling the orange. "Those who get axed go home with a pink slip. I go home with a fat paycheck." Another piece of orange skin was tossed into the sink.

"For a generous base fee, I guarantee a certain reduction in the company's overhead. I never fail to reach that figure, and typically I exceed it by laying off more people than estimated. For each extra employee who's fired, I get paid a bonus."

By now the orange had been peeled. He held it out toward her, but when she shook her head, he set it in the sink, turned on the water, and washed his hands.

"How did you get into that line of work?"

"I had a consulting business. Time management, basically. It was successful enough. I didn't drive a Jag, but I could afford the best cable TV package. One day, I was interviewing a prospective client, giving him the full-court press, promising a big turnaround in productivity, and, in passing, he said, 'While you're at it, trim the fat.'

"I asked what he meant. He said he would pay me extra for every lost cause, for those he could cut loose. Based on my opinion alone." He shook water off his hands and turned to her, eyebrows raised. "I saw a much more lucrative angle to my consulting work and went at it like a hound on the scent of blood. Since, I've done a lot of bloodletting. I get a little sick thinking about how cavalier I was while demolishing lives."

She said, "You're being unfair to yourself."

Using a bar towel, he dried his hands but didn't say anything.

"Without your analyses and recommendations, wouldn't the company continue on a downward spiral?"

"More than likely."

"Until it ultimately collapsed?"

He raised a shoulder that indicated the probability of that.

"If it was forced to shut its doors, then every employee would be out of a job, and the domino effect would have a negative impact on the economy of the whole community. More failed businesses, more lost jobs."

Meticulously, he folded the towel and draped it over the edge of the sink. "I tell myself that at lot. But it's a self-serving rationalization." He propped his hips against the bar and folded his arms across his chest.

"The evening of the shooting, I was celebrating my most lucrative project to date. Why? Because a goodly number of people lost their livelihood that day. Can you appreciate the irony?

"I drove away from there feeling so goddamn cocky. Gloating. Thumping my chest. A self-congratulatory, invincible superhero who nothing or no one could touch." He snuffled. "An hour later, a bullet went through my arm."

She assimilated all that, then said quietly, "Before the shooting, had you ever experienced misgivings about what you do?"

"Nope. Not a twinge of conscience. Never."

He pushed away from the wet bar and sat down on an ottoman, facing her, but with distance between them. "In that upstairs room in the safe house, Compton planted the seed in my head that maybe one of my...victims...was out to get me."

"That's why you were so broody afterward."

"That was one reason. The other was because you wouldn't even look at me." He waved his hand. "Another conversation."

He reorganized his thoughts. "This morning, when I looked up the name that Perkins had dropped and learned that Arnold Draper had relocated from Iowa to Dallas just months after his severance, I got a sick feeling in the pit of my stomach. Maybe Compton's theory wasn't so off the wall. Maybe Draper had moved here because he'd learned my headquarters is here. He'd been lying in wait, waiting for an opportunity to strike. I had to check it out. I had to nix their speculation that I was the intended target that day."

"I see."

"Draper's situation is pathetic, Elle. Truly. Heartwrenching. But when I learned that he couldn't have engineered the shooting at the fairground, or last night's, I can't describe the relief I felt. Because if I had been his provocation, if something I'd done had caused you to lose Charlie, I could never forgive myself. Worse—ten thousand times worse—I knew you could never forgive me."

Their long stare was interrupted when Compton walked in.

"Time's up."

Chapter 33

Calder had no choice but to end the conversation there. He couldn't interpret Elle's expression or discern what she was thinking. That bothered him, but for now there was no help for it.

As soon as the detectives were seated, Calder said to Perkins, "You said you didn't pick Draper at random. Explain that."

Perkins yielded the floor to his partner, an indication that it was going to be a somewhat lengthy explanation. She began. "Last night we were going through your files, running down the lists of people who'd been let go on your recommendation."

"That covers a lot of years. How'd you know where to start? Or were you just shaking the trees to see what might fall?"

"Basically that. In desperation. But moments before you

called and told us what was happening at the safe house, the name Arnold Draper grabbed Perkins's attention."

"Why?" Calder asked.

"At first I couldn't remember," Perkins said. "Then we had to drop everything and race to the safe house. It wasn't until later, while we were on our way back, that it came to me where I'd seen that name. Maxwell Supply."

"Supplier of what?" Elle asked.

"They manufacture steel pipe," Calder told her. "Generational family business. A few years ago, some disgruntled employees started a movement to go union. They made converts and began causing disruptions in production, which resulted in delayed deliveries and pissed-off customers. It got increasingly ugly.

"I didn't have a stance either way, but I was brought in by the owners, a pair of brothers, to try to quell the movement, smooth things over with the agitators, negotiate on some of their demands. If that didn't work, I was to weed out anyone pro-union or even anyone leaning toward it."

"How'd that go over?" Compton asked.

"I was subjected to sneers and jeers. A dead rat was left on the welcome mat of my hotel room. My car got keyed. Nothing violent, but that's why I now have the nondisclosure clause in my contract and why I use an assumed name when on a job. No one knows what I'm there for, and everyone thinks I'm just another guy who got fired along with the rest of them and has moved on."

He tried to gauge Elle's reaction to hearing all that, but she was looking at Perkins, who opened his laptop and, after a few keystrokes, passed it to Calder. "This was in your file."

On the screen was a picture that had appeared on the front page of the Des Moines newspaper. In the background was the foundry; in the forefront was a large group of people composed of both men and women. The pickets they carried distinguished which side they favored.

Lying on the ground between the two factions were three men. The caption said the three had been injured by bottles being thrown during the tense standoff. Only one had been identified.

"Arnold Draper," Calder said aloud, still staring at the photo. "I remember the picture. I wouldn't have remembered his name."

"I'd noticed the photo in your file," Perkins said. "Subconsciously, I guess I locked in the name, which is why it jumped out at me when I was going down that list."

"I don't even know which side he was on," Calder said.

"Union. It was voted down."

"In large part because of my influence." Calder returned the laptop to Perkins and dragged both hands down his face. "So now what? In my wake are thousands of Arnold Drapers who aren't afflicted with Alzheimer's. I profited from each one of them being fired. Are you going to go through every list and check out all of them?"

"Wait," Elle said. "This is absurd. It's nothing more than wild speculation. Howard Rollins was the first person to be shot. Perhaps he was the target. Have you looked into his past?

"The shooter could have hit Calder while aiming at me because my Betsy book made his four-year-old cry. Anyone who would fire a gun into a throng has only one purpose, and that's to cause death and destruction. He doesn't require motivation beyond his own villainy."

Calder could kiss her for saying that.

Compton said, "It was a lead worth following, if only for the purpose of elimination. But it left us at another dead end. We assigned a deputy to follow up on the other two injured men in the picture. He spoke to one of the owners, one of the brothers you mentioned. He identified the two immediately. Like Draper, both were let go, but both are now deceased. One died of an opioid overdose, the other of cancer."

A silence followed in which they all processed that; then Calder said, "Nothing came out of the investigation into last night's shooting?"

"Not yet. We have two crime scenes, remember," Compton said. "Three departments are involved. Ours. The other sheriff's office, which has lost two of their own, so they're struggling.

"The municipal police department that has jurisdiction over the Whitley murder is small and thin on personnel with experience in handling something on this scale. There are lots of moving parts to coordinate and form some kind of cohesion. And in any case—"

"We can't discuss it with you." Perkins's blunt statement stemmed the flow from his partner. "We don't trust you not to conduct your own rogue investigation. Again."

Compton added, "Calder, to do so could amplify the danger you and Elle are in. The shooter is still at large, and you're key witnesses who could put a needle in his arm. From now on, keep your head down and let us do our job. Elle's already heard this sermon."

She stood up. "If you're comfortable with this arrangement that Ms. Foster has so graciously extended, you can remain here. We'll post undercover guards on the street. It helps that the house is on a cul-de-sac."

"We're to stay here indefinitely?" Elle asked.

"Unless you want us to place you in another safe house."

She looked over at Calder, who kept his expression impassive. He wasn't going to press her to stay under the same roof with him, although he couldn't stand the thought of their being separated and of her under the watch of people whose vigilance he questioned. He had to bite his tongue to keep from telling her that she was staying with him. Period.

But his expression must not have been as cool as he'd thought, because she was fidgety when she turned back to Compton. "I hate to impose on Glenda's hospitality indefinitely."

"Perkins and I have discussed it with her. It's no imposition. She told us the house stays vacant most of the time, and she'll be recompensed for any expense."

"But I can't work here, and I have a deadline. I don't have my computer. I've got illustrations to turn out. My publisher is waiting on them."

"We'll retrieve your computer from your house and bring it here. We'll also get you whatever art supplies you need. Make a list and text it to me."

"It's not the same as working at my drawing board. What about clothes?"

"Ms. Foster looks like an expert shopper to me," Compton said. "Make a list for her, too."

Realizing she was up against an immovable object, Elle slumped back down into her chair.

"We'll have the undercovers in place within the hour," Compton said. "Stay put. We'll notify you of any developments."

With her in the lead, the two left the room. Calder could hear them explaining the situation to Glenda. He tuned them out and walked over to Elle. She was staring into near space.

"I know you hate this," he said. "You can call them back and insist that they make other arrangements for you. Or you could ask Glenda to stay here with us, and I'll take a sofa. Or I'll leave altogether and find my own—"

"Calder." She was frowning as though his monologue was interrupting her train of thought. Eventually she looked up at him. "Twice, this devil had derailed our lives. We're shut away in here, hiding from him, living in dread of what he'll do next if not stopped."

She wet her lips as though speaking her thoughts even as she formulated them. "We've got law enforcement, lady justice, and morality on our side, yet he's the one with all the leverage."

He hunkered down in front of her. "I'm listening."

She pressed her fist against her chest. "I can feel his smugness. I can sense his arrogance. Why not call him on it, publicly scorn him as a coward?"

"I like it. 'You're nothing special, asshole.' 'Wackos are a dime a dozen.'"

She smiled with uncertainty. "Something like that."

"I'm in. How do you propose going about it?"

She wet her lips again. "In an interview with Shauna."

Chapter 34

H ello?"

"This is Elle Portman."

The call had come in through the TV station's news line and had been routed to the extension in Shauna's cubicle. When she heard who was calling, she nearly dropped the receiver. Her heart gave a thump of excitement. At the same time, her insides roiled with resentment because of Calder.

However, she'd be damned before giving this woman the satisfaction of knowing that. Coolly, she said, "What can I do for you?"

Elle made a sound of wry amusement. "It's the other way around, isn't it? I've decided to grant your repeated requests for an interview."

Shauna could barely breathe. After the fiasco at the so-called safe house, the story was hot again, hotter than ever. The Fairground shooter had struck again! With a vengeance!

But she'd been hobbled. Identifying the key witnesses had been a journalistic coup, but in light of the three murders that had resulted, it was costing her. The news director had called her on the carpet and berated her for overstepping.

A news flash that sensitive should not have been aired without his approval and clearance from the station's lawyers. As her punishment, other reporters had been dispatched to cover the two stories that had broken overnight.

Since early this morning, she'd been on her phone, calling everyone she could think of, doing her manipulative best to get a tidbit of information significant enough to build a story around.

But Billy Green had been made an example. Since his abrupt eviction from the sheriff's office yesterday morning, it was as though every law enforcement agency in north Texas had been issued a gag order.

No one was talking. Not a single soul.

Her calls weren't being returned by public officials who previously had been flattered if she sought them out for a sound bite regarding an event as inciting as last night's.

She didn't take their cold shoulder treatment too seriously. It was temporary. The first time one needed face time on TV to reach his constituency, Shauna Calloway would be the first reporter he or she called.

Knowing what a girl crush Dawn Whitley had on her, she had tried to reach her by going through the hospital's phone system. But it was Dawn's mother who'd answered. When

Shauna identified herself, she'd gotten an earful of condem-
nation before the woman hung up on her.

It was rumored that Calder and Elle had made good their
dramatic getaway together and on foot, but Shauna couldn't
get anyone to corroborate that. How had they managed to
escape the gunman? Where were they now? These questions had been eating at her, and now, *now*, she had Elle
Portman on the telephone, offering to give her the holy grail
of interviews.

But she wasn't going to leap on it like a mongrel who'd
been tossed a bone. She said, "For reasons you're well aware
of, it's a busy news day. I'll have to check my schedule. Even
if I can work it in, it'll take me a while to round up a crew
and—"

"No crew, just you. You'll come alone and record the
interview on your cell phone."

What the hell? Shauna gnawed the inside of her cheek,
thinking through various strategies. *Appeal to her vanity.* "Your
camera-shyness is admirable, but you're a celebrity-in-the-
making because of your book, which has been flying off the
shelves since the shooting. People want to hear about your
journey since the tragic loss of little Charlie.

"From a broadcast standpoint, a cell phone recording
isn't ideal. Your first interview, your coming out, so to speak,
should be done right. It should be properly recorded in a
studio, where you can be shown to your best advantage."

"Lights, camera angles, a makeup person?"

"Yes."

"No."

"Ms. Portman, with all due respect, this is my field of expertise, not yours."

"But this is my interview. Do you agree to my conditions or not?"

"Your conditions will compromise the quality of—"

"Goodbye."

"Wait!"

Dammit! It stung that this picture book writer was dictating the rules of engagement. She may look as meek and maidenly as freaking Snow White, but she obviously had gumption. It would serve Calder right if he was having to contend with this intractable side of her.

And while she was still stewing and considering another intimidation tactic, Elle had the gall to say, "I have a busy day, too, Ms. Calloway."

Swallowing her pride, Shauna said, "Name your conditions."

———

Elle disconnected, tossed down the cordless extension of Glenda's landline, and turned to Calder. "Did you hear what she said? She implied how lucky it was that the shooting had amped up my book sales. My *journey*? When she said Charlie's name as part of that treacle, I wanted to scream."

"That was all a power play. She was champing at the bit; she just didn't want you to know it."

Elle shoved back a hank of hair. "At least the interview is on. She agreed to the terms."

"Don't take her word for it."

"If she begins to fudge, I'll walk out."

"Walk out of where? You told her you'd text her the location. Not here, surely."

"No. But I've given it thought. Glenda's dad keeps a boat in a huge warehouse on Lake Ray Hubbard. It's tricked out. Jukebox. Large bar. He hosts parties there. Otherwise, it's locked up tight and enclosed by a tall cyclone fence. No one will be around."

She took in Calder's visible worry. "What? You don't like that location?"

"It's not that. It's the whole thing, Elle."

"When I advanced the idea, you said, 'I like it.'"

"Now that I've had time to think, I'm second-guessing."

"Why?"

"For one thing, Compton and Perkins will go apeshit."

"This coming from the man who's defied and eluded them twice?"

"Which is why they'll go apeshit."

"If I ask permission, they'll confer, ponder, weigh the pros and cons, ask the sheriff himself, and ultimately the answer will be no. I'm doing it. I'll beg their forgiveness after." She could see that his concerns weren't assuaged. "What else?"

"I should go with you."

"No. Your presence would change the dynamic. The interview can't be about our triangle."

"It won't be. We'll stick to the subject."

"There's no way the three of us can be in close proximity and not radiate hostility. It's bound to come across. Besides, doing this by myself will have more impact. A challenge to the shooter coming from me will be much more effective than one coming from you."

"How do you figure?"

"An aggressive message would be expected of you, a male. I'm eight inches shorter and eighty pounds lighter. I'm a homebody who writes about clouds. Tears and trembling are what everyone will expect from me, including Shauna. I want to take her and the shooter off guard." She waited, then said, "I'm right. Admit it."

He didn't admit it, but he didn't relent, either. "It'll make for better viewing if you emotionally crumble. She'll push you for tears."

"I'm prepared for that."

"You're *not*. She's got a bottomless bag of tricks."

"Like what?"

"Like tripping you up, getting you to say more than you intended, admit something, deny something. She'll throw out a question so unexpected that it'll disarm you, leave you stymied. I've seen her do it a thousand times to people who have undergone training on how to handle the media. They're thrashed before they know what's hit them."

"What you're saying is that she's smarter than I am."

"Damn it, Elle. That's not at all what I'm saying. I'm saying she's more devious. Make no mistake, while she's murmuring sympathetically and looking at you with soulful eyes, she's homing in on your jugular. She's always after the bigger story."

"What could be bigger than this one?"

"Your arrest for leaving the crime scene last night."

That gave her pause, but she shook her head emphatically. "Compton and Perkins said they weren't going to charge us."

"It's not their jurisdiction. What they said was that they were advising the other sheriff's department not to charge us. I wouldn't put it past Shauna to be laying a trap for you. She could be setting you up to have your arrest caught on camera. *Her* camera. Nothing would please her more than to become an element of the story, just like she did when she broadcast our names."

"I don't think she'll do anything that exploitative again. Not this soon. She has a reputation to protect."

He looked at her from beneath his eyebrows and said quietly, "And an ex-boyfriend who is in love with the woman she's interviewing."

The profession was unexpected. It kicked the slats out from under her. But she armored herself with pent-up anger. "How dare you say that to me now."

He came closer. "I dare because we know how suddenly dreadful things can happen to change the course of one's life. Like that." He snapped his fingers. "I didn't want something dreadful to happen to either of us before I told you that."

He took her face between his hands. "My heart had been missing from my life for a long time, Elle. You found it and gave it back to me." He pressed a solid kiss on her mouth, then set her away and looked deeply into her eyes. "You're absolutely certain you want to do this?"

Trying not to reveal how shaken she was by his declaration of being in love with her and the affirmation behind his kiss, she said, "Absolutely certain. For Charlie."

Chapter 35

Glenda voiced her opinion of the planned interview. "It's crazy! Shauna Calloway has been like a circling shark. Why are you giving in?"

"I'm not doing it for her," Elle said. "I'm doing it for Charlie, and me, and Calder, and all the other casualties and their families."

Glenda eventually surrendered to what she called Elle's "stupid nobility" and agreed to drive her to her father's fancy boathouse.

Calder asked if, on the way, she would drop him at his temporary apartment. "I've got to get some clothes." In light of the current situation, Glenda's planned shopping expeditions for burner phones and clothes for him had been suspended.

"Compton and Perkins might have someone watching the building."

"They think I'm tucked inside here. You can pick me up

there on your way back. If I get caught in the meantime, I'll beg forgiveness," he said, shooting Elle a smile.

They quickly prepared to leave. Calder's laptop hadn't yet been returned to him, so he asked to borrow the one belonging to the house again and grabbed it and its charger as they left.

Although they couldn't be certain, they didn't think the undercover guards had been posted yet. There were no suspicious vehicles parked on the cul-de-sac, but they didn't breathe easily until they were clear of it.

His new apartment building wasn't that far. Within ten minutes, Glenda pulled her SUV up to the entrance. He got out of the back seat and waited for Elle to lower the passenger-seat window.

He was aware of Glenda watching them with unabashed interest from the driver's seat. He didn't care what she thought of him, but he didn't want to say anything that would embarrass Elle. "I'm keeping my phone turned on and within reach," he said.

"They could track it."

"Screw it. I'm leaving it on. Don't hesitate to call if something goes wrong. Promise."

"I promise."

"You have your phone?"

She patted the side pocket of a purse on loan from Glenda.

"Good. Keep it turned off, but call or text me as soon as you're finished. I'll be waiting to hear from you." He paused, then said, "Remember everything I told you."

"I will. I won't let Shauna trap me."

"*Everything* I told you, Elle."

She lowered her eyes for a second, then looked up at him again and gave a small nod.

"For godsake, say goodbye," Glenda said. "You set the time for this misbegotten interview. You don't want to be late."

Calder gave Elle a last, meaningful look before stepping back. With misgiving, he watched them drive away.

He entered the apartment building and crossed the lobby to the elevator. Since he'd spent only one night there, he had to remind himself which floor his unit was on.

It felt odd not to belong to any one place. But being displaced didn't distress him as it once would have. Everyone lived with impermanence; they just didn't realize it until a catastrophe befell them.

He let himself into the apartment. Because of his rushed departure yesterday morning, it was in disarray. He supposed the smaller suitcase he'd taken to the safe house was still there, but the larger one that he'd packed with clothes and shoes when he'd moved out of the condo was lying open on the living room floor, clothes strewn everywhere. He went around the room, picking up the garments he wanted to take with him now. The rest he left where they'd landed.

After repacking the suitcase, he sat down at the dining table, booted up the borrowed laptop, and accessed his own computer contents from the cloud.

First, he checked his emails, ignoring the business-related ones and sending a blanket one to friends who'd written frantic inquiries about his well-being after last night's harrowing events. In brief, he told them that he was well but eager for the ordeal to be over and the culprit in custody.

Then he went into his files on the Maxwell Supply job and clicked through them until the newspaper photograph came up. Compton and Perkins had scrubbed the theory that there was a connection between Arnold Draper and the shootings. Elle had called it absurd speculation.

However, despite their dismissal, Calder wasn't ready to let go of the notion just yet.

This reluctance to forget it and move on was bothersome and unwelcome. He couldn't explain it, except that he wanted to feel completely and wholly blameless. He resented Compton and Perkins for planting the seed in his mind that he might have been responsible. It seemed determined to germinate.

He stared at the newspaper picture, examining it for a clue, willing it to give up a secret if it had one. After several minutes, frustrated with himself, he closed the file, got up, and went into the kitchen to get a drink of water.

He checked his watch. It had been forty-five minutes since Elle had departed. Had Shauna shown up? Had they started recording the interview? Had they chitchatted informally first?

No, he couldn't envision that. It was more likely that Glenda and Shauna had gotten into a catfight and Elle was serving as referee.

Ironically, Glenda and Shauna were cut from the same cloth. When talking to Glenda last night, he'd recognized the personality traits they had in common. They could be sisters. Blood sisters, anyway, bonded as securely as blood brothers.

"All bastards have brothers."

Without forethought, Calder had said the words out loud. It was a quote, a line from a movie, he thought, meant to cause a chuckle. Or had he read it somewhere? The sentence had just popped into his mind with the suddenness and surprise of a jack-in-the-box. Why?

He stilled and let the idea take shape, then set down his glass of water, rushed back to his laptop, and pulled up the people-finder info on Arnold M. Draper. There were several other Drapers with male names in the list of possible relatives.

Also, drawing his eyes to it like a magnet, was the Drapers' telephone number. He debated, then, before he could talk himself out of it, punched the number into his phone.

On the fourth ring, the call was answered by a soft female voice. "Hello?"

"Mrs. Draper?"

"Yes."

His heart thumped. He cleared his throat. "Hello. My name is Calder Hudson. I'm—"

"I know who you are."

"Oh?"

"Of course."

"From recent news? From the Fairground shooting?"

"No, Mr. Hudson. All the way back to Maxwell Supply."

"I see." He rubbed his forehead. He thought of that sweet-looking lady, clipping her husband's fingernails and talking to him as if he recognized her and was following everything she was saying.

"Mrs. Draper, I'm aware of your husband's condition. I, uh, I was at the center this morning."

"That was you? One of the staff told me a man identifying

himself as Arnie's nephew had come to visit but had left abruptly."

"I changed my mind. I didn't want to disturb you."

"Well, it's had me baffled all day, because Arnie doesn't have a nephew. He was an only child."

"No siblings?"

"No."

"Stepsiblings?"

"No."

"Mrs. Draper, do you have children?"

"Unfortunately, no."

Calder's chest nearly caved in with relief. He blew out a gust of breath. "Oh, well, that's . . . that's . . ."

"Why did you come to the center?"

"I . . ." Why bother her with the initial reason? He had an excuse now that was every bit as valid. Maybe more so. "I wanted to apologize for the role I played in your husband's losing his job. If you hang up now, I'll understand, but I would like to apologize in person. Would you allow me to buy you a cup of coffee?"

"No, thank you." Then, after a beat, "But I'll make you one."

Chapter 36

Technically, it was an interview, but it felt more like a face-off, which would have suited Shauna fine, except that they had been at it for half an hour, and she had yet to crack Elle Portman's reserve. Shauna had wanted a dramatic meltdown. What she'd gotten so far was unfaltering composure.

Shauna was on the brink of losing hers because the setup was intolerable. The small tripod she'd brought along on which to mount her cell phone had failed to cooperate, so she was relying on Glenda Foster to hold the device steady and monitor what the camera was recording.

Before today, Shauna had known the real estate agent only by her reputation as a shrewd and assertive businesswoman who was charming only when she chose to be. She was the sales wizard to beat in the cutthroat Dallas housing market.

She now knew her to be a quintessential bitch. Several

times she had interrupted the interview in order to correct this or that—a distracting shadow, a muffled word. Usually the fault lay with Shauna, who suspected these pauses were calculated and unnecessary.

Elle Portman had remained cool throughout. Before they began, Shauna had given her a packet of tissues. "I've found these frequently come in handy."

The packet lay unopened in Elle's lap. Not once had her voice wavered or her eyes grown misty. They'd remained dry even when she had described in stirring detail the instant she realized that her child was gone.

Expecting an uncontrollable gushing of emotion, Shauna was momentarily at a loss as to where to go from there. She'd stumbled a bit. "Then...then later, it must have been difficult to learn that the bullet that had killed your son had actually passed through Calder Hudson's arm without doing any permanent damage."

Elle just looked at her. "That's a statement, not a question. If you're asking how I felt when I learned of that, I regretted that Mr. Hudson's courageous attempt to save Charlie resulted in his becoming a casualty as well."

"Surely you're not equating Mr. Hudson's wounded arm with the death of your child."

"Nothing equates with the death of my child."

Shauna knew that Elle's response made her look like a fool for suggesting such a thing. She moved on to the shooting at the safe house. "Where were you when the bullets began to fly?" To let Elle know that she had a sneaking suspicion of where she was, and with whom, she raised her eyebrow.

Elle didn't falter. "I can't speak to that. I wouldn't want to

divulge anything that could compromise the open investigation into the murder of the two deputies."

"They were downstairs, you were up?"

"I repeat. It's an open investigation. I won't answer specific questions."

"Did you fear for your life?"

"I feared for all our lives."

The perfect reply, dammit. Unselfish, eloquently expressed
in her alto voice, enhanced by the sincerity in her remark-
able aqua eyes. Shauna wanted to rip out her glossy black
hair follicle by follicle.

"Some have been very vocal about the laxity on the part
of those who were supposed to be protecting you against just
such an attack. Can you comment on that?"

Without a blink, Elle said, "Certainly. If not for your
reckless reporting, we wouldn't have required protection."

Shauna saw red. "It's my job to report the news."

"It's your job to report it responsibly. You could have broken the story about a new lead without making our names
public. Since you did, the arrangements to protect us were
rushed out of necessity."

Shauna's face was burning with anger. She'd been trying
to set a trap for Elle and had stepped into it herself. But no
harm done. She could edit out that segment.

"Detectives Compton and Perkins have spearheaded the
Fairground shooting investigation and so far have little to
show for their efforts. Do you blame their ineptitude for the
three deaths last night?"

"I blame only the person who pulled the trigger."

"Let's assume the assailant at the safe house was the Fairground shooter. It was awfully brazen of him."

Elle seemed to be choosing her words carefully before she said, "Brazen but not brave."

Finally, *something*. Shauna leaned forward, putting on her most earnest face. "Can you expand on that?"

"Brazenness requires only a warped ego. Whether inflated or trampled, that ego is controlling the individual's actions."

"You think it's this warped ego that's driving the unknown suspect?"

"Well, I'm not a psychiatrist, but what does bravery have to do with firing a semiautomatic handgun into a dense crowd of people who are defenseless? Nothing. That's not bravery, that's depravity.

"To kill a two-year-old doesn't take courage." Turning her head away from Shauna, she looked directly into the phone's camera. "It's the epitome of cowardice."

Knowing she'd been upstaged, Shauna said tightly into the camera, "Well said, Ms. Portman. Point made. Thank you for speaking with me." Then to Elle, "We'll end it there. I'll do an intro and closing remarks in the studio." She stood, took her cell phone from Glenda—who was unsuccessfully trying to contain a smirk—and clicked off the camera.

"When will it air?" Elle asked.

"On the five o'clock news."

"It's after three now," Glenda said.

"Which is why I need to rush off. It'll be a quick editing job."

She wished now she hadn't already videoed a promo for the exclusive interview. The ads would be aired repeatedly during the station's afternoon programming. She'd unwittingly painted herself into a corner. She had no choice other than to air the interview in which she'd been surpassed by an amateur.

Smiling stiffly, she said to Elle, "Will you walk me out? I'd like a private word with you."

"Of course."

Glenda said, "I'll close up."

Shauna and Elle fell into step as they walked toward the wide door, their footsteps echoing hollowly in the vast space. "You used me, didn't you?" Shauna said. "To send a message to the shooter."

"We used each other. You got the interview you've been after. I got to address the bastard who killed my son. I only hope he sees the interview."

"And the implied challenge at its conclusion." When they stepped outside, she stopped and turned to face Elle. "Why would you want to thumb your nose at him, practically daring him to make another attempt on your life?"

"Off the record?"

"Yes."

"Can I trust that?"

"I'm affronted that you would ask."

Elle looked at her with derision. "You've done nothing to inspire my trust."

"It's off the record, all right?"

"All right." Still Elle hesitated before saying, "To someone as sophisticated as yourself, it'll sound sappy."

"Possibly, but give it a shot."

"The characters in my books are smarter than I am."

"That does sound sappy, seeing as how you created them."

"They're in my subconscious. When they're ready, they reveal things to me. It can be something as small as the next word of dialogue or as vital as a life lesson. They know it before I do."

"Never mind sappy. That's psychotic."

Elle actually laughed. "I suppose. To an extent."

"Give me an example."

"In the first book, there's a bully among the community of clouds. Like all the other younger clouds, Betsy is intimidated by him. By the end of the story, she's gathered her courage and stood up to him."

"She's no longer afraid?"

"Oh, absolutely she is. Very afraid. But she's no longer willing to live in the shadow of her fear."

"Ah. She goes on the offensive." She eyed Elle up and down. "Did you and Calder cook up this idea together? While in bed?"

Elle gave her a Mona Lisa smile. "Thank you for the interview." Then she turned and walked to where her friend stood waiting for her.

—◆—

As Glenda drove them away from the boathouse, Elle did as promised and phoned Calder. He answered immediately. "Hey. All done?"

"For better or worse. It sounds like you're in a car."

"Which was it? Better or worse?"

"I got my message across, and Shauna accused me of using her for that purpose. During the interview, I charged her with irresponsible reporting. We'll never be friends or even friendly, but we didn't draw blood. I can tell you're in a car."

"The Jag."

"What?" With consternation, she glanced at Glenda, who mouthed *Alpha male*. "We're on our way to pick you up."

"Don't bother. I left."

"In your car?"

"It was getting lonesome there in the garage."

"It's the most conspicuous thing on the road."

"Appearing on TV isn't exactly keeping a low profile, Elle."

"Where are you going?"

He told her about his conversation with Arnold Draper's wife and what he'd learned from it. "No siblings of any kind. No kids. It's a relief, Elle. I can't tell you how much of one."

"I'm relieved for you. How was she?"

"Hard to gauge, but she invited me over for coffee. Not with what I'd call abundant warmth but no overt hostility, either."

"Hmm."

"What's that mean?"

"Just hmm."

In her tone, he must have heard the disquiet she couldn't account for. He said, "I saw her and Mr. Draper together at the center this morning. Trust me. Neither poses a threat."

"Okay. What time will you be back?"

"By five o'clock because I want to watch your interview. But that's rush hour. If I'm delayed, record it."

"Of course. Listen, have you talked to Compton? I've had two missed calls from her."

"I've had three in the last fifteen minutes, which I ignored. She and Perkins must have discovered we're no longer holed up. In which case, Compton will be volcanic. Vesuvius."

"I'll call her as soon as we hang up. I'll be contrite when I confess to sneaking out to do the interview, but she'll want to know what you're up to."

"Say I'm on an errand, but don't tell her the nature of it. I'd really like to clear my conscience with Mrs. Draper face-to-face and in private."

"I won't give you away."

"Thanks. See you in a couple of hours."

"Calder," she said, catching him before he disconnected. For some reason, she was loath to break that contact. "Please be careful."

In his low, gruff sex voice, he said, "Count on it. I've got plans for later that I don't want to miss."

She clicked off and held the phone against her cheek as she stared absently through the windshield, recalling the erotic sounds that resonated through his chest, the various textures of his body as it moved against hers, the feel of him inside her.

"You like him, don't you?"

Elle turned her head and looked across at Glenda.

"I mean ... Well, you know what I mean."

"Yes," Elle said softly. "In spite of trying hard not to, I like him how you mean."

Glenda nodded sagely as she returned her eyes to the road. "I always give credit where credit is due."

"You found something about him to admire?"

"Uh-huh. He looks damn good in a spa robe."

Elle's light laugh was interrupted by her phone's jangle. "It's Compton," she said to Glenda, and answered.

"Where are you?" The detective's mood wasn't quite volcanic, but close. "Where is Calder? And what's this about you giving an interview to Shauna Calloway?"

"Where'd you hear about it?"

"Channel seven is hyping it during every commercial break."

"The interview was conducted at an unlikely place. No crew, just her. It was perfectly safe."

"You've avoided her like the plague. How'd she twist your arm?"

"She didn't." Elle told her how the interview had come about and the essence of their on-camera conversation. "I decided to come out of hiding."

"Without clearing it with us first."

"I was afraid you wouldn't approve."

"You're damn right we wouldn't approve. Especially the sneaking out part. I'll withhold judgment on the interview until after I've seen it. Was Calder in on it?"

"We thought it would be better if he wasn't."

She chuffed. "No doubt of that. So where is he?"

"I'm not sure." Which wasn't a lie.

"Elle, stop playing with me. He's not at Ms. Foster's secret hideaway, he's not at his new apartment, and his parking space is empty. We've looked."

"He's running an errand but said he would be back at Glenda's house by five o'clock to watch the interview."

"Should Perkins and I prepare ourselves for some shocking disclosure to come out of that interview?"

"No. I swear I didn't say anything that would impede your investigations into the Fairground shooting, or the safe house, or Frank Whitley's murder. Speaking of, have you gotten a progress report on Dawn?"

"Health-wise, she's improved. Otherwise, a mess. She's still under observation. The group therapy doctor."

"Dr. Sinclair? That's good."

"Back to the interview, Calloway didn't sabotage you by—"

"She tried."

"Elle was the better saboteur."

"Who was that?" Compton asked.

"Glenda. She's chauffeuring me even though it's eating up her workday."

Glenda waved that off.

Compton asked, "Where are you now?"

"En route back to the hideaway."

"And Calder's zipping around in his own car, which is about as discreet as the Batmobile." Compton blasphemed under her breath. "You're both taking unnecessary risks, Elle, and not just to yourselves. You're putting Perkins and me in jeopardy. If something were to happen to you two, like what was done to Frank Whitley, Weeks and Sims, Perkins and I would be crucified by our own colleagues.

"We don't like having to monitor you any more than you like being monitored. But we're not playing around here. This isn't a game of hide-and-seek. The stakes are life or death."

"I understand that. So does Calder."

"I don't think you do. Because you're sure as hell not

behaving like you're targets for this guy. He murdered three people within hours yesterday, and we have no idea who he is. What we do know is that he's audacious and smart as hell.

"To people like Perkins and me, who are the knowledge-able veterans here, not a couple of would-be Nancy Drews, that combo of audacity and smarts is terrifying. Especially the audacity. So far he's got us all flummoxed, and that'll embolden him. He'll wonder just how far he can push it, how much more he can get away with."

Elle sighed. "I accept everything that you're saying."

"Good. Get to the hideaway house and stay there. Calder won't answer if I call him, but he'll pick up if you do. Tell him to get his ass back to that house, that Perkins and I will see you both there no later than five o'clock, and it's not optional. Some things have cropped up that we need to check with you."

"What kind of things?"

"Discrepancies."

"In what?"

"Not over the phone and not with your sidekick listening in. Five o'clock. You and Calder had damn well better be there."

She disconnected before Elle could.

"Whew," Glenda said. "She's steamed. I was going to ask if we could pop into my office for a few minutes, but I'd better get you straight back to the house."

"No..." Elle thought through an alternate plan and made a decision. "*You* pop into your office."

"While you're doing what?"

"Not something that Compton and Perkins would favor."

Chapter 37

H ello, Mr. Hudson. Come in."

"Thank you for the invitation, Mrs. Draper."

"I welcome the company. Dorothy." She stuck out her right hand and he shook it. "I've got coffee ready."

He followed her into a living area. "Have a seat. I'll be right back."

She disappeared through an open doorway, and he found himself alone in a room that appeared to be rarely used. All the accoutrements of a standard American living room were there, but it looked like a stage set waiting for the actors to enter from the wings.

The tinkling of china announced her return. She came in carrying a tray. He stepped toward her. "Can I help?"

"I've got it, thank you." She set the tray on the coffee table and motioned him onto a sofa. "Cream and sugar?"

"Black, please."

Her manner was pleasant and polite. She was a pretty lady who in her younger years might have been a beauty. But strife had taken a toll.

At the corners of her eyes were lines etched by perpetual tension. Although she smiled at him, her pale lips were bordered by parentheses of sorrow.

She filled a cup and passed it to him on a saucer, then poured one for herself, adding milk from a small pitcher. After taking a sip, she said, "I was surprised to hear from you. Have you fully recovered from your Fairground shooting injury?"

"A little stiffness in my arm. Otherwise, I'm fine." He paused, then said, "When you saw my name in association with the shooting, did you recognize it instantly, or did you have to search your memory for where you'd heard it before?"

"Instantly. To many who worked at Maxwell Supply, your name is memorable."

He grimaced. "That job marked a turning point in my career."

"Oh? How?"

"I lost my innocence there. It was the most volatile situation I'd been in. After Maxwell, I began using an assumed name when on the job."

"You fear reprisal?"

"Not fear, exactly. I just don't want to leave myself open to it."

She set her cup and saucer on the table. "You wouldn't have had to fear it from me. I despised that foundry. It's dangerous work by its very nature. But machinery broke down often. Accidents happened. Arnie was burned. Here." She touched her forearm. "The skin graft was badly done by low-rent surgeons retained by the owners. To this day, Arnie bears an ugly scar.

"That was one reason he was strongly in favor of unionizing. But I wasn't gung ho for that, either. Some of their methods were extreme. They created strife, dissonance. I actually celebrated when Arnie was fired from that place."

"How did he feel about it?"

"Angry at first, then worried about our finances, naturally. But he livened up when I suggested a fresh start. We sold ourselves out of Des Moines and came down here.

"He got a job almost immediately at a plumbing company and worked there until..." She stared into the middle distance for a moment. "Until he could no longer find his way home from work or even remember what street he lived on."

"I'm very sorry."

"Thank you." She watched him over the rim of her cup as she took a drink. "Forgive me, but I sense an apology wasn't the only reason you came to the center today looking for Arnie."

"No, it wasn't." He set down his coffee cup, then laid out for her the hypothesis that the Fairground shooting hadn't been random. "Given my professional history, it seemed possible to the detectives that I was the target, the shooter's motive being revenge, and the other casualties simply being at the wrong place at the wrong time."

She flattened her hand against her chest. "How awful for you."

"Yeah."

"You thought Arnie might have been that someone holding a grudge?"

"I didn't remember him, or any altercation, cross words, nothing like that. He was suggested to me by the detectives because of a picture—"

"The one from the newspaper."

"Yes. For my own peace of mind, I had to find out what was going on with Arnold Draper. Simultaneously, and unbeknownst to me, the authorities were also tracking him down as a possible suspect."

"I was told that two sheriff's deputies came to the center asking about Arnie."

"We would have intersected if I hadn't split when I did." He looked down at the patterned rug between his boots. "I saw the two of you, realized the impossibility of your husband having any involvement, and decided not to bother you.

"Then, later, it occurred to me that he might have siblings who were out to avenge him. That's when I called you. Otherwise, I never would have imposed. I appreciate your seeing me. You've relieved my mind considerably. I can't thank you enough."

"I'm sorry you were guilt-ridden even temporarily."

"It wasn't pleasant." He checked his wristwatch, then stood. "Thank you for the coffee. I hate to rush off, but I have a mandatory meeting at five o'clock with the detectives. At this time of day, the traffic will be working against me."

"You can dispel their theory that the shooting was an act of revenge committed by Arnie."

"And the other two men in that picture are deceased, correct?"

She nodded. "One worked in the payroll office. Arnie didn't know him personally. We heard he died of stomach cancer. The other worked on the production floor with Arnie. After leaving Maxwell, he suffered a severe back injury in a motorcycle accident and got hooked on pain medication."

"I was told he died of an opioid overdose."

"It was ruled a suicide. Because of that stigma, his widow desperately wanted to get out of Des Moines. Knowing Arnie and I had settled well here, she called to ask me about the cost of living, the housing market, and such. I gave her the name of the real estate agent who'd found this house for us. That's the last I heard of her. I don't know if she made the move or not."

They'd been moving toward the front door. Calder had been only half listening. He was planning the most expeditious route to get him back to Glenda's guesthouse by five o'clock.

But as Dorothy Draper's words began to register, they raised the hair on the back of his neck. The relief and peace he'd felt just moments ago began to evaporate. Creeping back in like a malevolent fog were the misgivings that had haunted him for days.

"What were their names?" he asked her. "The suicide and his widow?"

"Uh, Smithson. Jim and Marjorie."

"When did she call you?"

"Oh, mercy. It was before Arnie went into the center. Two years ago, maybe?"

"You said she asked about housing. Who was the real estate agent you recommended?" Calder held his breath.

"Foster Real Estate. Glenda was the agent's name."

Glenda looked at the readout on her cell, then clicked on. "Calder?"

"Glenda, listen. I need you to do something for me."

"You're asking a favor? You've got—"

"Please? It could be important. How good are your records? Do you keep a record of all the people you sell homes to?"

"I keep excellent records, thank you very much. We do periodic mail outs, send out Christmas cards, and—"

"Are you where you can look up somebody? Like *now*?"

"Actually, I'm at the office. What's the name?"

"Smithson. Marjorie."

He was still parked at the curb in front of Dorothy Draper's house. He'd thanked her profusely for her time, the coffee, and the information, then had run to his car and called Glenda.

Now he was impatiently tapping his fingers on the steering wheel. "How's it coming?"

"Just a sec. This computer is being as slow as bloody Christmas."

"Did you take Elle back to the house?"

"No. She didn't want to go back. Oh, here it is! Marjorie Smithson. I sold her a house in 2021. Why's she important?"

"What do you remember about her?"

"I've sold a thousand houses since then, but if I'm remembering right, she was buying it alone. I mean, without a husband or partner."

"Widowed?"

"I think so. She was living on a pension and Social Security. That raised red flags with the mortgage company, but

I got creative on the financing, and she was approved. She wanted a quick close because she was relocating from somewhere out of state."

"Iowa. Anything else? What did she look like?"

"Brownish hair. Plump. But I couldn't describe her features if my life depended on it. It was during Covid. We were all wearing masks."

"*All?* Who else was there?"

"Me, her, and her daughter."

"Daughter? How old was she?"

"Christ, Calder, I don't know. She had on a mask."

"Ballpark."

"Twenty-something. Collegiate or marriageable age. I remember her being taller than average."

Calder's breath caught; then he began to hyperventilate. Smithson had had an adult daughter. "Do you have her name? What was the daughter's name?"

"Hold on. I'm scrolling. They're on our mailing list for birthday cards. Here it is." She paused. "Huh."

"What?"

"The daughter's name was Dawn. Isn't that—"

Calder's breath came out in a whoosh. "Oh my God." Then, "Oh my *God*! Put Elle on."

"She's not here. Calder, what is going—"

"What do you mean Elle's not there? She's not with you?"

"No. She—"

"*Where the fuck is Elle?*"

Chapter 38

E lle?"

"Hello, Dawn."

"I'm surprised to see you. Aren't you doing an interview with Shauna Calloway at five o'clock? They've been advertising it."

"We recorded it earlier."

"Oh."

Her hair was damp, and she had a vacant stare that Elle attributed to her concussion and the shock of her husband's murder. "Dawn, I can't express how sorry I am about Frank. I apologize for showing up unannounced, but I wanted to tell you in person how distraught I was when I heard."

"It hasn't quite sunk in yet."

"I know exactly what that's like. Some days I still expect to turn around and see Charlie or hear his voice."

Absently, Dawn nodded. "How'd you know where I'd be?"

"I went to the hospital to see you. I stopped at the reception desk to get your room number. The lady called upstairs and was told you'd been discharged. She gave me your mother's address."

"She's not supposed to give out personal information, is she?"

"No, but she recognized me, and since you and I have been through so much together, she understood why I wanted to see you."

"That was sweet of you. To go to the hospital and all."

"I've been worried about you. How are you holding up?"

"I'm okay. Come in." She pushed open the screen door.

"Are you sure?" Elle asked. "I don't want to intrude, and I can't stay but a few minutes."

"You're not intruding." Dawn stood aside and motioned her in. As Elle followed her, she noticed that her feet were bandaged. She was walking tentatively in a pair of terry cloth slippers. Compton had mentioned cuts on the soles of her feet.

"Things are kind of a mess," she said over her shoulder. "Mom isn't the best of housekeepers to start with, and we haven't been home long. Just long enough for me to take a shower."

The living room into which she led Elle was indeed a mess. It was cluttered, and the layer of dust on hard surfaces attested to general neglect.

Dawn lifted a hospital-issued plastic bag from the seat of an armchair so Elle could sit down. "Just some toiletries and bandages they sent home with me. My clothes were taken as evidence. Sims's blood had splattered on everything."

"That must've been so traumatic for you."

"It was."

Before coming, Elle had been uncertain how Dawn would receive her. She wondered if she held it against Calder and her for leaving the safe house without her. But if she was resentful, she wasn't showing it. She wasn't exhibiting much emotion at all, not even when she'd referenced Sims's blood on her clothing. She was moving and speaking like an automaton to an extent that was eerie.

But Elle remembered how she herself had been during the days immediately following the Fairground shooting. She'd gone about in a trancelike state, it being easier to shut down completely than to try to cope with the tragic reality.

"Would you like something to drink?"

When Elle declined the offer, Dawn sat down on the sofa, facing her.

"How did you do?"

"How did I do...?"

"With the interview."

"Oh. Fairly well, I think."

"Why'd you do her that favor? She double-crossed us."

"I didn't do it as a favor. I—"

She cut Elle off. "I guess you know by now that I told Frank the location of the safe house. I'm to blame for the place being shot up." Her mouth twisted. "Are you mad at me over that?"

Elle didn't go down that path. Obvious to her was that Dawn was mentally and emotionally unstable and should never have been allowed to leave the hospital. Clearly, she needed supervision.

Easing into that topic, she said, "I was surprised to learn that the doctors discharged you so soon after you'd suffered a concussion."

"The doctors didn't. I got Mom to sort of push it through. We had to sign a bunch of paperwork, relieving the hospital of liability."

"Why were you in such a hurry to leave?"

"I was tired of everybody watching me. I didn't have a minute's peace. I think they were afraid I'd hurt myself. You know, because of me being to blame for those deputies, and especially Frank."

Elle looked at her with empathy. "Don't take all the blame on yourself, Dawn. There were many contributing factors."

"Maybe."

Elle noticed that her fingers were linked together in her lap like an intricate knot, so tightly clasped that her knuckles were white. "Did you see Dr. Sinclair?" she asked.

"A few times."

"Was she helpful?"

"Yes. Well, I mean, I guess so."

"Do you have thoughts about hurting yourself?"

"Not you, too." She shook her head with annoyance. "I wish everyone would stop asking me that."

Suddenly, in place of the automaton was a woman in a state of irrational anger and vehemence. Elle backed down. "I'm sorry. I didn't mean to—"

"How did you get here?"

Taken aback, Elle had to think for a moment.

"From the hospital," Dawn said with exasperation. "How

did you get here? I didn't see a car, and you couldn't have walked all that way."

"I...I took an Uber."

"What about Mr. Hudson?"

"Calder?"

"Yes, Calder." She rolled her eyes. "You know, Calder Hudson?"

"What about him?"

"Where is he? I know you must be in contact with him. Y'all were getting so lovey-dovey. Where is he?"

Unsure where this hostile inquisition was coming from or where it was leading, Elle answered carefully. "Compton and Perkins have found another safe house for him."

Dawn's eyes narrowed on her. "Where?"

"You know I'm not at liberty to say." Now distinctly uncomfortable, especially since she hadn't notified anyone of her plan to visit Dawn, she began plotting a graceful means of escape.

"Calder has been concerned about you, Dawn. I know he'd like to speak with you. I'll call him for you." She reached for her handbag, but Dawn stopped her.

"No, that's okay."

Elle tried another tack. "Once Compton and Perkins learn that you've left the hospital, they'll want to make provisions for your safety, too. They won't approve of your being here alone."

"I'm not alone. Mom's here." She glanced toward a hall-way that Elle assumed led to bedrooms. "She's resting." She leaned back against the sofa cushion and fixed a hard stare on Elle. "Are you sleeping together?"

"Excuse me?"

"You and Calder. And don't tell me no. I wasn't born yesterday. Frank was actually jealous of him. He kept asking if he was going to be there in the safe house, too. Like he and I would be sneaking off to screw while cops were all over the place."

She shook her finger at Elle. "But you two found a way. When the firestorm started, he was up in your bedroom, wasn't he? That's how you and he conveniently got away. That's so romantic," she said and fluttered her eyelashes.

"Dawn, I—"

She laughed. "Shauna Calloway would shit a brick if she knew. Or does she know?" Her eyes were agleam with malice. "I hope she knows. I hope the bitch knows and chokes on it." She drew her feet up onto the edge of the sofa cushion and hugged her raised knees.

And that's when Elle saw it: a starburst of blood on the toe of her white slipper. It couldn't have seeped up from the bandage protecting the sole of her foot. The spot was bright red. Fresh.

Forcibly concealing her panic, Elle tried to keep her hands steady as she reached for her handbag again and took her phone from the side pocket. "My Uber driver said he would stay close by and come back for me as soon as I called him. I really shouldn't have stayed this long. You should be resting."

Dawn lunged off the sofa and snatched the phone from Elle's hand. She threw it across the room at the fireplace. It smashed against the bricks and landed on the floor.

Elle didn't hesitate, she elbowed Dawn in the stomach

and pushed past her. She ran into the hallway, yelling "Help me!" and flung open the first door she came to.

But the older woman sitting propped against the head-board of the bed was beyond helping anyone. Her head listed toward her right shoulder. Her eyes were open. A hole marked the center of her forehead. Behind her, on the wall, was a grisly mosaic.

Elle clamped her hands over her mouth.

Dawn *tsk*ed and said from behind Elle, "After Frank, after the safe house, she was getting cold feet. I told her a thousand times that everything was going to be fine, that they'd never suspect us.

"But, no. She said our luck was sure to run out. She started making noises about us turning ourselves in. She said maybe if we surrendered ourselves to Compton and Perkins, they'd go easier on us than if we got caught." She laughed. "Have you ever heard of anything that crazy?"

Chapter 39

The deputy who'd been stationed outside Dawn's hospital room was getting his ears blistered by Compton. Her tirade was interrupted midsentence by her ringing cell phone.

She yanked it from her belt, looked at the readout, and passed it to Perkins. "It's Hudson. Tell him to stay at the house until we get there, or there'll be hell to pay. Tell him it could be a while."

Perkins took the phone from her and answered. "This is Perkins. I'm on Compton's phone."

"It's Dawn."

"What?" Perkins put a finger in his ear in order to hear Calder above the dressing-down his partner was giving the deputy.

"Listen to me. It's *Dawn*. I don't know if her mother and husband were in on it, or if Dawn carried it out by herself, but she was behind it."

"Behind—"

"The Fairground shooting," Calder shouted. "All of it. In reprisal. Her father was one of the men in that picture. The one who died of the overdose. Smithson was his name. Jim. Mother Marjorie. Daughter Dawn."

Perkins snapped his fingers several times. Compton stopped berating the deputy and turned to him. He hitched his head toward a storeroom, and she followed him into the tight space, which was stocked with extra blankets and bedpans. "He says Dawn Whitley is behind the shootings."

"*What?*" Compton exclaimed.

"That's what he says."

Calder was shouting into the phone, "It's Dawn, I tell you! Perkins, are you hearing this or not?"

"I pulled in Compton. You're on speaker with both of us now."

"Where are you?"

"At the hospital."

"Aw, good. Have you seen Elle? I got a text from her that she was going to see Dawn, but now I can't raise her on her phone. She needs to know about this ASAP."

"What time did you get that text?" Compton asked. "Elle was supposed to be on her way back to the hideaway house."

"She persuaded Glenda to drop her at the hospital so she could visit Dawn. Glenda's been at her office, waiting for Elle to call her to come pick her up. She hasn't heard from her. She must still be with Dawn. Get her the hell away from her."

The two detectives exchanged a look. Perkins slipped out of the storeroom. Compton remained on the line with

Calder. "What makes you think Dawn was behind the shooting?"

"I'll tell you everything when I get there. Just keep Elle away from her. Dawn should be taken into custody. For questioning if for nothing else. As a person of interest. Whatever. If her mother is there, she probably should be arrested, too."

"They're gone, Calder."

"What do you mean gone? Gone from the hospital?"

"Dawn checked herself out."

"Jesus. When?"

"A little over an hour ago. We came to question Dawn further about some discrepancies regarding her husband's—"

"Later. Where is Elle?"

"Perkins has gone to check. How'd you get onto this about Dawn?"

"From Mrs. Draper. I went to see her. Almost in passing she mentioned the opioid guy's widow moving to Dallas. I followed up. But all this can wait. *Where is Elle?*"

Perkins returned in time to hear that. "Elle was here, but she came and went," he said, more grim than usual. "She stopped at the reception desk, was told Dawn had been discharged, and left."

"Left how? Left for where?" Calder demanded.

"The security guard at the main entrance thinks it was an Uber. Doesn't know where to."

Calder's panting breaths came through loud and clear. "Nobody knows where she is?"

"We'll track her down," Compton said. "Go to the house. Wait there. We'll meet you— Calder? *Calder!*"

He had disconnected.

Dawn stamped hard on Elle's phone. "I think it was already busted, but you can't be too careful."

Elle was back in the living room, in the same chair, but this time there were bands of duct tape securing her to its arms. She hadn't put up a fight. Because not only had she felt Dawn's warm breath on the back of her neck, but the cold muzzle of a gun had also been pressed against it.

Strangely courteous, Dawn had steered her away from the ghastly scene in the bedroom and back into the living room. She'd motioned her into the chair and produced a roll of duct tape from the drawer of an end table.

"Mom stores things in the oddest places," she'd said. "It's one of her quirks. Once, I found a tin of lighter fluid in the silverware drawer." Her affectionate smile was, to Elle, obscene. It caused bile to fill the back of her throat.

Elle hadn't resisted as Dawn had ripped off a length of the silver tape with her teeth, passed it to Elle, and ordered her to wind it around her right arm. "No cheating. Pull it tight."

When that arm was secured, Dawn laid the menacing-looking pistol on an ottoman and used another strip of tape to bind Elle's left arm. "There. You may lose some circulation in your hands and fingers. I guess it depends on how long it takes Calder Hudson to get here."

"He won't be coming. He doesn't know where I am."

"Oh, he's smart. He'll figure it out. He'll come. And when he does, I'm going to kill him."

"Like you did your mother."

"And Frank."

"How…how did you manage that, Dawn? You were at the safe house."

"Well, I didn't pull the trigger. But it was my plan."

"Who pulled the trigger?"

"Mom. See, that way, I had a perfect alibi. But today the cops kept saying that Frank must have known the 'unknown assailant' because there were no signs of 'forced entry' and that the weapon had been fired at 'close range' and that there were no 'defense wounds,' and the 'time of death' was 'curious.'"

Elle remembered Compton mentioning "discrepancies" that she wanted to check with Calder and her. Did they relate to Frank Whitley's murder? She thought it probable.

"Mom had done exactly what I'd told her. She got over there soon after the deputies had taken me away. Frank was distraught. She made out to comfort and reassure him. He never felt a thing. It was supposed to be an imitation of the staged suicide at the fair. But," she sighed, "all that questioning about the crime scene was making her edgy. That's when she began suggesting that maybe we should call it quits."

"Who shot up the safe house?"

"Well, duh, Elle. Mom!" She kicked Elle's inoperative phone aside and sat down on the sofa. "See, after we moved down here from Iowa… Do you know about that?"

Elle shook her head.

"Well, it's a long story. I won't bore you. But we came down here for the purpose of killing Calder Hudson."

Elle swallowed with difficulty. "Why?"

"He ruined our lives."

"How so?"

Elle didn't mind if it was a long, boring story told by a

deranged individual. She had to give them—Calder—time to find her. She'd texted him only that she was going to see Dawn. He would have assumed that she meant at the hospital. She glanced at the clock on the dusty mantel. Three minutes till five o'clock. When she failed to arrive at the house in time to—

"So I put him out of his misery."

The jarring statement pulled Elle from her thoughts. "I'm sorry? What?"

"Daddy. After he got the boot from Maxwell, he couldn't find another job, especially not after the accident, which fucked up his back something awful. He could barely walk, much less work.

"Our car had been repossessed, which is why he was riding that damn motorcycle. Medical bills piled up. We had to sell the house and move into this crappy apartment. All because Mr. Calder Hudson had gotten Daddy fired. He's to thank for him getting hooked on the meds, too."

Elle remembered that one of the men in the photograph had died of an overdose. "Opioids?"

"Yes. Daddy was pitiful. Pathetic. One day he told me he would be better off dead." She shrugged. "I agreed."

"You put him out of his misery."

"Eventually he probably would have offed himself, accidentally or on purpose." She leaned forward and reached for the TV remote. "Show time."

Elle looked at the clock. One minute till five. *Soon, soon.* They may all already be there. They would be calling Glenda to ask where they were, what the holdup was. But not even Glenda knew that she hadn't stayed at the hospital.

She hadn't told her because she hadn't wanted an argument against this visit with Dawn. With misplaced compassion, she'd felt she owed it to the younger woman for leaving her at the safe house.

She'd planned to make it a brief courtesy call, then return to the hospital before anyone realized she'd come here. Then she would have called Glenda to come pick her up and begged forgiveness after the fact.

"I feel like I should be popping popcorn." Dawn grabbed a throw pillow and hugged it to her chest.

As Dawn had said, Calder was smart. He would figure it out. Compton and Perkins would have people—

"You look sort of washed out," Dawn remarked.

Elle looked toward the television. Shauna was opening the interview with her falsely warm greeting. Elle did look washed out. She said, "We were under fluorescent lighting."

"Hmm."

"Dawn, what about the death threat?"

She giggled. "Oh that. I planned that soon after the shooting. I was certain no one would ever suspect me, but *just in case*, Mom and I worked out the wording of a threat on my life—being sure to mention that kid's tattoo—which would have eliminated any suspicion that I was the culprit.

"Mom got this simpleton who walks the neighborhood looking for her lost cat—who's said to have been dead for ten years at least—to buy her a burner phone that she could use to call me, leave a message, then ditch the phone. We rehearsed it a lot. As you heard, she got real good at disguising her voice.

"When blondie there"—she nodded toward the TV—"broadcast our names, I thought it would be a good time to pull out the death threat. It would practically force the police to round us up, which would give me access to him."

"Calder?"

"You, too. See, by then, I'd already decided that the two of you together might not be the safest thing for me, and that I... well, you know." She ran her index finger across her throat, then returned her attention to the television.

Elle's hands were beginning to tingle with the lack of blood circulation, and her mind was reeling. But, to buy time, she must keep Dawn engaged.

"So, your mother shot up the safe house?"

She continued to watch the TV. "Uh-huh. She had a busy day and night and was really cranky when I arrived at the hospital here in Dallas."

Elle mused out loud, "You weren't calling Frank from the safe house. You were calling your mother, giving her directions there. Information on the layout." Then, "Dawn, how did she know she wouldn't hit you in the barrage?"

Dawn looked across at her and frowned, seemingly over Elle's stupidity. "Practice. We brought all of Daddy's guns with us when we moved down here. We'd go out in the country and practice. She and I both became very proficient."

"Did Frank know what you intended?"

"God, no. Frank would never shoot anybody. He didn't have the nerve. I only married him so Mom and I would have a scapegoat if we ever needed one. But he was a good husband. He liked taking care of me. A little too much sometimes. He hovered, you know?"

"How did you—"

"Shh. I want to hear this." She focused on the TV,

where Elle was talking about life after Charlie. "*Just getting up in the morning was a challenge*," she was saying. "*I didn't want to face another day without him. I would think about all the days to come that I would have to face without him, and grief would paralyze me.*"

Dawn looked across at her. "I didn't mean to kill your little boy. I was going for Calder Hudson. I fired a nano-second too late. He'd already moved past you. The bullet struck that old man next to you instead. I fired several more rounds—I lost count of how many—in Calder's direction, but they were misses, too, because he had hit the deck.

"Of course, by now people realized there was a shooter among them. They were panicked, running crazy in every direction. I figured I'd blown it, missed my chance, so I ran, too. That's when I banged right into your stupid stroller.

"But it actually turned out to be fortunate. Because when I glanced back to see if anybody was coming after me—no one was—there was Calder Hudson, hero, trying to catch the stroller before it went over. As he reached for it, I got off a lucky shot.

"Figuring he was dead, I thought, 'Yea! You son of a bitch.' But," she sighed, "the shot wasn't as lucky as I'd thought. He didn't die. The damn bullet went straight through him. So he's to blame for your kid dying, Elle, not me." She turned her attention back to the TV.

Elle was thinking that by now they would all be looking for her, but how much time did she have? How much of the interview had Shauna edited out? How long would it run? Time enough for rescue to arrive? When the interview was over and Dawn was no longer distracted by it...

She had to keep her talking.

"How did you know that Calder would be at the fair that day?"

"We followed him. All the time. Well, whenever he was in Dallas. He went out of town a lot on his jobs to fire other people from theirs. Sometimes we'd have to wait months at a time for him to come back. But when he was in town, he kept a fairly routine schedule, and we kept track."

"There must've been nights when Calder was out late. Didn't Frank become suspicious of your...excursions?"

"I'd tell him that Mom was having one of her spells and that I had to stay with her."

"What kind of spells did she suffer?"

"She didn't really suffer spells, silly. I only told Frank that."

"He believed you?"

"There was no reason for him not to."

Elle knew she was dealing with someone who'd lost all touch with reality. To keep her talking, she would continue to feed her ego. "You must've been very clever stalkers for Calder not to catch on."

"Oh, we were. Shauna never caught on, either. We knew where they lived, of course. High-and-mighty people like them never notice people like Mom and me."

Her features tensed into a hateful expression that chilled Elle to the bone. To divert her from whatever thoughts had caused it, Elle said, "You were going to tell me about the day of the fair and how you knew he'd be there."

"Oh, yes. Well, he'd been working in a downtown

skyscraper for several months. Every weekday, we followed him out of the parking garage when he left. He was driving this mediocre car, pretending to be a nobody.

"But that day, he left the parking garage in his Jaguar. We followed. Which wasn't easy, let me tell you. He drives like a bat out of hell. On that day, he was going even faster than usual. He drove and drove until we had about decided to turn around and wait for another time.

"Then, when we realized he was going to the fair, I knew it was the perfect place. Just dark enough. Tons of people. We could get lost in a stampeding, terrified crowd. I told Mom to get ready."

"Ready?"

"With our disguises. We kept them in the trunk of her car at all times."

"Your ball cap."

"Um-hum. So at a glance I'd look like a boy."

"But how did you know about Levi Jenkins? The tent he was in, all that?"

"We didn't." Again, she looked at Elle with impatience. "We're not clairvoyant, you know."

"It really was an ingenious plan," Elle said, looking at her with feigned wonderment.

Dawn beamed. "Yes, I know."

"I'm just trying to understand how you pulled it off."

"Well, we knew that when I started shooting—"

"Where did you have the gun?"

"Inside the pocket of the windbreaker. I shot through it. I dropped the cap on purpose."

"Weren't you afraid of leaving DNA on it?"

"No. Weren't you listening? Compton said they couldn't test any DNA on the cap until they had a suspect, and I certainly wasn't one."

She laughed. "See? Nobody would suspect a *casualty*."

Chapter 40

Calder ended his call with Compton and Perkins, swerved out of his lane and onto the shoulder of the freeway, then brought his car to a shuddering stop. He called Glenda again.

She answered with "What's going on?"

"The Smithson woman. What's the address of the house you sold her?"

"Calder, where is Elle? She hasn't called—"

"I know."

"Why haven't I heard from her? Tell me what's happening."

"*Give me the fucking address!*"

After a put-out sigh, Glenda rattled it off to him.

"Thanks."

"Wait!"

But he didn't. He hung up and repeated the address to his car's navigation system. The map appeared on his touch screen. "Fuck fuck fuck!" He was traveling in the opposite direction, and the estimated time to get there from his current location was twenty-two minutes.

He whipped the Jag back onto the freeway. As he took the next exit so he could turn around, he called Compton. "I've got the address for Dawn's mother."

The traffic light at the bottom of the ramp turned red. He looked both ways, saw a narrow opening, then hooked a sharp left turn. On the other side of the underpass was another red light. There were cars in front of him waiting to turn left onto the access road.

"We already have her address," Compton said. "We're on our way, just leaving the hospital now."

"Well, step on it. Have you sent a SWAT unit?"

"SWAT unit? Calder, we haven't even questioned Dawn yet. We can't send a—"

"Why the fucking hell not?" The traffic light turned green. He waited impatiently for the cars ahead of him to go. "Move already!" he shouted at them, and then to Compton, "This is the Fairground shooter, for chrissake."

"We don't know that. *You* don't know that."

"It feels right." He reentered the freeway, dodged his way between several slow movers until he found a reasonably clear lane, and floor-boarded the accelerator.

Compton was saying, "We don't have any evidence on which to base an arrest. We'll talk to her, then—"

"*Talk?* What is the matter with you? You're the one who advanced the idea that somebody had a vendetta against me. Now we have a likely somebody. Take her into custody first, then talk."

"You saw the individual who tipped over the stroller. You identified him as male. It wasn't Dawn."

"It could have been. She's tall. Easily attainable cap, remember? Never mind all that now. We'll talk details later. Just—"

"Dawn was a *victim*. She dropped where she was shot, and the bullet removed from her leg was fired from the same gun that wounded and killed the others, including you."

"Look, I don't know how she did it. But I know that she was somehow involved. I feel it. And Elle's with her. So send the fucking badasses to that house. Make fools of them, yourselves, make a fool of *me*. But if I'm right—"

"We can't barge into someone's house only because it feels right to you. We have civil rights laws in this country."

"Yeah, while you're clinging to that, I'll violate more than the rights of anybody who harms Elle."

"Calder, listen to me. You need to calm down. You're overreacting." After a beat, she added, "Remember what happened to Charlie Portman when you acted on impulse."

As though he'd been slapped, Calder blinked to clear the red haze of fury from his vision. "Fuck you."

Realizing Calder had hung up on her again, Compton cursed him. She looked over at Perkins. "You heard him. What do you think?"

He pondered it for all of one heartbeat. "Send in the badasses."

Calder made the twenty-two-minute trip in twelve.

The street address was in a neighborhood barely hanging on to a middle-class designation. All the houses were constructed of brick, but their wood trims needed fresh paint, the shrubbery was scraggly, and the roofs sported curled shingles.

He located the house number, and the name printed on the dented metal mailbox at the curb confirmed that Marjorie Smithson lived there. A Ford compact was parked in the driveway.

He drove the length of the block and around the corner and parked in front of a run-down playground. He felt conspicuous as he alighted from his car, but the houses he walked past were shuttered. He got the impression that this was a neighborhood where minding one's own business was probably the best policy.

He wasn't as impulsive as Compton had accused him of being. He wasn't going to "barge" in until he had some idea of what was going on inside the Smithson home. If anything.

Maybe this was a fool's errand. He would prefer that it was. But his gut was telling him otherwise.

Two doors down from the Smithson residence was a house with a for-rent sign in the yard. It looked like it had been there for some time. Banking on the house being vacant, he waded through the weeds in the front yard and down the side of the house to the backyard. A dog from somewhere in the vicinity began to bark, but he ignored it as he walked across the next backyard. It was separated from Marjorie Smithson's by a chain-link fence. Calder climbed over it.

There, he stopped, waiting for a challenge, listening for any indication from inside the squat, square house that he'd been seen or heard. When nothing happened, he moved to one of two narrow, vertical windows on the back of the house, cupped his hands around his eyes, and peered through the pane.

The woman looking directly back at him through the window glass was only a yard away from him. But her open eyes were unseeing. The sight was so unexpected, so grotesque, he reflexively stumbled backward, huffing breaths through his mouth.

Collecting himself quickly, he took his phone from his pocket and sent Compton a text. **Woman, guessing Marj, fatal GSWH. Bedroom, NE rear corner of house. I'm going in.**

He made certain that his phone was silenced, then cautiously approached the block of crumbling concrete that served as a back stoop. The outer door was screened. He held his breath as he tried it. It was unlocked, but the hinges squeaked when he opened it. He waited. So far, so good. He wedged himself between the screened door and the solid one and tested the knob. It turned. Heart thudding, he pushed the door open.

He was surprised to hear a familiar voice: Shauna's.

He listened for several seconds and, when he heard Elle's mellow voice, he realized he was hearing the broadcast of their interview.

He stepped into an untidy kitchen. The television would help cover any noise he made, but he wished he had on shoes other than his boots. His footsteps —

Dawn's voice froze him.

"Weren't you listening? Compton said they couldn't test any DNA on the cap until they had a suspect, and I certainly wasn't one. See? Nobody would suspect a *casualty.*"

The TV sound track continued but became like white noise to him. He crept forward across the kitchen and passed through a doorway into a small dining room. On the opposite side from the kitchen was a wide opening into the living area.

A framed mirror hung on the wall to his left. In it, he could see Elle reflected, seated in a chair. He experienced a momentary surge of relief to find her still alive, but upon further inspection, he saw that her arms were taped to the chair.

She hadn't noticed him. He mentally tried to telegraph her of his presence. At the same time, he didn't want her to react in a way that would alert Dawn.

"How did you plan to escape?" Elle asked.

"As Mom and I followed Calder through the entrance, I noticed the game tents off to the right. I'd told Mom to make her way toward the first one in the row as soon as all hell broke loose and that we'd look for each other somewhere near there.

"In the panic, I doubted anyone would notice me passing the pistol and the windbreaker off to her. No one did. Everyone was trying to save their own skin. I trusted her aim. She was supposed to injure me, but not too bad."

"You planned all along to be *shot*?"

"Well, yes. Our success depended on it."

"I see."

"We decided my calf was a safe place for me to be injured."

"You could have been crippled for life, Dawn. You took a huge risk."

"The whole plot was a risk. But one worth taking."

Elle said nothing.

"Anyway," Dawn continued, "after Mom saw that I was down but not seriously injured, she ran into that tent. There stood the dopehead." She laughed. "Mom told me later that he about scared her to death. He didn't say anything, just gave her this stupid, glazed stare. When she realized he was stoned, she walked straight up to him and shot him in the head. He never flinched, she said. The cops figured he'd saved the last bullet for himself, but, actually, it was sheer luck there was one left for poor Levi. Seems like it was meant to be, doesn't it? I mean, he was a wasted life."

Jesus, Calder thought.

She continued to babble. "Anyway, Mom had the presence of mind to put the gun in his hand. She stuffed the ruined windbreaker up her sweatshirt, then slipped through the back of the tent and went yelling and screaming toward an exit like everyone else.

"Later, she played out the whole 'I can't find my daughter' thing. Frantic-like. Hysterical. You know. When Frank got to the emergency room, even he was convinced that both of us had been traumatized."

"Getting yourself shot was quite a sacrifice," Elle said.

"A necessary evil."

"Explain that to me."

"Well, it couldn't appear that Calder Hudson had been targeted."

Upon hearing his name, Calder's gut tensed.

"Because then they'd begin looking into his background for someone holding a grudge, and that might have led to us. It had to look random."

Elle was slow to respond. "But, Dawn, you thought you'd killed Calder. You said you'd got off a lucky shot. So, after you saw that he was down, why did you continue firing into the crowd?"

"Calder never cared how many people he hurt, did he? I'll bet he never gave a thought to secondary victims like Mom and me. We were collateral damage. He didn't give us any regard, so why should I care who suffered because of him?

"Besides, Elle," she added as though speaking to an ignoramus, "to qualify as a mass shooting, there have to be four or more people shot. I had to make it look good."

Appearing sickened by Dawn's callousness, Elle turned her head aside. When she did, she spied his reflection in the mirror. In involuntary reaction, her body jerked. He shook his head and held his finger up to his lips.

She glanced quickly at Dawn, but apparently Dawn was oblivious.

Calder leaned forward slightly to get a better view into the living room through the mirror. Before making a move, he wanted to know the layout. Dawn was seated on a sofa, her back to him. She had her head turned away from Elle, toward the television, he supposed.

In the interview, Elle was saying, *"I blame only the person who pulled the trigger."*

Sounding pleased, Dawn chortled, "You were talking about me and didn't even know it."

Shauna said, *"Let's assume the assailant at the safe house was the Fairground shooter. It was awfully brazen of him."*

"Notice that she refers to the shooter as him?" Dawn said with scorn. "Everyone does. As though a woman couldn't do it."

"Brazen but not brave," Calder heard Elle say.

"What?" Dawn screeched. "What did you mean by that?"

Calmly, Elle said, "I meant exactly what I said, Dawn."

"Can you expand on that?" Shauna asked.

"Brazenness requires only a warped ego. Whether inflated or trampled, that ego is controlling the individual's actions."

Dawn lunged to her feet. "You called me warped? How dare you."

"You think it's this warped ego that's driving the unknown suspect?"

"Well, I'm not a psychiatrist, but what does bravery have to do with firing a semiautomatic handgun into a dense crowd of people who are defenseless? Nothing. That's not bravery; that's depravity. To kill a two-year-old doesn't take courage. It's the epitome of cowardice."

"You *bitch!*" Dawn screamed. She hauled off and struck Elle hard across the face with the pistol.

Calder launched himself into the living room, hurdled the sofa, and knocked Dawn facedown onto the floor, then fell on top of her.

But he fell short.

She'd stretched her arm far out in front of her along the floor, putting her gun hand out of his reach. She got off three shots before the whole house seemed to implode as all the doors burst open and SWAT officers swarmed in from every direction.

Using that nanosecond of distraction, Calder pushed himself higher up on Dawn's back, reached as far as he could, and managed to grip her wrist. He anchored her hand to the floor and kept the shots she continued to fire aimed only at the baseboard.

She was screaming like a demon and trying to buck Calder off. A booted foot planted itself on the back of her gun hand. "Let go of the weapon! Let go of the weapon!"

Another SWAT officer pulled Calder off her and shoved him out of the way as others surrounded Dawn to disarm and subdue her.

Calder staggered over to the chair where one of the men in full gear was removing the duct tape from Elle's arms. As soon as she was free, she threw herself against Calder. He didn't see any blood on her, but as he clutched her to him, he asked if she'd been shot.

"No. You?"

"No." They clung to each other even as they were rapidly ushered through the front door and out into the yard, where EMTs rushed forward to assist them.

"She's been hurt," Calder told the first to reach them.

"I'm all right," Elle said. But there was a red welt across her cheekbone, and it had already begun to swell.

"This way, ma'am." The EMT took her arm to lead her toward the ambulance, which was just one of the emergency vehicles parked haphazardly in the street. Reluctantly, Calder released her into the medic's care and fell into step behind them.

"Calder!"

He stopped and turned. In long strides, Compton and Perkins were closing in on him. Compton was huffing. "Are you all right?"

"Yeah, but Dawn hit Elle in the face with the pistol. May have broken a bone. I don't know." He turned and started jogging toward the ambulance.

"Calder!"

He stopped and turned again. Compton said, "What I said about you acting impulsively at the fairground? I owe you an apology."

He divided a look between her and Perkins. "Save it. You were right."

Chapter 41

After the dramatic takedown of the Fairground shooter, Calder was hounded by the media. He was unable to leave his apartment building without having to run a gauntlet of microphones and cameras. After five days of it, he cleared himself with Compton and Perkins and struck out for California by car.

He told himself that he was going for his parents' sake, to show them in person that he'd survived the ordeal, that he was well and whole. But in actuality, he was running home like a child with a skinned knee, seeking comfort and reassurance, needing to hear that a scab would form, that what ailed him would eventually hurt less and get better.

He'd needed them to tell him that he wasn't to blame.

They were thrilled to have him. He and his dad, whose latest scans were clear, spent a lot of time in the loungers on the back terrace that overlooked the ocean. One afternoon, Calder bounced off him an idea he'd been contemplating.

"It's a new business plan. Rather than going in and weeding out borderline employees, I would evaluate their weaknesses, coach them on how to improve, or suggest a task within the company that's more suited to their strengths.

"By doing so, I'd help create a happier and therefore more productive workforce, which would result in increased revenue, which would please the bigwigs. I don't know. It's still on the drawing board. You're the first person I've shared this with. What do you think, Dad?"

"I like it. Positivity, not negativity."

Calder grinned. "That might be the tagline on my new business card."

That was as serious as they got. Most of the time, they talked about nothing consequential. They used the silliest anecdotal recollections as excuses to laugh until their eyes leaked tears.

Ponderous things, such as how they felt about life and its often-cruel vagaries and the depth of their feeling for each other were communicated more subtly during companionable silences when they'd exchange a look and smile with mutual understanding.

His mom was more demonstrative. She fussed over him and fed him, having pledged she would put five pounds on him before he left. She was even more affectionate than usual, hugging him often for no specific reason, holding him close and whispering in a voice made ragged by emotion, "Oh, Calder, we came so close to losing you, our baby, our boy. I feel for that poor woman."

Elle. Elle who had lost her baby, her boy. He thought constantly of her and of the pain she still experienced. Knowing that it would reside in her for the rest of her life anguished him.

He spent hours each day walking alone on the beach, staring out across the undulating Pacific, or lying on his back in the sand, gazing at the nighttime sky, seeking absolution, asking the heavens: *Am I to blame?*

———

To the consternation of the media, Elle was even more reclusive than she had been following the Fairground shooting. She declined every request for an interview and kept to her house. After a few discouraging days of getting nothing from her, one by one the journalists camping out on her street packed up their vans and left.

Her parents came to spend a weekend with her. As usual, it was intended as a caring gesture, but Elle was relieved when they departed. Her agent, Laura, had called every other day or so to check on her. Given the circumstances, the publisher had extended her deadline by several months. Therefore, Laura was surprised and delighted when Elle told her she was ready to get back to work.

"Thank them for the gesture, but I won't need the extension. I'll get the book in ahead of its original deadline."

She had a voice mail from Jeff, telling her how glad he was that her ordeal was over. She called him back and congratulated him on the birth of his son.

Other than returning the calls of established friends, she

maintained a low profile and spent long days at her computer and drawing board. Closure had freed her mind and jump-started her creativity.

However, she couldn't entirely escape the specter of Dawn Whitley. She'd had several meetings with Compton and Perkins, giving her account of the erratic events leading up to her confrontation with Dawn and recounting for them everything Dawn had told her. Her recollection skill was of tremendous help to them in filling in the blanks.

The detectives told her that the death threat voice mail had already raised the eyebrows of their audio specialists. "They said it was 'hinky.' They were in the process of analyzing it when we got the frantic call from Calder that Dawn was our culprit."

Elle was also told that Dawn had initially remained silent and defiant during their interrogations. But after they played for her the recording that Calder had surreptitiously made on his phone while hiding in the dining room, her staunch avowals of innocence had begun to weaken.

In that dialogue with Elle, she had practically reconstructed her crimes and boasted of her cleverness. After hearing the recording, her court-appointed attorney impressed upon her that if she was tried and convicted of even one of the capital crimes for which she was accused—for instance, the murder of Charlie Portman—she would be eligible for the death penalty.

At her arraignment, she entered a guilty plea for every charge.

"Dawn's sentencing hearing is pending," Compton had told Elle at their last meeting. "Because of her homicidal tendencies, she'll probably be sentenced to spend the rest of her life in the psych section of a penal institution, where she'll be kept in solitary confinement. Prior to sentencing, you can address her and the court if you choose to."

"No, thank you," Elle had said.

Compton also had told her that the judge had denied Shauna Calloway's request to interview Dawn from her jail cell, even via video. "He put it in the form of a chastisement for her even proposing it, telling her that a mass murderer shouldn't be elevated to celebrity status. To quote, he said, 'The perpetrators of such wanton criminal acts as mass shootings should instead be ground into obscurity. Request denied.'"

At the conclusion of their meeting, Perkins had passed Elle a business card. "From the president of an advocacy group for victims of violent crimes and their survivors. He asked that you call him. He'd like to invite you to speak at a conference this summer. I know you shun publicity, but think about it, Ms. Portman. You could do some good."

For Perkins, it was a long speech. Elle became emotional as she took the card and thanked him for passing it along. "I'll think about it."

This evening, she related that exchange to Glenda, who'd brought carry-out Thai for their dinner. They were lingering over a glass of wine in her living room.

"As I said my goodbyes," she told Glenda, "I realized that, in an odd way, I'm going to miss them."

"They're like the counselors at summer camp," Glenda said. "Over a short period of time, you form a bond and then never see them again, but you also never forget them."

Elle smiled over the analogy.

"And if you do make an appearance at that conference," Glenda continued, "I'll get Daddy to contribute lots of money to the organization. You'd be terrific."

"I'm thinking about it."

"What happened to the other two?"

"The other two what?"

"Key witnesses. You told me there were five of you."

"Oh. The older lady got a new pacemaker. She's out of the hospital and doing fine. The young widower had been taken to relatives in Arkansas, where he's decided to stay." She looked wistfully into her wine. "I hope he recovers, finds happiness. Peace."

"I hope *you* do." Glenda hesitated, then said, "Elle, Calder has been conspicuously absent for the past three weeks. As you know, I was leery of him and of the two of you together. But I've come around. As men go, he's okay."

Elle laughed. "High praise indeed."

"So, where's he been keeping himself, and what's your status? I hope that for some reason I'm unaware of, you're not about to burst into tears because I asked."

"No, it's all right. Mutually, we decided to stay apart until things settled down. There were spotlights on us, and things were complicated enough. We didn't need another issue to explain or try to conceal."

"Hmm, that sounds dense, and I don't have time for density tonight." She drained her wine and shouldered her purse.

"What's your rush?"

"I've got a date."

"Oh, someone serious?"

"Yes. He's seriously rich."

They laughed as they hugged goodbye. "Thank you for bringing dinner."

"I'm glad you liked it."

"And, Glenda, thank you mostly for being my friend."

When Elle set her away, Glenda said with all seriousness, "Not a problem. You're the one who has to work at being mine."

They held gazes for several seconds, then Elle walked her to the front door and waited to see her off. Just as Glenda was getting into her car, an unfamiliar Jeep pulled up behind it.

Calder climbed out. Elle's heart began turning cartwheels.

He acknowledged Glenda with an absent-minded wave. She shot Elle a cheeky look over her shoulder, then got into her car and drove off.

Calder started up the walk. "Like it?" he said, hitching his thumb over his shoulder at the Jeep. "It's new."

"You traded in your Jag?"

"No. I still have it. We just needed space from each other."

She laughed. He joined her on the porch, and then they just looked at each other. Eyes on her bruised cheek, he said, "Does it still hurt?"

"No. It only looks like it does. It's been slow to fade, but it will."

His eyes reconnected with hers, and he asked softly, "Are we still talking about the bruise?"

She gave him a wistful smile. "It's no longer a shooting pain, just a dull ache." He nodded understanding. "Come in."

"Thanks."

She turned and entered the house. He followed her inside. She asked, "How was California?"

"We had a great visit."

"Lovely. Your dad?"

"The poster child for curing cancer with early treatment."

"That's wonderful!"

"Yeah. I talked to him about a new business venture. He came up with a great slogan."

"Really? What?"

"Later."

"You look excited."

"I am. It feels good, Elle. Honest. Work I can actually talk about."

"I'm glad for you."

"Me too."

"When did you get back?"

"This is my first stop."

"Oh?"

"Yeah. I left something here that belongs to me."

"Your signed Betsy book."

He shook his head. "You." He moved in, backing her into the wall, and, gently cradling her face between his hands, kissed her. Kissed her softly but ardently.

And then hungrily.

He unbuttoned her top far enough for him to pull it off over her head. When her hair fell back onto her shoulders, he buried his face in it while his hands went around her and unhooked her bra. She shrugged it off.

His mouth was hot and wet and eager on her breasts. Her head fell back against the wall, but her hands were busily unbuckling, unbuttoning, freeing him. When she wrapped her fingers around him, he swore, then prayed, "God save me."

He bunched up her skirt, stroked her thighs apart, moved aside her underpants, and caressed her until she was glazed with want and rocking against his fingers.

He broke a deep, delving kiss and rasped, "Take them off."

Battling cloth and urgency, she removed her panties while he shoved his jeans past his hips. Then he lifted her onto his thighs and pushed into her.

For a time, they held like that, his forehead pressed against the wall, even with her chin. Their breathing was heavy and hot, loud like the beating of her pulse against her eardrums. She bent her head down and pecked kisses along his brow, against his closed eyelids, across the pale freckles that dusted his cheekbone, all the while chanting his name in fervent whispers.

"Elle," he groaned, and began to thrust.

He was fiddling with the glittering stud that she'd replaced in her navel. "If I'd seen this beforehand, I wouldn't have lasted the thirty seconds I did." They were lying face-to-face in Elle's bed. Clothing, which had been an impediment, had been done away with.

She leaned forward and bit his scruffy chin. "But it was an amazing thirty seconds."

He arched his eyebrow and gave her a wicked smile. "Yeah? How amazing?"

She swatted his shoulder.

He bent down and flicked his tongue over the tiny jewel. "Yeah," he growled. "It was amazing." He nuzzled her, tickling her with his whiskers, but when he returned his head to the pillow and reached for a strand of her hair to sift through his fingers, he set teasing aside.

"I'm a selfish bastard, Elle. I always have been. But having sex with you before talking about this was possibly the most selfish thing I've ever done. I guess I was afraid that if I didn't, I'd never get another opportunity."

She angled her head back. When her hair slid out of his grasp, she took his hand, kissed the back of it, and drew it to her breast. "Before talking about what? Although I can guess."

He sighed, lifted his gaze from the study of her beautiful breasts to her eyes. "I have to ask. Did you mean it when you told Shauna in that interview that you blamed only the person who pulled the trigger?"

"Yes."

"Because I don't want to fall deeper and deeper in love with you and then one day have you look at me and say, 'If not for you, Charlie wouldn't have died.'"

"I would never say that."

"But would you think it?"

"No." She leaned over him and took his face between her hands. "Listen to what I have to say, and then never ask me that again. Because if you do, it'll be as good as calling me a liar. All right?"

He didn't verbally respond, but he bobbed his head.

"First of all, Compton told me about the letters."

He felt a flash of anger. "It wasn't her place to do that."

"No, probably not. But I'm glad she did, because I don't

believe you would have." She reached up and ran her fingers through his hair. "It was an incredibly noble thing to do."

He had written a letter to everyone who'd been injured in the shooting and to the families of those who hadn't survived, apologizing for the part he'd unwittingly played in Dawn Whitley's pursuit of vengeance.

"I wanted them to know that I never even met her father, had never had any interaction with him at all. It wasn't as if we'd had a bitter dispute. I don't know what he looked like. I didn't even know his name."

"Calder," she said, pressing her index finger against his lips. "You don't have to defend yourself."

"I felt that I did. I wanted them all to know that I didn't know I had an enemy who..."

"Is mentally ill. She murdered her own parents for reasons her sick mind thought justifiable."

"Yeah," he sighed. "I guess. Anyway, I asked Compton to distribute those letters only because I didn't have anyone's address."

"She's received replies. She's holding them for you for when you're ready to read them. She says they're—"

"She read them?"

"She felt it was her duty."

"Duty, my ass. She was being nosy."

Elle smiled. "She says you'll be deeply touched by their contents." She traced the rim of the deep triangle beneath his Adam's apple. "You didn't send me a letter."

"I was hoping to hear your reply in person."

Looking into his eyes, she said, "I don't blame you, Calder. No one affected blames you." In a softer voice, she added,

"That is, no one except yourself. And if you— No, let me finish," she said when she saw that he was about to interrupt.

"If you allow this undue guilt to become ingrained in you, you had just as well have died in the shooting, because the life you could and should have had will have ended that day." She kissed him tenderly and left her lips against his. "Let it go."

He took a deep breath. "That may take a minute, Elle."

"That's an allowable amount of time."

They smiled at each other. He said, "Can I count on you to be there?"

"You're the one who's always running off, not me."

He sank all ten fingers into her hair. "I'm not going anywhere that I can't be with you."

"Then you were being truthful when you said you're falling deeper and deeper in love with me?"

"Yes. And it's killing me. I'll work on the guilt thing. I will. But I've got to have you."

She seemed to think it over. "The prepared 'it's not you, it's me' speech that you never delivered?"

"What about it?"

"What you said in summation was enough."

"What did I say?"

"You don't remember? It was profound."

"As I remember it, I wasn't trying to be profound. I was trying to get on you."

She laughed. "Well, what you said worked then." She ran her fingertips across his lips. "It works now. Tragedy brought us together, but I'm not going to let it keep us apart." She rolled onto him and kissed him gently. "So, here I am."

He folded his arms around her. "Here *we* are."

About the Author

Sandra Brown is the author of seventy-five *New York Times* bestsellers. There are more than eighty million copies of her books in print worldwide, and her work has been translated into thirty-four languages. Four of her books have been made into films. In 2008, the International Thriller Writers named Brown its Thriller Master, the organization's highest honor. She has served as president of Mystery Writers of America and holds an honorary doctorate of humane letters from Texas Christian University. She lives in Texas.

Sandra Brown.net

Faccbook.com/AuthorSandraBrown

X @Sandra_BrownNYT

Instagram @sandrabrownauthor

Reading Group Guide

Discussion Questions

1. The day of the fair, Elle did laundry and other light housekeeping before settling into her home office to work, all while taking care of Charlie. Discuss the idea of women doing it all versus having it all and how Elle's situation in this scene was very recently experienced by many parents during the pandemic.

2. In *Out of Nowhere*, Brown covers a mass shooting and its reverberations from a deeply human angle. How does the novel comment on the issue of gun violence in America?

3. Several conversations in the novel focus on the shooter's motivation. Compton, in chapter 5, lists a number of potential factors, such as radicalization, mental illness, and rage resulting from ridicule, shaming, or romantic rejection. Compare these fictional discussions to other contributing factors often discussed in current events, such as social media and anxiety.

4. Do you believe that we, as a society, can predict or prevent violent acts? Why or why not?

5. Calder refuses to recognize himself as a hero, while others reiterate again and again that his actions were not

only valiant but also selfless. Discuss where this hesitancy stems from in Calder's eyes and the concept of survivors' guilt.

6. After the shooting, Elle says that the only thing she wants is justice. In the aftermath of such a horrific event, knowing how much is often at play in these kinds of situations, what does justice look like in your eyes? Compare and contrast "punitive justice" with "restorative justice."

7. At the police precinct, Calder doesn't know what to say to Elle—he's afraid that whatever condolence he tries to convey will sound insensitive and insincere. Have you ever found yourself at a loss for words while trying to express grief or sympathy? Do you believe words alone can express comfort, sorrow, or regret? Why or why not?

8. Calder's relationship with Shauna falls apart after the shooting. Calder feels that Shauna lacks empathy for his situation, while Shauna feels that Calder is intentionally sabotaging any and all attempts to "return to normal." Have you ever had a viscerally different reaction to a delicate emotional situation than someone close to you? If so, how did the conflict—or resolution—affect your relationship?

9. Calder refuses to go on camera to discuss what happened at the county fair. Shauna, by contrast, claims that through story, she can humanize those who have been harmed rather than group victims together as "grim statistics." Did you agree with Calder's decision here? Or did you, in principle, agree with Shauna's argument?

10. Discuss Shauna as a character. Did you admire her relentlessness, as a journalist, in trying to break a story? Or do you feel that Shauna ethically crossed a line in her efforts to report on the Fairground shooting?

11. At the therapy session for family members, Dr. Sinclair discusses what survivors of traumatic events typically experience, such as depression, nightmares, and mood swings. Discuss the many ways in which people react to trauma and why they often vary from person to person.

12. In Elle, Calder finds a sense of peace he's never felt before in his life. What is the number one quality you feel is important to have in (or receive from) a life partner? Why?

13. In chapter 31, when Glenda and Elle are with Perkins and Compton, Elle has a very emotional moment in the bathroom, feeling gullible and taken advantage of, wondering why she ever let herself trust Calder. Have you ever been in a similar situation, where someone close to you broke your trust after you had given them a second chance? How did you process this betrayal? Ultimately, did you choose to rehabilitate that relationship or cut ties? Why?

14. In chapter 28, Calder asks Elle a question: "A tragic circumstance brought us together. Will you let it be the one and only thing that keeps us apart?" Discuss the layered ways in which Calder and Elle's relationship progresses throughout the novel. If you had been in Elle's position in this moment, how would you have answered Calder's question?

15. Calder, upon entering his apartment building in chapter 35, observes that "everyone live[s] with impermanence; they just [don't] realize it until a catastrophe [befalls] them." Do you agree or disagree with the statement? Why?

Backstory

For every book, I write an "in a nutshell" synopsis of the story, a basic "What's it about?" It's a tool I use to hone down four hundred plus pages into one concise sentence that will arouse readers' curiosity, plant in their minds subliminal questions, and leave them wanting to know what's going to happen and to whom.

Writing that summarized storyline for *Out of Nowhere* was difficult because the book begins with the most unspeakable occurrence in our society's new reality: a mass shooting.

Yes...it involves an egregious loss. But let me emphasize that this isn't a story about death. It's about *survival*.

So, the nutshell for *Out of Nowhere*: in an instant of unthinkable tragedy, the destinies of two strangers collide.

Allow me to add three more words: collide *and become entwined.*

That raises the question of who these strangers are.

Calder Hudson: age thirty-seven, overachiever, successful, affluent, charming, and self-confident to the point of arrogance. He has a storehouse of grown-up toys, an expensive wardrobe, and a gorgeous girlfriend who lives with him in a glitzy high-rise condo in downtown Dallas. His life couldn't possibly be more charmed.

Elle Portman: midthirties, author and illustrator of children's books; a stay-at-home single mom to the love of her life, her two-year-old son, Charlie. They live quietly and contentedly in a suburban neighborhood of Fort Worth, thirty miles west of, but a world apart from, Calder.

The "unthinkable tragedy" that causes that fateful collision?

A mass shooting at a county fair.

To say that's a distressing subject is an understatement. It's a topic I would ordinarily avoid. As I'm sure you do, I react to hearing of yet another with dismay and abject sadness. I can't even imagine what it would be like to find oneself in that terrifying circumstance, to miraculously survive it, and then to endure the strife-embroiled aftermath.

But, as storytellers are wont to do, I did. Imagine, that is.

Did I want to write about a mass shooting? Not really. But I was compelled to write about people trying to pick up where their lives suddenly had left off. How do they go about rebuilding when crucial pieces of the past are now fractured or missing?

And characters waiting restlessly in the wings have a way of applying pressure to the author to tell their story. Elle and Calder emerged from my subconscious as individuals whose worlds had entirely different landscapes... until those worlds were upended by a shared horrific experience. Now, each is struggling to reshape their here and now into some form of normalcy.

If not for that unpredictable, inexplicable, and tragic occurrence at the fairground, it's unlikely that they ever would have crossed paths. But because of the ruthless act of another, their destinies intersected. Because of a caprice of physics, they became intertwined.

Now, you're asking, How so? What happened?

I can go no further here without giving away too much. Much of the conflict revolves around Calder and Elle trying to reconcile their unfathomable connection with a most untimely attraction to each other. But *Out of Nowhere* is also a novel of suspense. A clear and present danger is bearing down on them. The resultant mind game leads to a wild chase that culminates in a twist that I hope you won't see coming. Yes, this story packs an emotional punch, but it contains all the elements that readers of Sandra Brown have come to expect.

If you take nothing else away from reading this backstory, please note this: I don't presume to know what it's like to suffer through a tragic experience like the one portrayed in this work of fiction. Many do, though. They're living their stories, and those are brutally real.

I did my best, with as much authenticity and empathy as I could, to depict their heartbreak, despair, and anger. I acknowledge that I fell short of capturing on paper the enormity of their struggle to stay afloat in the wake of a catastrophe.

I wrote this book in observance of those killed or injured in mass shootings—and those who have survived, whom I rank among the casualties.

Sandra Brown